AGAPE and EROS

An Autobiographical Novel

David Smith

 New Generation Publishing

This book is dedicated to Sri Raju Vasudevan, his wife Sini, and his two boys, Akil Raj and Dhadin Raj. They taught me the meaning of love and the art of patience.

By the same author:

Find the Gifted Child
Gifted Children at School
Dracula (A musical play for children)
A Song in my Heart (A musical)
Resources and Resource Centres
Death in Dibba

Prologue

The subject of this novel has been running through my mind for over ten years. I have actually put pen to paper on three occasions, but never got beyond the first few pages. It was not that I did not want to write, rather that the demands of my profession, as well as writer, academic, politician, actor, seemed to be much more urgent.

Writing has been part of my life. I always seemed to be either writing an article for a journal editor who was in crisis, putting together a factual book, penning a political speech, or writing a play or musical for children to perform. All these forms of writing were very different to novel writing. A novel allows your imagination to run riot to some extent. However, a novel set in a particular period of time with actual events being woven into the plot, needs to be accurate and carefully researched. Much of this story actually happened in the time frame I have chosen, and as memory can play strange tricks, I have had to undertake careful checking of facts. I hope I have not made any glaring errors.

Over the years I have been lucky enough to travel extensively around the world. Travel has broadened my outlook on life, and it has also allowed me to look at my native country in a different light, perhaps becoming more critical. I have lived for many years in Spain and Arabia and thus sampled very different cultures from my own. In 1993 I holidayed in Kerala in South India, and fell under its spell. With the help of my Indian friends, I retired in Kerala in 2003 and found both intellectual stimulation and a true paradise on earth.

The first two chapters of my book were written in the garden of the River Retreat Hotel, near Trissur, situated on the banks of the beautiful and sacred Bharatha River. It was the monsoon time and warm rain fell as if a tap had been opened, whilst I wrote in the shelter of a gazebo, cup of coffee to hand, and words tumbled onto foolscap paper – later to be transferred to computer. The hotel waiters, I am sure, thought this Englishman sitting in the garden and writing, to be quite mad. They took every opportunity to visit me to enquire after my comfort and find out what I was doing.

As I have said earlier, the vast majority of the events in the story actually happened. The characters depicted are real and behaved and spoke in the way I have indicated. Of course, their names and descriptions have been slightly altered to ensure their privacy as many are still alive today.

The bulk of the writing was undertaken whilst I was recovering from acute dermatitis, caused by poison from spiders' webs. Spiders in Kerala can be pretty nasty and the unwary, like me, can suffer badly from their poison. I was unable to go out in the heat of the day as it aggravated my spotty skin, and at night I was kept awake from the itching. Hence, I had time to write in the daytime and also into the small hours. I hope the condition did not affect the writing as my temper at times was not at its best. I am grateful to my staff for putting up with me over that period.

The book is dedicated to my great friend, Sri Raju Vasudevan and his family who have shown me such love over the years. It was Raju who first persuaded me to visit Kerala and made the path easy in order for me to live in India. He encouraged my writing and put up with my bad temper during my 'spotty period'. I am eternally grateful to him and his family.

India is the most fascinating place I have ever visited, with a wealth of culture, and its people are extremely friendly. There are so many contrasts that one cannot fail to be stimulated. Poverty and great wealth exist side-by-side, as does great beauty and extreme ugliness. Spirituality is to be found everywhere in temple, mosque, church and shrine as well as in the peace and tranquility of the countryside. It is in this culture that the views expressed in this novel were finally formulated.

The views I have expressed in this story are my own and formulated after a lifetime of experience. Perhaps some readers will be shocked by what I have written, but the real dilemmas of life have to be faced. They will not go away. Value judgments have to be made after a thorough understanding, and not be made through prejudice. I hope those who are contemplating ordination will find some answers in these pages.

Chapter 1

The lady in the three-quarter length leopard-skin coat and matching pillbox hat drifted elegantly down the platform of Leicester's Grand Central Station, followed by a fawning porter carrying an expensive overnight bag. She was tall and graceful and walked with confidence. Lady Isobel Barnett, star of the BBC (1) television's popular panel game 'What's My Line' and watched by millions, was on her way to anther recording session in London. She got into a first class carriage and her luggage was put on the rack above her head and the porter bowed his way out of the compartment.

The station, built in the 1890s, was probably one of the grandest in the provinces with wrought iron gates, Dutch gables, ornate parapets, a clock tower, fine dining room and a general air of opulence. Following closely behind the television star, and on a completely different mission, aware of who was preceding him, was a tall, slim, handsome young man, carrying his own overnight bag of canvas and plastic. He was also catching the same train but for a totally different purpose. The young nineteen- year- old looked for an empty seat in a second class carriage.

The huge platform was busy, typical of a Monday morning, with businessmen and shoppers off to the capital city. However, the front end of the train was almost deserted as he walked along the lengthy platform. For some, the walk along the long platform nearing the time of departure was intimidating, but not so this energetic young man. He got into a compartment in which there was only a middle-aged lady in the window seat. He took the other seat opposite. Lady Isobel would have her seat paid for by the BBC and the young man was having his seat paid for by Her Majesty's Government for he was on his way to commence his National Service (2).

The young man was setting out on a journey through life which would lead him into events and situations way beyond his wildest dreams and ultimately enable him to find his true self. It was said that National Service either made or broke a person. All conditions of youth rub together in the barrack room: rich and poor, intelligent and dull-witted, honest and dishonest, well-mannered and crude, jokers and serious, stable and neurotic, fit and not-so-fit – a whole gambit of the human condition. Most emerge from the two-year experience fitter, wiser and more able to cope with all life has to throw at them, while others learn bad habits that dog their whole lives.

David Earl was born in Yorkshire. At the age of twelve, the family moved to a small village near Leicester where his father had set up a business selling marble, granite and stone. Throughout his teenage years the family was always short of ready cash, though not poor, as his father had to put out large sums in order to establish his business. Two things his father did ensure was that he and his brother had a good education, and that the family went on a Continental holiday each year.

Educated at the local Grammar School, David did not show excellence like his brother who had a good memory and thrived on rote learning. David was sensitive, more interested in ideas, what made things happen, and as his mother would say, he always has some fantastic scheme in his head. Not that he was poor at school as he always came somewhere at the top in each subject, except Latin, which he hated with great vigor. His ability was different and education in the forties and fifties was not geared to such an intellect.

Schools in the forties and fifties were still steeped in rote learning – particularly the Grammar Schools (3) - where a good memory was all that was required. Because of this, David was not as highly regarded as his older brother. Imagination and ideas were frequently seen as reactionary and a threat to school discipline. Pupils were there to record the pearls that flowed from the lips of their teachers, and then to regurgitate verbatim for the examinations. It was a body of knowledge that was seen as valuable and not the ability to challenge and initiate.

Having put his canvas hold-all on the rack above his head, David settled in. The only other occupant, the middle-aged lady, was well-dressed and possibly about the same age as his mother. She did not have any luggage that David could see so he assumed that she was going on a day trip to do some shopping in London.

"We're lucky to get seats," remarked the lady giving David a smile. "Usually the train is packed. I always find this end is least busy. People won't walk. I often travel to London to see my daughter......lives in Chelmsford."

"I just followed Lady Barnett down the platform. You know, of 'What's My Line' fame?" David told his traveling companion eagerly. "She got into a first class compartment. No rushing to get a seat for her."

There was silence. He was wrong about the lady being on a shopping spree. Maybe his comment about Lady Barnett had offended her. After a minute or two she smiled at him. "I suppose she gets troubled with fans. Poor thing. The price of being famous." There was a pause while she appraised the young man. "Are you going as far as London?" she asked.

David smiled back. "Yes."

"Do you know London?" she enquired, obviously wanting to start a conversation.

"Not very well.......I came in '52 with my parents just before the Coronation (4)....to see the decorations." David smiled at her in his disarming way, which was typical of him.

He had not always found it easy to talk to people, particularly in his pimply teens as he was unhappy with his appearance, but over the last couple of years, since the acne had gone and he had had passed his driving test and become a school prefect, his confidence had returned. He was always amazed how friendly people were to him and his shyness was beginning to disappear. Not that he would ever be a pusher and aggressive, as it was not in his nature. He knew he was sensitive and easily hurt, but he was learning to hide the signs and to cope.

The lady looked the young man up and down. He has such a lovely smile. Very good-looking, although his nose was too long, but he was handsome, possibly sensitive but with determination in those beautiful blue eyes. Yes, he was a looker and if she had been twenty years younger she could have fallen for him. He was dressed in a dark green tweed jacket and beige cavalry twill trousers, both expensive, with a white shirt and matching plaid tie. His shoes were good and spotlessly clean. Obviously he came from a nice family where he had been taught to turn himself out well. Unlike some of the young men she knew who had those dreadful haircuts like a duck's backside –'DA' it was called (duck's arse) – his fair hair was short and neatly cut. Tall, yes, about six feet. Quite nicely proportioned, if a little skinny, but he would soon fill out. He had a lovely deep tan.

She wondered where he had been to get the tan. Not England, for it had rained for just about the whole of August....typical England. It was clear that he was a very nice young man. Yes, he was very polite and a good companion to travel with. These days one never knew who would enter a carriage. Some people were dreadful.

"You look as if you've been on holiday. Certainly not England," observed the lady.

"Spain, for a month. My father wanted me to have a good holiday before I start National Service."

"Oh, so you're off to serve Queen and country? My son served in the Royal Warwick's Regiment. He quite enjoyed it."

David thought for a while. "I've heard all kinds of stories, good and bad. My brother is exempt as he is reading science at university. My girlfriend's brother says he is going to find some way to get out of it. I just want to get it over with and then start university."

"You'll enjoy it, a fit young man like you. My son was not the fittest

9

but it really made a man of him. He put on weight and the discipline did him good."

There was another short silence. "What can I call you? We have a long journey together?" the lady asked.

"David Earl," he replied.

"Call me Beryl ..... Beryl Regent."

"Pleased to meet you," said David with a look of genuine pleasure on his face.

The train began to move slowly amidst whistles and puffs of steam. Suddenly the sliding door of the carriage burst open and a red-faced, portly man flopped into the seat beside David. "Oh, my goodness I'm not made for this." He was certainly out of condition as he was panting heavily and perspiration ran down his face. "Thought I would never make it.....traffic terrible....son drove me.....no parking. Had to run down the platform. No room. Standing in the corridors. I knew there would be room this end." He took out a large, spotlessly-clean white handkerchief and mopped his brow.

"Can I put your case on the rack?" David asked politely.

"Thank you son," the man wheezed, "I don't think I've got the strength to get it up there," he said indicating the rack above his head.

David easily lifted the valise onto the rack.

"Sorry to disturb you," apologized the man. "My name is Welch, Dr Peter Welch."

Beryly and David introduced themselves and courtesies were offered. There were smiles all round.

It was not until they had left Nuneaton Station (5) and two further passengers had entered the carriage that Beryl spoke again. "What regiment have you been assigned to, David?"

"The R.A.M.C. ...... Royal Army Medical Corps," he offered.

"Didn't you want to join an armored corps or the Leicester's?" Beryl asked.

"No.....I volunteered for the RAMC."

Dr Welch looked interested. "Why was that, David?"

"For two reasons really. I studied biology, physics and chemistry at school and wanted to do something useful with them. − You see I am going to be on the arts side at university − and I didn't want to learn how to kill. Don't get me wrong, I'm not a conscientious objector. We have to protect our country and our loved ones. But there is so much killing in the world, I just want to learn how to heal."

"Good for you young fellow," observed Dr Welch. "I went through the war as an RAMC medic. No, I'm not a medical doctor. Professor of Physics at Leicester University College. We need young men like you

10

who have principles."

Each of them now fell into their own pattern of thought and there was silence in the carriage apart from the clank, clank as it went over the rails. David felt slightly sick. Since getting on the train he had been occupied in conversation. Now there was a silence he reflected on the picture of his mother, tears streaming down her face, and father looking grim, waving goodbye at the barrier. He would not let them go any further as he did not want an emotional scene on the platform. In any case, he had been close to tears himself and he did not wish his family to see him weep. According to his father, men did not weep. He loved his mother deeply. She had been the one constant in his life, the one he could talk to about most things and she could be relied on to give good advice. His father thought him too sensitive and not manly, and his idea of becoming a priest was crazy. Neither of his parents was religious in the formal, accepted sense, but neither had they actively dissuaded him.

David knew that his nature was too sensitive. He had been hurt many times at school by comments that others would just brush away. A film, or play on television could move him to tears. He had discussed this with his mother and her view was that sensitivity was a good quality as long as it was kept under control. Yes, he was too sensitive but his mother proffered that age, and what the world would do to him, would harden him. David knew why he wanted to be a priest. He had seen poverty in Europe after the war when his father had taken the family to France and Italy. He had seen all around him how cruel one human being could be to another. 'Love thy neighbour,' Jesus had said. But how many practised this precept? He had lived through a world war and seen at first hand bombing and death, and a special picture his mother had kept for so long.

That picture. David had been sixteen when his mother had shown it to him and his brother. He could not remember what had sparked off the action but it was clear that his mother had been waiting for the right opportunity to come along in order to show it. It was a newspaper cutting, folded and beginning to go yellow, and dated 1945. What it revealed shocked both the boys into a stunned silence. "You lived through the war. You were only babies when it started but you grew up through the bombing and deprivations," his mother had said. "Your father and I tried to shield you from it as much as possible. Of course, at first, you were too young to understand, but it did touch your lives in many ways. I saved this cutting to show you why the war had to be fought and what terrible things were done against innocent civilians." With that she handed over the cutting.

The black and white photograph, cut from the 'Daily Mail', showed a vast trench stretching as far as the eye could see with line upon line of naked, dead bodies, men, women and children. The bodies were desperately thin with bones showing clearly through a minimum of flesh. Starved before being killed. The caption read: 'Belsen Death Camp Revelation' (6). Mother explained that the Germans had systematically rounded up Jews throughout Europe, put them in camps and then slowly exterminated them by gassing them in bogus shower units. There was no doubt about their authenticity. Richard Dimbleby, (7) a British wartime reporter, has wept when he entered Belsen as one of the first press reporters. (David was to meet his wife years later, after Richard's early death, and learnt of the horror that haunted him for the rest of his life.) The boys were told that this was not the only camp and that their only crime of these people was that they were Jews. It was a shock.

Born in 1937, David had been unaware of war until he was of school age. Shortages were taken for granted. What you had not experienced you did not long for. Sweets were a rarity, toys were made by father, who served during the war as a policeman, and luxuries like oranges and bananas could only be seen in books. There were dried bananas available on ration. When stewed they looked like turds and tasted equally as bad. Not that the family went without food as father took on extra land and his parents grew much of what they needed. What they could not grow, they exchanged with others who had a surplus.

Yes, he could remember the air raids. The sirens would go, they would be taken from their cots, wrapped in a blanket and placed in an oak chest under the stairs until the Air-Raid Warden (8) came to help their mother carry them down the garden to the air-raid shelter (9). Father was frequently on nights so mother was helped by a friendly neighbour or a Warden. The shelter was very comfortable and father had made it as blast proof as possible. Mr and Mrs Williamson, retired publicans who lived next door, would also use the shelter and bring something liquid 'to get us through the night'.

One Saturday his eight-year-old brother had brought a silver bomb home that he had found on a waste piece of land. It was put in a bucket of water and the Bomb Disposal Team (10) sent for. Another time, mother had just got the weekend piece of beef in the oven when a German plane came over. Out of the oven came the beef, and it and the children were taken to the shelter. No way was Heir Hitler going to spoil their hard obtained piece of beef.

Of course, they were all women teachers at school, as the men had gone to war. There were also evacuees (11) from London who spoke in a queer way and frequently had flees and lice. Children lost their fathers. Uncle Tom came home in his uniform. John Kelly, who lived opposite, had an unexploded bomb right through his bed – luckily John was not at home. But the war did not really impinge on what seemed a perfect childhood.

It was after the incident of the photograph that David determined to find out more. At grammar school the younger masters had just returned from the war. Some would talk of their experiences and other would not. One had been a prisoner in the famous Coldiz Prison Camp (12) but would say nothing of his experiences. Father Edwards, a priest in a local village where David would help by playing the organ or serving at mass, was an officer in the First World War, and talked about his experiences and his injured arm. In fact, it was the experiences in the war that had turned Father Edwards to the priesthood. As his wife was fond of telling, she married an army officer and now she was the wife of a vicar. Slowly a picture of war grew and David knew that war was a last resort and not the glamorous fantasy imagined by many young men.

It was not only David's understanding of the results of war that steered him towards the priesthood. His sensitivity and the desire to do something worthwhile in the world also motivated him. For him, making money was a selfish pursuit, although he was sensible enough to realize that one could do little without it. He had thought of psychology. Healing the mind was a worthwhile occupation, but he did not have the academic aptitude for it as two universities had indicated. Being a regular churchgoer, server and chorister, it was inevitable he should be attracted to the cloth. He liked the music, the ritual, the order and the peace that belief in God brought, and he saw that contentment reflected in other devotees.

David's was a simple faith. God loves us and all we need to do is worship Him with prayer, music and ritual and anything can be achieved. The pain in the world, brought from doing evil, is soothed, and if one keeps the precepts of the Bible then all will be well. It was Sunday School (13) religion, the sort that had been instilled in him from the age of seven and had hardly changed in adulthood.

National Service had been compulsory for all United Kingdom male citizens over the age of eighteen since before the Second World War (14) but was consolidated in the National Service Act of 1948 when it applied to all males between the ages of 18 to 26. The object was to have an effective reserve military in case of future wars, and many saw it as 'making men' out of spoilt youth. Those who did not believe in military activity, conscientious objectors, were give an alternative service like working down a coal mine. David was not a pacifist, neither did he see himself working down a mine. At his medical he could have been classified as less than A1 medically because of a large red-brown birthmark on his right shoulder. However, he lied to the doctor when asked if it troubled him, and said it was no problem. The truth was that it did bleed from time to time when caught by clothing or PE apparatus, but he was determined that he was going to do his service like other young men. He was passed A1 and now here he was on the train ready to commence National Service.

Some escaped Service, like his brother, who was reading Science at Nottingham University and whom the government regarded as important, and thus excused. He knew of one boy in his village, whose father was an old soldier, who had suddenly developed back pain. He persisted with his story and was exempt. David was sure there was nothing wrong with him and that his father had put him up to it. The boy and his father were 'money mad' and he openly agreed that he did not wish to give up his good wage, which he had been receiving after leaving school at fifteen. David was contemptuous of him, but people soon forgot the coward in their midst, some even admired his cheek in beating the system.

David's thoughts were pierced by Beryl asking, "I assume you are a keen Christian, David, with your desire not to kill."

"Actually," responded David, " I hope to be ordained at some time in the future."

"I'm not surprised," added Dr Welch. "From what you told us it follows."

"What denomination are you, David?" asked Beryl.

"Church of England," (15) he replied .

Beryl smiled. "That's nice, dear. I'm C of E. Our Vicar is such a lovely man... new...maybe you know him.....Rev. Petersen of St Paul's, Countesthorpe."

"Of course," David glowed, "he's the new Director of Ordinands (16) for the Diocese. I met him at a get-together in April just after he was inducted into his church. Tall, dark and a real live-wire. I liked him a lot. He was the one who finally got me accepted as an ordinand. He was chaplain to the Bishop in Matabeeliland (17) and knew the Archbishop of Central Africa." David smiled, "It's rather complicated, but the Archbishop is married to a friend of my mother's and so I got a good recommendation. Influence, I suppose."

"And a little of that is a good thing, young man," observed Dr Welch, "never forget it. You can have all the ability in the world but without that little push........"

"Thanks for the advice, sir," remarked David happily.

The train increased its pace and sped through the English countryside. The train had become rather full since stopping at the mining town of Nuneaton. Conversation was sparse now as the carriage was full and people were sitting on their suitcases in the corridor. It was a lovely day, sunny and warm. Not unusual for September. An Indian Summer (18) it was called, but David did not have a clue how the name arose. Some trees were beginning to turn into autumn yellow while the elders in the hedgerows were clustered with purple fruit. Oh, the taste of elderberry wine, particularly when you had a cold and sore chest. How different was the landscape of the middle counties to those in the north where David was born: green hedges defining the fields, cattle grazing lazily and lush, green grass, as opposed to gray stone walls and close-cropped fields and rather dirty sheep.

As the train began to reach Reading (19) the landscape changed and there were more modern hamlets, ugly in their red brick and stucco. The land was obviously swampy as there were many excavated holes now filled with water. Some had their banks planted with trees to enhance the rather barren area. On one long waterway, someone was water skiing. What might have been just an ugly pond had been turned into a leisure facility.

Reading emerged all too soon and what a dreary town it looked, even on a nice sunny day. It seemed as if it had been built quickly and on the cheap. Apart from one or two rather incongruous ulta-modern buildings, much was red brick and ugly. Quite a few people left the train, which was filled again by more traveling to the capital. A whistle blew and the diesel locomotive slowly left the station. Next stop London, Marylebone Station.

After goodbyes and wishes of luck from Beryl and Dr Welch, David changed trains and caught the 1.35 from Waterloo to Fleet Station in Hampshire. His army travel documents told him that he would be met by military personnel and then taken to the RAMC Training Barracks at Crookham. The journey out of London was one of dirty, busy streets, factories interspersed with rows of houses. Few cities appear attractive from a railway carriage and London is no exception. It seemed to take an age to get out of these bleak surroundings but once the countryside was reached the soft greens of fields and trees was a welcome respite.

On arrival at the small station at Fleet, he was surprised how many other young men like himself had traveled on the same train and emerged looking rather lost. The station was so small one could not fail to notice the military lorries in the car park and military personnel on the platform. They were rounded up unceremoniously by a sergeant and his two NCO (20) colleagues.

He had not noticed these young men on the train, but then he had been preoccupied with his thoughts. What would life be like in the army? He had never been away from home without his family before. How would he cope? He and his brother had their own rooms. What would it be like to live so close to others? He wasn't a prude as being an athlete he was not shy of nakedness. How often had his physical education teacher complemented him on his excellent body and then slapped his wet bum as he emerged from the showers. But there were things that his body did that he wouldn't want to share with others, and how was he to hide this? What did the other boys do? He liked his space, private contemplation, being able to sink into his own thoughts. Would there be time to read and what of prayer and meditation?

Prayer was not easy for David and Father Grant, his Parish Priest, had tried to help him but with little success. Mundane matters, the desire for breakfast or the homework that was not finished, or the desire for sex, frequently distracted him. He knew how to talk to God, to ask but not how to contemplate spiritual matters. Father Grant had told him not to worry that deeper things would come later when he was in training.

David was a virgin and had been teased unmercifully by the boys at school. He knew the biology all right, but was in fear of 'catching something', which would ruin his whole life. Some of the boys bragged about their encounters and pointed out the girls who were willing. One of his best friends at school had got his girl 'in the club' and his father had to pay an allowance for his son's mistake. The girl even brought the child into school for her friends to see. His girlfriend, Ruth, the famous school beauty, had thrown him up for an older boy whom David suspected did things he would not contemplate.

Yes, sex was a problem. He never opened up about his confusion to his parents. It was too embarrassing. In fact, sexual matters were never mentioned in his home. He knew his father kept a mistress, maybe two, as women were attracted to him, or was it the other way round? Anyway, it was a painful skeleton that his mother tolerated, as ladies were a weakness and had been almost from the start of their marriage. He had only found this out quite recently when one day his mother had been upset and had told him the truth. He and his brother had confronted his father who promised to behave, but he was not hopeful.

The RAMC Sergeant lined the recruits up in the station car park where there were trucks waiting. He checked their documentation and they were assigned to a lorry with their bags. There were no requests, just commands barked as if they were a pack of hounds. It brought

David up sharply. He was used to a polite way of living. Mother was always kind and gently and father sometimes shouted, but each member of his family gave the other due respect. He was in the army now and there was no going back.

His fellow recruits were a mixed bunch; city suits, jeans and bomber jackets, tweeds like himself. They were a cross-section of youth. Their ages were eighteen or nineteen but David could see that some were older, perhaps in their twenties. One boy looked about sixteen, although he had to be eighteen. Most were clean and tidy but there were one or two who looked as if they had slept in their clothes. David hoped they had not got fleas. He began to feel itchy.

Fleet was a funny little place with a single main street, and the army trucks soon left the town behind and made off towards Crookham where the barracks was situated. There was no countryside as such as houses, large and small, stretched along the roadside. The main gate and guardhouse of Queen Elizabeth Barracks was entered after about a twenty-minute drive and the vehicles were waved through by red-capped Military Police. The vehicles traveled along a tarred driveway and pulled up outside a long, low, wooden building.

"Out! At the double!" commanded the sergeant unceremoniously. The recruits emerged with their bags, bewildered and intimidated. It was chaos. There were frequent cries of "Shift your arse, soldier" and more common expletives. The sergeant and NCOs shouted and stormed and some semblance of two ranks was eventually produced. David wondered if it would not have been better, and more efficient, if the 'nice' sergeant had gathered them together and explained placidly what he wanted. As he was soon to learn, the army thrives on shouts and shouts and shouts. Reason is frequently out. Yours is not to reason why but to do or die.

They were sorted out by size. David was in the front rank on the extreme right. Next to him was a tall, blond boy and next to him a dark well-built young man of about twenty-three or twenty-four. Sergeant Black, the one who had collected them at the station, explained that he wanted a space between each of an arm's length and when he gave the order 'right dress' the right arm should be put out and space measured. The order was given: "Right dress!" The blond boy put his left arm out and clashed with the dark young man. There was confusion. Black walked up to the blond young man and thrust his face about five inches from him. "What's yer name, soldier?" he hissed.

"Peter," replied the boy.

"When you talk to me yer say, 'sergeant', he screamed, still face to face, "because I'm god." He bellowed even louder, "What's yer name?"

17

"Peter........sergeant."

"Peter what?"

"Peter Kennett........sergeant." The boy looked terrified.

"Which is yer right arm, Kennett? Show me!" commanded Black who had retreated a little.

Kennett was confused. His eyes rolled, his left arm began to rise but he saw the twitch in the corner of Sgt. Black's mouth and raised his right arm.

"Good. Then use it Kennett. Yer know soldier, ye're stupid. What are yer?"

Kennett did not know how to reply. Somebody whispered to him and he responded, "I'm stupid, sergeant," he said in a low voice.

"Louder," yelled Black. "We all want to know."

"I'm stupid, sergeant!" yelled Kennett for all to hear. There was general laughter but sergeant Black yelled "Quiet" and all laughing stopped immediately. This was a lesson for everyone.

An officer, a captain, emerged from the building opposite, immaculate in his uniform: shiny face, shiny boots, shiny belt and a shiny expression for the new recruits. The sergeant roared 'A-ten-shon' and gave a smart salute to which the officer offered a feeble response by waving his right hand in front of his forehead. Most of the recruits just stood and gawped at this soldier play, while one or two, including David, came to attention. David had been a soldier in a school play and had got a little drill from one of the masters, thank goodness.

"At ease," the officer barked. What that meant few understood. "I am Captain Berry," the officer continued in a rather modulated voice," your Training Officer and it is my job with the help of Sergeant Black and Corporals Iver, Edwards and Pugh to turn you into soldiers. Your progress will be monitored through the twelve weeks of basic training. During this period you will be selected for a trade and depending on what it is you will receive further training or you will be sent to a serving unit. The Camp Commandant, Colonel Scott-Brown, will be talking to you later on in the week when you look more like soldiers." He smiled weakly and looked around. "I'd like to remind you that you are in the army now so make the best of it. Oh, and if you thought of having a weekend off, forget it. You will not be permitted to leave the camp for six weeks. We can't have you dressed as soldiers and not acting like them, can we?" He grinned at the NCOs. "So tell your parents and girlfriends that they will have to forego your company for a while. If anyone thinks they are smart and wants to pull one over on the army, forget it. We hold all the cards. I'm sure there are lots of questions. This is not the place to ask them. Sergeant Black and his brother NCOs will answer questions in due course." He turned to sergeant Black, saluted and said, "They're all yours sergeant," and strode away.

Sergeant Black glared at the recruits. "Ye're a shower," he said, "a fucking shower. But we'll 'av yer sorted out in the twitch of a gnat's tail. And that's quick. Now. This 'arfternoon you'll be given a medical and some basic kit. Enough to last yer for a few days. Yer'll be shown where to eat and where to sleep. There will be three squads only this intake, A, B and C taken by Corporals Edwards, Pugh and Iver. They will be like a farver to you (guffors from the NCOs) and will give you further information. Questions?"

There were no questions as everyone was too scared to ask. Names were called and the three squads were eventually marched off by their squaddy (21) to their respective barrack room where cases and bags were left. 'Marched' was not the right word. It was a shambles. Some recruits did not know their left foot from their right, Kennett in particular, who kept giving David a kick as he could not keep in step. When Kennett's name had been read out for squad C there had been a perceptible groan from the squad and sighs of relief from the rest.

And what of David's fellows in squad C? They were a mix bag: tall, medium and short, fat, thin and well-proportioned. One boy was very small with a white freckly face, another fat and florid rather like a farmer. Yes, the army had a job on its hands to get this lot into shape.

The barrack room was a long, low wooden building with a central polished floor, iron beds standing on concrete, and wooden locker beside each bed. At the far end there was a door leading into the ablutions, and at the opposite end, where they had entered, was a small room where the corporal slept. The room was lit by a series of hanging lamps each with a white metal shade. The whole place was stark and unfriendly. David shivered as he put his bag on one of the beds. So this was his 'home' for the next twelve weeks. Would they ever make it friendly?

Everything is done 'at the double' in training and so there was little time to become morbid. They lined up outside and Cpl Iver marched them, in a fashion, to their medical. Iver was tall, dark, rather chunky and very smart in his uniform. It was obvious he was a Londoner by his accent, but he appeared to be a decent sort of person. He had told them he was a National Serviceman and due for demobilization quite soon. They filed into another low building where their papers were checked – name, address, religion, date-of-birth, distinguishing marks – and then they were told to strip.

David was not at all worried by this as he was used to the showers at school and visits to other schools with the cross-country and athletic team. However, some lads kept their underpants on and eventually were ridiculed into taking them off. There were lots of jokes about covering the smallness of their private parts. David was teased about the largeness of his 'chopper' but he was used to that from ribald comments at school.

The army had no mercy. They were give a jam jar and told to pee in it. It's hard to pee on demand but an orderly took the recalcitrant ones into a sluice and turned on the water tap. The job was soon completed. The jars were marked with name and number and sent off for testing.

A bevy of doctors in white coats prodded and poked the recruits testing their pulse, blood pressure, lungs etc. They coughed to test for hernia, had their balls and penis inspected, for who knows what, and a gloved finger put up their backside. It reminded David of a scene from D.H. Lawrence's novel "Kangaroo" that he had read at school where Lawrence describes his medical and being outraged because he was inspected up the backside. Lawrence's doctors were brutes but David felt that the present-day doctors were more courteous. They asked about David's birth-mark on his right shoulder but he assured them it was no problem.

"Lovely tan, young man," one of the doctors remarked. "Bet you didn't get that in the UK?"

"No, sir. Spain."

"You don't wear much.......and there's so much to cover," he said. David blushed.

"Don't tease him, Tom," said the other doctor with a twinkle in his eye. "He's jealous, son, as he couldn't dream of wearing such a bathing suit......too fat!" They all laughed and David went on to get dressed.

At the stores, where they had gone after the medicals, there was a policy of humiliating the new recruits. They were a ridiculous sight anyhow as they had not had enough time to dress properly after the medical and looked a real shower. The storemen set about making fools of them by giving wrong sizes and making them dress up and walk around to display a particular item. Berets were generally too large, pyjamas too small and underwear quite impossible. 'Taffy', the small, pale boy, who turned out to be Welsh, came in for a lot of ragging. He had to dress in enormous white combinations that turned him into a ghostlike creature. Fortunately, he had a sense of fun and flapped his arms and made a weird noise. Even Cpl Iver had to laugh. Peter Kennett received a lot of flack also. David got away lightly by having to parade in a beret that was miles too large and fell over his eyes. When he was given his dark green 'draws cellular', someone shouted –

he didn't know who it was, but he suspected it was Cpl Iver – "That's not large enough to cover what he's got." Everyone threw themselves around laughing, including David. One of the store-men shouted, "Lucky sod." Then Sgt Black arrived and order was restored, although he seemed to appreciate the hilarity. They signed for their stores, were lined up, loaded with kit, including eating irons, sheets, blankets, boots suspended around their necks, and marched back to their barrack room.

After an explanation by Cpl Iver how to make their beds and some tips about keeping their lockers tidy, they were marched to the canteen for food. The building was a huge structure with bare tables and a long stainless steel counter at one end where Catering Corps personnel were waiting. There was soup with lots of bread, a choice of three main courses and three sweets. Huge earns of frothing tea were on tables to one side. The food was hot and plentiful, although the tea did taste rather peculiar. After their meal, which was served on large white plates, they handed them in at a hatch and in an anti-room they washed their eating irons and mug in hot water. The meal lasted a half hour and as they left, the mess hall began to get busy. David was thankful that they were some of the first into the mess and realized that Cpl Iver had done this on purpose so that they would have an opportunity to relax a little rather than put them under more pressure. It was clear that he had some humanity, unlike Sgt Black who appeared to be a bully with no mercy. They walked back to the barrack room on their own; thank goodness they didn't see any officers as most of them hadn't the slightest idea how to salute.

That night Cpl Iver showed them how to put on their working denims, gaiters, belt and boots, which would be their standard dress for the next few days. He showed them how to wear their beret and where to put the badge. Each badge had to be polished and they were to buy Brasso (22) and dusters the following morning at the NAAFI (23) shop as well as black boot polish and a candle. Nobody at that stage knew what the candles were for but there were some strange suggestions. He also advised them to buy a lock for their locker so that valuables would be safe. The boot polish was for their boots – one pair for working which had to be cleaned every night, and a best pair for parades.

It was now night and the lights were on in the barrack room. They were adequate and that was all; to write a letter would have been a strain. The whole room became even more dreary than it was in daylight. David could not but think about his warm, cheerful home and the dingy place he was now in. Around eight o'clock, Cpl Iver left them to their own devices. Lights out was 10.30 pm and they would be woken up at 6 a.m. He explained where the NAAFI was and a few went off to explore.

Wherever there is a military establishment you will find the NAAFI or Navy, Army and Airforce Families Institute which was set up in 1921 as a place where military personnel can find warmth, friendship, food at reasonable prices and a welcome. It is a meeting place and offers brightness as opposed to the dingy atmosphere of the barrack room, and where the military diet might be supplemented. As David soon found out, the recruits were always hungry. Many soldiers drank the cheap beer to excess and by Monday their meager pay had disappeared.

A few of new recruits, including David, wanted to get themselves organized for the following day. Paul, the tall, dark young man who had been beside David on their arrival, stayed. He was married and hailed from Nottingham. The others were Welch Taffy and Peter Kennett, who seemed to have attached himself to the trio. They sat on Paul's bed and talked over the day.

"Didn't think things would be like this," remarked Paul. "God help us if every day is like today."

"You and I didn't come off too badly, Paul," added David, "but Taffy and Pete......."

"I hate that storeman," groaned Taffy in his sing-song Welch accent. "He just picked on me because I'm small."

"You did well, Taffy," observed David. "You should have seen his face when you ran around like a ghost. He thought Sgt Black might catch you and he would get the blame for giving you an obviously wrong piece of kit."

"Everyone enjoyed it, Taffy, "said Paul. "You made a lot of friends by what you did."

"Except that storeman," groaned Taffy.

"He's only a Private like you. What can he do?" David pointed out.

"Even Sgt Black saw the funny side," said Paul. "I saw him smirk and then he went all hard and shouted at us. Maybe he is human after all.

"No way," chipped in Peter after listening to them. "He hates me."

"You'll have to watch him Pete," David said. "He's got his knife into you. Watch your step."

Peter seemed to be miles away now. There were tears in the corner of his eyes.

"Penny for them," smiled David.

"Oh!......" He was startled. "I was just thinking of home.........I don't think I can stand this sort of life."

David's heart went out to him. He was sure there were many new recruits who felt just the same but Peter brought many of his problems on himself. He was thick, but he couldn't help it. What could he say? "Where's home then, Pete?" he asked.

"London, Kensington. My dad's a chef at the Savoy Hotel (24) and my mother's a secretary."

"Don't worry, Pete," put in Taffy, "we'll all try to help each other."

Just then there was a clomp, clomp of boots on concrete and a red-haired sergeant entered the barrack room. They all jumped to their feet and stood to attention.

"At ease," he said. "Just sit as you were before I came. This is not an official visit."

They relaxed, sat on Paul's bed again, and to their amazement the Sergeant sat with them. "I'm Sgt Arthur Walter of the Education Corps. You'll be meeting me later this week. Tonight I'm not on official business. I just want to let you know that there is a Christian group on camp. We meet each evening to say evensong at 6.30 pm in the chapel which is by the NAAFI. Do you know where that is?" They nodded. "If you are at all interested then you are very welcome to join in with us. There's a group of about six regulars and if we can be of any help.... Anyone interested?"

David and Taffy said they were and he took their names. He asked where the other recruits were and they told him at the NAAFI. He laughed. "It tends to have a bigger pull that the Lord," he joked. With that he said goodnight and left.

"Wow, I thought we were in for it," said Taffy. "When I see a sergeant I assume he's like Black. I just get the jitters. He seems to be OK."

"Education Corps....better brain......better attitude," remarked Paul with a grin.

"A quiet place to pray suits me," said David.

"And me," added Taffy.

"You holy Joe's then? "asked Paul.

David did not know how to reply. "No...yes. Well..... I want to be a priest."

The other three looked at him in amazement. "The guy with the biggest chopper in the squad wants to be a priest. What a waste!" laughed Paul.

"You're Roman Catholic, then?" Taffy asked.

"No, I'm Church of England. We are the ones who get married," David replied, blushing. He was proud of his chopper and the envy of the class at school. Of course he was going to get married. He didn't believe in celibate priests.

Taffy told them he was Church of Wales but that was the same as C of E and Paul confessed he wasn't very interested in religion. Peter kept quiet but took in the conversation. Then he said, "I'm Jewish and don't have a big chopper, but ....can we all be friends?"

They all collapsed in laughter. "Trust you to be different, Pete! Show us, show us! No wonder you're the sergeant's favourite! We knew something was wrong!" came tumbling out of them. Even Peter had to laugh.

One by one the other occupants of the barrack room came back from the NAAFI full of beans and chips and beer. Amidst laughter at the sight they looked in army pyjamas they went off to the ablutions to clean their teeth. Some had a shower before bed but most were too tired as the day had been both physically and mentally exhausting. Cpl Iver turned the lights out and wished them good night, reminding them that revaleigh was at six am.

David lay for a long while listening to the breathing of his fellows in the barrack room. He had not got to his knees to pray but lay there thanking God for his very existence, his food and clothes, a safe journey, nurture for his companions, his parents, and that all those he loved should be held in God's protective arms. He even asked that Sgt Black might become a little more human. This night, he hoped God would forgive him for not expressing his supplications on his knees. He ended with the Lord's Payer: 'Our Father who art in heaven hallowed be Thy name.................'. He was unaware when slumber came, of the thrashing around of some of the recruits in their beds, which made them creek like loose floorboards, a soft sob of distress and a name of a loved one muttered. The barrack room was seething with a myriad of stifled sounds whilst in the darkness each recruit dealt with his personal emotions in a different way. Each recruit would deal in his own way with the trauma of leaving home- perhaps for the first time like David- the loss of freedom, and the endless discipline. Most would survive but a few would be broken forever.

Chapter 2

"Hands off yer cocks. Up, up it's six o'clock," Cpl Iver shouted as he put on the lights and walked down the polished floor of the barrack room. "Breakfast is served from 6.30. Be ready standing at the side of your bed for seven and we'll go from there."

The recruits unwillingly rolled out of bed, rubbing sleep out of their eyes, stretched and perhaps wondered where on earth they were. It seemed as if they had only just got to sleep before they were up again. They made their way to the ablutions, some half naked in underpants, others with towels round them and some in pyjamas. The water was hot and stimulating and they emerged invigorated with shaved faces, brushed teeth and a healthy appetite. Beds were made according to the system Iver had indicated: one blanket was placed over the bed and then at one end a boxlike sandwich of folded sheets and blankets was constructed. David had to agree that it did look neat and tidy.

At seven o'clock Cpl Iver emerged from his room and inspected each recruit and bed. There was a lot of pulling at clothes and remaking of beds until he was satisfied that things were reasonable. "Ye're a scruffy lot," he complained, "but I'll sort yer out. You Kennett, you have got to get organized. Look at yerself, look at yer bed. What a disaster." And sure enough, he was a disaster. Late from ablutions, he was just in time to stand by his bed before the inspection began. When asked why he was late and his bed was unmade, he gave the excuse that he had lost his underpants when he came out of the shower. "Lost yer underpants? Lost yer fucking underpants, Kennett," fumed Cpl Iver. "You get on parade on time even if ye're bollock naked." There were grins all round. The confrontation would be interesting, to say the least, and Kennett was so stupid he would take the corporal's word. Cpl Iver told them that breakfast was not obligatory but any soldier who fainted on parade and who had not had breakfast would be charged. It was permissible to bring a mug of tea back to the barrack room. "Don't worry about the tea," he pointed out. "It's frothy and disgustingly sweet but OK. I'm told it contains bromine, and for those who don't know, bromine stops you feeling fruity. From what I saw this morning some of you need a number of mugs of tea." Amidst laughter they were then dismissed and went for breakfast.

After breakfast the recruits were marched on an orientation visit around the camp. The tour ended in a large lecture hall where they were addressed by the Camp Commandant and then the Padre. The Commandant, a short, fat ruddy-faced colonel was unimpressive and talked in short bursts rather like a machine gun. David had forgotten what he had said after twenty minutes, he was so uninteresting. However, the Padre was different, never to be forgotten.

After the Colonel there was a wait of about ten minutes and the recruits began to get restless. Suddenly a captain with the black insignia of the Army Chaplain's Department strode on stage. He looked like any other army captain, but they were soon to find that he was unlike any officer, or clergyman, they would ever meet again. Immediately he dismissed all the NCOs. "There go your warders," he laughed as the corporals filed out of the hall. "You can relax now boys. Mother will look after your boys," he said. He was now alone with some eighty recruits. His banter with the NCOs as they left was quite unbelievable. More like a stand-up comic swapping jokes with his audience. He actually made fun of them. "You can put your feet up for an hour, but don't burn them. Freshen your makeup if you must. Do your knitting. Have a sticky bun for me........"

David couldn't believe it.

The Padre then introduced himself. "I'm your Padre......Captain Gregory, but just call me Padre. Yes, I'm a soldier and I served in France as a young lieutenant during the Second World War. Now I'm a padre and they don't fight. Except when your NCOs do you wrong." There were giggles from some of the recruits who saw the double meaning in the remark. "We comfort the dying," he went on, "minister to the sick, contact the families of the dead, hold services and do a thousand and one things for the welfare of the fighting soldier. In your case, I am your friend, the person to come to if you're in trouble or unhappy. I'm sure there are a few of you who are already unhappy. Initial training is no picnic and some of you will find it hard. My office is at the side of the chapel to the north of the camp. If you have a problem, just knock on the door and come in. No formality. If I'm not there leave a note with my clerk – he'll be the handsome one in the dress - and say which barrack room you're in and I'll find you. I'm the Church of England padre but serve all faiths on this camp, unless you prefer someone else. Just ask and I can put you in touch with the Roman Catholic padre or the Rabbi."

He went on in a serious vein for about twenty minutes but slowly wove more and more humour into what he was saying. Some of the anecdotes were rather riske but everyone laughed. It was a relief to laugh. The padre knew how tense the recruits were and played to his audience. Ultimately, he had everyone rocking in their seats. If David had been less innocent, he would have recognized the whole performance as high camp, (1) but he took it as fun and missed the sexual inuendos.

At the end of the session the Padre passed round a collection bag that he called his 'dolly bag' explaining that the money was used to help recruits and their families who got into difficulties. As if by magic, the NCOs arrived to take over and the Padre was cheered off the platform. "Been giving you his usual bullshit, has he?" commented Cpl Iver. "Have to watch that one. Too fond of the boys," and he marched them off without further comment.

That same morning the recruits were taken along to the barber's shop where each one was to be given a haircut. There was no choice. "You've all to get yer hair cut," ordered Cpl Iver. "Orders. You can tell the nice man what style yer want, if you like. But he only knows one style and that's short. And when I say 'short', I mean short."

One-by-one they went in and one-by-one they came out bereft of curls, looking like newly shorn sheep. Somehow they all looked the same, and certainly they were very aware that their individuality had been lost. David felt degraded. He was no longer a person in his own right, just one of the crowd, a clone. The first few to be attacked, as that was what the barber did, like Sweeny Todd (2), were made fun of and called 'baldy' but the fun soon deteriorated into sullen acceptance. And they had to pay for this forced degradation of their individuality out of their own pockets.

It was all part of the army's policy to break the spirit and make the recruits conform. There was no consideration of the psychological trauma involved. All the military could see was the need for pliable, conformist individuals. The recruits certainly felt intimidated by it all and it was a very sober group that left the barber's shop that morning. Today, in the twenty-first century, there would have been a complaint to the Commission on Human Rights, (3) but fifty years ago there was no body that would protect them against the inhumanity of the State.

That evening David went with Taffy to the makeshift chapel. They were both subdued and needed some form of uplift. Sgt Walters was there with five others whom he introduced. After the introductions, they read evensong together. One was a sergeant who had a beautifully modulated voice, one worked in the sick bay, two were clerks, and the other was a corporal from HQ company. They were a friendly lot and David enjoyed their company and the feeling that all was not against them. Sergeant Walters told David that he was an ordinand and had been accepted by Kings College, London University. David was amazed, as he too was going to King's too, and so he informed Sgt Walters. He was delighted and they talked at length. They talked so much that they had to rush to get their meal from the mess, but David

27

and Taffy felt that they had made sincere friends who would guide them spiritually and help with problems during their period at Queen Elizabeth Barracks.

The days became routine. Breakfast, drill on the square, lectures on first aid and other associated subjects, nursing practice, physical education, more drill, education for those who needed it, and yet more drill. They learned how to polish their boots. You might regard that as easy but to get a toe-cap that looked like black glass for parades was no easy matter. Army boots have a surface like orange peel all over. Oh no, the toe-caps are the same. Now a sensible outfit would have had the toe-caps of smooth leather for ease of polishing, but the army is not sensible, just bloody awkward. It wants its soldiers to waste their time doing useless tasks like cleaning brass, which could quite easily be stainless. Back to the boots. The way forward is to heat your army issue spoon over a hot candle – that is where the candles came in - and then apply the back of the hot spoon to the toe-cap. After a few days of patience, the leather becomes smooth and polish can be applied. But easy, not so fast, it has to be 'spit and polish' literally. You put a blob of polish on your cloth, apply it to the leather and then spit on it, working it around with a circular motion. After doing this for several hours, a highly polished layer is achieved. But that is not enough. To get the mirror effect, one has to hold the toe-cap under the cold water tap, let the water flow, and gently polish with cotton wool. In this way a really 'bulled' toe-cap is produced. To think that the State and parents spend thousands of pounds educating their offspring to have them waste hours of valuable time bulling boots. And the terrible truth is that the boot would probably only last for one parade, as some fool would step on it and the process has to start all over again.

When on parade one had to look 'immaculate' as the NCOs would say. That meant boots perfect, brass on cap and belt gleaming, gaiters and belt duly blancoed (4) and your battle dress pressed and creased in a particular way. Now the battle dress (5) or 'bd' is made of rough khaki material that does not take a crease easily. Oh, by the way, the officers have fine worsted that does take a good crease, and in any case they have a batman(6) to do their kit. In order to become a smart soldier with fine creases everywhere, the material is slightly shaved with a razor where the crease has to be. The next task is to place brown paper over the intended crease, water it with a shaving brush, and then apply pressure with a hot iron. Little by little each soldier acquires the technique and queues to use the barrack room electric iron. Trousers have to slightly overhang the gaiter (7), and look smart. To achieve this, a piece of folded newspaper is put down to give a full appearance. With all this 'bull' (8) David found that evenings were spent ironing and polishing with a quick visit to the NAAFI for beans and chips.

Drill was something David enjoyed. He found that there was something very satisfying when the whole squad acted as one. To get perfection, where the squad marched as one man, was not easy and the drill sergeants were perfectionists. Drill was taught by the use of numbers and shouting those numbers out loud. "One pause, two pause," could be heard from various parts of the drill square. Little by little the squad got more efficient and looked more like soldiers, except for Private Kennett. He had little sense of timing or co-ordination. Corporal Iver despaired of him. "You could be tops lads," he would say, "but Kennett is ruinous."

David had only been in the army two weeks when Asian Flu (9) hit Europe. It was terribly virulent and people all over went down like ninepins. The military was no exception and soldiers were collapsing all over. The symptoms were classic: hot flushes, shivering, high temperature and fever, usually resulting in collapse. In David's barrack room young men either reported sick, or like David, fought the symptoms until they collapsed and were carried off by their colleagues or medical orderlies to the sick bay. David had been feeling rotten all day, did not go to the NAFFI, and was brought a mug of hot tea by Paul, who was just recovering after four days in the sick bay. David sat on his bed and visibly shivered. He just could not control himself but refused to report sick. To have to pack a haversack with all sorts of useless kit in order to report sick, when you felt so unwell, was beyond him. Finally he keeled over and was carried to the sick bay by his friends.

There was little he could remember of the next few days. His whole body ached and burned. He had no strength and he was terribly thirsty. It was at night that he felt most ill. He remembered waking up longing for a drink of water. He could see a light at the end of a black tunnel. Sweat covered him; the whole bed was wet. 'Why could he not get a drink? Would nobody help him?' He must have moaned or shouted out as an arm lifted his shoulders, and a spouted drinking mug was placed to his lips. "It's ok Dave," a voice said. David drank and then slumped back into oblivion again. He was unaware of his surroundings for three days. On the fourth day one of the Christian group, a medical orderly, came to see him and told him how ill he had been. "It often strikes the fittest the worst, Dave, and you had a real rough time." When he was stronger he was sent back to the barrack room and given three days of 'light duties' along with a couple of others.

On the fourth week of training, very early one Friday morning, all the recruits were woken up, told to wash and dress, and then bundled into army trucks and taken to, what David learned later, was a military range on Salisbury Plain. Just as dawn came up on a very cold and misty morning, they alighted from the trucks and in a large tent were given steaming mugs of tea and sandwiches. They were then split into groups and sent to various parts of the tented encampment amongst newly dug trenches.

Later David found that where he was sent was supposed to be an RAMC Field Hospital on the edge of a battle zone, and erected for the purpose of demonstrating to top NATO (10) military personnel what the RAMC could do. The whole was an exercise to show what the NATO partners could do in the event of another European War.

The recruits were supposed to be patients injured on the battlefield and so the military makeup team got to work on them. David was cold and frightened and was directed to lie on a table where immediately his trousers were torn by the makeup men, and things were done to his leg. Plastic pipes were inserted down his trousers and a rubber balloon put in his left hand on the other side from his supposedly 'shattered leg'. Apparently they doused him with plenty of 'blood' and bandaged his head. His face was whitened to make it seem he was in shock. All this took nearly two hours.

David was more worried about the damage to his trousers than what they were doing to him. How would he explain when he returned that he had not damaged them? Then a friendly voice observed, "Well son, if you could only see yourself. Looks almost real." It was one of the medical officers who were supposed to be doing the operation. "You've got a broken leg with the bone sticking through the flesh and gangrene has set in. We're supposed to be amputating. That thing in your hand is to squeeze to spurt blood. Fine job they've done."

David was silent.

Two more officers arrived, one the chief surgeon and the other the anaesthetist. "Are we going to put him under then?" one asked with a smile on his face.

"No, we'll do it cold," said the other with a wink.

David could only hear and not see as he was flat on his back. The idea of being given, or not, an anaesthetic was terrifying to him and he came out in a cold sweat.

"Don't worry son," came a reassuring voice – David did not know which officer it was – "we'll just put the mask over your face and pretend. But don't forget to keep that blood going."

David tried to smile: "Thank you, sir."

"Not been in the army long then?" asked one of them.

30

"Four weeks, sir."

"Bit of a rest for you today and tomorrow. Top brass from NATO coming round." The voice laughed, "What they see here won't help their digestion. They'll need a stiff whisky by the time they get back to the mess."

At about ten o'clock the first helicopters were heard landing and half an hour later the word came down the line that the VIPs were on their way. A mask was placed over David's nose and he heard the clink of instruments. "When I say blood," he heard a voice say, "squeeze that bloody balloon and stop when I tell you. Don't move a muscle or we'll have to actually put you out."

There was a scuffing of feet. "Blood," said a voice and David squeezed in a rhythmic way as he had been shown.

A new cultured voice said, "This gentlemen is our field operating theatre. What you see here is a leg being amputated."

There was a cough. Then a scuffle and a voice said, "Catch him, someone" and then the sound of people rushing about. David never moved a muscle, although he was feeling cramped. Silence. Then the sound of feet scuffing again and a distant voice saying: "In the next tent we have the recovery ward."

"You can stop squeezing now," a voice said. "Well done!"

As the voiced died away chaotic laughter broke out. "Poor sod, turned as green as a pea and passed out."

Another voice said, "The others didn't look too well either. That fat general looked as if he was going to spew up."

"What can you expect," remarked another medical officer. I bet they're all pen pushers and have never seen a wounded soldier before."

"OK sonny, you can relax now. Sit up if you want. We don't get another group until after lunch," said the voice. "You did a great job."

David was helped to sit up by a number of hands and for the first time could see where he was.

He was in a large tent equipped as a field operating theatre. There must have been about eight people in the team, three medical officers and other medical personnel, all male. They were all smiling and chatting. A sergeant brought in mugs of tea for everyone, including David. As he handed David the tea he observed, "You were fine soldier. Perfect. It looked just like I've seen for real."

Another medic dressed in white observed, "So real one of the VIPs fainted and had to be carried out."

The word came down the line that lunch would be served but David, like many of the other 'patients' had to stay where they were because of the complexity of their makeup. A private from the Catering Corps brought David a mug of tea and a steaming mess tin of all-in stew. "Cripes," he said, "you look bloody terrible. No wonder them bastards passed out." Then he was off to recount his meeting with a war wounded. So the word had got round about a senior officer passing out. Amazing how the informal communication system works in the army!

An afternoon and a further day passed with David being the star patient. He found the medical officers and staff very friendly and had lots of laughs between performances. Only one person passed out however, but a number were sick after witnessing the bogus amputation. The two days had been fun, if rather tiring doing nothing. Even his worries over his torn battle dress were overcome when one of the medical officers gave him a note of explanation. The storekeeper's only comment when he went for a new pair of trousers and explained what had happened was: "As long as they didn't amputate yer dick."

One rotten apple infects the rest and that is true of a squad of soldiers. A squad is a unity and acts together for the benefit and safety of all. David had learnt the value of comradeship with the Asian 'Flu incident and realized that survival depended on all working together. Unfortunately, Peter Kennett was the rotten apple and the squad was suffering. They had virtually taken over his kit: he rarely polished and bumped the central floor as he was so useless, and they even wrote his letters, but they could not do drill for him. He could now march to some extent and was beginning to learn his left from his right but his reactions were so slow. Drill was timed by shouting out numbers. 'One - pause – two' and the squad did the turn etc as one man, except Kennett. You could hear the feet stamp as one man and a split second later a single stamp – Kennett.

Staff Sgt Ali, the senior drill sergeant, would go mad and shout and ball but Peter Kennett was oblivious to his rampaging. He still went on making a mess of things and the squad had extra drill frequently when they should be at the NAAFI or having a rest.

The squad had tried everything to alter his ways. "Talk to him Dave," the squad had agreed. "He respects you. Maybe he'll listen." David had talked to him. He liked Peter but the guy was thick. Oh yes, he would try to do better, but it was to no avail. They had frog marched him to the sluice, stripped him and given him a cold shower two or three times but to no effect. Some of the squad had even blacked his balls with boot polish. No change.

One evening, Cpl Iver called a few of them into his little room by the entrance to their barrack room. He explained that he was concerned about all the extra drill they had to do because of Kennett. "You're a good group," he said, "and quite capable of winning the drill shield, but

Kennett is screwing things up for you. I'm due for demob quite soon and you are my last group. I want to go out on a high and I know you lads can do it."

"But what can we do corp?" asked Andy Grade who hailed from south London.

Paul groaned. "We've tried everything: reason, kindness, bullying......"

"There must be a solution," remarked John Kent, the Boy Scout who was behind Peter Kennett in the squad.

"There's got to be," Paul said, "I can't stand many more extra drill parades."

"But what?" asked Iver.

"We suffer while he just smiles," remarked Eric James, one of the older men in the squad. "The only time we have peace is when he goes sick."

David suddenly had a brainwave. "But that's it. We have to make him go sick so he doesn't do drill."

"You're right Dave," Paul observed eagerly. "But how do we make him go sick? Beat him up? No, we'd be inside before you could say Sergeant Ali."

They all looked at each other. There was silence.

Eric slowly said, "Suppose ....we can get him excused boots?"

"You mean bribe the MO, Eric?" asked David. "Impossible."

A sickly grin came over John Kent's face. "No, but we could make sure he had to get excused boots."

How come, John?" asked Cpl Iver.

"Well," said John, "you know that I stand behind him in the rank. Dave is at one side and Paul at the other. I know Dave has complained about getting kicked by him as he doesn't know his bloody left from his right. I get kicked and I suspect Paul does also."

Paul nodded his head.

"Well, let's give him what he gives us, only a lot more. If we all three kick his ankles then they'll swell up, he'll go sick, be legitimately excused boots and hay presto!"

"You're a bloody marvel even if you are a Boy Scout," Eric James observed gleefully.

"But that's not fair.....," exclaimed David. He went no further as they all were looking at him.

"We know you're a gentle guy David and are always honest, but what is the alternative.....? asked Paul. "It's for the good of the whole squad."

David thought. 'Yes, they were suffering because of Peter and he

33

didn't seem to care. Unity and comradeship was important.' "Ok,....
I'll go along with it, although Peter is a harmless sort of guy. It's only
because he's so thick that he lets us down."

"You can say that again, Dave," said Cpl Iver. "That's agreed then.
Paul, Dave and John will do their stuff."

The following day the plan was put into action. Left, right, left,
right, kick, kick, kick, kick...... There was no letup on Kennett's ankles
and within three days he had packed his haversack and gone sick.

Kennett had remarked to David: "You keep kicking me, Dave."

Paul had looked across at David as if to say, 'Now don't get soft and
screw things up.'

"It's your marching, Pete," David lied. "You've just got to get it
right." He felt terrible about it.

'Excused boots' was just about the best diagnosis the MO had ever
made. At least, that is what the recruits of squad C thought.

There were others in the RAMC who were not good at marching.
One afternoon Paul, Taffy and David were in the gym supposedly
polishing the floor. In fact, it was a sinecure as they were excused the
education lectures and Sgt Walters always found them something easy
to undertake. Sometimes it was stoking the fire in the education office,
and this meant keeping warm in front of the stove for an hour. On this
particularly frosty afternoon, they were inside the gym keeping warm
and going through the motions of polishing the floor. From the
windows they could see Staff Sgt Ali taking a group of eight 'sprog'
officers through their paces on the parade ground. One, like Kennett,
did not know his left foot from his right. Obviously intelligent, as he
was a doctor, he was uncoordinated. David hoped he was not a
surgeon!

Ali's voice could be heard, even inside the gym. "Your right fucking
foot, SIR," he bawled. "I 'ope you don't take out my bloody appendix."

He always ended his shouting with a loud 'SIR' showing the officer
he was giving him due respect. Ali was smart, tough and a brilliant drill
sergeant. Even the officers were a little scared of him as he had a way
of dressing them down if they messed things up on parade. He would
always say 'SIR' so they could not complain.

"If you start on your right foot, SIR, you'll get it right," he went on.

If looks could kill Ali would be dead. "Yes, Staff Sergeant," yelped
the officer.

"Can't hear, SIR," bawled Ali.

"My right foot, staff sergeant," yelled the officer.

'Poor guy,' thought David. 'Once Ali gets his knife into you....
You'll not sleep for a week.'

The group was given a break and Staff Sergeant Ali was seen making for the gym. Suddenly the place was a hive of activity. As he entered they jumped to attention, almost trembling with fear. Ai was a demon and just the sight of this little swarthy Indian or maybe Arab, gave most recruits nightmares.

"At ease," he barked. "Get on with your job." He took out a tin from his battle-dress blouse and a box of matches. He took a cigarette from the tin, lit it, drew from it and exhaled with a sigh of pleasure. He was not supposed to smoke in the gym, but who would argue with Ali? He sauntered over to David and watched him for a while. David was aware of his dark eyes piercing into his back but dared not turn around or stop the regular movement of the bumper (11) as he polished. "What's you name, soldier?" asked a voice.

Quickly David straightened up, dropped the stick of the bumper and came to attention. "933 Private Earl, Sir."

"At ease, son," said Ali, "this is informal."

"Sir!" responded David dubiously.

"You enjoy drill, don't you?"

"Yes, sir."

"I've been watching you. You're right marker for squad C."

"Yes, sir."

"I like the way you hold yourself. You're shaping up well. You've the makings of a squaddy."

"Thank you, sir."

"Unlike that little bugger out there," smoldered Ali. His eyes narrowed. "But I'll have him. Stuck up little fucker. Useless!"

David said nothing.

"Just because they're doctors they don't want to do drill. Who do they think they are, bloody Albert Schweitzer?" (12) With that he stubbed out his cigarette, returned the butt to the tin, placed it inside his battle dress blouse, and left like a whirlwind.

"Wow," said Taffy, "I thought we were in for it."

Paul gave David a push. "He obviously fancies you. He was quite human."

"He knows a good soldier when he sees one," laughed David as he raced for the door with the other two throwing polish cloths at him.

David was a good soldier. However, misfortune hit him hard one morning. They were late for NAAFI break through no fault of their own. It was busy and it took a long time for them to get served. The result was that they had to gulp down their coffee and sticky bun. Cpl Iver called them and they rushed outside swallowing what was in their mouths. As ill luck would have it, Sgt Black was standing outside like a vulture waiting for its prey. David was not the only one having a last gulp as he lined up, but he was the one Black picked on. "You eating, soldier?" he demanded.

It was no use arguing. "Yes, sergeant."

"What's your name?"

"933 Private Earl, sergeant."

"You're on a charge. Eating on parade. Cpl Iver will appear with you at 6 pm this evening in the Company Office. Take over corporal." With that he marched away.

The whole squad just gawped. They could not believe that the man could be so childish. David had been to a tough school where discipline was tight, but this was just ridiculous. He could accept punishment if it was deserved but this was just unfair.

During the rest of the day the squad showed great sympathy. Cpl Iver was tight lipped but the squad knew he was not to blame. At 5.30 pm the whole squad helped David with his kit as he had to appear in front of the Company Commander in his best kit. Cpl Iver marched him at the double there. Left, right, left, right, right turn left turn, about turn..... It was a nightmare but he achieved it with some dignity. Sgt Black was there breathing fire, but David had the distinct impression that the Company Commander disliked Black.

He was given five days of fatigues at the Company Office from 7 – 10 pm. It turned out that he did a little polishing, kept the stove in coal, washed the floor once and spent a lot of time talking to the company clerks. One evening the Company Commander was there and spent an hour talking to David about his family, his vocation and what life could be like at university. So he lost his freedom for five days but he made new friends. Oh, and as a footnote, David heard a year later that when Black was demobed, he was beaten up by a group of disgruntled ex-recruits. They were not all as forgiving as David.

Physical education was something else that David enjoyed, although it was not enjoyed by the majority. He was always the star at school. He found it easy. He was mostly chosen to demonstrate something new. The physical training instructors or PTIs, as they were called, generally had bulging muscles and bad tempers. David thought they had wonderful bodies and would have liked his to be as good. He never tired of watching them demonstrate on the apparatus for the sheer poetry of their movement. However, he was good in the gym, never crossed them, and they respected his ability and frequently he was asked to do a demonstration. Now some of the things they had to do required strength. Hauling oneself up a rope, for instance. David went to the top like a monkey and back down again. It was easy. Some boys had no strength in their arms and got shouted at. Others got up the rope, but having looked down were too afraid to come down. There were other activities that needed agility and some courage, like vaulting over a horse. Generally they all would have a go, but Peter Kennett was one of the boys who just refused to vault and was charged with failing to comply with an order.

The only thing that David disliked about PE was that there was never time to get dried after the compulsory shower. One had to dress wet and then dash off to a lecture that usually followed gym and sit for a very uncomfortable hour. The lecturer would drone on and he would feel his clothes sticking to him and chafing. It was an unhealthy situation and one would have thought the Medical Corps had more sense.

Army lectures were rather like painting by numbers. The NCOs who delivered them had just learned them parrot fashion with little understanding of their content. Paul, Taffy and David had 'A' levels and Eric was an ex medical student so when it came to the anatomy and physiology lectures they led the sergeant a dance with their questions. It was obvious that he knew very little and after a while he would refuse to answer when asked a question by one of the four. He frequently referred the questions of others to them when he was at a loss. It was all very simple and David began to realize that the majority of recruits were not very bright. Being educated at a Grammar School, he thought that everyone could read and write and had a wide knowledge. He was wrong. He, Paul, Taffy and Eric were a very small percentage of highly educated teenagers – about 2% of the population went to university – and the rest were destined for manual jobs. Apart from the four of them, all the rest of the squad had to attend compulsory education classes.

One Sunday morning after service, a group stopped to talk to the Padre. It had been a very stimulating service, and the voluntary, played on a large electronic organ by a local lady organist, had been particularly enjoyable. Taffy and Paul had been talking to the lady who came in to play each Sunday.

"Hey," cried Paul, "Taffy says he can play the organ."

"Go on then, Taffy," urged the Padre. "Let's see what you can do." He had a smile on his face as if to say 'Go on soldier, make a fool of yourself."

Taffy sat down at the console. There was no messing about as he obviously knew what he was doing. He sat on the long seat in front of the console and began his preparations. As David had played a little, he noted Taffy's confidence. Stops were pulled for all the three manuals. Then he began.

Three magnificent chords startled everyone in the chapel, including the Padre who was on the way to the vestry. David knew immediately what it was. He had listened to it on record many times. The Padre stopped, turned, listened and then slowly began to walk back to where the others were standing. Amazement was on every face. This little, freckled, white-faced Welshman, who was so self-effacing, was playing the magnificent 'Widor Toccata.' (13) It was like Quasimodo (14) sitting at the organ of Notre Dame and entertaining Esmeralda. He played magnificently and the sound so grand and spellbinding that they all stood silently until the last note of the fuge had died away. Then there was silence. Disbelief.

Suddenly they were all around him, patting him on the shoulders and ringing his hand. "You never told us Taffy. Where did you learn that? Magnificent. Play us something else," came hard and fast.

"Where did you learn to play like that?" asked the Padre.

"In Wales. You see I'm the assistant organist at Bangor Cathedral. I'll be going to Oxford on a music scholarship when I've finished service," he told them.

"If I'd have known you had that talent young man, I'd have had you playing before now," the Padre told him. What about it?"

"I'm not sure, sir," replied Taffy. "You see we sometimes have to do extra duty after Church Parade."

"Leave that to me young man, "offered the Padre. "When I tell the Colonel about your playing he'll offer you the world. Great man for music the colonel."

And so Taffy became the chapel organist alongside the lady organist. Sunday was a free day for him and he gave the congregation so much pleasure. He also didn't change as a person in spite of his fame. He was the loveable little Welshman who sometimes masqueraded as a ghost in his long, white combinations.

So the days continued their ordered momentum. Nights were spent cleaning and pressing with a quick dash to the NAAFI for egg and chips and a cup of strong tea. Although weekends started on a Saturday after lunch, there was the compulsory church parade on a Sunday morning and perhaps a visit to the camp cinema to see Jane Russell or Marilyn Monroe. (15) The daily prayer sessions were a comfort to David and most of the time 'Taffy' would accompany him. Sergeant Walters was always a great help offering practical advice on how to circumvent camp rules or put them to your own advantage. However, there was one event always in the minds of the recruits – freedom.

They had been told that after their initial six weeks of training they would be allowed off camp to meet their loved ones. It was not a weekend pass as they had to return to camp at night, but at least it was a reprieve from routine and isolation. Corporal Iver had warned them that they needed to demonstrate that they were smart soldiers and able to uphold the standards of the army off camp. His warning fell on stony ground as the recruits just did not comprehend the deviousness of the military.

David wrote to his parents of his 'release from prison' as he put it and they decided to motor down from Leicester for the weekend and stay at an hotel in Aldershot, the nearest large town.

On the Friday night before their forthcoming 'release', the boys fell to polishing and pressing as they had never done before. Every soldier wanted to see the outside world and if it meant cleaning kit until the small hours, it was a worthwhile price to pay for it. 'Freedom' was the pearl of great price that they all longed for. The stony ground was fertile but the hearts of stone were with the military as they were soon to find out

Late October can be one of the most beautiful times of the year. In the south of England the leaves fall later and around the camp the beech, oak and ash were still in full colour. The red, yellow and orange of autumn clothed the countryside as if Picasso (16) had danced in revelry throughout the night. Dawn saw a mist swirl amongst the huts and the day was bitterly cold. As soldiers trotted to the mess for their breakfast, mugs clanking, their breath streamed out like dialogue bubbles in a comic paper, there was an air of anticipation amongst the new recruits.

All this, and the expectancy of the day, encouraged the recruits to eat a hearty breakfast. (And the condemned man ate a hearty breakfast.) The morning tasks, drill, a lecture on first aid, more drill, NAAFI break and then simple nursing care in the nursing center completed the morning. At midday they were released and it became a race to get to the mess for lunch and then back to the barrack room to get into their best uniform. One o'clock was the release time and Cpl Iver helped by adjusting belts, folding trousers over gaiters and arranging berets so they did not look like flying saucers.

They were marched up to the Company Office where, of course, there was a queue formed. Other squads were waiting to be inspected. 'Oh no!' whispered David to Paul as he could see who was inside with the Duty Officer, Sergeant Black and Warrant Officer First Class Cogill. Now Black was an ogre, but Cogill was a bespectacled sadist who would stop at nothing to make the recruits squirm. He was the devil incarnate. Universally hated, David suspected that in civilian life the man would be a gangland boss with several murders to his credit.

The queue slowly moved along and each recruit emerged, face as long as a week, without the clearance paper that was so badly needed to get through the main gate. They all could hear the remarks as each recruit failed inspection and was told to go back and work on a particular piece of kit. "Call yourself a soldier," thundered Black to one soldier who was decently turned out. "Fucking disgrace to the army. Look at yer belt. Look at yer boots. Get back to yer room and clean up."

Cogill was just as loud and rude as if the two were trying to outdo each other, whilst the Duty Officer stood at their side, stony faced. "What shit is this?" came the demand. "Yer look like a sack of spuds. Not a crease in sight. Her Majesty don't want a mess like you on the streets. Back yer go sonny until I see better."

David thought of his headmaster who was pretty strict but would never behave in such an uncouth way. Most of these lads came from decent homes, and yet had to be subjected to foul language and loutish behavior. So this was what the taxpayer was financing?

David began to get nearer to the disaster zone and could see that each recruit marched up to a white line, came to attention and saluted the Duty Officer. He then stayed at attention while he was insulted, saluted when dismissed, did an about turn and marched out of the office, possibly trying to keep back the tears or the anger. He was about number six when the office phone rang. Black answered it, talked for a while and then looked around the room with his beady eyes. "Is 933 Private Earl here?" he barked.

David was dumbfounded. 'Why did Black want him? What evil intent did he have?' He came to attention: "933 Private Earl, here sergeant."

"Come to the front soldier," he commanded with menace in his voice.

"Sergeant." David moved quickly and smartly and threw a salute at the officer.

"Yer father's asking for yer. Seems e's talking to the Guard Commander at the main gate. Pally with him, is e?"

David never made a sound to the rhetorical question.

"What you father do, sonny. MP or somethin'?"

"No sergeant. He's a businessman."

"Well e's got the attention of the Guard Commander. Not that y're fit to go. Sloppy, that's what you are, but I've been told to let yer go. Take care soldier, I've met yer kind before." With that he got the officer to sign his pass.

David saluted, did a smart about turn and marched out of the office.

He was shaking with fear.

Corporal Iver met him outside. "You're a lucky one, you are," he said. "I bet you're the only one to get away today. Now go before someone changes his mind. Be back by ten thirty."

The distance from the Company Office to the main gate was covered by David in record time. Not that he ran. He marched with purpose. A free man for a few hours. When he reached the car park at the main gate, he saw why the Guard Commander had his father in conversation. In front of them was a brand new green and cream Ford Zodiac, the latest model and looking very smart indeed. Fit to turn all heads. The model was only just released and somehow his father had managed to get one. Obviously, it was a surprise for him. In the back seat was his mother, smiling ecstatically and, wonders never cease, the dog as well. The Guard Commander, a captain in the Military Police, waved David over. David gave a smart salute and showed him the pass. "Well young man," he said, "not only an afternoon out but a super car to ride in. I'll sign you out Private, don't worry. Pleasure to meet you Mr Earl." With that he saluted David's father and was gone into the Guard Room.

"Let's go, dad," David offered, "before they change their minds." And he got into the car. The dog went wild and his mother shed a tear saying how fit he looked, but a lot too thin.

And so 'freedom' for a few hours was achieved. But at a price.

The afternoon was spent in Windsor Great Park. (17) The dog loved it but would not go very far from David. 'Laddie' was a present for passing his eleven plus exam and as his mother put it, "The best seven-and-sixpence she had ever spent." Dinner was in a smart hotel in Aldershot where his parents were staying, and so good after army rations.

His mother had baked him a fruit cake and a neighbor had sent some freshly baked rolls so there was a parcel under his arm when he entered the main Guard Room to sign in. He came to attention at the white line and gave his name to the corporal who was at the desk.

"Ere's the one whose palsy with the Guard Commander," he shouted to his colleague in the back office.

The other, a lance corporal, came through. "Well, well," he pronounced, "and what 'ave yer under yer arm?"

"Cake, corporal," replied David politely.

"Don't the little nancy boy with the big car like army food then?"

David made no reply. He deemed it better that way.

"I arsked yer a question, soldier?" barked the corporal. "Give it ere." And he snatched the parcel.

"The food is fine corporal but my mother wanted me to have it."

"My mother wanted me to have it," he mimicked. "Yer got a fucking mother then?"

With that the two of them spent the next ten minutes – it seemed like an hour – making David right turn, left turn, about turn and anything else their warped little minds could think of to their great delight. 'So it was true what was said of the Military Police.' David thought. 'They were the dregs of humanity who took a delight in sadistic behavior.' He resolved that after training, he would gain some rank and somehow teach these two morons a lesson in manners. And so he returned to the barrack room, dizzy from his experience, to find that only two others had been released that day. So much for the promise of freedom!

Chapter 3

It is amazing how routine anaesthetizes the memory so that time appears to pass quickly. The recruits at Queen Elizabeth Barracks progressed from one day to another without even registering the weeks and months of training. They were certainly kept busy. There was no time to ponder their situation or consider what their training was about, just obey orders and go through the daily routine. To the army, they were slowly becoming soldiers.

A soldier is similar to a machine: he just does what his operator directs. There is no thinking process, just obedience to orders. In the foot regiments the soldier is a killing machine. The RAMC is slightly different. David and his fellow recruits were still to be machines, but not killing machines. The dichotomy was that sometimes they were required to think and other times to resort to blind obedience. Medics cannot be zombies like foot soldiers, for they have to make decisions, at its most simplistic about what first aid to give, and yet at other times were expected to just obeyed commands without question. Generally, the soldier in the RAMC is more intelligent than the foot soldier, and certainly in the case of David and his friends, except for Peter Kennett. The unit sent him to the Pioneer Corps – regarded as the pits within the military - to try and get rid of him, but he was sent back to the RAMC as he was of no use to them. He certainly made life difficult for everyone.

What was the real intention of government after the second- world-war? Was it to create a reserve of fighting personnel who could defend the country if attacked? Or was it more sinister? To create a young population conditioned to obey, and lacking in thinking skills, in case they might demand change. Their parents had been promised a better life and a safer world? Returning troops had seen much and had been promised much. Churchill had promised that every fighting man would be welcomed as a hero on his return to 'Blighty'. A better world and more equality for all was what those brave men and women fought for. But the reality was something different.

The fighting man was soon forgotten and ignored. There was mass unemployment. Returning troops found that men who had not fought had taken their jobs. Those Commonwealth troops who fought were not remembered until 2002 when in November of that year Queen Elizabeth II inaugurated a Memorial Gate (1) near Hyde Park in London, commemorating the efforts made by unsung heroes from the Commonwealth. The stay-at-homes, the ones who found an excuse not to be in the armed forces, who made money while others fought, were the ones who benefited from the war. The arms dealers, captains of industry, property developers and politicians, were the ones who had a 'good war' and it was the ordinary soldier, sailor and airman and their families who suffered. One Labour politician and his wife lived at the Ritz Hotel for most of the war. Many politicians made money out of the war and became the ones with power who were looked up to in post war Britain. The memory of 'Mr Average' is a short one.

The reason given by politicians for National Service was to provide a force so that Great Britain would never again be unprepared for war as she was in 1939. That was a noble and appropriate aim. But what kind of war would it be in the future? Would the 'zombie soldier' be relevant or would the requirement be for highly skilled technocrats? As it has been now proved, the training used during National Service was inappropriate for a new era. It was a waste of taxpayers' money.

Would there be war? The United Nations was created to ensure that there would no longer be wars. What a joke. Certainly modern wars have not been the large-scale conflicts of yesteryear. But they are more frequent now. The conflicts are equally as bloody and more civilians become involved than in previous conflicts. It could be said that it is safer to be a soldier than a civilian in modern warfare. The United Nations has failed in its task of stopping war and become an expensive talking shop dominated by the United States of America.

It was clear to most thinking National Serviceman that a country needs to be prepared but the training given to them was based on old social concepts of social class. The soldier is a servant who slogs along without question at his master's bidding; an appropriate concept for the eighteenth and nineteenth centuries when the masses were uneducated and unskilled. Leaders were officers and gentlemen. What good is a gentleman who is unable to think? In the modern post-war world the masses were better educated and ideas, initiative and technical competence was required more and more. David found that his officers, generally, were not particularly well education, except for the doctors. The greater percentage had come up through the public school (3) system, and whilst they were at home drinking pink gins in the officers' mess, they were poor leaders, preferring to lead from the back and not by example.

Training was just about as appropriate as learning how to ride a horse was in the First World War. (4) Obeying orders blindly may be fitting for an uneducated generation, but not for a generation that was as well educated as many of the officers who led them. In some cases, as David was to find out later in his army experience when he served with the Life Guards, he was better educated than many of the officers. Much was a waste of time, potential, and taxpayers' money and inappropriate for a modern fighting force. Where were the thinkers in the War Office (5) who should have designed training fitting for a changing world?

By the end of November the recruits should have reached the end of their basic training and be ready to be posted to a unit. There was some apprehension amongst the recruits as certain military theatres were notorious for loss of life, even in a post war world. In Cyprus the British were fighting a guerrilla war against Greek separatists under the leadership of General Grivas and his political master, Archbishop Makarios; (6) in Kenya Jomo Kenyata led his mercenary band called Mau Mau (7)seeking freedom from the British; in the Aden Protectorate (South Yemen) malcontents encouraged by President Nasser of Egypt (8) under an Islamic banner, demanded home rule; and there was the continuing menace of Russia in the Balkans and the partition of Berlin.(9) Each place had its history of loss of life and it was generally the young National Serviceman who faced the trouble as Britain had reduced its numbers of professional soldiers to a minimum. It was cheaper to send a National Serviceman at thirty shillings a week than a professional soldier at six times that amount.

David knew that he would not be posted to a unit directly after basic training as he had been selected for further training. His exam results were excellent and he was chosen to train as a radiographer. However, the Recruitment Officer sent for him some time later and persuaded him to change and train as an operating theatre technician. He made it sound very glamorous with what turned out to be false information. As David was to learn later, it was a bad decision for him. The military hospital at Millbank, London, where he was posted, was no picnic.

Eric had applied for a commission and was going for officer training and "Taffy" was to go to the Royal Military School of Music. David had thought about a commission and talked to the Recruitment Officer. It meant serving another year in the army and he didn't want to postpone his university studies any further. Paul, who had been top of the class with David and Eric, was posted to the Woolwich Hospital to train as a radiographer. John Kent was going to a plum posting in Germany. It was later rumored that the padre had helped him. What is certain was that the boy scout and the padre were very close and John spent a great deal of time off camp at the padre's home. The rest were being posted to various parts of the world including Aden, Cyprus, Kenya and Berlin. Peter Kendrick was posted as an orderly to Woolwich Hospital. As Andy Grade pointed out unkindly: "He'll be in

45

charge of the bog shoveling shit."

One of the most stupid three weeks that David and his friends had to spend during their basic training was on 'fatigues'. There were three activities that all had to undertake during that period: working in the tin room in the kitchen up to the elbows in grease cleaning huge cooking tins, riding the dust cart emptying dustbins, and peeling endless sacks of potatoes. In theory it was designed to break the spirit and mould the recruit into a pliable soldier who would do anything ordered by an officer. Of course, the military called this 'character building' and 'accepting discipline' but those with sense knew it was just a form of cheap labor.

There are other more effective ways of molding character and instilling discipline as H.R.H. The Duke of Edinburgh showed in his award scheme.(10) But the military did not have a lot of sense and were still motivated by class divisions. As a retired Army Colonel and Commander of a training camp (11) was to tell David at a later stage in his life: "Most of you were too intelligent and we didn't know what to do with you." In consequence, the recruits were treated like workers from the slums and made to feel dirty and humiliated.

Peeling potatoes using a special 'rumbling' machine was easy. The hard task was sitting and taking the 'eyes' and other malformations out of the potato one rumbled. There were sacks and sacks of them to deal with day after day by the team of six recruits. It was boring but not particularly nasty. Gossip and story telling helped the day along. The cooks from the Catering Corps supplied endless cups of tea and the vegetable room was comparatively warm.

The tin room was even warmer. There were huge vats of hot soapy water into which the greasy tins from the cookhouse were soaked and then scrubbed. Thick grease congealed round the edges of the vats and fatigue uniforms became embedded with grease. Arms, up to the elbows in water, turned pink from the hot water and soap. By the ends of the seven days in the tin room fatigues were ruined beyond the laundry and skin was wrinkled and sore.

The most miserable fatigue was on the garbage cart as the recruits were outside all the time in the bitterly cold November weather emptying dustbins around the camp. Many bins were filthy and stinking, and the rain generated putrid liquid to drip onto those who carried them. By the end of the day, David and his friends were wet with these drippings that stank to high heaven. Nobody would want to go near them until they had stripped off their evil-smelling clothes and had a shower.

The 1944 Education Act recognized that all should have an

education within their capabilities. Grammar Schools took those who were academically inclined and the Secondary Modern School provided for those who had more practical and less academic talents. It was not a perfect system as 'late developers' found it difficult to move from one system to the other. Generally, the Modern School suffered as it should have had extra funding because of its intended 'hands on' approach, but with the same funding it never could provide the kind of curriculum appropriate for those with practical talents. However, it was an attempt to recognize that social class does not necessarily limit ability and everyone should be given an opportunity to become unequal.

Equality of opportunity does not mean everyone is equal. What it does mean is that those with potential, whatever their social background, should have the right to prove themselves. Millions of pounds were put into education and what did the military do? They sent this expensive potential out on the rubbish cart or got him peeling spuds for days on end. What a waste of taxpayers' money, what a waste of potential, what a comment on the dull brains that ran the British military.

Just when the recruits were looking forward to their Passing-Out Parade, (12) a few days with their families, and an exciting posting, they were faced with bad news. Some egghead in the War Office had decided to send them on a mass casualty course for two weeks just in case the United Kingdom had to face up to a nuclear war. What the egghead didn't seem to understand was that a nuclear strike on the U.K. would not leave many alive and those that were would soon die. In any case, the course proved to be little about what could be done on the outer edges of radiation but just first aid as if a conventional war had taken place. It was something the recruits had already trained for in basic training. David was sure that someone in Whitehall had thought up the course to placate the politicians and convince them that the military was doing something in case of a nuclear holocaust.

The Passing-Out Parade came before they went on the course and was quite an event. David felt proud, as his squad – winners of the drill competition - led the parade. Of course, they were all bulled up: boots shining like black hewn coal, knife-edged creases in their battle dress, belts and gaiters blancoed to perfection like the front steps of a miner's cottage, and brass glinting in the sunlight of a perfect autumn day. They marched in unison and the stamp of feet was the crash of a single person. The NCOs who led them threw out their chests, particularly Cpl Iver, who had achieved his goal of senior squad on the eve of his demobilization from National Service. Heads were held high, shoulders were squared, and every man, except for Private Kennnett, who was excused boots, proved himself a worthy member of the Royal Army Medical Corps.

David's parents, like many others, had come down to Crookham to watch their son. It was a proud moment. Stripling schoolboys had been turned into men. They were physically fit, broader of shoulder, and now theoretically capable of being involved in the defense of their country. And yet, until they were twenty-one years of age they did not have a vote. They could, and did, die for their country but they were still disenfranchised.

Many fathers looked back on their forced enlistment in 1940 into a war that went on for what seemed an eternity. No parade for them, just a few weeks of hasty training and straight into battle. Many had tears in their eyes as they thought of their dead comrades and the experiences they tried to forget. Pride in their sons, yes, but sorrow for those who would never see their sons again.

The ladies had come dressed for the occasion. Smart in warm winter coats or tailored suits. Hat and gloves were still essential on formal occasions. David's mother wore a dark green tailored suit with a small, close-fitting, beige, feathered hat with gloves in the same color. His father had on a new brown suit he noticed, quite an innovation, as his father hated buying clothes and was happy in something old. Most parents who attended were middle class. David supposed that this was because these were ones who could organize their Friday without upsetting the boss. It was a pity. However, David was surprised by the number of parents attending the parade, and proud that he could introduce his parents to Corporal Iver and his friends in the squad.

In the afternoon David went with his mother and father once again to Windsor Great Park where they walked in the warm sunshine and told each other the latest news. It felt good to be in uniform. After tea in an old-fashioned tea shop in Windsor, David was taken by his parents back to the barracks, and then they drove home to Leicester. As David told his mother, "Not long now mum. I'll be home in no time."

On a cold, misty December morning the whole intake of soldiers was loaded into trucks with their baggage and driven the twenty miles to Keog Barracks where the Mass Casualty Course was to be held. The barracks were purpose built, not wooden huts, and the accommodation was much better than the training camp. Each room held ten men and there were excellent toilet and washing facilities. The mess hall was in the same building and the food provided by the Catering Corps plain and plentiful. There was a lecture theatre, classrooms, and good facilities for sport. The building had obviously been built for professional soldiers and not raw recruits.

48

The course was interesting in that most of the lecturers were either medical doctors or State Registered Nurses and not like the NCOs in training, who delivered their content like minor birds. However, the content was a repetition, possibly at a greater depth, of their training course and obviously had been put together without much thought. There were only three things that David particularly remembered.

A Medical Officer was lecturing on how to apply a splint on the battlefield and then make a plaster cast. He singled out a smart recruit from the audience to help him demonstrate. "Go behind the screen and take off your boots, socks and trousers," he told the soldier, "then lie on the stretcher." which was to hand. The audience was fascinated with the excellent lecturer and did not take much notice of the young soldier who eventually lay on the stretcher as directed.

The plaster was ready and the doctor turned to the stretcher. "I told you to take off your socks," he said casually to the soldier and then turned back to his audience.

"I have, sir," came a voice from the stretcher.

This time the doctor took more notice and inspected more closely. There was a deathly hush from the audience. It was plain to see that the soldier had not washed his feet for a long while as at a glance the dirt on them looked just like socks. "Corporal," said the horrified doctor, beckoning to an NCO standing to one side. "Take this man away and charge him with failing to keep basic hygiene standards."

The lecturer used this example to digress and talk about the importance of personal hygiene for RAMC personnel. "If we don't keep ourselves clean, how can we keep our patients free from infection?" he asked.

His question was a fair one but David could have told him of many soldiers who hardly ever washed. True, they showered after PE but that was superficial as there was little time to do things properly. There were no hygiene inspections while he was training. Beds and bed boxes were inspected, as were lockers, but as long as one had good creases in the right places and shiny boots one was a good soldier. Personal hygiene was an assumption.

A second incident that took place did not really affect David, but some soldiers, RAMC personnel at that, had a very rough time one Saturday morning. They were told that there would be a Mass Casualty Exhibition followed by an option to give blood. 'Option' was not really the right word as they actually found that they were all marched off to the mobile transfusion unit and goaded into, as Anthony Hancock (13) said in his famous sketch, 'to give an armful of blood'. The mistake was to have the mass casualty exhibition first. David reckoned that army logic said that the willingness to give blood would be enhanced by the exhibition. But army logic is quite often flawed.

The exhibition was extremely well done, so much so that it entered the realm of realism. Some of the burns victims were so gruesome as to make a few soldiers physically sick. Skin was peeling off arms, legs and faces and the human 'models' made it seem so very realistic. Of course, burns would be a major problem after a nuclear attack as well as the damage done to the body from blast. Broken bones and pierced flesh were not as dramatic as the horror of second and third degree burns however. It did not affect David as he was used to blood and the interior of bodies from cutting things up in biology lessons at school. He had to admit though, that some of the exhibits did churn his stomach and made him unprepared when it came to giving blood.

It was the first time David had given blood so he was a little apprehensive as to what would happen to him. After his finger had been pricked with a needle by a rather attractive civilian nurse, and the blood smeared onto a slide to go for grouping, he waited his turn to give 'an armful'. He had never really liked hospitals and yet he was to be a medic, although he was lucky enough to have kept clear except for a period in the isolation hospital when he and his brother had diphtheria. (14) After being asked some questions about his previous medical record, he was given a card with a number on it and told to wait in the queue. Some of his colleagues were visibly shaking, some were looking green, and a couple were sick and had to be helped away.

"Next," came a female voice and David got up rather shakily to go into the adjoining room. The room had some twelve iron beds in it and soldiers were lying on the beds with their right arm stretched out. Tubes protruded from their arms. The voice was a middle-aged, motherly lady in a white coat with a stethoscope hanging round her neck.. "Take your top off dear and then roll up your right sleeve." When David had done this, he was asked politely to lie on the bed close to him. Clearly, she was a civilian as the lady was polite for a change.

David wasn't quite sure what happened to him next as he did not want to look. He felt a burning sensation as the anurism needle (15) was put into his vein and he knew that his arm had been steadied by some form of support. Blood was obviously trickling into a bottle below somewhere as the sister checked everything was satisfactory. "Are you all right?" sister asked.

"Thank you, yes," David replied giving the best smile he could muster under the circumstances.

"I'll leave you for a while dear," she said reassuringly, "but I'll keep coming back to check. If you have any problems," she went on, placing a bell push in his left hand, "or feel sick then ring the bell and someone will come."

He must have drifted off to sleep as the next thing he felt was his arm being gently lifted. It was all over. "That wasn't too bad was it?" murmured sister as she placed a plaster over his vein. "You can dress in the next room," she went on without waiting for a response, "and there's a cup of tea waiting for you."

"Er...thank you," remarked David groggily as he got to his feet. "Thank you."

Whilst he was having his cup of tea and an enforced rest, a civilian nurse came along with his donor card. She had a broad smile on her face. "You're a very rare young man," she said handing him his blue card.

David was confused. "W..........".

"Well, you have a rare blood group - A negative - and frequently we have problems getting donors. Oh and by the way, you should carry your card around with you at all times just in case you need blood." She smiled again and was off out of the room.

"Rare bastard are you?" enquired the soldier next to him.

"Suppose so," retorted David. He had not really taken the implication in.

"Cupa tea and a rest....worth giving blood for," remarked the chatty soldier. "Nice bit o' skirt too."

David was still trying to comprehend what the nurse had said. "Mmm.."

"You ok mate?" asked the soldier. "Bit of a shock I suppose you being a rare blood group an' all. You gotta be careful if yer have an accident."

David looked at him, just realizing the implication of what was being said. "I suppose so. If my blood is in short supply........ then I too can be at risk."

"Don't worry mate," went on the soldier, "just think you're lucky being special." With that he got up, thumped David on the back, and was off for his weekend leave.

In training they had been taught how to carry a stretcher under fire in order to get the wounded to a field medical station. It is not easy and means carrying a patient long distances and even crawling on one's belly dragging the stretcher along when under close fire. The patient, of course, has to be strapped onto the stretcher in order to stop him falling off.

One dark, cold, misty morning they were told to dress in fatigues and be ready to undertake an exercise where live bullets were to be used. David and his friends knew that it was not going to be a happy experience as dressing in fatigues indicated that one would get very dirty. They were driven for about a half hour to what appeared to be a practice area for tanks. The ground was muddy and churned by many wheels. There were a few bushes around but the undulating ground was barren and forbidding as if a war had just taken place.

They were marched into this battleground to a spot that represented the front line. Divided into groups of five, they were spread along this front and told that the object of the exercise was to get a wounded colleague to the Field Aid Station as quickly as possible whilst under heavy fire. A whistle would indicate the commencement of the exercise and they were to make for a blue flag about a quarter of a mile away.

David's group had a real problem in the form of Peter Kennett. Nobody really wanted him in their group as he was quite useless. After some heated discussion and threats from a burly soldier from Liverpool, Kennett agreed to be the patient. The NCO in charge said he had to have a broken leg and serious bleeding. That was no problem. David could see that a couple of his colleagues were ready to make Kennett's injuries real if he failed to co-operate. However, they splinted his supposedly broken leg to his good leg as there was no wood or branch to use as a splint, and put a large field dressing over the bleeding to stem the flow. This done, the whistle went and the exercise had started.

All went well for a while, although the going was difficult. It had rained in the night and everywhere was slippery. Many of the hollows between the mounds were full of water, some quite deep, and before long they were all wet through and very muddy. Boots slipped on the inclines and often it meant slithering on one's backside as it was impossible to stand.

Suddenly something whizzed past David's ear. He was startled and slid onto his bottom making the stretcher wobble.

"Bloody hell," remarked his colleague on the other handle, "they're shooting at us."

David regained himself. "Gosh, that was close. We'll have to crawl over the tops of the mounds."

"Some fuckin' sharp shooter 'avin fun," observed the soldier from Liverpool.

They crawled up the next mound dragging the stretcher and looked over the top. A bullet whizzed overhead again. "We'll crawl over and you can slide the stretcher to us," offered David.

"What about me?" wailed Kennett. "I'll get shot!"

"You'll be OK Pete," encouraged David. "You're only a small target being flat. We're the ones at risk as we have to hump you around."

He wailed on: "But I'll be shot....."

"Shut 'yer fuckin' mouth pretty boy. Lie still or I'll drop you one," came the Liverpool accent.

Kennett knew it was no good arguing with the soldier from Liverpool.

Sliding and slithering with the stretcher they made quite good progress. There was still an occasional round of fire so they had to be careful. Some marksman was having a wonderful time. All was well until about two hundred yards from the blue flag. They were all very tired by that time as Kennett was no lightweight. He kept moaning about his rough ride. As they told him in rustic language, it was not really their fault. They were doing the best they could. Then the worst happened. The two leaders, one of them David, slipped and the stretcher fell into a deep pool of muddy water. Peter Kennett was almost submerged. He spluttered and yelled gulping in some of the brown water. "Oh!...help," he spluttered. "Get me out. You did it on purpose. Pick me up. I'm drowning."

Of course he was not drowning. His head was well above the waterline but the rest of him was mainly submerged. The four stretcher-bearers, tired and fed up, just sat on the slope and laughed at the strange sight in front of them. It was the best comedy scene they had seen for ages. Poor Kennett, soaked to the skin, wriggling in his bonds, spluttering and spitting foul brown water. "Suppose... we'd.... better.... do something," guffawed one of the soldiers.

"Leave 'im a bit," replied the soldier from Liverpool, rocking with laughter. "Nah' 'e's got something to moan about. Best bloody laugh I've 'ad for a long time."

"Ok Pete," smiled David, slithering further to help his colleague. "Sorry about the accident. But you do look funny."

"You did it on purpose," wailed Kennett. "I'll tell my dad. I'll go to the colonel."

He was interrupted by a burly figure at David's shoulder. "The fuck 'yer will. Can't yer take a joke. Accident. Any more threats and I'll mark 'yer for life." It was the Liverpool soldier again.

The fierceness of his gaze convinced Kennett that he was not to be messed with. He calmed down and did not say another word. As David thought afterwards, all the selfless actions of his colleagues to help Peter Kennett through his basic training had not really taught him much. It was an accident, funny in the extreme, but could have happened to anyone who was the patient. Yes, he was wet and uncomfortable, but so were his colleagues. The fracture treatment was intact, the field dressing would be wet but that was a hazard in such conditions, so they had done their job. Battlefields were no picnic and it was no good trying to save a life at the risk of losing two or three others. But Kennett could not see this. It was only self he considered as if he had never grown from a baby.

The course quickly came to an end and David was in civilian clothes for the first time in months, a railway warrant in his pocket, and a leave pass for seven days. He was to report to Millbank Military Hospital, London at the end of his leave. He knew he had broadened as his jacket was feeling tight and he was fit, probably fitter than he had ever been. Plain and plentiful army food with exercise and fresh air cannot fail to work for better health. Whilst he was still slim, he knew that he had a fit, muscular body as good as any he had competed with. He also had a brain, better than most, and certainly better than his father had ever given him credit for. He had come through the first period of his basic training and, given all the faults and drawbacks, he felt better about himself. But what would Millbank be like? He had heard stories...... Anyhow, he had survived basic training and he supposed he could survive anything else the army was to throw at him.

Chapter 4

Millbank Military Hospital, or as it should be correctly known, The Queen Elizabeth Military Hospital, is in the heart of London on the Embankment of the River Thames and right next to the famous Tate Gallery, famed for its works of art and easily recognized from the statuary in its surrounding garden. The hospital itself, a two-story, red brick and Portland stone (1) edifice, is impressive but of little architectural consequence, unlike the Tate. It is clean-looking in its red and white, just what you might expect a hospital to be. Built perhaps at the turn of the century, it has been continuously modernized with excellent facilities both nursing and medical and is considered to be one of the best military hospitals in Britain.

David reported to the hospital on a fine Sunday afternoon and was sent along to the barracks which was situated about a twenty minute walk away. Housed in a nineteenth century building actually built as a barracks, it was situated in a run-down part of Victoria (3) and was hardly prepossessing. He walked past it a couple of times before recognizing it as his destination.

The barracks is in marked contrast to the officer accommodation near the hospital itself. Again, the social gulf between officer and men is clearly stated in nineteenth century terms by the way each is housed. Officers are obviously of value and are to be pampered whilst the 'men' can live in a hovel from whence they came. Entry was through a red-brick arched gateway. The accommodation was built in the form of a square round a central courtyard. It could have been the run-down stables to a stately mansion.

Inside the facilities were equally depressing. A long whitewashed barrack room was the living accommodation with iron beds and standard wooden lockers. It was a dreary place and the electric light would have to be on most of the day giving it a Dickensian (2) feel. Another room was for night duty staff. There was a mess hall downstairs and no NAAFI as he was told that there were plenty of entertainment facilities in the area. He found that most soldiers looked for their comfort elsewhere as the place was so depressing.

David wanted to learn Greek ready for university but where would he study? He also found that there was nowhere to study for his nursing exams, other than this dreary and ill-lit barrack room. It was, he found, so typical of the military. Give the men nothing but provide officers with accommodation worthy of their status.

He slept badly that night. The week at home had gone all too quickly. It had been a round of visiting friends and talking with his parents. His brother was at university and so evenings had been spent at home with his parents recounting news of mutual interest. His best friend, a nuclear scientist some six years older than David, had been sent by his firm to Canada to work on a special project. There was a letter waiting for him when he got home containing a photograph showing a tall, muscular figure paddling a canoe on a Canadian lake. They used to play tennis together and go to the theatre. David admired him so much, particularly his fine athletic body.

All his friends at church wanted to talk to him and the vicar was interested in his spiritual life. He was kind enough to give David the address of a priest who had a church in Victoria saying that he could possibly be of help if he made himself known.

His first day at the Millbank Hospital was a disaster. The day actually started quite well, but it was not to remain so. He was woken with the other staff at five-thirty and by six-thirty he was walking with a friendly group to the hospital. David was the only new boy and so the others were eager to show him the ropes. They were a friendly bunch, some professional soldiers and others, like David, doing National Service. He took a keen note of his surroundings lest he had to return to barracks alone. The walk was exhilarating as the morning was frosty and dry with the dawn just coming up. At this time in the morning the streets were surprisingly busy. He was apprehensive.

One of his colleagues took him to matron's room where a sergeant clerk told him the ward he would be working on and rang down to say he was on his way. A fellow nursing orderly took him to the ward. His parting words were: "Well here you are and may God protect you."

The ward had an office, treatment room, kitchen, and interview room at the entrance and then opened out into a long ward with beds down either side. Each bed had a locker and could be curtained off by a system of overhead rails. At the far end was a sunny Day Room looking over the grounds of the Tate Gallery and next to it the sluice.

There were patients in the beds but apparently no staff as the ward was silent. David waited about ten minutes outside the office and eventually a nurse, a corporal, appeared. "What do you want?" she said rather rudely.

David was unsure of himself. "I'm new....been sent to this ward...."

"Oh yes. They phoned. Haven't got time at present," she said. "We're understaffed. Sister will be here soon."

"Can I help?" offered David.

She looked at him with some pity. "You won't know what to do. They never do. There are patients in the day room." She nodded towards the end of the ward. "Go and talk to them. Keep out of our way!"

"But……." David wanted to ask her so much but with that she turned on her heels and went into the treatment room. He went down the ward and pushed open the double doors of the day room.

There were two patients there, an elderly man with yellowing skin and a young man, very thin, who smiled and looked friendly.

David did not know what to say or do. "I've been……"

"Sent out of the way," offered the young man. "I assume you're new?"

"Yes."

"I'm Jack and he's Bill. We've been here a long time so we know the routine," offered Jack.

"Seems like a lifetime," added Bill.

"How do you know I'm new?" asked David.

"There's always someone new on this ward," replied Jack. "They come and they go."

Bill winked at Jack. "Sister's an angel!"

"More like a fallen angel. You watch her, son. A bitch if there ever was one."

Suddenly the double doors to the day room burst open and the 'bitch' was standing there breathing fire. She was of medium height, overweight, red faced and sporting large breasts. She had the usual pale gray uniform of a QARANC officer, (4) white wimple and red epaulets with three stars. She was very much a captain.

The Queen Alexander's Royal Army Nursing Corps was formed in the First World War. Later, the Act setting it up was changed, so that those nurses who held a State Registered (5) qualification, and with sufficient experience, could apply for a commission and receive officer status. An SRN is not a high qualification as far as nursing goes, and officer rank is rather excessive, however, these women had rank and used it. As David and many others in the RAMC were to find out, the rank was abused frequently, particularly to cover incompetence.

"What are you doing in here? You should be in the ward helping the nurses. Don't they teach you anything? Why is it I get all the lazy ones?"

As she stopped to draw breath David tried to explain: "I was………"

"Don't you talk back to me. I'll have you charged for insolence. You're nothing but a lazy, good-for-nothing and I will not have you on my ward……."

"Hold on sister," intervened Bill. "No good getting yourself into a state."

"I'll not be spoken to by a patient...." she started.

"For fuck's sake, woman, listen. If you won't, I'll go to matron and explain to her. The young man has been here for five minutes. He's been asking us what needs to be tidied as he's new." He winked at David. "Check with your nurses. They were too busy to tell him what to do and told him to tidy up in here. He just asked us what needs to be done as we're old hands, didn't you, son?"

"Y...es," David replied.

She looked flustered. "Well you better get on with it." She glared at him. "Report to me in my office when you've finished." With that she about turned and was gone.

"Fat cow," said Jim. "She's always like that. Shout, shout! Not very good with her staff. Most just apply for a move."

"Now son. What's yer name?" asked Bill.

"David,"

"Well David better get some work done." He went on. "Tidy those papers, put the chairs round the tables and empty the ash trays." David looked in disbelief. "Oh yes, the old bitch allows us to smoke in here."

David began to do as was suggested. "Thanks for the life saver," he said as he pushed chairs under tables.

"There are cloths, mops and polish next door in the sluice," observed Jim.

Before long David had the day room clean and tidy. "Hey, you're a real worker," observed Jim. "Silly bitch don't know what she's got, hey Bill?"

"Sure don't," added Bill.

"Thanks for the help," David said and smiled at the two patients.

"Don't let her get you down, son," observed Bill. "Take it from an old soldier. These women officers are all bluster."

David opened the double doors, smiled and offered, "Thanks again." That was the last time he saw the two.

His interview with sister was short. She rampaged at him about being inefficient and lazy. She sent a nurse to look at the day room who reported back that it had been done well. After that her anger subsided a little. He was given a white smock to wear and sent to make beds with one of the nurses.

"Sorry if we got you into trouble," the nurse apologized. "There were only two of us to do treatments and we just didn't have time."

David carefully folded the sheets under the mattress with hospital corners. "Don't worry. It all worked out quite well."

The nurse smiled. "I'm nurse Wells. You're Private Earl. I heard sister screaming your name."

"All the ward knows my name and that I'm a lazy good-for-nothing," David told her with feeling.

"The way she screamed at you the whole hospital could know," nurse Wells told him. "Her bark's worse than her bite. She's a good sister really but hasn't a clue how to treat people. She needs a good man around her!" She winked at David.

They got through the beds quickly. "You're not bad at beds," nurse Wells observed with a cheeky smile on her face. "Go down the wards and tidy the top of each locker. Matron will be on her rounds in about ten minutes."

Most of the lockers of the walking patients were tidy as the patients knew that Matron would be arriving for her morning inspection. It was typical of military personnel, each helped the other, and David was to value this lesson for the rest of his life. The patients were friendly and seemed to like Matron, however, they warned David to beware of the deputy Matron who it seemed was always in a bad temper.

Matron was short, motherly and courteous and had a word with each patient as she went around the ward. Sister was with her and a Staff Nurse as well as a clerk from the hospital administration who took notes. She seemed to know each patient and had something pleasant to say to everyone, even David. "Private Earl. You're new."

"Yes, Mam." David stood to attention.

"I hope you'll find your stay here not too arduous. Tomorrow you are to report to the ENT ward. Sister Thornton. It's a new ward that has just been re-furbished. Sister will want some real hard work from you as the first patients are due in a few days."

"Thank you, mam."

Matron smiled at him and continued with her inspection.

"Lucky blighter," whispered Nurse Wells. "Sister Thornton is lovely and the new ward is super."

David had been feeling down in the dumps but this news made him feel better. Confrontation with 'the Bitch' had had its compensations.

The following day David reported to the new ward. Sister Thornton was slim, of medium height, quite attractive with chestnut hair, a pink and white complexion and sparkling eyes. She walked with a limp – the result of an accident in her youth. David took a liking to her from first seeing her. She had an air of kind efficiency and explained what she wanted clearly and was open to suggestions as to how the work might be undertaken better. There was a team of eight, five females and three males. Sister explained their duties until the patients arrived at the weekend when two would be put on night duty.

Much of David's days for the first week were spent cleaning new equipment and preparing beds and lockers. The ward floor was of polished wood. Thankfully, it was cleaned by civilian cleaners with an automated polisher. The treatment room and the sluice had to be cleaned by the nursing staff and that meant getting down on hands and knees and scrubbing. Everything was new and had to be checked and double checked. David worked some of the time with another National Serviceman called Basil Evans. He was still a private after eighteen month's service and was looking forward to being demobilized.

Basil was tall, skinny and rather effeminate. His mousy hair was quite long for the military and made his pale face look even longer. In civilian life he was a clerk for Cardiff City Council and his hobby was performing in the local operatic and dramatic society. In his spare time he went to the cinema, and also read most of the film and theatre magazines. As a consequence, he was a mine of information on all the latest films and the best and bizarre in the London theatre. If you wanted to know who was getting married or divorced or who was sleeping with whom, then Basil would know. His friend, a handsome regular corporal male nurse, worked on an adjoining ward and they shared accommodation away from barracks.

David's other colleague was a lance corporal named Derek Douglas. He had been a steel erector (6) in civilian life but had decided to sign on as a regular soldier as life seemed to be better in the military. He was stocky, dark-haired and an aggressive know-all. David tried to like him, but it was difficult. He fancied himself with the nurses but they seemed to treat him with contempt, which made him even more aggressive. As it tuned out, David saw little of him as he was on night duty when David was on days.

The character on the ward was Elizabeth, a large, round roly-poly Jamaican ward maid. Head bound in a turban as bright as the morning sun, large flowered dress in equally jazzy material, yet incongruent colors, she had one pace and that was slow. She insisted on wearing bright pink furry carpet slippers much to the disgust of Sister Thornton. In fact, it was Elizabeth's slippers that caused the enmity between the two. Her laugh was infectious and the whole of her vast body rippled with mirth. David took a liking to her the first time he saw her and she to him. It was clear that Elizabeth looked forward to their meetings and always welcomed him with "I'z put a cup of tea aside for yer." She made excellent tea. David teased her unmercifully and she loved it.

Her job was to keep the kitchen clean, wash the dishes after meals before being returned to the central canteen, and wipe the locker tops each morning. She was slow, very slow, but thorough and kept the kitchen very clean and the staff and patients supplied with cups of tea, water, whatever was necessary. At times Sister Thornton asked Elizabeth to do little extra jobs like cleaning out cupboards. Elizabeth would refuse. "I'z not my job," she would complain. Sister and Elizabeth just did not get on. Then Sister would come to David and ask him to help. David always managed to persuade Elizabeth – a pat on her ample bottom and a little joke would do the trick.

The female nurses were quite pleasant except one. She was tall with an excellent figure and the face of an angel, but the morals of a sex-starved rabbit. David came to the conclusion that she was a nymphomaniac, although he had never met one before. She had been used on recruiting posters by the Army and this had given her certain status and this status had gone to her head. Corporal Gill Mays was very friendly with the Assistant Matron who seemed to think she could do no wrong. (In later life, when David had had more experience of the world, he came to wonder what sort of relationship these two were having. He later experienced lesbianism at close quarters and found that quite often nymphomaniacs could live in homosexual or heterosexual relationships. Certainly the Assistant Matron was very masculine.)

One morning David came on duty to be confronted by a very angry sergeant from the Scotts Guards. "Get rid of that fuckin' woman," he stormed. " Nobody slept. She's been having sex in the sluice most of the night." David was shocked. It was not just the sergeant complaining but patient after patient. Some admitted what a 'good fuck' she was and others that they had been stimulated under the bedclothes by her wandering hands. This was not the first complaint David had heard. What could he do, a mere private? He suggested that the sergeant talk to sister when she came on duty as he was a mere private without authority. So after many months of complaints by married patients on the ward – the single ones quite enjoyed the experience – and this final showdown with a very angry sergeant, Gill was moved to other duties in the hospital. She was not dismissed, just moved to other duties. That made one really think.

Days, weeks, and months passed. Up early, ward work until eleven in the morning, and then there were nursing lectures within the hospital complex for an hour and a half three times a week. A quick lunch was grabbed in the canteen, and then it was back to the ward for the afternoon until the night staff came on at seven. Nursing lectures were most interesting and consisted of anatomy and physiology and nursing techniques. The anatomy and physiology was easy as David had A-level zoology. He and another recruit, Justin Ames, were eventually selected by the Sister Tutor to give the anatomy and physiology lectures as the Sister Tutor, Major Inman, was of the opinion that they knew more than she did. The two did quite a bit of research on some areas but generally it was simple.

The nursing techniques were quite easy too. A good memory, knowing what was wrong with the patient and what the sister or doctor had to do was all that was required. He and Justin worked together setting up trays and trolleys and soon were way ahead of the ten others. After their first exam – a written test and a practical – they gained over 90% and were allowed accelerated advancement which meant going on to the next exam without the usual ward experience period in between. Much of this was due to the personality of Major Inman who was kind, encouraging and an excellent teacher. She was a devout Christian and had a shining humanity and yet could be tough with any soldier or nurse who tried to take advantage. David did not know this at the time, but he was destined to stay friendly with Major Inman years after his National Service finished.

One incident, which David never was to forget, was the delivery of his first injection. Of course, they had practiced many times on a rubber manakin in training. Sister Thornton told David one morning, "Today Private Earl, you must give your first injection. There are a number of patients who have to go to theatre so you can give a pre-med. Choose your time and one of the nurses will supervise you." David wanted to give the injection and yet.... Suppose he made a mistake? A real person was involved and he might do some harm...... He would do it....sometime that morning.

The morning went on and still he had not plucked up courage. He liked all the patients. How could he inflict a painful injection on one of them? Suddenly Nurse Walker arrived with a kidney-dish, syringe and cotton wool soaked in alcohol. "Right David. Now or never," she said with a smile on her face. "Private Elliot down the ward. Come on." With that she marched down the ward to where Private Elliot lay grinning.

"Don't worry Dave, I'll be fine even if it hurts like hell," he laughed. "Come on, we all know you have to do this or Sister will kill you." With that he rolled over to show a bare bottom ready for treatment.

David looked at Nurse Walker and she looked back with look of 'well get on with it' on her face. 'Here goes,' thought David. 'Upper and outer quadrant.' He cleaned the area, raised the syringe and bang, in it went. Private Elliot was a six foot hunk from the Guards and never felt a thing, or at least he didn't show it. Out came the needle but oh....there was a drop of blood. 'What have I done? I've put it in the wrong place,' thought David.

Nurse Walker smiled at him. "Fine, couldn't do better myself."

"Never felt a thing," responded Private Walker as he rolled over onto his back. "Give me another if you like," he said with a twinkle in his eye.

"But there was bl......" observed David.

"Oh that's nothing. Often happened with big fat rumps," said Nurse Walker winking.

"Hey, who's got a fat rump?" complained Private Elliot.

"You have," smirked Nurse Walker. "But I quite like it." And with that she walked up the ward.

"Now she's quite a girl that one," laughed Private Elliot. "I'd show her my rump any day."

David's first stint of night duty was to last for a week. On duty at seven in the evening until seven the following morning. There was not a great deal to do once the last treatments had been undertaken until the following morning when patients had to be woken, washed and shaved, if they were bed-bound, and the first treatment of the day given. The day staff came on at seven and helped with breakfast and any other extras the two night staff had not completed.

As the ward specialized in ENT and ophthalmic (7) cases there tended to be quite a turnover of patients and very few who were confined to bed for long. Sometimes a patient with a detached retina (8) remained a while in bed and had to be handled carefully, but generally patients could do things for themselves. Whilst night duty was easy physically it was tiring mentally. As David was still doing lectures, he had to stay up three mornings a week for the lecture and then grab a few hour's sleep before duty again. It was exhausting and the early hours of the morning were always a fight to keep awake.

The night duty room back at barracks was of little help as the sounds from the traffic outside could easily be heard. Sleep was difficult and so after twenty-one days of 'cat-naps' the night duty staff went off on their seventy-two hour pass merely to catch up with sleep. David managed to get home for a long weekend as trains were quite frequent to Leicester. At least he could sleep at home. There was no chance of a decent sleep in barracks. He was also finding the opportunity to study impossible and he wanted to learn Greek ready for university. He had enrolled on a correspondence course but found little opportunity to do any work. There was nowhere quiet to study.

One morning he was bemoaning the problem to Basil Evans. "Why don't you apply for a living out pass and allowance," suggested Basil. " I get one. Tell them you want to study and can't find anywhere quiet.

You've got a good argument if you need Greek for university."

David thought about it and decided to try. 'If you don't ask, you don't get', he said to himself. He wrote a letter to his commanding officer and signed it 'your obedient servant' as was the archaic way in the military and dropped it in at the Company Office.

Three days later he found on company orders that he was directed to report to the Company Office at 11 am. on the following day. On checking with Basil, he was informed that he had to go in full kit with boots and brasses polished to perfection as if he were on parade. He had a sickly feeling in his stomach. He knew this meant trouble, stamping feet, saluting and doing everything at the double.

Of course he was right. When he got to the office ten minutes early, the sergeant major was waiting for him. He brought him to attention and inspected him in detail growling like an untamed tiger and making David feel like an offender ready for a prison cell. There was nothing he could put his finger on, as David had prepared well, knowing that any slight wrong would be jumped on and used against him. There was no justice and little freedom in the army. One was a number and democracy went out of the window as soon as one entered the gates of the barracks to become a soldier. For officers, it was different. They were treated with great dignity. David supposed that all the dignity and justice had been used up by the military on the officers and there was none left for other ranks.

The 'tiger' spoke. "Cheeky little bastard aren't you?"

The question was rhetorical and David said nothing. What could you say to a raging beast with probably little intelligence and a warped sense of duty.

"Want a living out pass? Not satisfied with barracks? What makes you special?"

Standing to attention, stiff as a board, is not conducive to small talk. In any case, when the interlocutor is walking round you and you have no eye contact, sensible discourse is most difficult. David felt it was better to give him the opportunity to rabbit on. Maybe when he had vented his spleen and worn his tiny mind out, he would be less brutal.

"God knows what Cap'n Davis will say. If I had my way I'd give you a week's jankers for being so cheeky. Cheeky little bastard."

A voice from within yelled "Next" and off David went at the double. Leftrightleftrightleft....right turn, attention, salute.

A chubby, elderly captain faced David. "Name, rank and number? he asked in a quiet voice.

"933 Private Earl, sir," responded David in clipped tones.

There was silence as the officer shuffled papers on his desk. "Ah yes," he at last uttered having read David's request. "You do know private that soldiers are not entitled to make request such as yours and quote Queen's regulations."

David was amazed. He had found the relevant passage in regulations where a soldier was entitled to make a request and quoted it in his letter. He remained silent.

"Soldiers are not permitted to read Queen's regulations. They are not able to understand them," he went on.

David could not believe what he was hearing. If regulations governing the rights of the common soldier were not available to them how could they establish their rights? Surely, this was against all the laws of human justice? In 1957 when most of the population was as educated as the officers, perhaps more educated, a denial of access to Queen's Regulations was an anachronism.

"A cheeky bastard, sir," remarked the sergeant major.

"Quite so sergeant major," remarked the captain. "So you want to live off barracks. You are trying to study Greek before you enter university. Have you already been accepted?" He looked up at David.

"Yes, sir. I have a place waiting for me at King's College here in London as soon as I finish my service."

"Why didn't you learn Greek at school? Didn't you know you would need it at university?"

"I did begin to learn classical Greek in the sixth form, sir, but the Greek I need is New Testament Greek which is something different."

"I see." Captain Davis thought for a while. "Have you started a course of study?"

"Yes, sir. I enrolled in a correspondence course when I first came to the hospital and I have been trying to study."

"You say there's nowhere quiet."

"Yes, sir."

"I'm told by Major Inman that you are an exceptional student in your nursing studies. How do you find quiet to study for that?"

"Well, sir, the anatomy and physiology is easy as I did it at A- level and the nursing practice is just common sense. I don't really need to study much."

Captain Davis looked David up and down. David stared straight ahead at attention. He could feel the captain's eyes burning into him.

There was silence for what seemed an age. "All right, permission granted. See to the paperwork Sgt major."

"Yes, sir," replied a startled sergeant major.

"Dismissed," the captain intimated quietly.

"Salute, right turn, leftrightleftright........" and out of the office

65

David was marched at the double with the sergeant major breathing down his neck.

In the outer office David was halted and stood at ease. The sergeant major came behind David and quietly spoke into his ear so that he was not overheard. "Y're what I said. A cheeky bastard, soldier. If I 'ad my way I'd bloody slaughter you. 'Owever, I admire your guts. Git out of my sight and don't let me see your pretty face in 'ere again."

David marched very quickly out of the office, intimidated but satisfied.

Chapter 5

It was not hard finding accommodation in Victoria, that area of London nearest the hospital, as it was an area of large run-down houses that had been used for bed-sitters for many years. With the help of Basil and his friend at the hospital, David found a spacious room in St George's Drive. A hundred years previously St George's Drive had been a smart upper middle class residential area. The houses were spacious three-storied buildings with elegant pillared porticos and large ground and first floor windows. The rooms on the first two floors were spacious and led from a long, narrow hallway and elegant staircase. Now the properties were too large for family accommodation and had been converted, most very badly, into bed-sitting rooms with shared bathroom. Often the owner lived on the ground floor and the rest of the house, including the basement, was let. That was the situation at 24, St. George's Drive.

Simply furnished with double bed, wardrobe, easy chair and a washbowl in one corner, David's room was quite self-contained. There was an ancient gas fire so he could make toast, and with an electric kettle, he could supplement his diet quite well. The bathroom was down the hall: a barn of a place with a gas heater for hot water and a coin meter that seemed to gorge itself on the shillings slotted into it. The huge Victorian bath, standing on four clawed feet, took ages to fill, but the water was hot and the old iron bath roomy. The place was quiet for study and with his own key David could come and go at will. He rarely saw the owner as he crossed the lino-covered hall and went up the stairs, being careful not to trip in the holes of the threadbare carpet.

Night duties were still difficult as he had to wait from coming off duty at seven to eleven o'clock for his lecture. It was nearly one o'clock before he got to his room and four hours sleep for three days a week was not really enough. The staff nurse on his ward gave him 'something to keep him awake' when he was very tired and 'something to sleep' when he complained of not sleeping. All the staff seemed to take tablets. However, a room of his own, which he made comfortable with little things he bought, was better than sleeping in barracks.

He did not have much money. Pay was around thirty shillings a week and supplementing his accommodation allowance left nothing to spare. There was nothing much left for entertainment, even if he had time and the inclination to sample the delights of London. His parents had driven down to see him and provided an electric kettle and other little comforts. It was not a bad life.

At the hospital on the oncology ward was a four-year old boy who had cancer of the nasal passages and throat. By the time he came into hospital, one could see the cancerous tissue coming down his nose, and his left eye was beginning to be pushed to one side. He was a beautiful child: golden curly hair, flawless skin, blue eyes and a rosebud mouth made him look like a living cherub. Fold back the sheets and look at his body and he was just skin and bone. David would go on the ward every night before his duty began to see the child and ask how he was. The nursing staff knew David loved the child and prayed for his recovery. Not that the little boy knew of David's presence as he was always sleeping under heavy sedation. David would stay a while, hold the boy's tiny fingers in his own, and offer a prayer to God for the safe recovery of the child.

It came as a terrible shock when one night the boy was no longer there. "Sorry, David, he died this afternoon while you were off duty," the Duty Sister gently told him. She looked at David with such compassion. "He had no pain...... We're all shattered." There were tears in her eyes.

David tried to control his own emotions but a tear rolled down his cheek. "Why, oh why did God allow this to happen?" he muttered and walked off the ward.

Night duty was a blur that night. He couldn't get over the picture of the dead angelic child. This was the first death he had had to face and he knew that there would be many more in life. Death was inevitable for everyone and one could expect the old to depart this life. But why had such a young life been taken out of the world when it had hardly begun? He knew of the doctrine of original sin (1) according to St Augustine. But how could God allow the sins of the father to harm an innocent child? Surely God was not that unjust? David had always felt God to be loving and caring and not angry like the God of Israel in the Old Testament. A young child could not be such a sinner as to bring down the wrath of God, surely? There had to be an explanation as to why. He worried most of the night.

A thought struck him in the early hours when there was little to do. He would go and see that priest his vicar had recommended. He did not like to ask the army chaplain who came occasionally around the wards. He seemed to be a rather hard person, devoid of compassion. Father....What was his name? He had it written down somewhere...... Yes, Father Royce. He had a church in Victoria somewhere. He would telephone him and ask for an appointment.

The appointment was made for the following Sunday when David had completed his night duty. Father Royce sounded very warm and friendly. David explained his problem over the phone and was invited to the Sung Mass (2) and then lunch. For the rest of the week his thoughts kept turning back to the little boy.

Night duties tended to drag on except for the activity of administering the late night treatments, and those before the day staff came on. It was boring. However, when you were a Night Special and required to work all over the hospital, things could be a bit rough. That week David was Night Special and it had been a particularly busy week with a number of emergency admissions and some sick patients on Nightingale Ward, the cancer ward. By Friday, many of the night staff were exhausted, including David, who was still having to hang around for lectures.

The Duty Night Sister was a Captain Bell, about thirty and not noted for her patience or tact. She tended to get agitated rather easily when under pressure and screamed at the staff no matter how hard they worked. Generally, the staff ignored her outbursts. She was not a very good sister and covered her incompetence with bluster. On that particular night a doctor had made a mess of catheterizing (3) a patient with a prostate (4) problem and a staff nurse had taken over. Sister blamed the nurse. An old soldier from the Chelsea Hospital had messed his bed and demonstrated his predicament by holding up a handful of faeces. He was old, incontinent and unable to comprehend what he was doing. David had to clear up the mess and sister blamed him for the situation. "You should have seen what he was doing," she yelled. "Clean the mess up. I can't trust anyone." How one could see under the bedclothes a patient messing himself was quite beyond David's comprehension. He said nothing and got on with the job.

It seemed that wherever Sister Bell went there was trouble. Yes, the hospital was busy but calm and efficiency was called for and not shouting and undue criticism. The other Night Special, Corporal Newsome, a regular soldier and with an SRN like the sister, had been abused as well. Over a quick cup of tea in the kitchen of Doughty Ward, the night staff exchanged their experiences. Nobody had had any respite let alone a food break and five minutes of rest would recharge their batteries. They all had suffered under Sister Bell and were feeling antagonistic. The two nurses, one a staff nurse, had also smarted under sister's sharp tongue.

Suddenly the door slammed open hitting the kitchen unit behind it and startling the occupants of the kitchen. Sister Bell stood there like an angry bull at a correda.(7) "What are you doing?" she demanded in a voice loud enough the waken the ward. It was clear what they were doing. Having a break after a very busy night. "I've never come across such a lazy, good-for-nothing lot of staff in all my life," she yelled going red in the face. "Get back to your duties."

This was too much for Corporal Newsome. "Wait on, sister," he responded quietly. "None of us here have had a break all night. Now it's quiet we're having a cup of tea. We've not had any food or break as we are entitled......."

"You speak to me when I've given you an order....." she yelled going even redder in the face.

"Listen, woman," went on Newsome. "You've had a break and food. I know as I covered for you. We have not."

"We have been on the go none-stop for nine hours without a break," added the staff nurse."

"Shut up!" screeched Sister Bell.

With that Corporal Newsome threw his cup of tea at sister. The cup missed her but the contents splashed her uniform. "Christ, woman, don't you ever let up. Don't insult another professional."

"I'll have you charged," wailed Sister Bell.

"Do it," responded Newsome. "Staff nurse and I are equally well qualified and you treat us like dirt. Nurse here is about to receive her SRN and Private Earl is probably the brightest of us all with university entry and you treat us all like dogs. Your rank is superior and nothing else. God knows how you got your SRN as you can't even do a simple catheterization. Charge me, but I'll spill the beans and I'm sure my colleagues will give evidence."

Sister Bell knew when she was beaten. She glared at them, turned about and left the kitchen. "You're in for it," said staff nurse.

"No way," replied Corporal Newsome. "She's all mouth. I've met her type before. All bluster and no brain. She knows she's inefficient. Charging me will cause a stir and that's the last thing she wants. In any case, she had a break when we did not. They would want to know why she left her post if we were so busy. No, she will not go through with her threat."

And she did not.

The church of St Peter's was a large neo-Gothic structure of red brick down a side road off Victoria Street. Church and clergy house were a unity as was the fashion in early Victorian times so that the clergy could get to services easily. The interior of the church was rather dark, but the gloom was overcome with spotlights focused on statues and Stations of the Cross. The altar was of pink alabaster with a central crucifix surrounded by saints, and had a myriad of cherubs blowing trumpets. There were six candles on the altar in candle-holders of gilded wood and the frontal to the altar was finely embroidered in gold thread. It was typical of churches of the Oxford Movement (8) and David expected the Mass to be colorful and dramatic.

Mass was certainly dramatic with plenty of 'smells and bells'. If one had not known, the casual visitor would have expected the service to be Roman Catholic rather than Anglican. The young man carrying the thurible swung it with great professionalism so that clouds of incense permeated the church. There were numerous servers and a second priest as master of ceremonies. Father Royce was the celebrant and a monk from a religious order was the preacher. There was quite a good choir and the service was full of ceremonial as well as symbolism.

David's own church at home was 'spiky' and thus he was not unusually disturbed by the service as some Anglicans might have been. However, it was not a 'high church' like St Peter's. At the hospital chapel the service was very simple, typical of most Anglican churches. Both were acceptable to him. He could not always receive communion on Sundays as generally he was on duty. The Padre did bring round communion, but David felt that this was for the sick rather than the able bodied. Sister Thornton would let him go to chapel if they were not busy, but frequently they were short staffed, and he had to make do with a quiet prayer in the sparse chapel after duty. He reasoned that he was serving God by helping the sick and that this was a form of worship. His attitude to ceremonial was that as long as it did not detract from the main purpose of worship, then it was fine. If well done and not intrusive, he felt that it enhanced the spirituality of worship. He could not understand the extremes of bigotry within the Church of England: those who were opposed to pomp and those who took the alternate view. If music and beauty helped one receive the Holy Spirit then fine. If God had intended man to do without music and beauty then He would not have allowed man to develop such skills. Skills of the Devil? David could not believe that the Devil was capable of creating such sublime skills. To dictate how one obtained spirituality was misguided, and there was room in the Anglican Communion for many approaches. Did not Jesus say that in His house there were many rooms? That was why he was an Anglican and not a Roman Catholic. Rome was far too insistent in telling people what they should believe and how to obtain grace, and thus there was little room for individuality.

The congregation was smallish consisting of old ladies mainly, and a few young men. Many London parishes were like that. Few people lived in the area but many worked there. It was a pity as the service was full of color and movement: the choir sang well and the hymns were carefully chosen to give the congregation a part in the proceedings. The sermon was about giving, based on the story of the Widow's Mite from the Gospel of St Luke, but encompassed not just the giving of alms, but of giving love, and time, to others. As could be expected from a Franciscan monk, the sermon was down-to-earth and of practical value. Highly theological sermons had their place, but ordinary people wanted advice and uplift, which would see them through the following week. David had no time for the priest who tried to be clever and ended up mystifying the congregation, rather than informing and teaching. On the whole David was impressed and felt much better for the experience.

What David thought was so very nice was that Father Royce and the Preacher were in the church porch shaking hands with the congregation and having a word with each one. It seemed that Father Royce knew his parishioners very well, as they responded to his comments with smiles and banter. When it got to be David's turn, Father Royce shook his hand warmly looked into David's face with his piercing gray eyes. "So you must be the young man on the end of the telephone, David? How is Father Garrett?"

"Yes, father," David replied with a smile. "Father Garrett is fine. In his last letter he asked to be remembered to you."

"When you write tell him all is well here. Now then, you'll have to excuse me a moment. Parish duties. Frank here will take you round to the clergy house."

With that he summoned a tall, broad-shouldered young man whom David had seen acting as a server at the service.

"Frank, this is David from Leicester by way of the RAMC. Take him round to the house and make him comfortable. Do you drink sherry, David?"

"Yes, father. Thank you. Pleased to meet you Frank." They shook hands.

Frank took David round the side of the church to a gate in the wall, which led through a rather untidy garden into the clergy house. In the sitting room were two other young men sipping from sherry glasses, both were handsome and in their early twenties. They all appeared to know each other. Frank introduced David to the other luncheon guests. He poured David a sherry from a decanter on a side table. Eric was from Coventry and worked as a sales assistant at Harrods, the famous store in Knightsbridge, and Alan worked for a merchant bank in the City. David learned they had completed their National Service three years previously and had met Father Royce during that period. They were now lodgers at the vicarage.

Frank, it appeared, was still in the services, a Corporal of Horse in the Life Guards. David thought how fine Frank would look on a horse in the uniform of the Life Guards: tight white trousers, knee-length boots and red jacket, for he was a fine looking man with what appeared to be an excellent body. He was typical of the two young men you can see sitting like statues on their horses outside Horse Guards Arch (9) as you go through to Horse Guards Parade. He had been told by patients from the Life Guards who had been on the ward, that many girls slipped notes with their phone numbers into the knee-length boots of the guards.

Frank's natural charm soon put David at ease. Quite soon they were joined by Father Royce and the monk, who was introduced as Father Jacob from Walsingham, (10) a community based on the famous shrine. The jolly crowd went into the adjacent dining room where a cold lunch had been set out by the housekeeper. The conversation was not particularly religious, although Father Royce did ask David what he thought of the service. David had thoroughly appreciated the service and the sermon and said so.

"Did you find it rather high church?" Alan asked.

"No, not really," David confessed. "It was rather like the service in my own parish church."

"David's vicar and I were at St Stephens together," remarked Father Royce. "It will be about the same in the St Stephen's tradition.

"Father Royce tells me you have been accepted at King's College here in London," observed Father Jacob. "That will be somewhat different......very..... Anglican."

David wasn't sure what that meant, but assumed with was less 'spikey' than what he had experienced today.

'I'm told it's middle of the road, Father," he remarked.

"Approved of by the bishop and archbishop, David. Unlike we of the Oxford Movement who are viewed with suspicion," laughed Father Jacob. "They think we're about to bring back Popery." (11)

"Well aren't you?" enquired Eric mischievously, a smile on his face.

"Now Eric........" Father Royce interrupted, "we'll have none of your mischief."

"Eric's a Baptist, David," observed Father Royce. "We're not averse to Baptists here." They all laughed.

"Well you've got a good bishop, Father," observed Frank. "Bishop Stockwood has come out in his true colors quite recently. I'm told he wears a mitre as big as the Pope."

"No, bigger," added Alan.

They all laughed again.

"He certainly shocked one or two people," noted Father Jacob. "I was surprised when I first saw his vestments. He's a left winger as well. Quite a few at the top of the Church of England have had to sit up and take note. These Tories in the House of Lords will have to watch out"

"No more shop," said Father Royce changing the subject. And there was no more. The conversation ranged over the theatre, literature and Maria Callas's (12) latest outbreak of temperament.

Around three o'clock Father Royce suggested they all went for a walk in Hyde Park, (13) which was not a great distance away. It was a lovely spring afternoon and the park was quite busy with locals and tourists wandering lazily around the lake or sitting on the grass in the sun, sometime obliterated by the canopy of the great trees that had been planted centuries before. The group paired off and David found himself with Frank who pointed out the sights surrounding the park. A band was playing in the bandstand and for a while they all stopped to listen to a selection from the operas of Gilbert and Sullivan.

"Do you like music?" Frank asked David.

"Yes, very much," he replied. "I play the piano but get little opportunity to touch it nowadays."

"That's a pity."

"I did think of becoming a concert pianist at one stage, but I felt I was not good enough."

"You must play well then."

"I did but not well enough. You have to be really good as the competition is so great. Now, after nearly a year of not playing, I'm a little rusty. I can sight read anything, but the fingering is dodgy."

"You must come round to my place, David, and listen to some music. I like classical music. What about you?"

"Me too," David replied, thrilled that he had been invited to somewhere other than his bed sitter. "Thank you, that will be great." He heard little music on the ward and what there was tended to be pop – Cliff Richard mostly.

"I assume you like Beethoven, Tchaikovsky, Chopin?"

"Yes. I'm not much into pop."

"I've a huge collection of records. Phone me and we'll get together when both of us are not on duty." Frank stopped, wrote his phone number on a piece of paper and handed it to David.

"Thanks Frank, I'll look forward to that," David replied with enthusiasm.

Father Royce, who had been talking with Alan, caught up with them. "David needs to talk to me Frank," he said. "Actually that was the point of him coming to lunch. But it's good to see you getting on so well together. You make a handsome pair. I'll sit with David on a bench here in the park and you all can wander back home. I'll be there for evensong."

Frank gave David a big smile. "See you David. I'll not be at evensong as I'm on duty this evening. Give me a ring." With that he joined the others and they began to wander towards Hyde Park Gate.

"Now David," he began, "what seems to be the problem? By the way", he went on, "I hope you don't mind sitting in the park having a discussion. I feel it's better than being in a stuffy study, particularly on a lovely afternoon like today."

"No, not at all, Father. This is lovely."

"So what is the problem, David? You gave me an outline on the phone but tell me again," continued Father Royce.

David explained the death of the child and his difficulty in reconciling this with a loving God.

Father Royce listened quietly, not seeking to interrupt, until the narrative and dilemma was enunciated. "You say you cannot accept the doctrine of 'original sin'. The psychologist Young, the pupil of the father of psychology, Sigmund Freud, proposed something similar – 'archetypes' he called them. Fears that we inherit from our ancestors and repress because they make us afraid. Shadows in the night, monsters we have never seen but can conjure up. St. Augustin's concept of original sin is something similar. Why do some young children need to have a night light in their bedroom? Yes, they are afraid of the dark, or what's in the dark or a past fear inherited from a parent."

David thought for a while. "But such fears are not necessarily sins, Father. Fears could have been put into the mind of the child by the parent. What about the fear of thunder and lightning? My brother and I were never afraid as my parents never made a fuss about a storm, but some people are. In any case, fears are different to sins. A sin is something wrong that you do knowingly."

"True," interjected Father Royce, "but sin is an offence against God's designs for us and natural law."

"But if you are unaware of God's designs and ignorant of the natural law, how can you be a sinner?"

"We are all sinners, David. It does not matter if you are ignorant or unaware. If you go against God's will, then you sin."

David thought for a while. "Sorry Father but I can't accept that. If you are too young to know God's will then how can you sin against Him?"

"A child can do wrong not knowing it is wrong. An infant will bite or spit without knowing it is not acceptable. The parent has to teach that it is wrong."

"But reason has to play a part somewhere. The child cannot be blamed until he knows the reason for the bad action, even if that reason is the disapproval of the parent. After all, we are animals and animals spit and bite if provoked. If you are an ignorant savage, unaware of God, and you kill to protect you family, you are doing what is right for the family. If you kill anyone you come across you are going against the natural law. If you are a Christian and kill, knowing that the Ten Commandments say "Thou shalt not kill" and also Jesus asks us to turn the other cheek, and forgive seventy times seven, then you are knowingly disobedient and a sinner."

"I'm afraid David that we have to accept that we are all sinners, knowingly or not," said Father Royce, "and accept the concept given by St Augustin."

"But I can't, Father. We have been given a brain, the power of reason, so surely God meant us to use reason?"

Father Royce closed his eyes and thought for a while.

A family with two small children passed by and David was reminded of his small cancer patient. What did these children know of right and wrong? They knew that which their parents had taught them, and some instinctual universal laws that were essential for our existence. Surely there was nothing in their short lives that caused such sin as to be denied the right to live?

"There is another way of looking at the problem, David," remarked Father Royce opening his eyes. "The concept of vicarious suffering."

"What does that mean, father?" responded David awakened from his thoughts.

"Vicarious suffering is when God uses the suffering of a person as an example to ordinary people. It's a sort of teaching method to explain or highlight something rather complex. Our Lord suffered on the Cross in order that the sins of the world were taken on His shoulders. Many of the Saints suffered as an example to we sinners to sin no more."

"I find that even more of a problem," David said slowly. "I can accept Our Lord suffering for the world. He is God and it was His will to do so. But for God to choose people to suffer without their agreement as examples to 'we sinners', as you put it, seems a wicked concept."

"Many of the saints willingly suffered. In their prayers they said 'Thy will not mine, Lord'," replied Father Royce.

"I can accept that, father, if they were willing," responded David, "but how does this apply to a small child who died of cancer? Was he mature enough to say 'Thy will not mine?'"

"That is a mystery David. We puny humans with our limited brain power cannot possibly understand the workings of God."

"But that's a ...." David started a reply but decided to say no more. He wanted to say 'but that's a copout, father, an excuse because you are unable to give a rational answer' but he left it unsaid. He didn't want to offend Father Royce. Instead he went on, ".....an argument I shall have to consider."

There was silence for a while. It was clear that Father Royce had finalized his argument. And David?

They parted at the underground station by the park gates. Father Royce told David to visit him any time and suggested that he might like to serve mass one Sunday morning when he was not on duty. David felt that it was a nice gesture and agreed to phone him when he was free. They shook hands and went their separate ways. St George's Drive was not far from the park so he decided to walk. It would give him time to think. Original sin was unacceptable if your concept of God was that of a loving God, whilst vicarious suffering seemed even more wicked. All things being a mystery was just an excuse for not having an intellectual argument. The dilemma was still there. He thought for a while. Why not ask Frank and maybe Sister Thornton? Maybe they had come across the problem and had an answer.

Work impinged on David's thought patterns and it was a while before the dilemma rose in his consciousness. He was helping sister check the stock in the treatment room when sister mentioned that her disabled brother was ill and that she would be taking leave to be at his bedside. "I'm really sorry, sister. I hope he will be OK." He did not want to ask what the problem was as it seemed like prying. There was a silence and he decided to pose his question. "Can I ask you something personal, sister?" David proposed. "It's not really personal ....I mean.....rather to do with how one looks at things."

"Is there something troubling you Private Earl?" ask sister. "I've noticed a time or two that you seemed to be lost in thought. I didn't like to press too much."

David spilled out his story of the little boy, his dilemma over the suffering and the explanations of Father Royce."

Sister thought for a while, counting the bottles of scopolamine that David passed to her and checking them in the drug register. "You know, David, in nursing, death is something one has to accept. Of course, we fight to let a patient live but we don't always win. To become emotionally involved with patients is not healthy for the nurse or the patient. When I lose a patient, I just tell myself that it's God's will. Does that help, Private Earl? "

"Well......," David did not know how to explain to her that it was the sort of copout Father Royce had suggested.. "You see, sister, it does not really answer my question but I'm grateful for you being so frank."

"I've never given such things much thought really. I just accept what I was taught at Sunday School and what is communicated in church."

"Me too, sister, until quite recently."

"You know, Private Earl, I believe that you are a very bright young man, far brighter than the usual National Servicemen we get here. Sister Tutor tells me you are way ahead of the others and could become a doctor. Certainly you could apply for a Commission. It is quite understandable that you want to ask questions and sort things out in your own mind."

David did not know what to say. Praise tended to embarrass him. He knew that he was bright as he did not work hard at school and he was always somewhere near the top of the class. However, his father always ridiculed him and praised his brother, but somehow he knew that he had a good brain. The trouble was he was not interested in facts. Ideas were more important. "Thanks for being so frank sister," replied. "A commission would be fine. In fact, the Recruiting Officer at my medical suggested I go for a commission, but it means an infantry regiment and three years in the army and three years postponement of university. I don't want to do that."

"Maybe you're right Private Earl," continued sister. "I assume you wanted the RAMC on religious grounds?"

"Yes. Not that I'm a complete pacifist. That's another dilemma in my life. I don't like to kill and yet I recognize that there are times when one's family and country has to be protected."

"An unhappy pacifist then?"

"I suppose so. Joining the RAMC and learning how to heal rather than kill seems the sensible compromise."

"I wonder how many other young men join the RAMC for the same reason, Private Earl?" asked sister.

David wondered. They finished the drug inventory in silence both respecting each other's thoughts.

David telephoned Frank and a meeting was arranged an evening a few days later. Frank lived in an apartment block overlooking Hyde Park, built specially for members of the guards regiments. The apartment was on the fourth floor and David had to climb the stairs as there was no lift. Frank opened the door to a rather hot and breathless David.

"Come in, David, and let me get you a cold drink. Those stairs are killers," he said motioning David to a comfortable chair. The room was simply furnished with G-Plan (14) furniture – a bit too modern for

David's taste, but comfortable. It was quite artistically decorated with one or two good modern prints on the walls. He was quite surprised really as Frank gave the impression of being uninterested in artistic things.

Frank returned with an ice cold Coca-cola. "What do you think to my pad David?"

"Well....," David began, trying to be diplomatic. "It's very comfortable."

Frank laughed. "No need to be a diplomat. Tell me the truth."

"It's very comfortable and homely, Frank, but well...it's not my style of décor."

"No problem, David. What is your style then?" asked Frank.

"Oh, I'm much more for the traditional – antiques and all that."

"Fair enough. Too expensive for me, even reproductions."

"Me too, but I can always dream," replied David with a smile.

David sipped his drink and Frank settled into an armchair. "Now, David, on the phone you mentioned a problem. Shoot"

David related the death of the child, his dilemma and the discussion he had had with Father Royce and Sister Thornton. Frank listened intently, only interrupting when he wanted to clarify a point. At the end of his account there was silence while Frank closed his eyes, pressed his fingertips together and thought. During this period of silence, David had time to study Frank. Yes, he was certainly very handsome with his aquiline nose and wavy black hair. He had broad shoulders and a small waist and very muscular legs showing through his rather tight jeans. David wondered how he got into them.

After a while Frank opened his eyes, smiled and spoke slowly and deliberately. "I'm no theologian David, just a soldier who rides a horse and takes orders. In fact, it took all I could do to pass three 'O' levels. My faith is strictly traditional and I just accept what the clergy tell me. I have to be honest that I am more impressed by the music and ritual of the church than the boring sermons that the clergy provide. An honest answer would be that I don't know. Maybe Father Royce was right when he said it was a mystery and our puny brains cannot understand."

"As I've already mentioned, I can't accept that Frank," David replied. "It's just a way of denying the knowledge of an explanation – a copout."

"Maybe you're right, David. Maybe there is no explanation. Certainly, if the child had been mine I would have been asking why, and 'It's a mystery' would not have satisfied me. I don't have a child, but I do have a wife."

"Oh, you're married?" responded David with some surprise.

"Separated. We were together for two years and then she left. I've not seen her for five years now. That's the trouble with getting married so young. I take it you're not married, David?"

"No. I'm only nineteen."

"I was nineteen when I got married. Do you want to get married?" asked Frank.

David thought for a while. "I've never really thought about it."

"Don't like girls?" asked Frank.

David blushed. He had always felt a bit intimidated by females, although there were many girls at school who pursued him. He had taken Ruth, the most desired girl in the school, to the cinema a few times and they had kissed. She threw him over for an older boy who he knew went much further than kissing. "I don't know much about them Frank. I had a girlfriend at school........"

"Kissed her?"

"A few times."

"Go any further?"

David was a bit shocked. "No, no of course not."

"Why not?" asked Frank.

"Well....," David did not know what to say. "It's wrong."

"Ok, fair enough."

Frank got up to make some coffee. David had the chance to pull himself together. He had never been interrogated before about his sex life and he was left feeling uncertain. It hade never really occurred to him whether he liked girls or not. Everyone at school had a girlfriend and it was natural that he should have one too. Many girls liked him but he was too shy to respond. Some of his classmates had had sexual relations with their girl, but as far as he was aware, none of his close friends had gone so far. Girls who 'gave' themselves were no good and to be avoided. Pamela Evans had had a baby to a boy he knew quite well. She had brought the child into school. Whilst she was made a fuss of by her classmates, the general opinion was that she had ruined her life by her rash act. The father, however, was seen as quite a hero whose masculinity was in no doubt. For David, it was an unfair world where the girl was degraded and the boy made into a hero.

There was now a chance to look around the room. He had been taught not to be too inquisitive in other people's homes, but he was always interested in other people's decor. It gave an indication of their character. It really was quite nice. There was a huge collection of mainly classical records in a rack in one corner and a Philips Stereo Player. Everywhere was neat and tidy, quite unusual for a male. For such a masculine person Frank was really artistic. There were one or two nice pieces of porcelain on an occasional table. One in particular took David's eye. It was in pure white and depicted two beautiful male figures wrestling. Certainly it was in the Greek style, exquisitely modeled and rather expensive looking. David got up from his chair and went over to look at it. Lovely.

At this point Frank emerged from the kitchen with a tray of coffee and a plate of biscuits. "Ah, I can see you like beautiful things," he observed putting down the tray. "That's my pride and joy. Nimphenberg and very expensive. I bought it at Harrods when they had an exhibition of fine porcelain."

"It's lovely, Frank. Beautifully modeled."

"I think it's based on a Greek sculpture."

"Thought so," responded David.

"You like things like that?" Frank asked pointing to the male figures with his eyes.

"Yes. I think the male body is very beautiful."

"Good. When we've had our coffee I'll show you some more beautiful things."

They sat and drank Frank's excellent coffee and ate chocolate biscuits. Conversation was about David's knowledge of London. He really knew very little as he always seemed to be on duty. He had seen Westminster Abbey and the Houses of Parliament, Hyde Park and Green Park but little else. Frank had been in London since he was nineteen and knew the place like the back of his hand. He suggested so many places to visit and described them with great enthusiasm. David had never seen the Changing of the Guard at Buckingham Palace, or the Queen's Birthday Parade in which Frank had taken part on a number of occasions, or the great museums in South Kensington. (15) Whilst David did not really like big cities he found central London fascinating. As for the rest, the urban sprawl, it was ugly and unfriendly, and made him feel claustrophobic; to be confined to such environs for the rest of his life would be like putting him in a cage; his was a free spirit, a countryside spirit.

Eventually the coffee cups were cleared away and Frank brought out two large photograph albums. The first held family pictures and his wedding photographs. It was revealed that Frank came from Southampton and had two sisters and an elder brother. All were very good looking and David commented on what an attractive family they were. Both his parents were dead, but their photographs showed a family likeness with his father being the double of Frank. His sisters and brother were married and there were lots of photographs of children and babies. Towards the end of the album, there were lots of

81

photographs of the growing, rather gawky, Frank and his friends. The last couple of pages showed Frank in his Life Guards uniform looking so smart and handsome and full of confidence. There were a couple of pictures of him on the beach – Brighton he said – in rather tiny swimwear showing his fine body.

"You look good," David remarked as they thumbed the pages.

"Like the body?" asked Frank.

"Mm...really great."

"Oh, I'm better than that now," replied Frank. "I've been lifting weights for the last five years and have developed somewhat." With that he went to the other album that was bursting with photographs of the developing Frank and others who frequented the gym he attended. There were some beautiful bodies as good as any Charles Atlas.(16)

They finished the album and Frank suddenly asked, "Like to see my body, David?"

It came as quite a shock and David did not know what to say. Deep inside he would love to see what Frank looked like, but men didn't usually admire each other like that. Anyhow, he had no choice, as Frank got up, took off his shirt and pulled off his jeans, and there he was in skimpy, white briefs showing his fine body. It really was quite magnificent with a tiny waist, broad shoulders and arms that would be the envy of any male. His thighs were muscular and he had good calves worthy of any short-distance runner. Short black hair grew across his chest and over large pectoral muscles and a thin swathe of it followed his stomach down to the top of his brief. As the nurses in the hospital would have said, he was a 'hunk'. "What do you think, Dave?" he asked.

Speechless at first, David offered, "Magnificent Frank. You are as good as anyone in the films. Wow!"

"Feel those biceps," he said flexing his arms. "Come on, feel them."

David got up hesitantly and put his hands on the bulging muscles. They were like iron and he said so.

"Put you hands on my abdominals and see how hard they are," commanded Frank.

They were a perfect set and like iron when David touched them. "Gosh," he said I never knew stomach muscles could be so hard.

"Now feel my thighs," requested Frank and David did as asked. He didn't know why but something between his legs had stirred and he didn't know what to do. As David stood back from Frank, he notice that Frank had a large bulge in his briefs.

Their eyes met and Frank took David's hand and placed it over the erection. "That's big as well David," he said smiling with his bright blue eyes. "See what you do to me."

It was wrong, David knew it. Men just do not do that to each other. Yes, they had played at school when he was younger but that was growing up, finding out. Now he was a man and no longer open to boyish pranks. "Frank.... I....we mustn't ...... I better go," he said moving towards the door. Thank you for a fine evening. You are beautiful....I think you.....have a wonderful body. I mustn't......we mustn't do this kind of thing......it's wrong." With that he opened the door and fled down the stairs and into the darkened street.

Out in the street David was shaking like a frightened rabbit about to be slaughtered. What had happened? He just did not understand himself or Frank for that matter. He had loved watching Frank' body and feeling his muscles and fascinated by the huge bulge in his briefs. To be honest, he had an erection as well during that episode. He was very attracted to Frank and yet he knew it was wrong for such feelings and actions. It was against all Christian teachings and illegal for two men to be attracted by each other. What was wrong with him. Was he sick? And yet, this was not the first time he had had such feelings for a male. There had been a boy at school he could not keep his eyes off, then his friend who was now in Canada, and now Frank. Frank....He still could see those broad shoulders and muscular body and the look of pure puzzlement on his face as David fled down the stairs. He would phone him tomorrow and apologize. Frank would understand even if he did not.

Chapter 6

David did not ring Frank. He had spent a sleepless night worried by what had gone on. He told himself that it was clear Frank liked to display his body and got a kick out of it. Narcissism, (1) that is what it was called. Maybe he was frustrated: he was a married man and he had not seen his wife for a number of years. But David did not understand his own feelings. Should he try to seek advice? No. Such feelings were wrong and he was embarrassed to discuss them. Maybe he was sick? He knew that boys at school did things and had special friendships but that was adolescence. He would not see Frank again, at least not alone, and put himself in a position he knew to be against what he had been taught.

The weeks went on as usual and then one day Sister Thornton told him that Matron had instructed her to send him to work in the operating theatre, as this is what he had been selected to do on completion of his basic training. It would be a trial period to see how he got on. David had forgotten. He was happy on the ward and did not really want to move.

When the nurses found out that David was leaving to work in the operating theatre, they gave him dire warnings about the theatre sister, Sister Anthony. "She's a bitch of the first order, David," remarked Derek Douglas who just happened to have called in on the ward and generally said little to him.

"You'll be back," remarked Nurse Walker, a cheery, chubby newcomer to the ward who seemed to have inside information.

It did not sound good so David was very nervous when he reported to theatre on the following Monday morning.

Sister was around forty, of medium height, stout and without an ounce of humor in her entire body. When David introduced himself military fashion, she just glared at him and passed him on to one of the nurses. From the start he seemed not to get anything right. No matter how hard he tried, how hard he concentrated, sister always had criticisms and she voiced them for all to hear. It was clear she had no management skills whatever and no manners.

At coffee break one of the other theatre orderlies told him not to worry. "She's like that with everyone who is new in theatre. You get used to her. She's really very good at her job. The trouble is she has no idea how to handle people." With a twinkle in his eye he went on, "You see she hates all men. Rumour has it that she was raped by a Chinese during the Korean War, and since then she takes it out of us all. She's fine with the girls, but we males get it all day, every day. It's not that you are poor at the job, Dave, but that she is never satisfied."

"How do you put up with it?" asked David.

"You get used to it," he replied smiling. "Been in theatre four years and I just close my mind to her and get on with the job. Good theatre sister though. She'll chase you for the next year or until you break."

"I don't want two years of misery thank you," David observed and from that moment he decided at the end of his duty he would ask to be returned to his ward. He was not a career theatre technician and his future did not depend on his performance. Maybe he would tolerate this insensitive human if it was but..."

He went to see Sister Thornton that evening and caught her just as she was going off duty. She had a knowing look on her face. David explained the situation, and Sister promised to see Matron first thing the following morning. He would have to stand another day of the terrible woman, but he did not mind if the agony was to be short lived. In reality, he had to stay for a week and the fact that he had asked to be moved antagonized Sister Anthony further, so that life was a week in hell.

He was moved back to his usual ward, but not for long. Something like a month later he found that on Orders he had been posted back to the RAMC barracks in order to be assigned to a foreign posting. It came as a shock, and yet it was a relief. He had been six months at Queen Elizabeth Hospital, six months of excellent experience and he was ready for a new challenge. His brush with Sister Anthony may have had something to do with it.

He did not get any leave but had to dispose of his belonging in his bed-sitter as best he could. Three days notice was all that was given. He phoned his parents for help and they agreed to drive down to London at the weekend and remove the belongings he could not take with him to Queen Elizabeth Barracks. It was unfortunate that he did not see his parents, but he was on his way to Crookham, and a new chapter in his military experience.

He reported to HQ (2) Company Office at the barracks and was allotted a bed in a long barrack room where there were other recruits waiting to be posted. He found that he had been promoted to full corporal and was to be sent to the Aden Protectorate in South Yemen. He was not sure where Aden actually was, but he knew it was one of the 'hot spots' around the world like Cyprus and Kenya. Eventually, he learnt that there was some kind of fight going on backed by a Colonel Nasser, the ruler of Egypt. It was not the worst posting he could have been assigned to like Kenya or Cyprus, but it was not cushy like

Germany. His parents were quite worried when he phoned them to tell them the news. Obviously they knew more about the situation there than he did.

Because of the nature of the posting, he had to undertake a whole series of injections: typhoid, tetanus, cholera and yellow fever. After being pricked and prodded, kitted out with the appropriate uniform for the climate – khaki shorts, shirt and long canvas trousers with a most ridiculous sun hat – he was sent home on leave for ten days before embarkation to Aden.

The journey to Leicester was a pleasant one as it was May and the sun shone warmly. It was with a feeling of freedom, of regeneration, that he undertook the train journey. For him, London was a place of busy, dirty streets and endless buildings. Oh yes, there were parks, beautiful large parks, but it was not the same as the freedom of the open countryside. He was a county boy at heart, used to open spaces and green fields. Fields that were visible from his bedroom window and acres of farmland to be walked where one met the occasional human. Crowds of people had their place but solitude was also important. In London it was impossible to get away from people.

The countryside displayed its rebirth from winter to spring with the leaves of the stunted trees backing the railway showing fresh shades of green before being blackened by railway pollution. The cows in the fields were clean and fit and munched away at the luscious emerald grass spotted with yellow buttercups, contented and well fed. In the hedgerows the hawthorn displayed its flowers like white lace, and the occasional clumps of bluebells, protected from the jaws of the plough, danced in the gentle breeze among the low spring grasses.

He was a corporal now with two stripes on his arm. There was pride in being a soldier and a new confidence showed in his manner. His uniform was immaculate with knife-edge creases in the sleeves of his tunic and trousers. David knew he looked good in his uniform. Being tall was an advantage. There was a swagger in his step adopted by many soldiers who were aware of their distinguished look.

Home was a pleasant relief from the bed-sitter in Victoria and his mother spoiled him, obviously proud of her soldier son who seemed broader, fitter and more grown up than he had been before he went away. There was even an air of pride in his father, who did not usually show his feelings. Not once did he offer a word of criticism. And yet David was not in perfect shape as his right arm was aching like mad. The arm began to swell and he began felt really unwell. He said little but in the end it got so bad that his father noticed and made him see the local doctor.

"You'll have to rest David," the doctor advised. "For some reason your yellow fever jab has gone wrong and you have an infection in your arm. It's bed for you for a few days or there will be complications."

"But I'm due back in barracks in four days for a foreign posting," he told the doctor.

"No return to barracks and no posting yet, David. It's rest for you my boy."

"What do I do? I'm in real trouble if I don't return on time," David observed, rather worried.

The doctor thought. "Do you have a phone number for your barracks?"

"Yes,"

"I'll telephone you commanding officer and explain the situation. Now don't worry. "It'll be all right."

The local doctor was as good as his word and the message came back that he could have another ten days of leave and a new travel warrant would be sent to his home.

The extra leave was spent recovering from the reaction to the yellow fever injection. He was quite poorly for about five days with a fever and high temperature. The doctor came to see him each day. Slowly the fever-like symptoms subsided, the sweating stopped and his aching body began to feel like normal. The red and swollen arm took longer to reduce and was still quite painful when he finally traveled back to barracks. One of the Medical Officers had a look at him and pronounced him not fit enough to be sent overseas immediately. He told David that such a reaction was quite rare.

The Staff Sergeant in charge of overseas postings, Sgt York, decided that David was to be put to work helping him rather than just sitting around. "I need someone with brains," he said, "and I'm told you've got them, corporal." They got on well and David soon learned about documentation, kitting out and what injections were required for various postings. It was interesting work as most were individual postings rather than large groups and each one was different. There was a manual to consult, but the job was so easy and David did it with great efficiency. Sgt York was a regular soldier, efficient and friendly and they worked well together. David was quite surprised that on Orders one day he found he had been promoted to acting sergeant for the duration of his stay with HQ Company.

"Gives you a bit of status, David, to help you with the job" was all that Sgt York offered.

Now David had never uttered a bad word in his life. He was of the opinion that expletives were a lack of sufficient vocabulary as well as wrong. Whilst his father swore on rare occasions, his mother did not, and so the family was not really used to bad language. On commencing National Service, David was amazed at the use of derogative terms both in range and frequency. Bad language was a way of life in the military and even officers took part in the practice. Of course, many of his contemporaries came from homes where bad language was the rule, and it shocked him at first. In time, he came to ignore it. His English teacher at school had argued, a devilish smile on his face, that one did not 'know' a language until one could swear in it. However true that may have been, David had not succumbed and did not intend to.

One morning Sgt York received word that a War Office Colonel was on the way to pay a surprise visit and a guard of honor was required.

"Scoot up to Hut 46 David and get that lazy bunch down here as fast as you can. I've already phoned to tell them so they should be ready for parade," he reported.

David marched double quick to the top of the camp where about twenty soldiers were forming up. They were a rag-tag bunch and it took a while to get them assembled.

David gave the order: "Parade....parade...'shun. Right turn. Quick march. Left, right, left, right........"

What a bunch. It was a wonder they could walk at all. They dragged their feet and were so slow. An officer appeared from out of the blue. "Eyes right," and David threw him a smart salute to which the officer just raised his swagger cane in a half-hearted wave. Some of the officers felt it was beneath them to offer a decent salute. David had been told that it was not the man who was being recognized but the Queen's uniform. Perhaps a 'stuffed shirt' inside a stuffed shirt could do no more. "Eyes front," and they continued but so slowly.

David increased the pace....left, right, left, right, left, right....but they still dragged their feet. He had to get these men to move more quickly. Why not play them at their own game in a language they could understand? And so David's rule of no expletives was broken. "Get your fucking feet moving or I'll kick your arses. Leftrigh, leftright, leftright," he bellowed. It was magic. It hit them in the right place, wherever that might be, and to a man they quickened their pace. The rot had set in and from that moment onwards David became a user of expletives, not in general parlance, but when necessary. 'If the cap fits, wear it,' he thought.

One night David was returning from a visit to Aldershot when he was summoned into the main Guard House by a lance corporal of the Military Police lingering in the shadows. David was in civilian clothes and thus his rank was unknown. David knew him to be one of the soldiers who had made such a fool of him when he was in basic training.

"Where yer bin soldier?" the lance corporal asked in a bullying way.

David just looked at him without comment.

"'A said where yer bin?" he snarled again.

By this time, a full corporal had arrived from a room at the back. "Stand to attention when yer talk to us," he ordered. "Answer 'is question."

David did nothing and said nothing.

"Stand to attention yer bastard, or I'll charge yer with dumb insolence," roared the corporal.

"Seen 'im afore," the lance corporal said to his colleague, a leer of recognition coming on his simple face. "In training a few monfs ago. Private. Remember, we made a right nancy of 'im."

"Ye," replied the corporal. "Na soldier do as yer told or yer aint seen nofin yet."

There was silence. They expected David to crumble under their stare but he did not.

Their simple brains could not work out what to do next.

"Bastard, stand to attention when 'a talk to yer," yelled the corporal.

"Fuckin' thick if yer arst me," replied the lance corporal.

David had had enough. "You stand to attention you sniveling little runts," he roared, "or I'll have your guts. Don't you know a senior NCO when you see one?"

They froze. They were now unsure of themselves.

"You horrible pair," David shouted. "Insulting a superior officer is an offence," he roared.

Immediately they snapped to attention.

"Yes, you made an idiot of me when I was a recruit. It's clear you do it for sport," he growled at them. "Now I'm back as a sergeant. I could have been an officer. What then?"

They were silent and looked fearful. They were too thick to realize it was his word against theirs.

For a while he kept them standing to attention until they were suitably frightened, then he stood them at ease.

"If I ever hear of you abusing your authority again, I'll put you on a charge," he told them. "You've got off lightly with a warning, but any more nonsense and ……."

They looked relieved. Bullies always are cowards underneath.

"Understand?" David asked. They nodded their heads. "Now get out of my sight."

They moved very fast inside the inner office whilst David walked away satisfied that an old score had been settled.

After nearly two months with HQ Company the War Office in London asked questions as to his whereabouts and the Medical Officer agreed that David was now fit enough to take up his posting in Aden. Sergeant York and the officer commanding HQ Company would have liked him to stay on but one cannot argue with the Top Brass. And so, early one misty morning, David was sent on his way to RAF Lynham (3) where he would be flown out to his new posting.

Chapter 7

The Aden Protectorate (now the Republic of South Yemen) is a strategic wedge of land situated at the southernmost end of the Red Sea where it narrows before entering the Arabian Sea. Saudi Arabia is to the north, the old Yemen abuts the territory and the State of Oman is to the east. Its original purpose of occupation was to protect the British route to India but later, after the oil refinery was built at Little Aden, it became important as an oil port and refueling center. At a time when Arab nationalism was on the rise in the 1950s, fuelled by Gamal Abdul Nasser, the military ruler of Egypt, it was an anathema to the Arabs. The British were not only fighting an unofficial war with their communist Yemeni neighbour, (1) but also with Arab nationalist locals. Unlike a formal war where each side wears a recognizable uniform, these fighters were indistinguishable from the locals and one did not know friend from foe. It was a dangerous place to be.

Aden Port is a huge deepwater bay surrounded by volcanic hills of little use and limited greenery; an ugly place; hot, dusty, smelly and unfriendly, green areas irrigated daily from underground wells. The British Residence, of palatial proportions, as if to remind the populace of the power of Empire, sits on a hill overlooking the town along the waterfront known as Steamer Point. It lies under the shadow of an extinct volcano, has a few good shops, an hotel, sprawling administrative buildings, an excellent hospital run by the RAF, narrow alleys of lesser shops leading to an assortment of primitive dwellings in various stages of disrepair. Poverty abounds and some locals are so destitute that they even live in large Kellogg cornflake boxes just to get a little shade. It is such a contrast to the opulence of the home of the British Ambassador and the comfortable homes of the many European employees.

Behind the modern settlement of Steamer Point, and inside the volcanic hills, is the crater of an extinct volcano holding the old town of Aden itself, a mass of tiny un-swept streets, wandering goats and chickens, white-walled houses and the inevitable mosque. It became a 'no go' area for British troops as the residents were known to riot and throw stones should a 'heathen' enter their town. To the north of the city, at Khormaksar, is a Royal Air Force base, and the airport run by the RAF, with civilian flights to the interior by Aden Airways, and some distance around the bay the oil refinery at Little Aden.

The refinery is a huge area with its own 'city' of neat prefabricated bungalows for refinery workers. Each bungalow has a small garden and there are excellent recreational facilities for refinery workers: cinema, Catholic and Anglican Churches, the Bureka Club and a beach protected from the inevitable sharks. There is a seaport for ocean-going tankers and an excellent road round the bay, some ten miles long, to the town shops and airport. The refinery itself is an immense complex of pipes and cracking towers like some futurist nightmare. It was the job of the British military to protect this installation.

Aden was considered to be a 'punishment posting' not only for the military but for civil servants as well. The intense heat of southern Arabia, around 70 - 80 F in the cooler part of the year to up to 110 - 120 F in the summer, with an 90% humidity, takes some living with, particularly if one does not have air conditioning.

It is into this intense heat that David arrived. The flight was full, mostly of civilians returning to the colony, and the hours spent in an ancient prop-driven aeroplane was tiring but uneventful. Having refueled in Malta, he slept most of the way. When the doors were opened he was hit with a gust of hot air as if an oven door had been opened. It was almost dawn and the 'cool' part of the day, but his shirt became wet with perspiration within minutes, and by the time his documentation had been checked and his kitbag put into an army lorry, he was visibly dripping wet.

That first night, or early morning, was spent in accommodation belonging to the military hospital set on a hill above Steamer Point. The hospital was run by the RAF, but the overall medical services were administered by the RAMC. None of the military installations had air conditioning, only roof fans, and as the day wore on it got hotter and hotter. After breakfast in the hospital canteen, David reported to the office of the Director of Medical Services. A very blond, freckled-faced clerk with rather thick glasses, told him he was to report to the York and Lancaster Regiment situated near the airport and a military Land-Rover was ready to transport him. The clerk was very friendly and told David that he could be found off duty at the NAAFI Club, which was where most servicemen met, situated beyond Steamer Point, just below the hill where the British Embassy stood.

As the Land-Rover approached the airport, David could see some fine accommodation blocks and his spirits began to rise as it was now almost midday and very hot. Even in his khaki shirt, shorts, socks, puttees and boots he felt exhausted already. He longed for some cool, a fan blowing away the oven-like heat and a cool drink. But no, it was not to be. Just to the left of this accommodation was a tented colony, the old transit camp, and now home to the York and Lancashire Regiment, which was David's destination and not the luxury of the

RAF.

As the Land-Rover tuned into the entrance to report to the guardhouse, David could see lines of tents rather dirty and fading after long use. Yes, the guardhouse was smart with white-painted stones, red fire buckets and a whitened rope in front and a sign with the regimental name and crest, but all this smartness was superficial, top show. His felt decidedly depressed . The RAF accommodation was new and modern; the army accommodation was old and medieval.

So this was where he was to spend the next twelve months? He looked over at the RAF purpose-built accommodation with envy and back at the army accommodation. Why, oh why, did the army have little respect for its personnel to let them live under such conditions? If the RAF could treat their servicemen well, so could the military.

He found later that this compound was deemed a 'transit camp' and was of a temporary nature where processing could take place for other postings. But it had been in existence for two years as a home for a full regiment when it was never meant to be thus. The War Office in Whitehall had 'forgotten' about it; perhaps they did not even know where Aden was. The regimental officers were fine in their accommodation outside the camp, and they had failed to push their case for better for the men, and deterioration had set in. Generally, officers lived in rented accommodation outside the camp or in hotels at Steamer Point. It soon became clear that the senior officers seemed to have nothing but contempt for the ordinary soldier.

After meeting the Regimental Sergeant Major, who stood David to attention in the heat and provided a diatribe in correct military dress, he was escorted by a regimental lance corporal to a tent shared by three other RAMC personnel. There was the usual iron bed and wooden locker and one of his colleagues, who had just returned from eating lunch, took him to the store to collect his bedding and two white plates of substantial make. There was an electric fan in the middle of the tent and the tent flaps were rolled up on three sides to assist in cooling further. It was still hot and two of his colleagues were lying naked, except for a cloth between their legs, trying to doze in the heat. David introduced himself to the others.

They had been told that another RAMC person was to arrive. Simon, one of the group, explained that 'tiffin' was over but that it was not worth eating, like most of the food on camp.

"We'll take you to the NAAFI on the RAF compound later for some tea and a bun if you're not too hungry now," another explained, whose name was Wilf.

David agreed as he was not very hungry. He had eaten a good

breakfast and in any case the heat was too oppressive to be hungry.

"Best have a ziz while it's so hot," suggested Andrew who had taken David to the store.

"I'd like a pee first," requested David. "Where do I go?"

"I'll show you," offered Andrew who was in shorts and shirt, unlike the other two.

"Don't forget your newspaper," offered Simon with a smirk.

"No toilet paper or is it to read?" offered David, bewildered by the comment.

"Nope," smiled Simon. "There's paper....usually. It depends if the cockroaches haven't eaten it or not. It's to whack the bloody flies. They're terrible."

As they left Wilf yelled, "And let him hold his own dick, Andrew."

Andrew blushed under his tan and said nothing.

The 'bog' was everything Simon had predicted and more. Flies buzzed in huge clouds and the smell was terrible. The latrines, as the army called them, were just holes in the ground with a sort of bucket over and a minimum of canvas around them as a sop to modesty. Most of the canvas was torn so one could converse directly with one's neighbor. David soon appreciated the use of the newspaper.

Andrew waited for David, who was feeling rather queezy after his unpleasant experience of going to the toilet. He explained, "They are supposed to be kept clean by local Sudanese civilians but they are lazy and nobody seems to supervise them. The officers don't care. The M.O. has tried to get something done but he's a National Serviceman too – a lieutenant – and his senior in the regiment takes no notice. He's too nice. You'll meet him. Lieutenant John Morrison. He's quite brilliant and all the other MO's around seek his advice. He's studying for his Royal College of Surgeon's examination."

After getting over the initial shock of being virtually naked on his bed, David realized that there was method in the madness. Underpants just got wet with sweat whilst the naked body cooled as the sweat evaporated. One just had to get used to it. He could not sleep although, he felt tired, but this gave him the opportunity to do a little thinking. Things were rushing around in his mind as events had moved so fast in the last few days. Here he was in a tent in Aden in baking heat whilst forty-eight hours ago he was in cold, rainy England. Now he was in a godforsaken place of sand, heat and a myriad of flies ensconced with three new colleagues who were lying on their beds virtually naked, succumbed to sleep, and seemingly impervious to the intense heat of mid-afternoon. As the fan whirred overhead and the occasion fly itched his skin, he tried to assess his fellows.

He liked Andrew who was gentle and thoughtful. He had been such a help. Without his willing smile and considerate behavior, finding his way around the camp would have been hell. Apparently he came from Hastings in Sussex. He told David that his father was a lawyer, and that he intended to become a lawyer also and go into the family business. Like David, he was doing his Service before going to university. Andrew was not good-looking, but he had a face that one could not help but like. Surrounded by black curly hair, perhaps a little longer than army regulation permitted, his features were classic. He also, David noticed, had the most hairy legs he had ever seen. No hair on his chest but thick curly hair on shapely legs that made them look black. He had a good tan and obviously kept himself fit. He told David that he spent a lot of free time at the beach and had offered to take him to Elephant Bay, a private swimming area some miles out of town.

David was not sure about Wilf. He did not like to rely on first impressions as some people were better for knowing. He appeared to be a 'know all' with a snide sense of humor. Wilf was a regular soldier and the senior of the group. He had informed David of that soon after he arrived in the tent. Short, stocky with mousy short-cropped hair and short, fat legs his upper body seemed to be too large in comparison with the rest of him. He was older than the others, perhaps twenty-six or twenty-seven. His strong Liverpool accent gave away his antecedents.

Simon was quite different. His good looks could not be questioned and his physique was that of an athlete. David suspected that in spite of his air of lethargy, he was physically very active and took part in many sports. He assumed he was a good rugby player. His accent was 'upper crust' and laid back, possibly he was the product of a good public school and a parental residence somewhere in Surrey. He had brown hair cut short, but not quite a 'crew cut'. Nakedness did not seem to worry him as he had a small towel just hiding his private parts, and David could see the thin line of hair from his chest right down to his pubes. English public schools not only provided an air of confidence in their pupils, but frequently a disregard for modesty perhaps as a consequence of living so close together in a dormitory.

At around six-thirty David was wakened by Andrew who told him they were taking him to the NAAFI and skipping the meal on camp. He presented him with a mug of steaming tea. He must have dozed off as it was getting dusk.

"It's hot but it'll cool you down," proffered Andrew handing him the mug. "I took the liberty of taking your own mug to the canteen. Tea's not bad but it has bromide in it. That gives it the froth. Supposed to lessen your sex drive. Don't know it does much for me."

95

David laughed. "Come on, Andrew, that's just an old wives' tale."

"True. The cooks told me."

"Oh well, I suppose it reduces the number of hand jobs." David had quickly learnt in training the common parlance for sexual relief, although in innocence he thought at first he was the only one to operate such a practice. He soon learnt differently.

"Simon has gone for a shower. Drink your tea and I'll take you. I'm afraid it's almost as bad as the bog. Got some soap?"

David affirmed that he had.

"Wear flip-flops. Got a pair?"

"No....."

"I'll lend you my spare pair. But get yourself some as it's a wet business and you can't wear boots or they'll be ruined. Just put a towel round your waist and nothing underneath. There's nowhere to hang things and underpants tend to fall off the door into the wet."

"Sounds delightful," David observed.

"Not like home," Andrew smiled. "You'll get used to it. The facilities here are terrible but the lads are great. They all come from northern England and once you get used to their funny accent you'll find them very friendly. I'd be glad to have any one of them beside me in battle."

Showering was not quite as bad as David expected and he supposed that once you got into a routine all would be home from home. The 'bathroom' was a corrugated affair open to the sky, but over the years the iron had rusted and holes had appeared between each cubicle so, like the toilets, there was little privacy. The duckboards were useless as they were wet and rotting and very slippery. In spite of the heat, everywhere was wet and slimy; it all needed a good clean. Hygiene was minimal. When they returned Simon was waiting in shorts and jazzy shirts with leather sandals on his feet

"Where's Will? David asked looking round. "Isn't he coming as well?"

"He's on duty in the medical center this evening. We take it in turns with the regimental staff as assistants. It's just Andrew and I"

"Tomorrow," observed Andrew, "when you meet the rest of the medical team, you'll see how we work. It's quite good really.

When David and Andrew were ready they went through the camp and reported out at the guardhouse. They had to sign out and in as a matter of security. Whilst generally the locality of the camp was safe, some areas were not and knowledge of whereabouts was essential. It was clear that they were well known and respected as there were shouts and waves from various tents. David was introduced to two soldiers they met on their way out, both regimentals and from the north of England. Their names were a haze when he tried to remember later.......Sidebottom was the surname of one rather stocky soldier who was obviously a bodybuilder. How could you forget a name like that? As for the other, well he was tall and blond with freckles but ......yes, Proberts?

The RAF camp was minutes away across the road and the NAAFI was a large building near the center of the camp. It was easy to find as music from the place could be heard right across the camp. Inside was bright and cheerful with chintz curtains to the windows, cream painted walls, a stage at the opposite end to where they had entered with red plush curtains, and against the left hand wall a long counter displaying all kinds of goodies beloved by young healthy males, including pretty girls behind the counter. There was catering to suit almost every whim. Tables were dotted around and the music came from a juke box in the right hand corner. The place was not too crowded, although Andrew informed him that later on, after the camp cookhouse closed, the place became very crowded. They lined up by the cafeteria, took trays and pondered their choices.

"It's on us tonight," Simon told David. "A sort of welcome to the team."

David was embarrassed and started to protest but Andrew intervened: "It's a tradition in our tent Dave. We do it to all newcomers. At least they did it when Simon and I came. Will came with the regiment so I don't know what happened to him."

"Take you pick, Dave," said Simon. "I'm having bangers,(2) beans and chips and jam sponge and custard."

"Sounds good," said David. "I'll have the same if that's ok?"

"And me," affirmed Andrew. "Beer to follow?"

"No thanks, I don't drink beer," David told them. "A mug of tea will suit me."

"Same here," affirmed Andrew.

"And me," agreed Simon. "Beer only blows you out and gives you a fat belly. Now a nice glass of wine....."

"Tell me more," observed David. "Can you get wine out here?"

"You can but only in certain places, but we are not allowed to visit them," Andrew responded. "Only for officers."

"And gentleman," added Simon with a sly smile. "The Shenaz Hotel at Steamer Point sells wine as does the Bureka Club at Little Aden, but other ranks are forbidden there."

"On pain of death," laughed Andrew. "You see we're too common to be let lose in a decent place."

"To be fair," interrupted Simon, "the behavior of some soldiers in this place does give some sense to such a ban."

"I suppose so," observed Andrew, "but it's unfair."

By this time they had moved to a table and got settled, one of the girls behind the counter brought them three huge plates of bangers, beans and chips. The servings were enormous and the mound of bread and butter and mugs of hot, sweet tea turned it into a feast. Little was said while they ate. The jam sponge and custard was just as huge and very good. David felt as if this was the best meal he had ever tasted.

It was comforting to sit back and relax after the meal and listen to Cliff Richard singing his heart out and Chubby Checker (3) rocking and rolling. Simon and Andrew asked David about himself and where he had been working. He told them of his family, school, about his university intentions, basic training and then his spell at Millbank Hospital. They were both amazed that there was a would-be priest in their midst and said they would take him to the RAF church on Sunday.

"So what's your nursing qualification, Dave?" Simon asked. "You seem to have been doing a lot of studying since basic training. Andrew and I were posted to this regiment as soon as we had done our three month's basic training."

David thought a while. "I completed my C344 just before I got posted....accelerated advancement meant I did it in half the time. Somebody told me it was equivalent to State Registration."

Andrew looked at Simon. "Bright Simon, bright. We've got a brain here."

"Will won't like that," observed Simon. "He thinks he's the boss because he's a regular but he's got only basic qualifications like us."

"I won't tell him if you won't," commented David. "No use causing a war."

"Crafty with it as well," smiled Simon. "You're right. No use altering the status quo. It would put Sergeant Wright's nose out of joint as well if he knew. Mum's the word."

David looked puzzled. "Who's Sergeant Wright?"

"A regimental sergeant who's the regimental MO's buddy. They've served together for many years apparently. He fancies himself. Knows nothing."

"Someone to watch closely – creepy?" David asked.   They both nodded in agreement.

"Dave likes swimming so I offered to take him to Elephant Bay on Sunday," offered Andrew tactfully changing the subject.

"Great," commented Simon. "I like the beach too but I won't be able to get as I'm on duty. We'll all go another weekend. Be careful though

Dave as the sun is very hot and burns quickly. Sunburn is an offence in the military and you can be punished for it."

"He's got quite a good tan already," observed Andrew. "Where did you get it?"

"London, the Serpentine…Hyde Park. We had quite a good summer this year and I did get a little time to relax."

"Don't know how you did it with all that study," observed Simon.

"Good use of time and in any case the exams were not too difficult," commented David. "My father took me on a months holiday to Spain before I started National Service so I was pretty brown to start with. In fact, at my medical I became a center of attraction with the doctors." He smiled at the thought of the medical.

"Why?" asked Andrew.

"You know what happens Andrew," David said looking directly at him. There was a smirk on both their faces.

"Naked and peeing in a jam jar….," commented Simon.

"Well I had the smallest 'tide mark' you could imagine and the doctors were 'intrigued' I think the word is. They all gathered round to look. I didn't know whether to run or feint," David laughed.

"How embarrassing," remarked Simon.

"Not only that," went on David, "but they commented on the size of my dick as well."

"Never! I certainly would have feinted," remarked Andrew seriously.

"Suppose they were either amused or envious," laughed Simon. "What did you do, wave it around and give them a thrill." They all laughed.

The evening just flew and soon it was time for them to leave as lights out was at ten- thirty. David had gleaned a little about Simon during the evening. He had been to Charterhouse School, (4) one of the top English Public Schools, and had ended up as house captain as well as rugby captain. His father was a banker in the City of London and they had a country estate of some five hundred acres in Surrey. Simon was a socialist and did not want a commission in some fine regiment. In any case, he wanted to serve for two years only as he had been accepted at the London School of Economics to do an economics degree. He was an unhappy pacifist and thus had volunteered for the medical corps. Andrew too had pacifist leanings and asked for the RAMC when he joined up. David was the only one of the three who did not attend a public school, but he had no feeling of inferiority or was made to feel that way. It was clear they were bright lads who were serving their country and justifying their ideals at the same time.

The following morning was Friday and David reported to the camp medical center with Simon and Andrew. Will was allowed to sleep in as he was duty medic and had to remain in the center the previous night in case of emergency. It was a tented complex with a small room at the rear where medical personnel slept when on night duty and sometimes where a patient was put when under observation. Sergeant Wright was there to meet him and took him round the center to show where everything was kept. He was about forty, stocky with a large stomach and very military in the way he spoke and carried himself. David was surprised how pleasant he was and only later was told that it was all show because he was new and they were short of staff.

There was a queue of about thirty soldiers all reporting sick with their full packs as per regulations. Andrew told David that most days were busy as there was lots of sickness on the camp. The two MO's arrived together in Captain Price's vehicle, but Lieutenant Morrison took the sick parade while the captain went to a meeting of regimental officers. David came to attention and saluted when the sergeant took him into their office to meet both officers. They were very informal and shook hands welcoming him to the team.

"You're supposed to be on light duties for the next two weeks corporal Earl, but we are short-staffed and I'm afraid you'll just have to muck in," commented Cpt. Price. "You don't look pale and insipid like the regular newcomers so perhaps you'll adjust easily."

"I'll try sir," offered David.

"Right corporal, Lieutenant Morrison will be taking the sick parade. Sergeant Wright will see to the regimental organization and you RAMC chaps see to the treatments. If you have any questions Lieutenant Morrison will be glad to put you right."

The lieutenant, a slim, fair-haired young man of medium height and friendly smile, just nodded his assent. David saluted, about turned smartly and marched out into the treatment room where the others were waiting.

"Regimentals over?" asked Simon playfully.

David nodded.

"Good. Here's your white coat. Let battle commence," remarked Andrew as the first soldier was marched in front of the Lieutenant by Sergeant Wright.

The morning went along so quickly that it was eleven o'clock before they had time to realize. By then there were only two soldiers still waiting. The majority of cases were suffering from diarrhoea, heat stroke, and a few from prickly heat. One soldier had a badly infected toe that he had stubbed against his bed and failed to keep clean and another, a rather nasty cut on his arm from a bayonet he had been cleaning. The toe took some time to clean and the cut needed careful preparation before Lt. Morrison put in eight stitches. There was a bit of a panic when the MO asked for a tray to be set up so he could do the stitching. Simon explained that Will usually did things like that and that he and Andrew really were not too sure.

"No problem," explained David. "Watch while I do it and you'll know the next time. It's just a matter of thinking what he's going to do and putting out what he needs."

David set up the tray and the MO came through into the treatment room to undertake the task.

The soldier in question never flinched when the injections went in around the wound to deaden the pain of the stitching; he watched every stitch that went in without a murmur. Simon and Andrew watched also, fascinated, and David was sure they would know what to do next time they were confronted with such a request. Lt. Morrison was quick and skillful and David was very impressed. He could see that he was an excellent surgeon. Amazingly he even thanked David for setting up the tray. Quite a turn-up for the record as usually doctors are so arrogant that they almost throw things at you. Here was a gentleman in every sense of the word.

"Coffee?" smiled the MO at Andrew after he had finished and washed his hands.

"Gosh, sir, I'd forgotten," he apologized looking at his watch. "That was so interesting.

"We'll have a break for thirty minutes, sergeant," he said to Sgt. Wright, "then we'll see the last two patients, unless of course they are at death's door?"

"They'll live, sir," responded Sgt. Wright with a grin.

"Strong as usual and no sugar, corporal," he said to Andrew and disappeared into his room.

"I'm off to the mess for my coffee," Sgt Wright told them." With that he turned on his heels and was not seen for the rest of the day.

"Coffee my foot," remarked Simon. "Beer for certain. Look at his gut!"

It seemed that most days there was very little time to get over to the canteen where tea, coffee and bread and jam was readily available so they brewed up with an electric kettle in the back room. A NAAFI break was an entitlement but as they were mostly under pressure from large sick parades there was rarely time to take it. The coffee tasted good and Andrew even found a few biscuits, which he said had been purchased from the NAAFI shop. Apparently, the three of them pooled their money each week and bought coffee and biscuits and sometimes Lt. Morrison would bring in a jar of Nescafe.

"I'm surprised Lt Morrison doesn't go to the officers' mess for his coffee," observed David.

"Sometimes he does," Andrew replied," but he prefers to drink with us. There's not much time if there is only one MO here. I'm not sure he really likes the atmosphere of the mess here. He calls his brother officers 'toffs'."(5)

"Brilliant but shy," observed Simon.

"Right lads," the MO put his head round the door, "bring in the next one."

Simon went out and accompanied the soldier into the MO's room. He had tinea, a series of round one-inch sores on his back and chest. They were caused by a fungus in the air and too infrequent showers. The MO prescribes Mycota cream rubbed on the sores three times a day and more showers.

"I know your problem of keeping clean, private," he told the soldier, "and that you sweat a lot, but try or the problem will get worse. Do you swim?"

"No, sir," replied the soldier.

"Well even if you don't swim go to the beach and splash around in the sea. The salt water will help to keep you skin fungus free. But not too much sun, mind."

The second soldier complained of itching in his groin. After removing his trousers and dark green army-issue under drawers, the MO had a looked for the cause. The area was rather red from scratching, but it was only close scrutiny and a magnifying glass that revealed the problem – crabs. These are tiny crab-like mites that inhabit the pubic area and are generally passed on from person to person. The MO had the three medics around to look as the case as it was not particularly common. Shaving the pubic hair and a few applications of benzyle benzoate lotion was a fast cure. Simon undertook the job and the MO warned him to wear surgical gloves and to make sure all hair was burnt afterwards. All three boys were amazed afterwards when Lt. Morrison told them that they were generally caught through sexual contact and that perhaps the soldier had been with an unclean woman. He hoped the soldier had caught nothing else. Such is innocence.

There were treatments to undertake at mid-day and an evening treatment at five-thirty, but they were generally not too busy. They all did the mid-day one but only the duty medic stayed in the afternoon and did the evening session and throughout the evening and night. The night staff had the following day off. However, on Sundays one person was on duty all day so that the others had one free day a week. It meant that every month one worked on Sunday as Sgt Wright took his turn too. The MO's took it in turn to be on call so that the center was covered twenty-four hours a day, seven days a week.

On Sunday Andrew took David to the RAF Church. It was a large white-painted building with a tower on the roof similar to some churches found in the deep south of the United States of America. The RAF did things well. The Anglican Communion service was simple and effective. The Padre had a clear, sincere voice and his homily on the power of faith stimulating. David felt at home here as if he had been present in the village church at home. He and Andrew received communion and after the service, which was well attended, the Padre was waiting at the door to have a word with each person as they left.

The Padre obviously knew Andrew and shook his hand vigorously teasing him about his unruly hair. "In a rush as usual Andrew? Lack of a comb in your hair gives the game away."

"You won't believe it Padre," Andrew responded, "but I took great care with my hair this morning as I knew you'd comment."

"The Lord will be pleased you wanted to look your best for him," smiled the Padre.

"And for you, sir," continued Andrew.

"Andrew, I'm flattered. Don't take your unruly hair to heart. My wife is always on about mine, but I've not much to be unruly," he laughed.

Andrew then introduced David.

"Pleased to meet you, David," the Padre responded. "You're obviously new here. Welcome. I hope we'll see a lot more of you in church."

"Thank you sir," David replied.

"He's going to read theology at King's, padre," Andrew blurted out.

"That so, young man?" observed the padre with interest. He thought for a while. "You wouldn't like to come and serve for me at communion next week? I just can't get a server."

"I'd be glad to help, sir," offered David, "if I'm not on duty."

"Perhaps we'll see you at evensong and I can show you the routine then?"

"Fine sir. We'll be there," David replied looking at Andrew. "I'm sure Andrew will keep me company."

They shook hands again and the Padre was chatting with the next of his congregation as they left the church.

"Good chap," observed Andrew as they walked back to camp. "He really works hard and is our padre as well as for the RAF. Many of our chaps have been helped by him. His wife is lovely too. You'll meet her at evensong."

They walked back in silence to the camp, each with his particular thoughts resulting from the religious experience achieved in love and simplicity on an RAF camp in the depth of Arabia. David thought how fortunate he was to have Andrew as a friend. Someone with the same religious ideals, a kind and thoughtful person who obviously cared about people and was prepared to stand up for his beliefs. The legal profession would be better off with such a person in its midst. Not all lawyers would be the sharks that Charles Dickens had painted in his novels and perhaps the words from 'Die Fleidermaus' – "Go to law and go to ruin, litigation's your undoing:" -would not be so frequently true' (6)

Elephant Bay was a half hour drive in a taxi from the camp. It was a series of thatched huts on a white, sandy beach. The owners had created a shady garden where one could have coffee or eat, and there was an air-conditioned restaurant, changing rooms and showers. A huge sea wall, built of immense rocks, ran out to sea and was open at one end to enable the tides to flow in and out. The huge swimming area was protected from sharks by a metal 'net'. The sea wall was some ten feet wide, concreted so one could walk along it and often used by fishermen to catch huge moray eels. It was extremely pleasant and well-worth the cost of a taxi.

The entrance fee was reasonable, and when David and Andrew got inside they felt that they had temporarily left the military behind. There were quite a few young men there as well as families with some quite small children. Everything was seemingly informal and, except for the indoor restaurant, people tended to sit around the place in their bathing costumes having coffee and snacks. There were lots of palm trees around giving plenty of shade and on the beach were palm-thatched umbrellas. It was almost like a little piece of Hawaii.

After changing and leaving their clothes in a locker, David and Andrew went for a coffee and baguette (7) before lazing on the beach. They found a spare umbrella for shade and hired two sun-loungers. There was a pleasant breeze, the sound of waves splashing on the sand and children's voices. They rushed into the warm sea to cool off. The water was crystal clear and quite salty so swimming was easy. The waves were gentle, and beyond them the water was calm, so David could float on his back. He was quite a good swimmer but Andrew was better. He swam under water and emerged for a breath and was then off again. After a while, they staggered out of the water breathless, tired but well satisfied. "Makes me feel as if I'm on holiday once more,"

David commented.

"Me too," responded Andrew lazily. "It's nice to get away from camp."

"I assume you come here quite a lot?" David asked.

"Yes. Hence the tan."

"You do have a good tan," offered David. "I want to improve mine. Black. Like you."

"Strange, isn't it," Andrew observed. "The white want to become black and the black want to become white. There's no satisfying the human condition."

"Mm," responded David and he was soon asleep.

He was awakened by the sound of voices. He looked over at Andrew to find a group of young men talking very loudly. Andrew glanced across. "Oh, you're awake. Did we startle you?"

David slowly realized who these young men were. He had met one at the RAF hospital, the blond clerk with the thick glasses. "Hi," David responded and smiled. "I wondered who was making the noise. It's the RAF."

"One RAMC and three RAF," the blond corporal replied. "Good to see you. Have you settled in all right?"

"Yes, thanks."

"We come here most weekends," added the blond corporal. "Join us any time you like."

"Thanks," Andrew and David responded in unison.

"We'll leave you in peace," the blond corporal said. "See you again." With that all four turned on their heels and returned to their towels further along the beach.

"Do you know them, Andrew?" David asked.

"They work at Steamer Point at the hospital and I think the blond guy with the glasses works in the Director General's office. I've seen them around. Not really my types."

"Oh!" David replied mystified.

"A bit too effeminate for me. They all go around together and have a bit of a reputation."

"Reputation?" responded David still at a loss for an explanation.

"Andrew looked at David in a sympathetic way. "Dave, I can't believe it. You really are innocent. You don't know about gays?"

"Gays?" David asked.

"The name given to homosexuals. Couldn't you see the way they looked at you. Those 'come-to-bed eyes'?"

"I saw them staring but......"

"They fancied you. I can see why as you are very good looking and have an excellent physique," offered Andrew.

David was embarrassed. He had never been confronted so openly with talk about homosexuality before. Of course, he knew about it. He knew that he had feelings for some males but he had never had it presented to him so openly before. There was silence between the two for a while. It was Andrew who spoke first. "Have I embarrassed you, Dave?" he asked.

"No.....no. It's just that I have never heard it discussed so openly before."

"Sorry," Andrew replied. "You see at home....in my family....we are encouraged to be open about everything. I can discuss anything with my parents."

"I wish I could," David offered. "My mother is ok but I couldn't discuss sex with her. My father.....well......it's difficult to open up about anything. He has very strong opinions and is never wrong. I found the best policy was to shut up."

"Poor you. Don't mind about me, I'm prepared to discuss anything without making a moral judgment. It's the lawyer in me."

"So do you approve of homosexuality?" David asked.

"In principle, yes. Sexuality is not black and white. There are all shades, if you like. People cannot change what they are. What I can't stand are the very effeminate boys who show off."

"Like the ones just now."

"Yes. They give everyone a bad name."

"I suppose so," David added without conviction.

"I have no objection if two males, or females for that matter, love each other. What they do in private is their business. I do object to it being blatantly advertised. Nobody expects a heterosexual couple to advertise what they do in bed so why should the homosexual?" Andrew remarked.

David made no further comment. He was confused. There were certain males who caused feelings to stir in him. Were they homosexual feelings? He did not wish to face those feelings.

The time to leave soon arrived as the sun began to sink over the horizon and people drifted back home. It was nice to sit in the cool of the evening and just enjoy the comparative silence, but all good things come to an end. The talk with Andrew had been interesting and David was determined to raise the subject again when the time was ripe. He wondered about Andrew. Had the gay boys recognized something in Andrew, perhaps also in himself? Andrew was not handsome but certainly attractive. There was something in his personality that one could not help but like. The visit to Elephant Bay had been enjoyable but also disturbing.

Chapter 8

Whilst new regimental postings were given 'light duties' there was no respite from the heat and humidity for David: he was thrown into full duty from day one and had to take part in the complete shift system. To be fair, he was working under shade with an electric fan helping to dissipate some of the heat, whilst the foot soldiers were out training in the blazing sun. Some of the officers worked the newcomers to the maximum and there were many cases of heat exhaustion, some so bad that they had to be hospitalized. In David's view, an officer who put his men at risk in such a way, should have been court martialled, but nothing was done. The attitude of the officers in the York and Lancaster Regiment had not changed since the nineteenth century. Men were something one used to achieve an objective, no matter how much they suffered.

One medical officer, a famous athlete, on a project from the War Office to do with response to heat, drove his men to ridiculous lengths. One might say even to cruel lengths, so that they collapsed in large numbers of heat exhaustion. Each day some of his men had to be sent to the RAF hospital at Steamer Point, as they often fell into a coma and needed specialist attention. Nothing was done about this use of National Servicemen like guinea pigs in the name of research. Although, to be accurate, they were volunteers and did get extra pay, but David suspected they were initially unaware of what could happen to them. But is not that like prostitution? Putting oneself at risk in order to get extra money. The general public did not know, just as they did not know about service men being used for radiation experiments immediately after the Second World War, (1) until it was too late. Why is it that a few men in government with warped moral arguments can get away with using their fellow beings in such a way? No man, however poor or uneducated, should be treated less than his peers. All men are equal in the sight of God and to use one's fellows, with or without their consent, in an experiment that harms their health without fully understanding the consequences, is a sin against God.

The days seemed to pass so quickly that two months went by without even noticing. David wrote to his parents regularly and they to him. He did not really have time to be homesick, but there were times when there was a hollow feeling in his chest when he thought of home. Andrew and Simon turned into true friends and they were inseparable. Will, being a little older and a regular soldier, was not quite as close and in any case he had his long-standing friends in the regiment. They went often to Elephant Bay to swim at weekends and to the NAAFI Club at Steamer Point.

After only three weeks, David was ordered to go on a convoy into the interior to relieve a medic who needed a break and dental treatment. He was to be there for a week. A convoy of one Land-Rover for the officer, and two three ton trucks for the men followed the beach north and then cut west into the interior following a wadi. All the twenty soldiers in the trucks were heavily armed, except David, who was RAMC, and a machine gun was mounted in the rear of the Land-Rover. The possibility of an ambush was real and the regiment was taking no chances. The ride along the beach was pleasant as the sand was smooth and the drivers could get up speed, but the wadi (2) was something else.

The track was rough and the three-toners threw their occupants about so that soon they were all feeling bruised. Each truck raised a great cloud of dust, and although David was not in the last vehicle, he was soon coughing and spluttering. Poor occupants of the second truck! There was no shade and the content of their water bottles, although sparingly consumed, was soon at an end. This part of the desert was rocky with clumps of a coarse-brown grass, low thorn bushes and sand and more sand. There were herds of camels here and there eating something or other and an occasional flock of desert partridge would rise up from the scrub. In one way the desert was beautiful as the sand changed from gray and blue, to pink and red as the light changed: but David was glad of his companions and hoped the trucks would not break down as, for him, the desert was an unfriendly place.

On one occasion, a great deal of interest was aroused when a snake slithered across their path. Someone said it was called a 'sidewinder' as it moved in a sideways motion and was very poisonous. David was glad he was in the truck and not on the ground as he detested snakes. He had always had a fear of them. When he and his brother were taken to see the film "Sabu" about an Indian boy, he remembered hiding his head behind the person in the seat in front so he could not see what a particularly large snake was up to. His mother had told him when he could look again after Sabu had narrowly escaped death from the leviathan.

By late afternoon, they arrived dusty, thirsty and tired. The outpost was a tented encampment surrounded by a barbed-wire fence with a second encampment a hundred yards away. David learnt that this was for the Life Guards who, as well as being soldiers seen on ceremonial parades on horseback in their white and red, were also an armored brigade. They were there with their armored cars to give support and protection to the foot soldiers of the Yorks and Lancs.

David was allocated to share will Cpl. Brown, whom he was to replace for a week. His tent was rather crowded but it was only for one night. Brown was a thin, wiry fellow, a regular soldier of about thirty. He welcomed David with a mug of tea and showed him where to find the shower. This consisted of a tank raised on a platform, with corrugated iron sheets to provide five cubicles, and taps to regulate the water flow. Apparently, the water came from a bore hole. It was ice cold and plentiful and as Cpl. Brown had got David there quickly after his arrival, so he was head of the queue. The late-comers had to wait in line. Cpl. Brown explained that he washed and shaved in the medical tent as a small water tank had been installed at the rear so he had water for medical use. It was filled every day - a perk for being the medic on the camp.

The medical tent was a dark green affair about twelve feet square with a table at one end for equipment, a lockable cupboard for drugs, three chairs and a stretcher on a stand for treatments. There was matting on the floor and the place was spotlessly clean. David remarked how clean and tidy it was.

Cpl. Brown explained: "I get quite busy sometimes and there's only me. It's much easier to work in order than chaos. And I'm a tidy person anyway, I suppose."

"Me too," replied David.

"Good. We'll get on fine then. Perhaps you'd like to help me with the sick parade this evening?"

"Ok by me. It'll help me get into the routine."

The sick parade went without a hitch. Mostly it was dealing with sore feet, cuts from the scrub that surrounded the camp and the inevitable tinea.(3) David found that the men were far more healthy than the ones down in Aden. He raised this with Cpl. Brown.

"Healthier and happier," he remarked.

David was puzzled. "Why?" he asked.

Well....that camp is badly run for a start. The officers don't care as they mostly live off camp. Up here we all live and work together. The facilities are simple but effective and they are clean. As you perhaps noticed when we ate, the senior NCO's eat with us as there are only seven of them and the five officers eat in a tent near ours and have virtually the same food. We are such a small community and we all rely on each other so very much."

"Practical democracy?" suggested David, "and I did notice how good the food is."

"I suppose so," Cpl. Brown responded. "Our officers and NCOs are excellent here and we value them as they value us. They care about us.

We all like it up here. None of us want to go down to Aden. I'll be glad to get back after my teeth have been seen to. And the climate is better - cooler because we are not by the sea and at a higher level. Some nights it's quite cold." A mug of cocoa was then brewed on the medical center primus and slumber came quite easily.

David was up at six, summoned by a bugle call from the Life Guard's lines, washed and shaved and into breakfast by seven. He would have a shower after sick parade at eight and after Cpl. Brown had left. Breakfast was excellent: porridge, bacon and beans, toast and marmalade and as many cups of hot sweet tea as could be drunk. The other solders were friendly and eager to meet the new medic. The mess tent was a little crowded as there were twenty relief soldiers extra, but that would balance out when twenty others went down to Aden for a spot of leave .

Cpl. Brown handed over the keys to the drug cabinet and David signed for them and he was suddenly on his own ready for his first-ever personal sick parade. He felt nervous. He would have to make decisions that the MO usually made. It was a bit like appearing on stage to do a performance. He remembered his first school play and the way he felt waiting in the wings. Basically he felt the same now.

Looking back, as he showered in peace around ten-thirty, it was all over and completed. His first sick parade on his own had gone like clockwork. The lads knew the routine. They sat on benches until called. They called him 'doc' and explained their symptoms. David made an examination when necessary, gave them treatment and recorded details in his daybook. Only one soldier had been a problem. He had a very bad blister on his left foot so much so that it had begun to bleed. Give him his due, the soldier wanted to do his duty. David gave him a chit for his officer requesting 'excused boots'. One of the officers came to see David to ask about the soldier. David explained the condition and said that the soldier really should not be using the foot for a day or two until the blister healed. He also explained that the soldier wanted to continue with his work. If he could do his job wearing flip-flops for a couple of days then all would be well. The officer was quite happy with the situation and promised to find the soldier light duties until the foot had healed. The officer seemed to want something else. "Can I help you at all, sir?" David asked.

"Well….." the officer hesitated. "I get a lot of headaches and Cpl. Brown gives me Paracetamol.

"How frequently, sir?" asked David.

"Two or three times a week," he replied.

David asked: "Do you wear glasses, sir?"

"No,"

"Do you read at night, sir?"

"Yes, I always read for about half an hour before I go to sleep."

"Me too," replied David. "But that may be your problem. You are perhaps affected by the bright sun, then you strain your eyes in bad light at night."

"I suggest, sir, that when you next go down to Aden you have your eyes tested."

He smiled. "Do you know, corporal, I did think of that but never did anything about it. I do find the sun rather bright. I don't wear sun glasses because my fellow officers don't, but I will. And I'll get my eyes tested. Thank you."

David gave him some codeine and he went off happily.

Altogether, a most successful morning.

In a way life became quite boring as apart from the sick parades, which were not busy as everyone seemed to be very healthy, David had little to do. He was glad when he was told that on the fourth day they were going out on a patrol which would mean them sleeping out for one night. Everyone was up before dawn and as the sun came up above the horizon they set out in convoy. Two armored cars led the way followed by eight Land-Rovers filled with soldiers armed to the teeth, and a truck with supplies followed behind. In the rear were two more armored cars. Three of the Land-Rovers carried machine guns. David took along his portable medical kit.

The going was tough as the wadis were uneven and wound around large rocky outcrops. By midday it was intensely hot and conserving water was paramount as there was nowhere to refill a water bottle. Thank goodness for the shade from army-issue sunhats, as the vehicles were open to the elements. The landscape was similar to the one coming up from the coast except the scenery was grander, and David was aware of large purple-blue mountains in the distance. Perhaps they were six or eight miles away, or more even as the atmosphere was perfectly clear except for the shimmering of the ground as the thin, hot air rose up from the sand. Where the wadi was wider and flatter there was the mirage of water and occasionally camels came into view close to the convoy. Mostly the wadi was narrow with occasional clumps of thorn with acacia in the midst. It was clear that in places water was just under the surface as indicated by the trees and thorn bushes. Surprisingly there were quite a few birds about in these thickets.

Where the terrain was narrow the place had to be picketed in case of ambush. This consisted of the two leading armored cars going ahead whilst one of the rear armored cars took the lead. The convoy moved slowly only on the signal of the picket vehicles who were in radio contact. Safety was paramount, and David appreciated the skill of the Life Guard's as they nosed out the safest route. Lunch was emergency rations of biscuits, dried fruit and hot, sweet tea brought in large flasks by two of the Catering Corps and carried in the supply vehicle. They were very efficient and fed thirty people quite quickly. Then off the convoy went down the rough track to where? David did not know and had failed to ask.

Rounding a bend in a wadi, they came across a dead camel and surrounding it were about twenty huge vultures. They stood nearly as tall as a man and were quite startling. The men in the two armored cars had not bothered to drive them away as they, like the rest of the troops, were fascinated with the scene. Vultures are ugly creatures with bald heads and necks of red, wrinkled skin and terribly sharp beaks. This is so that they can thrust their heads into an animal and tear out its entrails without feathers getting dirty and in the way. They squabbled incessantly, flapping their wings and hissing at each other as one bird got in the way of another. It is survival of the fittest.

The convoy watched for a while as they tore the animal apart. After enough of the horrible scene, they went on their way. One or two birds rose into the air and then landed by the dead animal again, but most just got on with the task of tearing the creature to pieces. As someone remarked amusingly, "We could do with those in Aden to get rid of some of the shit on the transit camp!"

At about five-thirty, the vehicles came to a halt and a camp was set up quite quickly as obviously they had done this before. Camp was hardly the word for it as there were no tents, just a ring of vehicles and a camp-fire at its center. David did a quick sick parade – a few cuts from being jolted around in the vehicles. Each soldier put his waterproof cape on the ground to sit on and later to sleep on. They were to sleep under the stars. The cooks prepared an 'all-in stew', which meant opening tins of meat, vegetables, fruit etc and putting their contents into a huge pot and heating it. This was the first time David had used his mess tin and eaten such fare. It was eventually filled with a steaming brown broth with lumps floating in it. Goodness knows what the lumps were but it tasted good. Eaten with dry biscuits, David thought its flavor was a little like goulash, but who cared: anything would have tasted good as everyone was so hungry. It was all washed down with a mug of steaming, frothy tea.

The sunset was marvelous, although few noticed it. The sun dropped quite quickly behind the distant hills and as the shadows lengthened there were a myriad of colors across the rocks and sand of the desert:

gold, orange, then red, purple, and the blue rocks turned to gray and then black in silhouette. Yes, the desert could look beautiful. Darkness comes quickly in Arabia and four or five kerosene lamps were soon lit. The main light, however, came from the fire around which everyone sat, except for some soldiers who had to do sentry duty. Those at the front, nearest the fire glowed gold, whilst those at the back were black silhouettes with no identity. There was lots of chatter and laughter and David felt part of the group. One of the sergeants started to sing 'Ten green bottles' and soon the whole group was singing, beating time with their mugs of tea. One song followed another and as one would expect from a northern regiment the inevitable 'Ilkley Moor Bar Tat' raised the roof, if there had been one. As it happened, the soldiers on each side of David were from the Life Guards, both from London and, of course, they provided a couple of choruses of 'Maybe it's because I'm a Londoner".

Around nine o'clock the lamps were put out, new sentries posted and everyone got as comfortable as they could on the stony ground. Ablutions consisted of a pee in a trench dug in a designated area and a quick wash of hands and face in baths of water put on the ground for that purpose. David found it difficult to sleep, although he was very tired. He rolled up his towel for a pillow and shuffled the stones beneath his cape to give a little comfort. The night was clear and he could see the stars bright above as he lay on his back fully clothed. It was not cold. A wild dog, or possibly a fox, barked somewhere out there in the darkness. David hoped the sentries would do their duty well and sense anything that might constitute an attack. But these were York and Lancs, excellent chaps who took their soldiering seriously, so what could happen to them? He thought of the snake they had seen. 'Let's hope there are none about here,' he told himself and then shuddered. He thought of the vultures and their grizzly existence. But scavengers were needed to keep nature clean. He chuckled at the comment about vultures and Aden and then...........

It was still dark when he was shaken by one of the Life Guards. "Come on 'doc' we'll be moving out soon. Drink up and eat yer breakfast." He was given a mug of tea, some dry biscuits and a date bar. The camp was stirring. He felt very stiff, paining all over from his monastic-like bed, and he was a little cold. The tea revived him and after a good stretch and a 'crap' in the 'trench for the use of', he was fine. As the sun came over the horizon, they moved out along another wadi that looked just the same as the one on the previous day. How they found their way around was a complete mystery to David.

The second day was uneventful with one exception. It was the practice of the leading Land-Rover carrying the senior officer, a captain, to go back and forth along the convoy checking and giving orders. This was done at quite a speed. Just after lunch the vehicle passed David and suddenly came to a halt. The captain leapt out and dashed into the scrub. David though he had been 'taken short' but no, a minute or two later he emerged with a large lizard held by its tail. It must have been eighteen inches long, quite fat and pure white. The captain held it up for all to see as the convoy went past. Just as David's vehicle came alongside the lizard, or gecko as it is correctly called, swung upwards and buried its teeth into the captain's hand just below the thumb. He yelled and dropped the gecko, which wriggled off into the scrub. The hand was bleeding and he tied a handkerchief round it, got into his Land-Rover and was off again.

When the convoy got back to the base camp the captain came to see David. His hand was quite swollen, the flesh had been pierced but there was no deep cut. David cleaned the area and applied anti-hystamine cream and gave the captain a tetanus injection. He assured David that the creature was not poisonous but David was not so sure. However, the following day the swelling had gone down and the officer felt fine. 'Lucky,' thought David. 'He should know better. Unless you're an expert don't mess.' In training they were told of an officer in Arabia who shot a desert fox. He did not realize, but he only wounded it. The silly man picked it up and it bit him. The officer caught rabies and had to be flown back to the U.K. for treatment. He was very ill and nearly lost his life.

After the patrol, the time went quickly and Cpl. Brown was back with newly filled teeth and a mass of essentials only obtainable in Aden itself. As he explained, living up country was fine but obtaining simple things like toothpaste and decent soap was difficult. Generally there was always somebody going down to camp at least once a week for supplies, and they tended to take a list of requirements with them. David was given a dozen letters to be posted and a request to come back when he could. His kit was put in one of the two trucks that had arrived the night before and he said his farewells. Even two or three Life Guards came over to say goodbye to the 'doc'.

They bumped along the wadi and by midday they had reached the beach where they were given food and allowed to splash in the waves. Most soldiers just stripped off and dashed into the sea naked. David had showered at school naked but never bathed in the nude before. He found the new experience exhilarating, the most natural thing in the world. Of course, there were ribald comments about dicks and arses but that was to be expected from a group of lively young men – still schoolboys really. David could not imagine why people made such a fuss about nudity. The young human body was beautiful. Maybe not as one got older and acquired a gut, but even then he could not see it as being sinful to bathe thus. After a while everyone became tired and found a place to snooze. Some found shade at the side of the vehicles, while others sunbathed on the sand at the water's edge letting the wavelets lap over them. It was an ideal break but all good things have to come to an end and soon they were in the vehicles racing along the sand towards the transit camp.

Nothing had changed on camp and David soon got back into his usual routine of sick parades, off duty visits to Steamer Point, the NAAFI complex and to Elephant Bay. However, there was an increase in stomach upsets, some so bad that they had to be sent to the RAF Hospital at Steamer Point. Sometimes, on an afternoon, when he had an evening duty and did not have the time to go into town, he went to the RAF pool. It was a strange place. The sides of the pool were some ten feet above the ground and a wooden staging at each end served as a sunbathing area. It was clear that the pool was built thus so that sand did not easily blow into the water, for sandstorms were quite common. It was not used a great deal, and those who did use it were mostly RAF personnel. David soon got to know them. They would swim, play a form of water volleyball and sunbathe on the boarded area.

One afternoon David was aware of being watched. A fellow some yards from where he was lying kept looking at him and smiling. David smiled back. The guy, finely made with brown short-cropped hair and a small white bathing suit, could have been a model as his excellent physique and handsome face was well tanned and photogenic. Eventually he came over to where David was lying and placed his towel beside his.

"You're new around here," he stated.

"Yes," responded David with a smile. "I've been in Aden for three months now but I don't get a lot of time to come here."

"Mm..I've seen you here a few times." He held out his hand. "I'm Alex. I run the cinema here." They shook hands.

"Are you RAF then?" asked David.

"Yes. National Service."

"How come you get such a cushy job?" David questioned.

"Easy really. I work in the film industry in civi-street and my father is a film director."

"So the RAF put you to work," observed David.

"Suppose so," replied Alex with a smile that was really electric. "You're army?"

116

"RAMC," David replied. "National Service like you."

"I've eight more months to do. What about you?"

"Nine more months now," responded David.

Alex stretched out on his towel. "Great life here. Sun and a pool at the taxpayers' expense."

David thought for a while, stretching out too. "Never thought of it that way. Some of us live better than others," he offered, pointing to the RAF accommodation.

"True," Alex responded. "Your camp's a bit grotty."

There was a silence for a while, and then David commented," Some of us may have to go into action if Col. Nasser keeps up his rhetoric."

"Mmm...," responded Alex lazily. "Will you?"

"Maybe if things flare up and the York and Lancs are called on."

There was silence for a while as the two soaked up the sun.

"You've a great body," Alex observed looking David up and down.

"A bit skinny I suppose," remarked David.

"I like your physique," went on Alex. "Slim, fair and muscular. Great."

David looked at Alex, at his body and at his features. He really was quite beautiful, something like those marble statues one can see in the Uffizi Gallery in Florence. (4) "You've a great body yourself. Sort of film star quality...... leading man and all that.......our hero."

Alex laughed. "Nice of you to say so but there are plenty of guys around with good bodies."

"What's special about me then?" enquired David, mystified as to why Alex liked his figure.

"You're....don't quite know how to express it."

"Go on," said David intrigued.

"Well, you're....sexy." responded Alex a little embarrassed.

"Sexy?" How do you mean?" He had never been called sexy before.

"You have great looks; a lithe, muscular body like a cheetah or a leopard. There's an energy about you also," he went on.

"Oh, I've got lots of energy. I'm always on the go," responded David. "Not that I don't know how to rest, but I tend to put everything into whatever I do. If that's sexy," he laughed, "well I suppose I am."

I'd like to have that blond hair on my chest like you," observed Alex.

"You like hair then?"

"Yes, I've always wanted hair on my chest but it's not to be."

"You've got hairy legs though."

"I'd like more," went on Alex.

"I'm afraid we can't have everything we want. You have to put up

117

with great looks and a super body and...."

"Ok, I give in," laughed Alex. "Suppose I am fortunate really. My dad says I'm lazy. Wants me to be a doctor, but I don't have the brain or the inclination. I like the theatre, films. They're my kind of people." He yawned.

There was silence for a while but David was aware that Alex was watching him.

"You ever sunbathed in the nuddy," Alex asked suddenly.

David was taken aback. He just didn't expect the question. "Not until I came out here. When I was on holiday in Spain a couple of years ago I just wore a thong. That was almost nude. The other week when we'd been up country we all bathed naked. But that's all. I've never purposely bathed naked."

"What did you think to it," asked Alex.

"I liked it. There's a feeling of freedom"

"What about you?" David asked.

"It's great. As you say, you feel really free. We have a pool at home and nobody wears clothes." Alex told David.

"Even your parents?" David enquired in amazement.

"Yes. In the theatre people are not narrow minded like elsewhere."

"Well...," David hesitated. "I don't mind. But where can you bathe nude here?"

"Easy," explained Alex. "At the back of the camp here there is a beach that hardly anyone uses. There is a way through the wire fence. A few of the lads sunbathe there naked. I do often. Look." Alex turned down the side of his bathing costume to reveal a brown thigh with no white mark. "Want to try it?"

David found himself saying, "Yes....but is it allowed?"

"No, but nobody bothers," replied Alex.

"Come tomorrow if you can make it," offered Alex.

"OK then," agreed David. "Is it safe to go through the wire?"

"Of course. Be outside the camp cinema at two o'clock. You'll need to bring some water to drink as there's no shade."

"I'll be there."

David carried on reading his book and after about twenty minutes Alex said goodbye and left as he had to get the film ready for the evening showing. After a short snooze David also left.

The following afternoon David met Alex outside the RAF cinema. Alex showed David where there was a hole in the wire fence that they crawled through, and after walking about a half mile along the beach they reached some small sand dunes where Alex suggested they should stay. It was a great spot with the sea some two hundred yards away and a grassy hollow in the dune where they could sunbathe unobserved. They put their towels down side by side and stripped off. Alex suggested they had a swim first as they were hot from the walk. The beach was deserted and anyone approaching could be seen far off. They ran into the sea, everything flapping in the breeze, as naked as the day they were born. The sea was wonderful and after a period of jumping the rather large waves they went back to the dunes.

"Better put on some oil, Dave," Alex suggested, "as its hot and even with a tan you could burn quite easily."

"You're right," agreed David and he went into his bag to get some sun oil.

"Use this," said Alex offering him a bottle of white liquid.

"What is it?" David asked.

"Cocoanut oil. The best thing you can get for sunbathing. You'll smell like a cocoanut after using it but it's great. I always use it."

"Ok," offered David and Alex handed over the bottle. It was easy to rub it all over his legs and chest but when it came to his shoulders and back there was a problem.

"Let me," said Alex taking the bottle. He put some oil in his hands and began to massage David's shoulders and back. It was a lovely sensation and David began to get aroused. He saw Alex look down but he said nothing. "Now you can do my back," he told David.

Alex got down onto his towel, face down, ready for David's massage. David pored a good quantity of the oil into his palm and began to rub gently massaging the muscles of Alex's back and buttocks.

"Oh, that's heaven, keep going. You do it perfectly," Alex crooned.

"I've never done a massage before," David told him.

"Ooh, lovely!" went on Alex flexing his muscles under David's hands.

David had a feeling in his groin that he could not stop. He was getting hard.

When he had finished, he gave Alex a slap on the bottom and turned over on his stomach quickly to hide his growing erection. Alex turned over immediately onto his back. David could see that he was hard and erect. Alex smiled at him. "Look what you do to me Dave."

"Sorry," David apologized. "Didn't mean to get you aroused."

"No problem," laughed Alex. "It was a lovely massage and my erection feels great. What about you?"

David did not know what to say. He was hugely erect now and rather embarrassed. "I....suppose.... I..... enjoyed .....the massage too."

"You hard too?" asked Alex.

"Mm....," replied David.

"Let's see," asked Alex. David turned over.

"My god," was the reply he got as Alex stared. "You're a big boy."

They both turned back onto their stomachs and nothing more was said. They read and dozed for an hour and then Alex suggested another swim in the sea as it was very hot. They both were no longer aroused, although David did notice Alex glance at him as they raced down to the water. It was so good to cool off, although the water was as warm as a tepid bath. One or twice as they frolicked in the surf Alex's hand brushed against David's crotch but he thought little of it. When they got back to the beach and David looked at his watch he found that it was time for him to make a move. They quickly dressed and wended their way towards the hole in the wire. Outside the cinema they took their leave promising to do the same another afternoon. Alex told David that he could always be found around five-thirty in the cinema and showed him a back entrance to the projection room.

On the way back to the camp David reflected on the events of the afternoon. It was clear Alex had wanted to see him naked. David had not objected to that. Why? He supposed he was flattered by his attention and the compliments about his body. Nobody had ever wanted to see his body or made flattering comments until he had become a soldier. Certainly nobody had said anything at school and he felt his father thought him weedy. What about his own feelings? Well he did find Alex attractive just like Frank. Andrew was different. He did have excellent legs but he found Andrew fascinating as a person. With Alex and Frank he knew there was something else. He wanted to touch them, to feel their bodies against his own, and yet he knew that was wrong. Everything in his being told him it was wrong but......it aroused him. What was wrong with him? Maybe it was the climate that made him like that or being away from loved ones. Maybe.

Chapter 9

The mess accommodation on camp consisted of two large tents open on all sides and, trestle tables with wooden benches to sit on. Each table could hold six down each side. The wooden tops were wiped down after each meal but David could never remember seeing the tables scrubbed. Food was collected from a line of tables to one side supervised by the Catering Corps. Outside the mess tent two galvanized iron baths of hot water were placed for washing eating utensils, and a large dustbin for waste food. The systems was that you scraped your waste into the bin, washed your plate and 'eating irons' as best you could in the first bath of water, and then rinsed off in the second. Primitive but effective, if organized correctly. The problem was that the water was changed infrequently, and it got very nasty with a greasy scum on its surface: the first few to use the water were fine, but if you happened to be the twentieth or fiftieth then your plates remained greasy and unclean. No amount of complaining seemed to change the system.

A second problem was the food. Breakfast was not too bad but the two main meals were frequently uneatable. Most soldiers tended to eat in the NAAFI on the RAF camp or in town. One lunch-time, having picked at what was supposed to be a meat pie, David decided to fill up on rice pudding, so he allowed the cook to give him a large dollop. He took it back to his seat and started to eat. The taste was not bad, but on taking a second spoonful he saw a large beetle, about a quarter of an inch long, in the pudding. He fished it out with his spoon and put it on the side of his plate. A fourth spoon revealed another and another. There was always an officer or senior NCO on duty so he took his plate up to the officer who happened to be the catering officer.

"Please sir," he said, "I've found beetles in my pudding."

The officer looked at him in disgust. "You're lucky laddie," he snarled, "don't tell the others, or they'll all want them." With that he turned his back on David and walked away.

When he got back to his seat Andrew asked what happened.

"You saw him, Andy," David said and told him what was said. "He just walked away. He doesn't care."

"I bet he eats well enough," observed Andrew. "I never told you before, Dave, but I wrote to my parents about this place and our treatment. I'm getting really fed up."

"Strange," remarked David but I did the same.

"Had any reply yet?" Andrew asked.

"No. Early days yet. I did it after being up country. If they can live decently there, why not here? Have you had a reply?"

"I expect some comment in the next week or two," reported Andrew. "My dad gets very busy, but I'm sure he'll do something. You do know we could get into trouble for complaining?"

"No, but I'm not surprised. We seem to have no rights in the military. They're all living in the Dark Ages."

A few days after this incident, on a Sunday morning, David woke up feeling weak and with a strange feeling in his stomach. He did not manage to get to church the previous Sunday as he was working, so he was determined to serve for the padre at Communion, even if he felt unwell. He pulled on his clothes and set off. Andrew was on duty so he was alone. The custom was that the padre and server never spoke before the Communion service so that they could concentrate on God alone. As the service progressed David began to feel worse. Something was really wrong with him, however he managed to get through without a hitch. It was a matter of will as he felt so terrible. In the vestry as he and the padre disrobed he began to feel dizzy. The next thing he knew was a voice saying, "Now old chap does that feel better." A cool cloth was placed over his brow. "Get him a glass of water Marion," said the voice. It was the padre and his wife. He had suddenly collapsed on the vestry floor.

After some time, he began to feel less dizzy and when he could stand the padre bundled David into his car and drove him to his own house on the RAF compound. The padre and his wife between them helped him to an easy chair in the parlour, and then brought him a cup of tea. "You need some food old chap," observed the padre, Marion will get you some breakfast. You're dizzy because of going without your breakfast."

"No, no thank you padre," groaned David. "No breakfast. I feel terrible. I think I'm going to be sick."

"Marion, get a bowl," the padre yelled. "He's going to be sick."

The bowl came just in time. What was inside him came spurting out. "I need to go to the bathroom," David groaned. So he did. Both ends were erupting.

"Looks to me like dysentery," the padre's wife said.

"Lots of it about on that camp," offered the padre. "Poor lad."

After the initial shock of being sick and the embarrassment of rushing to the toilet, David began to feel a little better but still rather dizzy. He was not erupting for the time being so the padre drove him back to the sick bay on his own camp. Fortunately, Lt. Morrison was there, having been called out to a whole spate of dysentery patients. He examined David, asked him a few questions about how he felt, gave him some white tablets and sent him with Andrew back to his tent where he was to stay in bed unless he had to go to the toilet. A bucket was placed by his bed so he could spew his heart out. Andrew and Simon promised to look in and take care of his medicine and to bring him plenty of fluids. There would be no need of food in the near future.

For three days David was unaware of the world around him. He could remember someone taking him to the toilet, someone holding him while he vomited, someone giving him water when he was burning up, but the rest was a blank. Simon told him afterwards that he was delirious and talked a whole lot of nonsense, and Andrew said that Lt. Morrison was very worried and was about to send him to hospital.

Everyone had rallied round and taken it in turns to be with him. Will had sat through the night and Private Sidebottom and his friend had given up their afternoons to sit at his bedside. The Padre had been in a couple of times to see how he was. Even Sgt. Wright and Captain Price had paid a visit.

It left David very weak and it was nearly a month before he got back his energetic self. By then he had received a letter from his parents. His father had written in his rather brief style. It was quite an event. His father hardly ever wrote as he left it to his mother, who rambled on without full stops and with many misspellings. When David had teased her when on leave about her spelling she said with a twinkle in her eye: "It's Shakespeare dear." His father wanted to know more details and wrote that he would take it up with their local Member of Parliament. He also asked if David had been ill recently for his mother had woken with David's voice crying out in her ears. She was very worried. It was strange, but that was not the first time his mother had had a premonition.

David had the time to reply after his illness as he was on 'light duties' for a week. He explained his illness and said that he was recovering well and not to worry. At his father's request, he gave him more details about the camp. He told his father that many soldiers had suffered the same fate. He related the different diseases that the men were suffering from, probably because of the conditions. One thing he did ask his father, and this advice had come from Andrew's father, not to reveal his name, rank and number as if discovered the military was more than likely to take retaliation. Andrew had given his father many details also. Apparently quite a few servicemen had made complaints.

Three weeks later, David received a letter from his father explaining that he had contacted their local MP but he was not prepared to do anything. His mother was outraged with the man's attitude. She had spent many years on the local Conservative Party Committee as a fund-raiser for him. She resigned in disgust and 'gave him a piece of her mind'. David smiled knowingly as his mother could wither a person with a few words when she was angry. A business friend of David's father had told him that there had been some correspondence in the 'Yorkshire Evening Post' about the bad conditions. David's father also told him that he was going down to London to the House of Commons to meet the Labor MP, Bessie Braddock, (1) whom he had been told had taken up the case.

An afternoon trip David undertook with Andrew and Simon was to the Sheba Tanks. The tanks were situated on the side of the extinct volcano that was Aden and overlooked Steamer Point. Reputedly, the tanks had been built to hold rainwater two thousand years ago by the Queen of Sheba, (2) when Aden had a rainfall. Now they were empty as the rainfall in Aden was virtually nothing. In fact, David experienced a half-hour shower only once while he was in Aden, but the rain dried as soon as it hit the ground.

The three tanks, constructed of hewn rectangular pieces of rock that fitted together perfectly, were probably sealed with mortar to reduce the loss of water. They approached them down a long drive shaded with trees. The taxi had been left at the main road. The area was very green and obviously was irrigated from a modern bore well, certainly not the tanks as they were empty. A lovely garden surrounded the tanks - hibiscus, oleander and bougainvillea. It was a peaceful place, away from traffic and the bustle of Aden town and Steamer Point. Each tank was connected to the other by an overflow channel and the last tank must have overflowed into a stream that wound down the hillside.

A large notice in English and Arabic, provided by the Government of Aden for the education of tourists, gave an explanation of the origin and purpose of the tanks. They were only 'reputed' to have been built by order of the Queen of Sheba but were certainly used to provide water for the settlement that existed some two thousand years before. David and his colleagues could only marvel at the ingenuity of that early civilization. It also made them realize how the climate had changed in that part of the world.

They sat on a wooden bench in the shade of a tree and enjoyed the comparative cool. Shafts of sunlight flashed around them as the trees gently swayed in the breeze. Somewhere in one of the numerous large trees, a parakeet squawked in agitation at its neighbor. "We could be in England," Andrew observed with a sigh.

"Maybe," agreed David.

"Except in never gets as hot as this even in the best summer and we don't have parakeets," Simon remarked.

"You're just not a romantic, Simon," grumbled Andrew. "I was just meaning the greenery is a little like England."

"Homesick?" asked David.

"A little," Andrew admitted. "I'm just fed up with bloody sand, bloody flies and continuous sunshine."

"I thought you like the sun, Andrew," observed David.

"I do.....but you can have too much. Wouldn't it be nice just to have a downpour of rain for a change?"

"You bet," enthused Simon. "Nice, warm rain on your face."

"Trouble is," David reminded them, "it's never warm rain and it never knows when to stop in England."

"I don't care," mused Andrew. "Warm or cold it would be very welcome."

"You're a little Englander, Andrew," laughed Simon. "You'll be telling me next that you fancy roast beef and two veg."

Andrew grimaced at him. "Well what's wrong with that? I suppose I am very English in a way and I love my country."

"And me," added David.

They both looked at Simon. He thought for a while. "Yes, I love my country but....."

"But what?" they said in unison.

"But there are other places where I'd like to live – America, Australia. England is all right but we need to change, to stop looking at our past and look towards the future."

For a while there was silence, each with his own thoughts. David was quite struck with what Simon had said. He loved his country but it had its faults. There was still too much class distinction, as the army had revealed. Privilege was still a problem. The country would get nowhere until people were judged on merit and not on their school or parentage. Yes, Simon was right, Britain needed to change or it would be left behind. America and Australia had a future. Anyone with energy and ability could make good in the New World.

One afternoon, a few days before Christmas, David was on duty in the Medical Centre when a sergeant wandered in and asked for the Medical Officer. "Sorry, he's not here," offered David. "Can I help?"

"Well, a sergeant's been electrocuted in our tent.....," he went on without any degree of urgency.

David jumped up, grabbed his medical bag, and commanded, "Show me!"

"In the sergeants' tents," he offered.

David knew where they were and he ran, while the sergeant ambled along at a leisurely pace. As he got to the senior NCO lines, he saw another sergeant beckoning him.

"Over 'ere mate," he shouted.

David got to the tent and there on the floor, on his back, was another sergeant looking very pale, almost blue, making a faint spluttering sound.

"He was fitting some fairy lights.....," one sergeant said.

"Is the electric switched off now?" David asked as he bent down to feel the pulse. He did not want to be electrocuted as well.

"Ye' it's off," was the answer.

David could not feel a pulse and the spluttering had stopped. He started to give artificial respiration. "Send for the MO, Captain Price," he told one of the gaping sergeants as he continued the treatment. "Quickly. And get an ambulance."

David carried on for what seemed like hours with the artificial respiration. There was commotion round him, but he was concentrating on the man under his hands. He began to get tired but he could not stop. He became aware of a figure by his side feeling the man's pulse. It was the MO, Captain Price. David kept on as the MO listened to the heart with his stethoscope. "I think he's dead," he said quietly. "You can stop now Cpl. Earl."

David sat back on his haunches and looked at the body beside him. He could not believe the man was dead. He'd seen the sergeant around the camp, a man of about forty years of age, married with children, according to the photographs by his bed. Dead from trying to fix Christmas lights. David must have looked dazed as Cpt. Price said quietly, "I'll carry on now corporal. If you like to return to the center."

That evening David went to the RAF Church. He could not get the dead man out of his mind. 'Did I give the treatment correctly?' he asked himself. 'Suppose I didn't try hard enough?' The man had been alive and well a few hours ago as David had seen him with his platoon arriving from a training exercise. 'Christmas. How will his family receive the news? Terrible.' David could see the two wires running down the central tent pole that the sergeant had been trying to tap, and the fairy lights fallen to the floor. Tears welled up in his eyes. 'Christmas is a time of joy, a time for the family, but for this family it would be nothing but sadness.'

He didn't know how long he had been in church kneeling at the altar, but he had prayed to God for the man's family and for the man himself. It was an accident, a terrible accident. He thought of others who would suffer at Christmas: the poor, the sick, the unwanted, those involved in war. When he was a child Christmas had been a wonderful

126

affair, magic, with Father Christmas bringing presents to everyone and the Baby Jesus in his crib. As he got older, the magic had gone and the commercialism had taken its place. The rich indulged themselves whilst the poor frequently got into debt in order to provide for their children. It was not a time of giving but a time of grabbing. His face was wet with tears but he didn't care.

"David," a voice impinged on his thoughts. David looked up and the light reflected on his tears. "Gracious, what's wrong?" asked the voice. It was the padre come to say his office.

"I...., someone.....," David broke down and sobbed.

"What is it? Tell me," the padre said. He put an arm round David's shoulders.

Suddenly everything rushed out in a series of words and sobs. "A sergeant died...electrocuted...I gave him...... artificial respiration........maybe I could ......have saved him....married...children....if only I'd been earlier....." and the tears again streamed down David's face.

The padre waited.

David's tears began to subside and his sobs got less frequent. The padre lifted David up and took him to a pew where they sat in silence, the padre holding his hand.

"You've had a shock, David. I expect you've never seen death before?"

David nodded. He had not seen the young boy in hospital die.

"Don't blame yourself. I'm sure you did all you could. Was the MO there?"

David nodded.

"It wasn't your fault. An accident you say. These things happen. None of us know when God will call us to his bosom."

David began to shiver. It was warm outside but he felt cold. "Come on, old chap, my wife will make you a nice cup of tea."

For a second time David was driven to the padre's home. His wife was at the door as the padre had telephoned from the church.

'Mrs. Padre', was kindness itself. It is often said that behind every successful man is a good woman. In his case this was true. The Padre and his wife lived their religion day by day. David knew that the men on both camps respected him, even those who never came to church – the so called 'four wheelers – the ones who came on four wheels to be baptized, married and buried. Marion, for that was what she was called, asked David to recount exactly what happened. In the telling David was able to get things in perspective. With a little prompting from Marion, he began to realize that he had done everything possible to help. He was not responsible for the death. Life was not all plain sailing and if he was going to be a priest then he would come across death frequently.

Changing the subject, the Padre suddenly said, "Come to us on Christmas Day, after morning service. My daughter will be here and a couple more of the chaps."

"Yes, do come David," Marion concurred.

David was told that the officers would serve lunch on Christmas Day, but the tented mess area at the transit camp was no place to celebrate. It would be quite miserable really when compared to Christmas with his family. "Thank you," he said. That would be wonderful."

Fortunately, David managed to wangle the whole day off on Christmas Day as he had worked two Sundays in succession because of sickness. Andrew lost his voice and had swollen glands and Will ended up with exactly the same. Believing that prevention is better than cure, David gargled with salt and water and it did the trick. Will was not bothered about working at Christmas, and as long as Andrew could go to church in the morning, he was not too bothered. Simon was going to the home of a girl he had met whose father was something to do with the British Embassy. There was a Christmas lunch on camp but most were going to the NAAFI Club in order to drink beer and get high.

David served at communion at eight o'clock. It was well attended. He dashed back for breakfast and changed into white slacks and a pale green shirt and then he was off to morning service at ten thirty. He would not have missed the service for anything as he loved to sing carols and to listen to the readings of the nativity. It reminded him of his childhood, the years of innocence before the spell was broken, and he realized that Christmas had become a marketing bonanza and a glutton's paradise instead of a religious experience. The church was full and he was thankful to be a member of the choir and not to have to fight for a seat. There were lots of families and he noticed quite a few teenagers who had obviously flown out from the U.K. for the holiday. Everyone was in a joyous mood, particularly the small children, whose beliefs had not yet been shattered.

'O come all ye faithful' was the first hymn and everyone sang with such gusto. At 'oh come let us adore Him' the women sang alone and at the third repeat the men joined in. It was so beautiful and so touching. The two lessons were read by senior officers from the RAF and in between there was 'Once in Royal David's city..' - David had a feeling that he was being watched – and later came the old favorite 'While shepherds watched their flocks by night.....'. The Padre's sermon was short and to the point. He talked about "A Christmas Carol" by Charles

Dickens and the message of sharing and love found in the household of Bob Cratchet and Tiny Tim's 'God bless you everyone.' It was most moving and very appropriate holding his young congregation spellbound. The service ended with 'Good Christian men rejoice' and David was sure the roof rattled from the wonderful singing. At the end of the service the Padre shook hands with everyone, wished them a happy Christmas, and joked with almost everyone so that the whole congregation left with laughter and bonhomie in their hearts.

In the vestry David found that 'Mrs. Padre' had placed a huge tray of mince pies and two thermos jugs of hot coffee for the choir. There was a little note saying "Thanks for the support you have given the church. Happy Christmas." 'Typical,' David thought, 'of the padre and his wife'. Andrew, who was also a choir member, stayed a while for a mince pie and a chat and then went off to do the sick parade with Will. Alex put his head round the door and wished David a happy Christmas. He looked fit and very handsome.

"Where've you been, Dave I've not seen you for ages?" he asked.

"Sick," responded David. "I thought you knew. I got dysentery. Bad, very bad."

"Poor you. Tied to the bog for a while?"

"Sort of," responded David. "It left me terribly weak and I just have not had the energy to go to the beach."

"Call round sometime," he yelled and then was off with a group of RAF types.

The Padre and his wife arrived having said goodbye to the congregation. "So you know Alex?" questioned the padre. "His father directs films. Famous family. Knows all the right people right up to the Air Marshall."

"I knew his father directed films but I didn't know he was so well connected," David said.

"Has all the right things to be an officer but would rather just be an aircraftsman. Socialist views I believe. Doesn't approve of privilege," offered the Padre.

"So he told me," David reported.

By this time the Padre had taken off his robes and was ready to leave. There was a girl of about eighteen with the padre's wife who was introduced as their daughter, Audrey. She had just started the first year at Leicester University College (3) where she was training to be a teacher. The padre bundled them into his Austin car and off they went to his home.

RAF married accommodation consisted of neat, white bungalows each surrounded by a small garden. The gardens were maintained by

Airforce personnel and planted with flowering trees. It was all typical of the RAF: good standards for everyone. There was a concrete drive leading to a car-port on the side of the bungalow and a small white-painted latch gate that led up to the front door.

At the house, the padre and his wife were greeted by two young men of about David's age. One wore an apron with poinsettias on it and the other was in gray slacks with a bright red shirt. They certainly were in the Christmas spirit.

"Everything under control," smiled the Apron.

"Leave it to us, we never fail," laughed the Red Shirt.

"That's a relief," responded Marion. "I expected the turkey to be in flames."

"The only trouble we had was getting it into the oven," observed the Apron with a twinkle in his eye. "It refused to go in. Kept flapping its wings."

"We had to bash it on the head before it submitted," observed the Red Shirt.

It was clear that they were jokers. "Oh, David, these two wonderful boys are Ray and John. This is David, boys, from the Medical Corps. Both are RAF and great cooks. They promised to do the whole meal for me so I let them. I know Ray (Apron) is going to an hotel school when he leaves the RAF, and John (Red Shirt) comes from an hotel background. But he's going to be an actor."

David shook their hands happily. "Smells good," he said. "You've got my gastric juices going already."

"Talk of getting juices going," chipped in the padre who had just come in from parking the car, "what about a sherry before lunch?" There were welcoming noises from everybody. "We need six sherry glasses Aud." Audrey went off into the kitchen.

David had wondered how the padre's wife could cook a large and complex lunch like the one at Christmas, and also attend church. Now he knew – volunteer cooks.

The lunch really was superb. Ray and John could certainly cook. They were so friendly as well, wisecracking as they served the various dishes. For the first course there was avocado vinaigrette and then the usual roast turkey and all the trimmings. They paraded the turkey into the dining room, did a circuit of the table dressed in Father Christmas red hats, and placed the huge bird in front of the padre to carve. The chestnut stuffing was wonderful, and so were the roast potatoes, sprouts, bread sauce, sausage and gravy. It was like being back home in the UK for David's mother was a good cook too. The conversation was lively as the boys had a myriad of stories to tell.

To herald the pudding, John and Ray had put on grotesque false noses, and Ray blew a paper trumpet to announce its coming. When the flamed pudding arrived, and was served with brandy sauce, David felt a little nostalgic. This was his first Christmas away from home and the excellent food and merry laughter reminded him of his family. Christmas was a religious and a secular festival. It did not matter really when Jesus was born, or where, the important point was that He was born to save the world: to bring a love into the world that no other religion preached. The secular present-giving and feasting was part of the love to fellow human beings that Jesus had preached. Such was the message of Christmas and David was experiencing it amongst friends. But that was not the same as being amongst family, however excellent the company or food.

David thought he was going to burst. A little exercise was called for and so when the meal ended he volunteered to wash up with the padre and Audrey. Mrs. Padre fussed around putting things away while John and Ray had a rest. It did not take long to get things ship shape and then everyone retired into the parlor to read the papers and generally relax. At about five the padre excused himself and went off to read his office and on his return, Audrey produced a tray of tea and the Christmas cake. It was a lovely cake. "Brought out from England by Audrey," Marion explained honestly. "Getting all the ingredients out here is quite a problem."

After tea David felt he should be moving as he did not wish to outstay his welcome. When he suggest it there was unanimous agreement that, unless he had another engagement, he should stay for the rest of the evening.

"We're going to play charades (4) later," Marion said. "John is going to impress us with his acting ability."

"You'll be disappointed then," laughed Ray. "He's terrible."

"Come on, I'm not that bad," laughed John. "Besides, when you've seen Ray's ability I'll look like Lawrence Olivier."(5)

"Daddy's good," offered Audrey. "He gets lots of practice from the pulpit." There was a twinkle in her eye.

"Well I suppose there's something in that," responded the padre. "But teachers have to be actors too, young lady."

"Ok, dad, I give in," offered Audrey.

"You haven't mentioned the housewife," pointed out Marion.

"They're the greatest actors of all," David said. "My mum is better than Sybil Thorndike.(6) She puts on a great act with my brother and I when she gets angry."

Everyone laughed. "Yes, yes," they said looking pointedly at

Marion.

The teams were formed: John and Ray, David and Audrey and the padre and his wife. They all went off into corners to discuss their titles and, after the padre had spun a coin to decide who would go first, John and Ray were to be the leaders. They chose a song, "An easy one to start," they said. It was easy really when you knew what it was, but the mime was hilarious, and they laughed so much at the antics of John and Ray that it took a while to guess. They offered the whole word first. John strutted and pouted like Marilyn Monroe (7) and then when they could not get that they did 'girls' and 'friends'. 'Girls' consisted of the two holdings hands and prancing around the room. Audrey got that one. Then they did friends by shaking hands and later kissing each other when shaking hands only produced the word 'gentlemen'. Suddenly David had an inspiration and got that one. Before they could do 'diamonds' Marion suddenly shouted out 'Diamonds are a girl's best friend' and it was over. The padre told us later that he got it quite early on but enjoyed the fun so much that he couldn't end it.

David and Audrey chose the film 'The Wizard of Oz' (8) and after David's mime of doing magic and Audrey and he linking arms like Judy Garland and the Tin Man for the whole word John got it easily. David tended to be rather shy doing party games but he found that the company was so relaxed that he never thought of fear. The padre and Marion acted out the book 'Pride and Prejudice' (9) and were very funny conveying pride but found 'prejudice' difficult to dramatize. Eventually Audrey got the correct title but they were almost ready to give up. After a cup of coffee and mince pies the party broke up. It had been a wonderful day and David thanked the padre and his wife enthusiastically. He said goodbye to Audrey and went part of the way home with John and Ray. On parting they said they hoped to see David again. "Do you go to church?" David asked innocently. "I've never seen you there. We could meet up there."

Ray and John looked at each other. "Well, actually Dave," Ray said," we don't go to church. I'm Jewish, although I don't go to the synagogue, and John is an agnostic."

John added, "We respect the padre because he respects us. You see....," there was a pause and they looked at each other. "I believe we can trust you, David," John added.

Ray went on,"... we're gay.....lovers..... not openly. It's not allowed in the forces. We could not help ourselves."

"We tried to forget each other but...," John added. "We were worried."

"And so we went to see the padre for advice," continued Ray. "He does not make judgments or discriminate and has been so helpful. He and his wife are wonderful people and they love us for us and not our sexual orientation."

"I see," David said.

"He gave us advice. My religion was no barrier for him. He regards it as just another means of approaching God," added Roy. "I hope you don't mind?"

Quite without being able to explain his action David put his arms around Ray and then John and hugged them both. "You're lovely guys," he said. "Of course I don't mind."

His walk back to camp was thoughtful. What was it that caused him to bump into so many homosexuals? Of course, as a priest he would meet all conditions of men. Did not Jesus do exactly that? Everyone, saint and sinner was encompassed in His love. Surely, if two men or women really loved each other what was wrong with that? There was too little love in the world anyway. Why was the homosexual condemned so when the hyper-active heterosexual, rushing from flower to flower, was just regarded as 'one of the lads'? To David's mind, producing a child that was not intended, wanted or loved, for 'a bit of fun' was as great a sin as premeditated murder. The world was a crazy place.

It was just before New Year that David received a letter from his father to say he had been to see the Labor MP, Bessie Braddock, at the House of Commons. She had received him with great courtesy and listened intently to what he had to say. She informed him that she had had many similar complaints and had taken it up with the appropriate Minister. She also informed his father that a number of journalists were on their way out to Aden to see for themselves as the newspapers in the north of England had received complaints also. It was her feeling that the government was concerned and embarrassed and something would be done. She said she would do all she could to exert pressure.

Just after New Year some visitors did come round the camp. David did not see them but Andrew had been told by his father over the phone of their visit. Andrew's father knew a number of top people in the military and in politics. He had used his contacts to cause a stir in the corridors of power. Things then moved very quickly. Within a month, orders indicated that the regiment was going home to the U.K. by troopship. David had been posted to the RAF hospital at Steamer Point. Andrew and Simon were to go back with the regiment as they were due for demobilization within three months of leaving. They all promised to keep in contact, but like many friendships they were not kept. Andrew and Simon did write once but that was all. They had their lives to get on with. Later on when David was at university he bumped into Andrew in Oxford Street. They had lunch together and discussed old times. He never met Simon again but read of him in the newspapers. He married a young starlet and within a year divorced her. Such is show business.

Chapter 10

After only a week at the RAF hospital working on the E.N.T. Ward, David was sent up country to a place called Mukkeras in the mountains. He traveled by Hercules transport plane, a monster of an aeroplane that could accommodate trucks and armored cars as well as troops. It took nearly two hours of unpleasant flying, as the plane kept dropping suddenly because of the air currents over the desert and mountains, and then up it went as a current and its engines took it upwards. The sudden swoops downwards and then the slower assent again was rather like being on a rough sea. The RAF personnel were used to it, and David seemed to be the only one feeling slightly sick.

As they arrived, he could see from above a rough desert airstrip at the foot of a range of high hills. He had been informed by the aircrew that often planes were strafed with machinegun fire from those hills. He hoped it did not happen this time. The sky was clear and the visibility excellent. Looking down was like inspecting a model landscape one sees displayed in a museum.

There were two clusters of tents, each on the top of a small hill, with a small valley between. One cluster of canvas was large and the other one quite small, with no more than about a dozen tents. On another small hill was a larger e-shaped, white painted building, which he was told was the Officers' Mess. He could see that it had a small garden where the center of the 'e' should have been. He learned that the small group of tents was for the British forces and the other was for the Arab Levy Third Battalion. (1)

By the time he landed on the rough airstrip his hearing was impaired and he looked decidedly pale. It took a while for his ears to right themselves, and he felt rather unsteady as his feet touched the ground, which was very rough and stony. It must have been about eleven o'clock, the sun was high and it was very warm. There was no shade. He had been told by one of the crew that nights were very cold, which was hard to believe.

On the ground great clouds of dust were raised by the huge plane. Three trucks and two Land-Rovers came out to meet them, being careful to approach upwind, but leaving their own cloud of dust. There were troops in the trucks and they almost immediately began to unload the plane of the stores intended for the camps. The first Land-Rover with its officer collected the mail and other special items, while the second Land-Rover collected David. It was driven by an Arab driver and by his side was a Medical Corps Captain who introduced himself as

Peter Dennis. The captain explained on their drive back to the smaller camp that David was taking over from another RAMC medic who had gone back to England for demobilization.

There were about thirty British troops in the camp – Royal Artillery, Catering Corps, Life Guards and some Royal Corps of Signals with ten British officers – and the rest were Arab troops with their own officers. The British officers lived in an old palace – the white building David had seen from the air – and the British troops lived in a compound with their own mess and cookhouse. The medical center was in the Arab compound but David would be collected each day by Abdullah, their driver, as the distance between camps was about a quarter of a mile and in any case it could be dangerous as Yemeni often shot at them from the hills.

David was driven to the compound where he was to live and Cpt. Dennis left him with Sgt. Major Evans, a Royal Artillery NCO, who was the senior NCO on the compound. He was a big man, Welsh, six foot two and broad shouldered. He welcomed David and got one of the gunnery privates to take him to a tent he was to share with four other NCO's. Cpl. McKinnon was Catering Corps and in charge of the kitchen, Cpl. Bennett was a gunnery corporal, Cpl. Brewster was Intelligence Corps, and Cpl. Finn was Life Guards and ran the armored car section, but none of them were there when David arrived. McKinnon, Bennett and Finn were at work and Brewster was on leave.

The usual iron bedstead and wooden locker were awaiting him and David soon made himself comfortable. Suddenly the flap of the tent opened and a ruddy faced soldier of about thirty dressed in blue and white checked trousers and white jacket - the dress of the Catering Corps - appeared with a steaming mug of tea. "I heard y'd arrived," he said with a smile on his face. "I'm Bob McKinnon the most important man in the camp." He handed David the cup of tea. "Ye'll be needin' that after the flight on that monster."

"Thanks," David said. "I'm David Earl. Good to meet the most important man on the camp."

"You're the second," went on McKinnon.

David did not quite understand. "How come?" he asked.

"You're a medic. They all need the medic just as they all need a cook. I keep them well fed and you treat them when they're ill. We're a team. The lads look after us as they recognize our importance to them."

"We're a team then," laughed David and he shook hands.

"And no jokes about the medic putting right what the cook made go wrong," laughed Bob McKinnon.

David smiled. "I'm sure your cooking is excellent, Bob?"

"It's great up here," went on Bob McKinnon. "Best posting I've ever had. Och, we get fired on most nights, but apart from that the sergeant major is a great guy, a pussycat, and the officers never bother us if we do our job well. The colonel's a gentleman. You'll meet him. He often comes down for a piece of my apple tart. Says it's the best he's ever tasted."

"Sounds beyond belief," David said trying to cut into the flow of Scottish bonhomie.

"Where've ye come from?" asked Bob.

"The RAF Hospital and before that the York and Lancs."

"Poor you," he cut in. "They're a rotten mob, at least the officers are. We had them up here for a while."

"They've been sent back home. The camp was terrible and there was a big row over it."

"About time. They told me how bad it was. You'll get good food here, Dave, or my name's not Bob McKinnon." He looked at his watch. "God, it's nearly time for tiffin. See you later," and with that he was gone.

Bob McKinnon was right in blowing his own trumpet. He was the best army cook David had come across. His chicken pie, potatoes and carrots were excellent. The main course was followed by jam sponge and custard, a favorite of David, and then coffee. The mess tent was in the center of the camp and at its side a corrugated iron structure that was Bob McKinnon's kitchen. It became obvious that the sergeant major was a great builder and the facilities in the camp were excellent as he and his gunners had time to 'fix' everything for comfort. There were only thirty British troops in all and they all ate in the same tent, the three sergeants and the sergeant major on a table of their own.

The only disturbing thing in the camp was that fastened to a chain attached to an iron post in the ground was a huge ape called "Nobby", for obvious reasons. His large pink 'thing' always seemed to be erect and hanging down. He was a ferocious beast, and as you went by him, he would bear his teeth and jump up and down. The lads threw their beer cans at him. He had a keeper, a gunner named 'Dave', the one who had brought David to his tent, and he was the only one the ape would allow near him. Dave even fondled him without harm. Nobby was a sort of mascot and whilst everyone teased him by throwing beer cans and getting him jumping up and down, they all liked him.

Not only was there an ape on camp, but a pelican named "Knocker" who David saw had a broken wing. Sergeant Major Evans had a chicken coop at the rear of his tent and he frequently supplied eggs to the mess, and on special occasions, chickens for roasting. The waste food was mainly given to these birds and they were fat and healthy. The sergeant major, David found to his cost, would talk endlessly with his lilting Welsh accent about his chickens. He was a real father figure and greatly respected by everyone.

A further hazard was the 'shite hawks' as the soldiers called them. David was warned that if he took food back to his tent, then he must cover it with a plate or these birds would swoop down and take the lot. They knew when it was meal times and would circle round waiting for an opportunity. At night the wild dogs would move in, howling to each other as they waited for darkness. There must have been thirty or forty each evening and although they were shot at and killed, more appeared. Generally, they were crafty, sitting just out of range of a rifle. They were scavengers and found ways under the wire around the compound no matter how often their entry point was repaired. One could hear them outside the tent at night sniffing and snarling.

The camp usually dozed after lunch during the heat of the afternoon but Bob McKinnon and Ian Bennett seemed to want to chatter, while Andy Finn slept through it all. As David had already found, Bob was not a dour Scotsman but an amiable, talkative and likeable colleague. Ian Bennett was different. He was rather overweight, slow of speech and not particularly communicative. He was a gunnery corporal, a regular soldier from Warwick, married with two children and, as David found later, had a drink problem. Ian informed David that he would need at least four blankets at night, as when the sun went down it got very cold being eight thousand feet up in the mountains. He offered to bring the blankets over later in the afternoon, as he ran the stores as well as being a gunner. From Bob, David learned that most nights they were machine gunned from the hillside opposite by Yemeni tribesmen opposed to the British. They did little harm and served as good target practice for the large guns sited just behind where the senior NCOs had their tent.

They were, however, in constant danger from ambush as rather than attack the camps, which were well-guarded day and night, the Yemeni tended to wait in the rocky wadis and fire on a convoy. Everywhere soldiers went, except for the airstrip that was in the sight of the camp, there had to be an armed escort and narrow wadis were picketed. There had been one or two skirmishes, but nobody had been killed thus far. The local ruler, the Naib, (2) had got his own private army and generally kept the locals in check.

In the late afternoon, Captain Dennis called at David's tent to see that he had settled in and to take him to the medical center, which was at the other camp about a quarter of a mile away. The reason for this was that the majority of soldiers were on the Arab site, and they made up the greater part of the sick parades. He told David that he would have an interpreter and helper called Mohammad. Each morning Mohammad would send Abdullah with the Land-Rover to collect him and then they would call at the Officers' Mess to collect Cpt. Dennis. David would assist the captain with the sick parade.

Captain Dennis worked with the local political officer inspecting civilian medical establishments and working with the local population in order to achieve good relations. This work frequently took him away for a day and thus David would have to take the sick parades himself. There would be times when they could go together, but generally the colonel liked one or the other to be on camp at all times.

The Medical Center was a large tent with a white sign outside with the RAMC insignia and the name in red. Mohammad, who would assist David and had some medical training, was waiting outside. He was small and slim with a lovely olive skin and dark shining eyes. David thought how handsome he looked in his headdress and military uniform. His smile revealed a set of perfect white teeth. Inside the center, the floor had cocoanut matting, cabinets for drugs, a refrigerator, electric light from a generator, a sink and running water, a desk for the MO, treatment table and three wooden chairs. In one corner was a pilot's seat from a crashed aircraft. Captain Dennis told David it was used for extracting teeth. He explained that almost everything happened in the medical center, except major operations, as they were some three hundred miles from Aden and often mist stopped any flights for days. They were thus on their own and had to deal with any emergency.

After giving David a set of keys for the drug cabinet, Captain Dennis explained that Mohammad slept in the medical tent, partly as a precaution against thieving and partly for someone to be on call. He left David to do the sick parade with Mohammad and pointed out that he would be on call for serious cases, but that otherwise David was in charge at night. The sick parade was easy and Mohammad's English was quite good so there was no problem with finding out symptoms. Mohammad told David that he was twenty-three and newly married. When he was eighteen, he had joined the Levy's as his family was poor and he had to support a widowed mother and three younger brothers. When the treatments were all completed Mohammad called a driver to take David back to his camp. He explained that Abdullah, the driver, was his friend and would collect David each morning.

That first night in camp David went to bed early. In any case it was very cold once the sun was down, and as the lighting was by kerosene lamp it was difficult to read. It would seem that most soldiers were of the same mind as Bob McKinnon, Any Finn and Ian Bennett were soon to follow. There was a generator in the mess tent and beer was available, but as it was so cold, few remained. He found that four thick army blankets were not really enough and so for the first time since being in Aden he wore his pajamas. Still he was cold and he put his greatcoat on the bed. He would ask for a couple more blankets in the morning. He usually said his prayers in bed, as in training he found it caused a lot of unnecessary comment to kneel by his bed. A prayer was a prayer said in public or in private, but to be disturbed by ribald comment from his communion with God was not acceptable. So prayers in bed was the norm.

Morning parade was very cold indeed and the sergeant major did not waste time. The custom was to collect a mug of hot tea from the mess tent, wash and shave in cold water and be ready for inspection at seven. They lined up in threes, the parade was brought to attention, names were called and then they were dismissed. Everyone was in summer kit and until the sun came up, one physically shivered with the cold. There were no showers as water had to be bought at a local well, and then had to be transported in jerry cans to the camp. Each tent was allowed a can of water a day and its conservation was strictly controlled. Water was saved for the weekly bath.

Breakfast was at seven fifteen and eaten with much chatter. At a quarter to eight, Abdullah arrived for David, and he was joined by a cook private and a gunner who were reporting sick. It was custom for the British sick to accompany the medic, unless they were too sick to walk. They were then driven to the other camp, which took about five minutes. Captain Dennis said he would come later as the Land-Rover was full.

When David got there he found about twenty Arab soldiers sitting on benches reporting sick. Mohammad had got everything organized and sharply at eight fifteen, just fifteen minutes after David had arrived, Abdullah drove up with Captain Dennis, having been back to collect him. He soon got to work and saw the two British soldiers first, as there was always fewer of them, and they took less time. The cook had a nasty burn on his left arm, which had been kept clean and not messed with. It would heal on its own unless infected. David carefully covered the burn with a sterile paraffin-wax gauze and bound it carefully. The gunner had trapped his middle finger during an exercise and the nail had been shattered. After cleaning it the MO felt that the nail would come off naturally and a new one would grow. The finger was badly bruised but not crushed. There was a suspicion of infection so a shot of penicillin was administered. The soldier dropped his pants for the injection. He could not believe it when David told him it was over and to pull his trousers up. "Gosh mate," he said gratefully, "never felt a thing." David smiled knowing the agony he had gone through perfecting his technique.

The Arab soldiers were quite another thing. Most of them were just looking for an excuse to get off duty and as Captain Dennis explained, they were masters at feigning sickness. Many had just got a cold and had a slight fever which the ordinary British soldier would just shrug off or take a couple of aspirins. Not these soldiers. They dramatized their symptoms and kept pointing to their arm and saying "*Ibra, ibra.*"

"What do they want?" asked David.

"Oh, they want an injection," replied the MO. "They think that an injection will cure all ills. In fact, some of the corrupt government medics at the rural medical centers sell an injection of sterile water. They make a bomb."

"There is a medical service then?" asked David.

"Yes, sort of. There is a good hospital down in Aden for civilians and the government has set up primary medical care centers up country. Those who run them know very little and many are corrupt. One of my jobs is to inspect the ones in this area. I'll take you with me next time I go."

"Thanks," David replied, "that sounds interesting."

"Well, if I'm not here, then it's your job to do the inspections for me," Cpt. Dennis went on. "Now let me show you something."

The next patient was a tall Arab soldier who according to Mohammad's translation felt ill, had a headache, and whose body ached. The MO sat him down and through Mohammad asked him to open his mouth and put out his tongue. A thermometer was then put under his arm. "Don't put it in his mouth, David," the MO said because he'll chew it." The soldier looked ill and his tongue was furred. He had a temperature of just over one hundred. His mouth still remained open and his tongue hung out. The poor thing looked quite ridiculous. "Notice, David, that he does not close his mouth unless you tell him to do so. These men are very simple, primitive possibly, and obey every order without question. You have to tell or show them everything, even how to take their medication. It is always better to give their medication here in the center. If you don't they may not take it, or they may sell it and come back for more saying they lost it. If you give them pills make them drink water. If not they may spit it out when they get outside"

It was clear that the soldier had flu' and was feeling ill. The MO explained that many of the Arab soldiers came from villages miles

141

away from civilization and had never come across influenza before and had little resistance to it. It did not mean that they were not tough but that European diseases attacked them easily. Codein three times a day and keeping warm worked wonders. He would be fine within three days. Cpt. Dennis explained that modern western drugs worked amazingly on these people as they had no built-in resistance inherited from parents as westerners have.

The sick parade went on and on with Mohammad translating and Cpt. Dennis using some Arabic phrases he had picked up in the course of his duties. Much pantomime was used to discover exactly what was wrong and at times it became hilarious. So many of the soldiers had simple colds and a headache and were not really ill. They just wanted time off.

"These guys are not really lazy as we would define it," Cpt Dennis told David. "They are not used to sustained work. It's not part of their culture. They do a job that needs to be done and then they sit around until the next one is needed. The military keeps them working all the time and they find it difficult."

"It makes running an army a problem, I suppose," observed David.

"Yes. They are fighting a different culture all the time. They make good terrorists but poor regular soldiers," Cpt Dennis went on.

"Mohammad told me he is Yemeni," remarked David. "I thought they were our enemy and we were here to fight them?"

"True, but many of these troops are from the Yemen and not from the Aden Protectorate. They will fight for whoever pays the most."

"It's difficult to know who to trust then," observed David.

"Exactly. Did you notice the stores compound as you came to the medical center?" Cpt. Denis asked.

"Yes."

"Well, a few weeks ago about sixty empty jerry cans (3) disappeared from inside the compound. They are worth a lot on the black market. You know how those cans rattle when empty. The place is guarded with armed guards day and night and the fence patrolled. The wire was not cut. Nobody saw or heard a thing."

"It's almost unbelievable," commented David. "Inside job?"

"Most likely but nobody is telling. The colonel moved the soldiers concerned to another unit but there is not much more he could have done. That is why Mohammad sleeps in the medical tent. He has been told that it is his responsibility and if anything goes missing, he will be blamed. Hang on to those keys corporal and don't let anyone else handle them."

It was nearly eleven o'clock before the sick parade was over. Just as the MO was about to leave a civilian was brought into the center by one of the guards at the gate. Apparently, the colonel and political officer encouraged a certain amount of civilian work as it promoted good local relations. The man who arrived was in shirt and 'footah', a sort of skirt round his waist made of a single piece of cloth. He had a dirty cloth wound round his head. He complained of a headache. On sitting him down and removing the cloth the MO showed David a form of primitive medicine used in that area. On his forehead and on the back of his scalp were burn marks where he had been branded. It had been purposely done, the MO said, using the theory that the pain of the branding would counteract the pain of the headache. "Sometimes," he said, "they tie a piece of string tightly round the head to counteract the pain of the headache." The man had no temperature so was given two aspirin and escorted away. "It could be his eyes," offered the MO, "but getting him tested and then wearing the glasses will be a real problem."

It became clear to David that things were very different in this part of the world. The ancient cultural and religious traditions that were ingrained into the community made change very difficult. For instance, Cpt Dennis told him that no matter how ill or how anxious an Arab is to have an injection he will not permit it in his bottom. He just will not lower his trousers and show his rear. (4) The injection has to be given in the deltoid muscle of his upper arm and a long course of treatment could be a problem. He demonstrated this with a patient who asked for an 'ibra'. "Tell him ok Mohammad and to lower his trousers so I can put it in his bottom."

Mohammad translated. There was a look of horror on the man's face. He shook his head. "*La*, la," he said meaning 'no, no.' and left the medical center as quickly as possible.

Poor man. Let us hope he did not hear the laughter that ensued in the medical tent.

Around midday David returned to his camp. Lunch was at one o'clock and then, apart from the guards, most people had a sleep in the heat of the day. The contrast in temperature from day to night was quite amazing. Tent flaps were up during the day to allow the breeze, which seemed to be always present, to cool the tent, and at night the flaps were down and blankets piled on the bed. Even Nobby found some shade and dozed.

Abdullah collected him at five fifteen for the evening sick parade. It was not busy and he was just completing a new dressing on the leg of an Arab soldier when the Colonel walked into the medical tent. David quickly came to attention as he was on his knees doing the final bandaging.

"At ease, corporal," the colonel said sitting himself in one of the chairs. "This is an informal visit. Carry on with your work."

David finished the bandaging, got Mohammad to tell the soldier to report the following afternoon, and then stood in front of the colonel at attention."

"At ease corporal Earl. Sir down," the colonel said pointing to one of the chairs. "Thought I'd introduce myself and see how you're doing. Everything ok?"

"Yes sir, fine sir," David replied rather nervously. He's never actually talked to a colonel before. They were like gods and he had only seen them from afar whilst on parade.

"You'll find us informal here, corporal. We're a small community so we get on with our job with the minimum of formality. There are only a few British here as you will have discovered and they are mostly specialists like yourself."

David was about to reply, "I......."

"Oh, yes, I know all about you corporal. You're a bright lad. You are one of only a few RAMC National Servicemen who are able to achieve high qualification during their service. Very impressive. Do you intend to become a doctor?"

"No sir, I want to be a priest," responded David.

"Well, well," went on the colonel. "A priest. What denomination?"

"Church of England, sir."

"Where are you intending to study?" the colonel asked.

"King's College, London University. I've already been accepted on the B.D. course.

"That's good to hear," he offered. "Not a university man myself. Sandhurst. (5) Not all that good at school. Didn't like it much. Better at sport." He got up. David quickly got to his feet. "Welcome to the unit." He thrust out his hand. David hesitated and then shook hands. He came up to attention. "Carry on corporal," the colonel said and was gone.

David was a little put off balance. The colonel had come to see him and not the other way round. For the first time during thirteen months of service someone had said something complementary to him instead of him being shouted at.

He was brought back to reality when Mohammad said, "Colonel good man."

That night the Yemeni communist tribesmen sat in the hills and decided that the British deserved to lose their sleep. Sometime after midnight, machine gun tracers shattered the silence, and not long after the big guns at the back of the camp opened up and pounded the hills opposite. David woke with a start thinking it was thunder. He had not heard or seen the tracer bullets come from the opposite mountainside but the guards had. Corporal Bennett had been summoned and must have left silently as the gun crews mounted a barrage of fire. Bob McKinnon and Andy Finn took David outside to watch. "Come an' watch the fireworks David as we'll n' get much sleep tonight," Andy told him. They put their greatcoats over their pajamas and a blanket over their shoulders and watched from behind a pile of sandbags near the cookhouse. The gunfire was deafening in spite of them being some way from where they crouched. "They're rotten shots and in any case they're too far away," Bob yelled in a lull in the firing. "They do it to annoy us. To let us know they're there."

The large guns soon got their range to where the tracer bullets crossed the valley like a line of sparks from a child's firework. It was pretty if you didn't know what they were and how lethal they could be. The shells burst into the mountain and in the moonlight you could see the black debris smoke out from the impact. "The buggers only fire when there's a good moon," yelled Bob. "Don't know why. Maybe because they can't see us else."

"It's quite a sight," yelled back David who had never experienced this before.

"Ay, suppose so," voiced Bob, "but it ruins m' beauty sleep." There was a lull in the firing and then tracers came from a different spot. "Ach they keep movin' their positions," commented Bob loudly forgetting the lull.

"Cat and mouse," added Andy.

"Do they ever kill anyone?" David said loudly as his ears had become affected.

"Who knows," replied Bob. "We don't go and look and they certainly wouldn't tell us. Bloody heathens."

They watched for about a half hour. Suddenly there was quiet. "They're gone, the little sods," remarked Bob. "Come on let's try and get some sleep. They'll not be again tonight." For David sleep took quite a while. He heard Ian Bennett return muttering something obscene under his breath about what he would do if he caught an Arab. Then there was quiet. The howl of a dog could be heard in the distance. Bob lurched over onto his other side. 'This was real army life,' thought David. 'Quite different to the hospital, and quite different to the Yorks and Lancs. Guns and bullets.' Then he thought of the danger. 'Bullets can kill.' The enormity of the situation suddenly hit him. 'Danger is around the corner. But God will protect me.' It took him what seemed an age before sleep came.

Chapter 11

One morning after sick parade Captain Dennis took David in his Land Rover to the city of Mukkeras, which was some four miles from the camp. The area was not considered dangerous so there was no need for an escort. It was ruled over by a friendly tribal leader who quickly put dissidents in his jail. A good example of his control was illustrated by a local boy of about sixteen whose legs were shackled with iron rings. The boy hobbled about by lifting the fastening chain with a piece of string, thus stopping the rings chafing his ankles when he walked. David asked what crime the boy had committed and was told none. His father, however, had sided with the Yemeni opposed to the British and talked of joining them. To prevent him leaving the area and to punish the man, his first-born son had been prevented from walking and the father would not leave him behind. Thus, the father and the family was punished. It was rough justice but it worked

As they got near the city, it was clear that the barren land was inhabited as there were green paddy fields, vegetables growing, clusters of date palms and the occasional farmer working in the fields. It was all watered through a system of irrigation channels. The water came from ancient wells dug deep into the ground and serviced by a camel or a donkey. A primitive shadouf, consisting of a goatskin bag on the end of a rope over a pulley at the top of a high post, is lowered down into the water. The other end of the rope is tied to a hobbled camel. With the posts are a series of wooden pulleys, water is hauled up as the camel or donkey walk away from the well. The contraption looks fragile but does the job. A farm laborer tips the loaded skin into a trench as it appears over the side of the well, and the water runs down the channels to irrigate the fields. The beast walks towards the well again and the skin is lowered. It is a slow, but effective process, and slavery for both beast and human.

The town looked so romantic in the distance, shimmering white in the heat with its mud-brown outer wall and inside tall, white buildings of four or five storys. Surrounding each building was a walled courtyard with shady garden. Between the buildings were narrow lanes providing cool for the pedestrian. The buildings were built of whitewashed mud and timber and had glassless slit windows with decorated cornices in intricate Arabic patterns that made the architecture so appealing. Palm branches tumbled over garden walls indicative of cool, shady gardens perfumed by exotic aromatic plants. Perhaps there were trickling fountains and brilliantly colored birds.

There it sat looking like something out of 'The Arabian Nights'. (1)

As they got closer the illusion was soon shattered as the smell of open sewers, dirty lanes and unwashed humanity was the first thing that reached David. He had a sensitive nose and must have grimaced because Captain Dennis glanced at him and smiled. "Smell it? Illusion shattered, corporal?" David nodded. "It happened to me the first time I came here. Looks wonderful but as you approach...." Now he could see that chickens and goats wandered the streets eating the rubbish that the occupants of the houses threw out of their doors or over their garden walls. It was like a town in the 16th century, not the middle of the 20th century. There were one or two little shuttered openings in the wall that were shops selling an assortment of goods from food and clothes to kitchen utensils. Flies were everywhere and settled on anything and everything. A few boys in their early teens stood around the filthy shops, but the rest of the populace must have been at home or working in the fields as the place was deserted.

The boys were naked except for a swathe of cloth round their waist and their feet were bare. Their legs were caked with mud and their dark brown bodies dusty. They were handsome with good features, large dark brown eyes and rich black hair, which, alas, was mattered and very dirty. They looked strong enough and yet they could not have been particularly well nourished living in such an environment. Captain Dennis explained to David that these were children of the poor who did not have land or a well and had to buy water from those who did. They could not afford water to wash, only to drink, and as their loin-cloths became dirty and torn they fell off and a new piece of cloth, often stolen, replaced it. They lived on a primitive diet of rice, dates and perhaps a few vegetables, and yet appeared to be reasonably fit. They were generally immune to the disease around them, but easily succumbed to the diseases brought by Europeans and frequently died of pneumonia if not treated.

There was no schooling for these boys, except perhaps what they got in the mosque, and they were destined to poverty all their lives. Some left their home and went to Aden or Sala'a, the capital of the Yemen. Even then, because they had no education, they usually succumbed to crime or prostitution. The girls were never seen as they stayed in their home and helped with the rest of the family. Some got married at an early age, if they were attractive, others were sold and became domestic servants of the better-off farmers and were often physically and sexually abused.

Skirting the main part of the town and avoiding the main gate, their driver took them to a building standing apart under the shadow of the city wall. It was painted white with blue shutters and looked in better condition than the rest of the town's buildings. This was the government medical center where the people from the city and surrounding area could benefit from western medicine. The wooden door was wide open and three old men sat on a bench outside, their heads and faces covered to protect them from the burning sun.

Inside the building were white walls, two wooden tables, a cupboard and two chairs. On a second table was a pottery bowl of water for washing hands and a not-so-clean towel. The 'hakim' or 'doctor' as the local people called him was a young Arab of about twenty-eight years of age. "*Salaam Alicum*," he said bowing low. He seemed rather subservient and David did not like the way he did not look at you directly. He was too smooth.

"*Alicum* salaam," Capt. Dennis replied. "*Khefalak alium?*"

"*Zein*," replied the man who was introduced as Talal.

"He speaks English," Captain Dennis told David, "don't you Talal?"

"Yes, sir captain," replied Talal. "I speak little English."

The captain then spoke very slowly and in simple terms. "How... is... the... work? Do.. you... have... problems?"

"Work .. good. No many... patients. Like... old.... ways. Go....hakim.. in... town," he reported.

"It... take... many.... months, Talal. People... not... trust... new ...medicine. Be...patient. *Shwey, shwey*," advised the captain.

Tea in little glasses suddenly appeared, brought by a beautifully slim boy of about sixteen with laughing eyes. Talal introduced him as his cousin. "Probably his boyfriend," the captain whispered to David who did not quite understand the implication. The tea was strong and sweet and very refreshing. When they had drunk up, they turned their glasses upside down on their saucers to show that they had finished. This was a sign of courtesy as was the offering of tea to a visitor. Now the formalities had been completed the captain inspected the day book and the drugs cabinet. Everything seemed to be in order. The place was clean and well run. They made their farewells and drove off back to the camp.

"The place seems fine," David remarked on their way back.

"Seems to be," the captain replied. "But I don't trust the man. He's too smooth, too subservient. There are stories of him selling treatment, particularly injections, but we can't catch him."

"He seemed a bit of a smoothy," David observed.

"Very smooth. He's known to like young boys. Mind you lots of Arabs like young boys. It's part of their tradition. The women are taboo until they are married and so they go for the boys. That boy helper is no more his cousin than I am."

David's eyes opened wide. "I never knew that. Isn't it illegal out here?"

"Yes, according to British law. But who is going to try to enforce the law here? It's part of their culture. Been doing it for thousands of years. If someone tried, they would all clam up and deny everything unless you caught them in the act, and they're too clever for that."

When they got back to camp, Mohammad was waiting with a local tribesman whose left arm was bound with a dirty piece of cloth. However, the man was someone of importance as his shirt and *footah* were comparatively clean compared with the usual locals and of a good quality. He had a broad leather belt round his waist and in it a curved dagger some ten inches long in a silver sheath. David could see that the sheath was finely worked with intricate patterns and that the hilt of the dagger was made of ivory. Mohammad explained that he was the brother of the local ruler, had been in a fight and been slashed with a knife by his adversary. He wanted us to treat his wound.

He was taken into the medical tent and seated at the side of the treatment table with his left arm on the table. The bloodstained rag round the wound was removed to reveal a four-inch gash. It was not deep and miraculously the artery had been missed. David prepared a tray with sutures, needle, forceps, syringe of pain-killer and the usual cleaning materials. The MO slowly cleaned around the wound and then injected the pain-killer. It took a little while to act and then he further cleaned the wound. "You see, corporal," he explained, "out here they often put hot sand into a wound to stop the bleeding and to heal it."

"But that surely introduces bacteria from the sand. It can rarely be hot enough to cauterize," observed David.

"Exactly," continued the MO. "To some extent it does help to stop bleeding, but as you say, it introduces other nasty things." By this time he had cleaned the wound and began to put in the first stitch. The Arab never flinched even though there must have been some pain in the process. "It's what we were talking about earlier, 'tradition'. They've been doing this for centuries and to some extent it works. The bleeding stops and if you're lucky there is minimal infection. If you happen to put in really dirty sand and the patient is weak then all kinds of infections may result and that could send you off to Allah."

Captain Dennis was quite skilled and twelve neat stitches were soon in and the job looked really tidy. David put a sterile dressing over the wound and bandaged it carefully, sealing it round with sticky tape.

"We'll give him an injection of penicillin, corporal," the MO told David with a smile on his face. "We won't insult him by suggesting it goes into his bottom. He's too important."

David gave the injection of penicillin into the man's deltoid muscle. It was difficult to give as the powder had to be mixed with sterile water and tended to become thick and to set like concrete, unless handled quickly. David was very deft at giving this form of injection as he had administered many hundreds of similar injections in the hospital in London. The MO watched and commented, "Well done corporal. Nasty stuff that. Gives me problems at times."

And so, with a feeling of achievement and elation, David was driven off to tiffin. Only the Sister Tutor at Milbank Hospital had ever offered any praise for David's efforts and now Captain Dennis. Everyone needed a pat on the back once in a while, but in the military praise was a rare commodity. Motivation tended to be by bullying and fear. Negative reinforcement works for a while but in the long-term is destructive. This was another example of archaic methods used by the military. What might have been right in the Napoleonic Wars (2) was no longer acceptable in the mid twentieth century.

It came as a shock to David one day when the guards brought two veiled women and a boy of about eighteen to the medical center. It was almost time for tiffin and the MO was just getting into his vehicle. Usually women were rarely seen and when in public their husbands were always with them. One woman was heavily pregnant. Through Mohammad, it was explained that the pregnant woman's husband worked in Aden and that the young man was her brother and the other woman her mother. The woman had started with labor pains but they had stopped.

"Ask her how long ago the pains stopped," Captain Dennis told Mohammad.

"She say one week," Mohammad translated.

"What?" asked the MO. "Ask her again, Mohammad."

"One week, sir," came back the reply via Mohammad.

Captain Dennis looked alarmed. "My God," he uttered. "We better have a look at her. Get her on the couch Mohammad."

The brother and mother got the pregnant woman on her back on the couch with her legs drawn up. As a Muslim it was more polite to let her family touched her unless it was really necessary. "Ask them if I can examine her," directed the MO.

"*Iowa*," came the reply. "Yes."

"Tell them to expose her down below," suggested the MO.

The old woman pulled back some way her daughter's voluminous and very dirty skirts whilst the MO put on a rubber glove ready to undertake an inspection. When he looked closer he gasped. "Oh, no."

he said quietly. "Poor thing. Come and look corporal."

David went forward and there protruding from the vagina was the dome of a child's head. By no stroke of the imagination could the baby be alive.

"You see corporal, the head is stuck. In a good hospital there are instruments to aid such a delivery. Here there is nothing. Unless something is done very quickly this woman will die. We have to get her to hospital as soon as possible."

The woman was lucky as there happened to be a flight on the airstrip that day. Captain Dennis was all action. "Is the aircraft still on the ground, Mohammad? Go and look. If it is then get Abdullah to drive down and tell the pilot to hold the plane. Tell them it's the colonel's orders."

Mohammad returned to say it was still there and Abdullah had gone to hold the flight

The woman and her relatives were informed of her grave condition and that she must go to hospital at once. There was the possibility of a flight and treatment at the government hospital was free. They assured the MO that they would go and made many salaams. "Keep them here, corporal, for ten minutes," he told David. "I'll have to ok this with the colonel and also send a signal down to Aden. If I don't return that means good news. I'll send Abdullah back in the Land-Rover and then you can bring them to the plane. I'll get another vehicle and see you there. It will save time. We don't want to hold the plane for long."

With that he was away, shouting for his driver as he went.

It all worked as planned. After ten minutes the woman was eased into David's vehicle and driven to the plane where the MO joined them. David had already explained to the pilot the nature of the emergency and assured him that there would be no birth on the flight. A signal had been sent to Aden and an ambulance would be waiting to whisk the woman away to hospital.

David and Captain Dennis watched in silence from a safe distance as the small plane bumped along the runway and rose into the air leaving a huge dust cloud behind. It was a beautiful day with a clear blue sky and they followed the silver aircraft as it disappeared into the distance and the dust settled back over the desert.

After a while, as they walked back to the parked vehicles, David asked, "Will she make it, sir?"

"I hope to God she does, corporal," came the response from Captain Dennis. "I've been told of difficult births by my father - he's a doctor too – but I bet he's never seen a case like this." He thought for a while. "Maybe she'll make it if her system has not been poisoned. They have the equipment in Aden. What a life these people lead. There is little concept in the developed world of what others have to suffer."

It must have been about three weeks later that the Political Officer for the area heard that the woman was alive and well but, of course, the baby was lost.

One morning a few days after the incident with the pregnant woman, Captain Dennis suggested that David might like to join a convoy of four armored cars and some Arab troops that were going out on patrol. The idea was to 'show the flag' and make people aware of the existence of British forces in the area. "I don't know if you know it, corporal, but we are on a plateau some eight thousand feet above sea level," he said. "The patrol is going as far as it can to the very edge of the plateau. It's a wonderful sight. I've been and I'm sure you'll find it exhilarating."

"Thank you, sir, but….." David commenced as he wondered who was going to do the sick parade.

"Don't worry, corporal. I'll do the sick parade with Mohammad's help. It's a chance in a million for you as they don't often go that way. Go. It's an order," he smiled.

Riding in Andy Finn's armored car was an experience. However, it was something not soon forgotten, as the bruises from being thrown about inside the vehicle as a result of the uneven track remained for a week. Whatever discomfort there was, David was more than compensated by what he found at the end of his journey. The scenery on the way was spectacular. He spent much of his time looking out of the conning tower of the vehicle. There were high mountains always in sight and in the early morning they were shrouded in mist, which disappeared as the morning heat caressed the rocky terrain. The wadis were generally quite wide, and in one or two places water dripped through the rocks to form black ponds, goodness knows how deep. Nearby these were fields, always carefully irrigated and manicured by the grazing sheep and goats, but no sign of man. In other places, there were huge boulders scattered as if some giant had thrown them around in anger. Here and there a thorn bush would be miraculously growing out of what looked to be solid rock. Large lizards could be seen sunning themselves on flat rocks, and once a two-foot-long silver snake glided into the shadows, disturbed in its sunbathing by strangers.

At one moment the leading vehicle seemed to be slowly climbing a slight rise, and then suddenly it disappeared, dipping downwards to where there was the edge of the plateau right in front of them. It was a strange experience, rather scary really. The four armored cars pulled up side by side, and the other vehicles with troops in them, parked behind. Everyone got out. Pickets were posted just in case of an attack.

The edge of the plateau was about a hundred yards away with an eight thousand foot drop to the desert below. There were shouts of amazement from some who had not been before, including David. The view was quite beyond belief as it was possible to see some forty miles as the air was so clear. On the floor below was a silver-gray road snaking away into the distance to Dhala, making its way round what looked like small molehills, but in fact were hills around one thousand feet high. The orange-red sand stretched for miles and the shadow of the hills changed its color from orange to purple and to black. It was like the film set of some bad space movie, and yet here it was in reality.

Tentatively, David walked to the edge of the plateau, as there was an actual edge of hard rock, which some brave souls actually sat on for a photograph, dangling their feet into space. David was not so brave as he did not like heights, and it was almost a sheer drop. He did get Andy to photograph him giving the illusion of being on the edge, but he did not trust himself. Drops seemed to draw him forward. His father was fearless and used to stand right on the cliff edge at home when they were on holiday, whilst he would shout all kinds of warnings, but to no avail.

They had brought packed lunches and there was no rush to return. An eagle soared in the distance using the thermals to glide in front of the rock face, and some of the lads threw bits of bread into space hoping to attract it. Strangely, some seagull swooped after the bread. On closer inspection, David could see that the drop was not sheer in places. There was a goat track some way away winding up from the floor below. If there was a track then something must come up. Was it man or beast?

The answer came later in the afternoon whilst they were resting. Suddenly there was a click of rifle bolts and a shout of "Halt". Everyone got up to see one of the Arab guards, who had been posted as a lookout, pointing his rifle at a little old man and his two pack donkeys. The man had black, shiny skin and his skinny frame was covered with a minimum of clothing. A long ginger beard, died with henna, covered much of his face and a large knife in a leather sheath hung at his waist. There was an expression of bewilderment on his face. Like them, he had not expected to find anyone in this deserted area at the top of the world.

It transpired on questioning by one of the Arab officers accompanying the party that the man was a Bedouin trader who had been down to Aden to buy goods that he would sell up in the hills. He had been five days traveling and it had taken him the best part of a day to come up the goat track from the desert to the plateau. He was very pleasant and accepted the tea offered and then with a smile, numerous salaams and a wave of his hand, he was off. The bedou are very tough people and can walk huge distances without fatigue. A skin bottle of water and dates suffices as food and drink for many days. They mix cocoanut oil and gentian violet dye and rub it into their skin, which gives them the shiny, black appearance. It keeps them warm when the night temperature drops.

David had proof of their toughness a few days later when a Bedouin was brought to the medical tent complaining of toothache. He had a string tightly tied round his head and there was evidence of brand marks on his forehead. The pain must have been great. The MO sat him in the old flight chair and inspected his mouth. The tooth was very badly decayed.

"Tell him that he should go to Aden for proper dental treatment, Mohammad," the MO instructed.

"He say no can go Aden," Mohammed reported. "He want you to take."

"Tell him I am not a dentist. I can take it out but it will be painful."

Mohammad did as he was asked. The bedou jabbered in Arabic.

"He say pain no problem," reported Mohammad. "You take."

"Ok. Set the instruments for an extraction, corporal. We'll give him some xylotox to kill the pain but I don't think it will be very effective," said the MO.

David set up a tray. Both he and the MO were dressed in white medical coats as was their usual practice. The bedou was black and oily and wore a long, colored cloth from across one shoulder to below the waist. A leather belt was round his waist holding the usual knife. "If you hold his head at the front corporal, I'll approach from the rear," the MO explained.

The man's mouth was open wide but as soon as the MO tried to give him an injection he snapped it shut.

"Tell him to open his mouth, Mohammad. Tell him I want to give him an *ibra* to stop the pain."

Mohammed translated. There was as discourse between the two. "He say no injection. Take tooth," Mohammad reported.

"Does he know it will be painful?" asked the MO.

"He bedou. He no injection. He strong man," reported Mohammed.

"Ok," said the MO with a sigh. "As long as he doesn't stab me with that thing around his waist when he feels the pain." He indicated the knife.

"Now corporal, let's try."

The back molar was a brute and it took almost twenty minutes to get the thing out. At one stage a piece broke off and the man thought they had finished. He had to be reassured, put back in the seat, and the work continued. In order to stop the man from being pulled onto the floor, David had to almost sit on his lap. Having seen the comic Norman Evans (3) doing his dentist comedy routine standing on the lap of his patient and tugging, David was reminded of the similarity of the situation. It was so funny really but in this case it was reality. By the time it was all over, the MO was sweating and both he and David were covered in black-violet grease from the body and arms of the man. Their pure white coats were a mess.

The pain for the patient must have been excruciating and yet, the man never uttered a sound throughout the extraction. After washing his mouth out, the bedou salaamed and was gone.

Captain Dennis announced one morning that he would be going down to Aden with the colonel for a week to some sort of conference. The Aden Protectorate was to get its independence and the Colonial Secretary, Mr Lennox Boyd, M.P. was coming out to the colony and would be coming up to Mukkeras for some kind of celebration, so preparations had to be made. David would be on his own and was to carry on as usual.

The first two days were uneventful but one morning a young Arab soldier in his twenties wandered into the medical center and asked to see the MO. David sent for Mohammad who had just gone for a break. The young man was holding one arm behind his back.

"I *hakim* -doctor," David told him. "Big *hakim* in Aden."

By this time Mohammad arrived and was asked what was wrong. The young soldier then brought his arm from behind his back and said, "*Shuft* – look!" The hand was bleeding profusely and three fingers were missing. David got Mohammad to sit the soldier down and immediately put a pressure bandage over the damaged fingers to stem the bleeding. Mohammed translated and the soldier told him that he had been tapping a bullet on a rock and it had exploded. He had the fingers in his pocket.

Again, fortunately, there was a plane on the runway and David raced the soldier down to the runway before it took off. The pilot was most co-operative when he heard the story and said he would radio ahead for medical attention. When he returned to the camp he reported the incident to the Arab Major in charge of the soldier who thanked him profusely. He hoped he had done the right thing. There was no way to deal with the fingers other than by surgery and then it was touch and go if they could be saved. Whether the fingers could be sown on was very doubtful. It was a stupid thing to bang a live bullet on a rock, but people do silly things.

A further incident involved an old couple who arrived on a donkey and had been sent with a note from the Political Agent. Although addressed to Captain Dennis, David had full authority to deal with any eventuality. The note explained that they were distant relatives of the local ruler and that the woman had an infected foot. It would be politic to have a look at the foot and do the best for her as good works would help politically.

They were an unusual couple in that she rode on the back of the donkey and he walked by her side. It was usually the other way round in that part of the world. The man generally was the peacock and the woman his slave who did all the work. Often you could see an old woman bent double, with a huge bundle on her back, walking, while the man rode on a donkey. Perhaps David should have had a prior warning from this deviation from the norm but he was unaware of the signal.

Inside the medical tent David sat the old couple down and asked Mohammad to get their story. The woman had grazed her foot on a stone or glass some months before and it had become infected. The local *hakim* had treated her but the foot had got worse. He had treated her a few times but now he refused to treat her any more. They had come a two-day journey as they heard that British medicine was good. The foot was now so bad she could not walk.

The right foot was covered with a filthy bandage and David had to cut most of it away as it was stuck and muddy. When he opened it up the stench of the infected foot was terrible. He could see Mohammad's face turn green and he was off outside, probably to be sick. To be fair, it made David feel sick, but he had to be professional and put feelings aside. The instep was white flesh and covered in yellow puss and the whole foot was red and swollen. David looked to see if there was a tell-tale line to indicate the infection running up the leg but amazingly there was none. With disinfected swabs and tweezers he cleaned up the foot. It revealed that there was a great deal of dead flesh and the whole foot was hot and sore. What to do? He remembered the MO saying that western drugs worked wonders out there. Penicillin? No, the other *hakim* had possibly used penicillin, which was confirmed by the old man. Why not try something new? He would use the new sulphonomide drugs. As yet, they were relatively untried. Without treatment, the woman would surely die. He wished the MO had been there. He was their last hope and he had to try.

He cut away some of the dead tissue with a scalpel as gently as he could while the old man looked on without a word. Over the area he put sulphonomide powder, then a layer of petroleum jelly net and bound it all firmly and stuck tape over it for safety. By this time Mohammad had returned and David got him to deliver precise instructions for the rest of the treatment.

"Take two capsules every eight hours for the next four days," translated Mohammad. "You must do as the hakim says or treatment not work. Come back in seven days."

The old people nodded their heads. They thanked him with many smiles and salaams. Finally Mohammad and the old man lifted the woman onto the donkey and they rode away. As they rode off David thought of Mary and Joseph. It was just like a picture from the Bible or maybe a scene from one of Cecil B. DeMill's Hollywood epics. (4)

When Captain Dennis returned David told him of the old couple and what he had done. "It's a long shot, corporal," he said. "Sounds like the beginning of gangrene even if you could not see the run of the infection."

The couple did return and when they looked at the foot there was a slight improvement. "Amazing," was all the MO could say. "Keep up the treatment corporal."

The old couple came six times in all. Each time there was an improvement to the foot. It was almost like a miracle.

"Tell them, Mohammad," the MO said, "next time will be the last. Foot is good."

They were delighted and so was the MO. "Do you know, corporal, that was very unconventional medicine but it has worked. Congratulations."

David felt really good but the last time he came he could have wept. The old lady walked at one side of the donkey and her husband was at the other. They brought gifts. All that they could afford to offer. There was one battered and rusty tin of Australian peaches and two live chickens, their legs tied together to stop them running away. To them, it was worth a fortune. David thought of the Bile story of the Widow's Mite. (5) He was so overcome with their gratitude that he had to walk away. Tears filled his eyes and he did not want to appear a cissy in front of his colleagues.

The foot was checked and the woman given a clean bill of health. That was the last he saw of them. He hoped they lived to a grand old age. Their devotion to each other was unusual in that harsh world where women generally were chattels. But it did his heart good to see how love can overcome all boundaries and triumph over adversity.

Chapter 12

Captain Dennis imparted bad news to David one fateful morning. He informed him that a signal from the War Office in London had posted him to the Life Guards in Little Aden. The Colonel had tried to get this posting changed but had not succeeded as they both would have liked him to stay with the unit. "When do I go?" asked David.

"Not yet," Cpt. Dennis responded. "The colonel will prevaricate as long as he can and see if he can keep you. There are things going to happen and he needs you. I can't say more than that."

The first major incident was bound up with the frequent machine-gunning of the camp. Most nights they were fired on and apparently the colonel had warned the Yemeni over the border that if they did not stop he would retaliate in some way. They took no notice. The top brass in the military decided that a town of some three thousand inhabitants, just over the border, would be attacked as it harbored these terrorist gunmen. Leaflets were dropped from the air by the RAF giving notice to the citizens of the forthcoming attack, and suggesting that they leave the town.

Three tanks were flown up from Aden and a huge convoy was mounted on the runway just below the camp. The field guns were attached to trucks, armored cars were made ready, and truckloads of Arab troops were put on alert. David and Captain Dennis with Mohammad and Abdullah followed the convoy in a Land-Rover with a portable field hospital and their equipment. It was quite a sight as RAF jets buzzed overhead. Nothing was done in secret. The whole open preparation indicated that there would be an imminent attack and served as a warning. Innocent citizens were given the chance to leave.

Arab troops erected the medical tent for them just behind a ridge that overlooked the city and beyond this the field guns were placed at the ready. The tanks waited in the background in case they were needed, having rumbled along slowly at the end of the convoy. It was not expected that there would be casualties as there was to be no hand-to-hand fighting. The idea was that the RAF would rocket the town and the field guns would also inflict as much damage as possible. The foot soldiers and tanks were there in case the convoy needed protection.

Once the tent had been set up there was nothing to do except watch the activity in and around the town. David and Captain Dennis settled on a ridge where they had a superb view. The town lay on a flat plane below them and was walled and had the usual tall buildings and the minarets of a large mosque. The surrounding area was cultivated with fields, water channel and wells. There was no sign of movement, not even a donkey, dog, camel or chicken.

The first thing that happened was a voice in Arabic suggesting over a loud hailer that the town surrender and hand over the gunmen. It was clear that the majority of citizens had fled as there was no movement and no response to the request. It was like a ghost town. Later there was some sporadic rifle shots towards the ridge from the towers of the mosque. Nothing more. A few armed figures could be seen moving along the town walls and some sort of defense had been mounted, but that was all. It was just as if some deadly disease had killed all the citizens. Strange and eerie. As a shot rang out from the town, black crows, startled by the noise, fluttered upwards from one or two buildings and then roosted again.

After a little time the noise of jets could be heard and then suddenly they were overhead, six of them, silver in the pale blue sky, going in to attack like determined mosquitoes. As they flew over the town, they released their rockets and David could follow the smoke as they flew to their target. There was an impact, a shower of debris rising into the air and then the noise of the explosion. It was just like slow motion seen in films, only this was real and there were a few real people down in the city. Rife fire could be heard as the jets screamed over, but a rife was no match for these machines. The defenders had nothing more than rifles and a single machine gun. What could they do except look heroic?

Once the jets had done their work, the field guns opened up from behind the ridge. David could hear the shells as they whistled overhead but, unlike the rockets, could not see them until they made an impact. The barrage went on for about ten minutes and the town just disintegrated in front of them. Buildings just exploded, towers swayed and crumbled and little by little the town was being raised to the ground in front of their eyes. Whoever was inside the town stood no chance of defending it.

The attack went on for about a half hour when suddenly a white flag was poked through one of the slit-widows in a damaged building. It was a surrender. Soon the tanks rumbled into place outside the crumbling walls, their guns pointing at the town, whilst armored cars raced towards the city gates which were hanging precariously from their metal hinges. A parley took place.

By mid afternoon the convoy was on its way back to camp having completed a successful mission. The Colonel had received a guarantee that the strafing of the camp would stop.

"They'll be back in a month or too," remarked Captain Dennis.

159

"You can't trust these chaps."

"I thought an Arab's word was his bond," noted David. "At least that's what they taught us at school."

"What your innocent schoolmaster taught and what is reality," observed Capt Dennis, "are two different things."

"You don't like them, do you?" asked David.

"It's not a case of liking, corporal," he replied. "It's just experience. We have trusted them so many times and been let down. Now we don't trust at all. Yes, there are individuals who are trustworthy, but as a race well....."

David felt a little unhappy. He liked the Arabs. They were handsome, proud people with a strong sense of family. Yet he had not been long in Arabia and only knew them from brief contact. Maybe he trusted too much. His mother said he was too trusting and maybe she was right.

"There is a Christian medical missionary living near here," continued Capt Dennis, "who has been here for thirty years. He has failed to make one conversion from Islam even though he is well respected for his work."

"Is Islam that strong?" asked David.

"It's a way of life, not just a religion," replied Cpt Dennis. "You will find that these chaps will milk you of all your western knowledge and eventually use it against you. I've seen it happen."

One morning after sick parade, David and Captain Dennis, with Abdullah driving, went off to the town of Mukkeras to see the wife of the local representative of Aden Airways. She had been diagnosed as having abdominal cancer and the husband wanted a second opinion. As the man was known both to the colonel and the political agent, there seemed no harm in seeing her.

The house where she lived was quite a large one on the edge of the city and had a high wall around it with a gate-house for the watchman. The wooden gate was about eight feet high, very sturdy with hand-made metal hinges and ornamentation. By banging on the gate the house was alerted and the husband, who spoke quite good English, let Captain Dennis and David in. They were taken across a paved courtyard directly to the women's quarters of the house.

In Arab houses, men and women inhabit different areas. They even eat in different places. The men are only received on request and then in a room set aside for this purpose unless, of course, the husband demands conjugal rights. The women are veiled, only their eyes showing, to all but their husband and close male relatives. It is rare for a stranger, particularly a westerner, to be received into the women's

160

quarters, but often there is an exception for the doctor, as there was in this case. David and Capt Dennis were handed over by the husband to one of the serving women and taken to a large airy room decorated in pale green with the walls painted with flowers and exotic birds. It was really quite lovely. Around the wall was a raised platform loaded with silk cushions in various colors. It is here that the women lounged.

The lady in question was at the far end of the room propped up on many cushions. She looked ill. Her head was covered but her face was not. She had black, hollow eyes and her skin was an unhealthy yellow. Her face was painted with ornate patterns, as is the custom, but they could not hide her sickness. In simple English, she made her greeting and offered tea as is the custom. There were four other women in the room whom she said were her relatives. All had covered heads but their faces were open to inspection, which was a great courtesy to their guests.

After the formalities, Captain Dennis asked if he could make an examination of the woman. This was granted and he went forward to inspect her abdomen. With very little effort the cancer could be easily felt. It was large and there were certain to be secondaries as it was clearly advanced. In fact, her palour was indicative that the cancer had reached the liver. The diagnosis took only about fifteen minutes. Captain Dennis was thorough as he wanted to be certain before he pronounced his diagnosis. On completion he thanked the woman for her co-operation and hoped it had not been too painful. He said that he would talk to her husband. They made their salaams and were escorted out of the room.

The news that Captain Dennis gave the husband was not good. He confirmed what was already known, that the cancer was terminal and that possibly other organs were affected. Life expectancy, he thought, would be in weeks rather than months, and he suggested that the morphine that had been prescribed should be slightly increased. The husband was quite shocked. He had possibly been expecting a reprieve. He thanked Capt Dennis and then rushed off to speak with his wife, whilst David and the captain were left to find their own way out. But when they got to the stout wooden gate they could not move it. It was locked. There was no key and no gatekeeper. Try as they may they could not get the lock to open. It was a wooden lock, hand crafted and very old, but no way could they get the handle to turn.

"I know I gave him bad news," whispered Cpt. Dennis. "I hope he doesn't intend to slit our throats."

David was unsure whether he was serious or joking. "It's a wooden lock," noted David. "Quite ingenious really. Surely it doesn't need a key."

They looked closely at the complicated and beautifully crafted piece of machinery and tried rattling it but nothing gave.

"Sorry to get you into this mess, corporal," offered Capt Dennis.

"Perhaps if we bang on the gate somebody will come," David offered nervously. "Then we shall know if they are going to murder us."

This they did and after what seemed to be an age the husband came along. Seeing their plight, he went back into the house and returned with a large wooden key.

"I so sorry," he apologized. "I concerned about my wife. Never thought. Watchman to village." He inserted the key into the mechanism and unlocked the gate. "Thank you, doctor. I sad - the news bad." He bowed low, salaamed and closed the gate.

Back in the Land-Rover on the way home the tension of the moment dissipated and they were able to laugh about the incident. "Phew," said the captain, "I thought we were in there for good. Eunuchs for the harem or maybe our throats cut."

"Surely, sir," David said innocently, "they would never have killed us, would they?"

"You never know, corporal, you never know. The Arab can change so quickly. One moment he is your friend and the next he is willing to cut your throat. A volatile race."

David had noticed this. He had treated a number of Arab patients who had knife wounds from fights. They could be violent with each other let alone foreigners. "I live and learn, sir," he responded. "My teachers at school were very wrong in what they told us. They said that Arabs were very patient and could wait for days for something"

"To some extent that is true. They can wait for days to catch an animal for example, but when the emotions are involved.....that's another matter. Honor and dignity are important as is the family, particularly the mother. Insult the mother and wow..... There's a lot of romance attached to Arabia. 'Desert Song' (1) and all that. It is romantic in many ways. But it's tough, very tough. We in the west just don't understand the culture."

David thought for a while. "I'm glad I was posted out here, sir. It is somewhere nobody ever dreams of going on holiday. It's quite an experience."

And the experience David had a few weeks later was unique and would stay in his memory for the rest of his life. The British Government had decided to grant the Aden Protectorate its freedom and self-government, and in a series of durbars throughout the protectorate, the Colonial Secretary, Mr. Lennox Boyd M.P., would enact the handover in spectacular style. For weeks preparations had been going on in the camp to receive the Minister and his entourage as well as members of the press. A special tented encampment had been built to accommodate some guests over night and the local ruler, or Naib, had erected a nomadic tent for a grand feast. The tent was made of goat skins, and according to Mohammad, had precious hand-made carpets on the floor, and inticate-patterned carpets from Afghanistan on the walls. Guests would sit on cushions on the floor and eat from silver plates.

On the day of arrival, David got the sick parade over quickly. The camp was buzzing with stories. It was said that thousands of tribesmen from all over the area had assembled. The Naib was providing a great feast to which the British officers had been invited. Captain Dennis was kitted in his dress uniform and looked very distinguished. He was also very nervous as he disliked these posh military occasions. He was at his happiest practicing medicine and not holding a gin and tonic and finding small talk at a mess party. There were many guests at the overflowing officers' accommodation and everyone was on edge. The world's press was there and nothing should go wrong.

The Arab troops forming the guard of honor had been drilling for weeks and were eager to perform before this important man from England. They looked wonderful in their flowing colorful headdress, beige shorts and shirts, puttees, boots highly polished and rifles gleaming in the sun. They were formed up some way from the path of the expected plane, and up wind, so that there would be little dust. A red carpet was ready to be rolled out and waiting dignitaries milled about.

David positioned himself on a rise above the camp with Mohammad and Abdullah so that he could see all that occurred. At precisely eleven o'clock a silver aeroplane of Aden Airways dropped out of the blue sky at the far end of the valley and taxied along the runway raising huge clouds of dust. Fortunately, the guard of honor and dignitaries had been placed correctly and were safe from the dust. Portable steps were placed at the side of the plane and the door opened to reveal a medium-sized man in a dark civilian suit. It was difficult to see what he was really like as David was too far away.

As he emerged, the guard of honor came to attention. Mr. Lennox Boyd, M.P. walked down the steps onto the red carpet, was introduced to various dignitaries by the Colonel, and in turn he introduced various people from his party. Then came an inspection of the troops forming the guard of honor.

163

The local Neib was present with his entourage, as David could see his gold-edged flowing robes and those of his party. There was an occasional flash from the sunlight on the sheaths of their gold and silver knives. Out of the corner of his eye to the far right of the runway, he could see many horsemen assembling, maybe two or three hundred. They seemed to have emerged from nowhere and were forming a line across the runway. All were armed to the teeth. David could see they carried rifles of uncertain age and their belts contained long, curved knives, which also flashed in the sunlight. Their colored robes and headdress made it a truly magnificent sight. It was rather like some medieval battle scene at one end of the runway and a modern flight arrival at the other.

When the inspection of the guard was over, at a signal from the Naib, the hundreds of horsemen charged in wild confusion towards the plane, firing their rifles into the air as they came. In many ways it was a fearsome sight as any one of them could have fired at the British party. They raced at breakneck speed and David wondered how they would ever stop. At another signal from the Naib, when they were only twenty feet away, they pulled up their horses in a wonderful display of horsemanship, their mounts raising the dust and prancing on their rear legs. It really was an incredible display and David marveled at the skill of these tribesmen. The Colonial Secretary, seemingly unperturbed, waved to them to show his appreciation and then the party was loaded into a fleet of Land-Rovers and drive off to the officers' mess.

David learned later that the Governor of Aden had been in the party as well as Foreign Office Officials and prominent journalists from various worthy newspapers from the United Kingdom. Journalists from Arab papers and the rest of the foreign Press Corps had been housed in the tented accommodation the day before. In the officers' mess they were provided with tappas and juice. No alcohol was served in deference to the Muslims in the party. The Naib and his party stayed a short while and then returned to their own encampment in order to prepare for the great banquet.

The following day Captain Dennis told David of the banquet and the food that had been served. It had been quite a massive affair with over six hundred people sitting down to eat. There were a number of huge tents made from animal skins and on the floor, as Mohammed had suggested, there were multi-colored hand-woven carpets of exquisite design. Guests sat cross-legged on the floor and down the centre were various silver pots and dishes containing the food. The main dish was mutton and rice cooked with saffron and herbs. It was scooped up from the communal dish with a piece of chapatti-like bread torn from a large pile and thrust into the mouth. Only the right hand was used. "It took a while to get used to using one hand only," reported Captain Dennis. "There were other side dishes that one scooped up in similar fashion."

"And what did it taste like, sir," David enquired with genuine interest.

"Well….better than I expected. I forgot about the hygiene, or lack of it just for once. Then my neighbor gave me a tidbit that he indicated was especially delicious. He produced a piece of what looked like meat about two inches square and dipped it into a green sauce. The taste was quite pleasant like boiled chicken done with a mustard sauce."

David was intrigued. "What was it?"

"I asked and that finished me," giggled Captain Dennis. "It was python meat with a sauce made from its gall bladder. Quite a delicacy I was told."

"Ugh! I couldn't have eaten that," responded David with a look of displeasure on his face.

"Exactly. It is when you know what it is that puts you off. I'm afraid I ate little after that and left as soon as I could."

"What about the other officers, sir. Did they like the food," asked David.

"Some did and some didn't. I suspect that most did not know what they were eating except for the mutton. There was plenty of fruit of all kinds. Had it flown in from India apparently."

"The banquet must have cost a lot if things were flown in specially," David commented.

"Suppose so," remarked Capt Dennis. "These guys look scruffy and poor but many of them are loaded. The carpets on the floor would be worth a huge amount in Europe."

"So everyone had a good time," remarked David with a twinkle in his eye, "except those who were offered python?"

David was glad he had not been an officer and forced to go to a banquet where guests were served such food. That day Corporal McKinnon had excelled himself and produced roast beef and Yorkshire pudding with jam roly-poly and custard to follow. There was beer to drink and good company so what more was required? There were times when it was better to be a simple mortal doing what was natural rather than playing a part, taking on a role. But at the back of his mind David longed to be important, to have status, value in the community, to be someone looked up to.

In life, not everyone had a choice. Those born into high office, kings, queens and princes, had no choice, unless they abdicated, but the taste of luxury and power can be difficult to give up. The uncrowned

King Edward VII of England (2) after his abdication soon found the importance of status, privilege and wealth and the loss of all three drove he and his wife to constantly travel Europe and America to find what he had lost. A man born into the lower echelons of society at least has a better choice; he could use the talents he has to advance to high office or reject ambition and be content. Every man is an island. Whether he remains so is up to him. David was ambivalent about his future. He wanted to serve his God and through Him, humanity. Being a priest was a means of achieving both. There were other ways, of course, but within David was a burning desire to be recognized. His father's constant comparison with his brother, degrading him and destroying self-image pushed him unknowingly into a non-competitive situation. A priest had status, value in the community, respect. It would be difficult to compare big brother with a man of god without some criticism of God Himself.

Chapter 13

All good things come to an end, and the happy time for David at Mukkeras with the Aden Protectorate Levies had come to an end. The Colonel himself came over to the medical center one morning with the bad news. "I'm sorry corporal Earl but I can't hang on to you any longer. The Life Guards are jumping up and down asking where you are. They are the number one regiment in the British Army and what they want they get. Sorry. I would have liked to have kept you and I know Captain Dennis would."

"Thank you sir," was all that David could muster. Things had developed far quicker than he had anticipated.

"However," the colonel went on, "I've done you a favor corporal, to show my appreciation. I'm sending you on leave to Mombassa, Africa, for two weeks at a leave camp. You are entitled to it and you've been up country far too long without a break. The War Office has sanctioned it and so you report back after your leave to Little Aden and the Life Guards. The company clerk will give you all the details. Good luck, corporal."

David could not believe his luck. Mombassa.... Africa. All paid for by the army. All things considered, the Matron at Millbank had done him a favor getting him posted. Not in his wildest dreams did he consider visiting Africa. To get there from the United Kingdom cost an arm and a leg. It was a holiday for the rich and here he was, 933 Corporal Earl D., going off on holiday to Africa, all expenses paid.

It was a wrench to say goodbye to all his friends. The night before he left there was a party in the mess tent for him. Somehow, Corporal McKinnon had managed to wangle extra rations and the Sergeant Major had sacrificed two of his beloved chickens. It was an other ranks party really but the senior NCO's arrived and Capt Dennis put in an appearance. "I'm not really here if anyone should ask," he said and stayed for over an hour. It was all good fun and David got rather tidily as he rarely ever drank beer.

The following morning, feeling a little the worse for wear, and after saying farewell to his friends, he was driven down to the airstrip for the last time by Abdullah. Captain Dennis had said his farewells earlier and Mohammad, nearly in tears, was remaining to help with the sick parade. His kitbag was packed into the aircraft hold and as he started to ascend the steps to the plane, Abdullah threw his arms round David and kissed him on both cheeks. "We miss you Corporal David," he said. "I love you." There were tears streaming down his face as he turned and ran back to where the Land Rover was parked.

"Somebody misses you mate," a burly RAF corporal at the top of the steps remarked.

David smiled. "My driver....and friend."

The last glimpse of Mukkeras as the plane rose into the clear blue sky was of Abdullah driving back to camp, the two camps on the hill, the white officers' mess with its surrounding almond trees, and in the distance, the mountains of the Yemen. David wondered if he would ever see the place again or meet the friends he had made there. Of course, they had exchanged addresses but in reality few ever keep in contact. Most people live complicated lives and the past is overtaken by the future.

The journey to Mombassa in East Africa was like a dream. Everything had been arranged in detail. David stayed the night on the air force base and joined other personnel, both Army and Royal Air Force, on a special flight the following morning. They were all dressed in civilian clothes and not uniform, and the holiday spirit came with the change of clothes. There must have been over a hundred individuals in all. Everyone was excited. The single men were going to the Leave Centre, unless they had arranged an alternative, whilst the families and officers were being accommodated in hotels. There were stewards to serve tea and coffee, and lunch was excellent. One thing David would remember for the rest of his life was the clarity of the sea as they flew down the coast. He pointed his camera through the window and hoped for the best. The water was so clear and shallow that sand-bars, coral reefs and beds of seaweed could be clearly seen in the azure water.

Kenya is around five hours flying time from Aden so the plane touched down in the early afternoon. It was such a contrast from Aden. Both places are hot but Mombassa was so green with cocoanut palm trees everywhere and the lush foliage of many tropical plants. An army lorry came to collect the dozen young men going to the Leave Centre at Nayali. Five were RAF personnel and the rest were Army. All were very cheerful and looking forward to sun, sand and some said 'sex'. David was told by one of his army colleagues that Mombassa was famous for its brothels and that he was looking forward to a bit of black 'cunt'. David was not sure what that meant.

The Leave Center was set right on the beach a quarter of a mile from the famous five- star Nayali Beach Hotel. Some of the officers and the families were staying at this hotel and taxis had been used to transport them. At the Centre there were a series of thatched bungalows set amongst palm trees. Each bungalow slept six people and had its own bathroom. There was a long palm-thatched wooden building, which was the dining hall; a recreation center, table-tennis and a library all staffed by European volunteers; tennis courts and a swimming pool; and there were also facilities for all kinds of sea-bourn activities. A regular hourly bus service passed the center and taxis were available on request. What could be better than this? Certainly it had as many facilities as the five-star hotel along the beach, but without the swank.

After unpacking, David had a wander around the resort to familiarize himself as to where everything was. Two of the RAF boys, who were also sharing the same room, came with him. It was strange, but they all seemed to like each other immediately they met. They were four or five years older than David and regulars. They had been to the resort before. Tom was of medium height, athletic with a mop of dark hair that tumbled around his face. He had a lovely smile, which made a rather ordinary face into something magic. His friend, Archie, was over six feet, powerfully built and blond. Unlike his friend he hardly ever seemed to smile and generally was rather introverted, yet he had rugged good looks and a dry humor, which he used sparingly.

"I wonder what's happened to the others in our bungalow?" David enquired without expecting an answer. They were looking at the tennis courts and considering whether to have a game the following morning.

Tom looked at Archie who was looking very serious. "Probably won't be back until their flight," he responded.

"Oh!" was David's puzzled response. "Why?"

"They're.......well.....otherwise engaged I would think," Tom said winking at Archie.

"Engaged in what?" David asked in all innocence.

"Fucking," offered Archie.

David was flustered. "Fucking! What do you mean?" he asked.

Archie looked amazed. "You know what fucking is?" he said.

"Yes, but...." David had a vague idea what they were getting at. Of course he knew what the word meant but did not see the connection to empty beds.

Archie was just about to make some other crude comment when Tom intervened. "Some lads come here just for sex, Dave. They sign in here and then go and pick up some Eurasian girl from one of the brothels, and live with her for the rest of the vacation. The girls are cheap, rooms are cheap, and they get what they have been missing for a long while."

"But aren't they scared of....of...?" enquired David who was interrupted by Archie.

"Clap?" Archie added.

"Yes, that's it, venereal disease," offered David.

169

"Where have you been all these years, Dave?" he asked. "When a bloke's on heat he doesn't think about clap, only a good fuck. It's later when his prick is sore and he pisses razor blades that he begins to worry."

All this was a revelation to David. Of course he had heard the boys at school talk about v.d. and the blokes in his barrack room made jokes about dicks dropping off, but he had never really considered it other than a joke.

"It's an offence to get the clap in the forces, but not much is done out here as blokes are away from their wives and girls," Tom informed David. "When they get back to their unit the MO sticks big needle in their bum and tells them not to be a naughty boy."

"I'd rather not get it in the first place," David remarked.

"You a virgin then Dave? asked Archie in his direct way.

"Well......" David blushed. "Yes.......I've never gone that far with a girl."

"Don't know what you're missing," remarked Tom winking at Archie.

The dinner gong sounded and David was relieved to be able to direct the conversation away from such a sordid subject on to a topic of more pressing importance, food. As they approached the brightly lit dining room, which was open to the outside garden, they could see that there were only a few tables occupied with maybe two dozen people in all. Each table could seat six. The African head waiter told them that many people went into Mombassa in the evening and ate in the town. He winked knowingly to indicate that there were other reasons as well as food.

After many months of army food and the best Corporal McKinnon could muster, the dinner really was excellent. Wine and beer could be purchased for very little extra cost and that gave the place that little extra status from being a military barracks to a proper resort. There was a choice of starter, main course and sweet all collected from the buffet table. Plates were cleared from the tables by African staff. Coffee could be taken either at the table or at tables out in the garden. As it was their first night, they all decided to have a brandy with their coffee. They went out into the garden with their cups and grunted approvingly from the full and satisfied feeling in their bellies. "That's the best food I've had for months," observed David. "Our cook up country was good but this is...."

"Bloody marvelous," offered Tom.

Archie made no comment. He had bought a cigar and with feet up on a spare chair he was puffing away luxuriously and occasionally sipping his large brandy with a look of utter pleasure on his face.

"Archie's in paradise," David laughed.

"Doesn't take much to keep Arch happy," observed Tom. "A beach, sun and sea and ...."

"Sex," suggested David with a laugh. "They say that is what holidays in Spain are about. Sun, sex, sangria and sand. Not necessarily in that order."

"Old Arch isn't even interested in sex. Just sun, sand, maybe sleep and a good cigar."

"What about you?" asked David.

"Me....well...sun, sand, sea I suppose. Not really bothered about sex. Got the clap once. Never again. We like to swim...... naked preferably."

"Oh!"

"Shocked, Dave?"

"No," responded David. "We always swam naked when I was in Aden. Just climbed out of the lorry, stripped off and in. Bit nervous at first but...Nobody bothered. Got used to it. Quite like the freedom really."

"Good. I'm glad we're sharing. Some guys are very prudish. Archie and I tend to wander around with not much on."

Doesn't bother me," remarked David.

There was a grunt from Archie whose eyes were now closed, but whose lips were still firmly planted round the butt of the cigar.

David and Tom chatted happily for about an hour while Archie puffed away at his cigar and eventually nodded off. Tom told David that he had been married, but his wife divorced him as she was fed up with army accommodation and overseas postings. "Found another bloke with a nine-to-five job in some ministry or other," he explained. "Relieved really. Fed up with arguments. Sex is over-rated anyway."

"Don't you want to marry again then?" David enquired.

Tom thought for a while. He had a far-away look on his face. "No....met Archie and we became chums. That and life in the RAF is fine for me. Everything found, no worries."

David was not sure what to make of this comment. "What do you do exactly?"

"Both of us are aircraft maintenance – electrical. Interesting. As senior technicians we get well paid and have no outgoings like the officers."

The night was balmy with just a slight breeze and waves breaking on the beach could be heard. A mosquito had an occasional nibble, but it was not a problem. From the recreation center the voice of Frank

Sinatra (1) could just be heard drifting across the lawn. The place was really peaceful. Tom looked at his watch. "Midnight. Come on Archie old chum," he said. "Time for bed. He's nodding off Dave. Booze got to him. Help me with him Dave."

They got one on each side of Archie and part carried and part dragged him to their bungalow. He was heavy. The cigar still remained between his lips.

They rolled him into his bed on his back, and Tom carefully slid the cigar from between Archie's lips. It had gone out a long time before. He was out to the world. Between them they got him undressed down to his underpants and Tom threw a sheet over him. "He'll be fine in the morning. Won't remember a thing and will eat a hearty breakfast," Tom told David.

"He's been like this before then?" enquired David.

"Oh, yes. Once in a while it happens. I've known him for ten years. No problem. Anyhow, thanks for the help Dave. Goodnight."

They both got undressed and Tom climbed into bed while David switched off the lights He lay in bed and said his prayers. He thanked God for his trip to Africa, for his new friends and asked for blessings on his parents, brother and his many service friends. "And dear God," he pleaded, "please forgive those who are absent tonight from our bungalow. Don't let them get the 'clap' even if they have misbehaved."

Tom was right about Archie. He was the first up the following morning and brought them a mug of tea, which he had collected from the dining room. It was seven-thirty, a respectable hour for them, and the cup of tea was a real luxury. For David, breakfast in bed had never been considered a luxury. Eating from a tray was uncomfortable and crumbs got down the bed. On the other hand, a cup of tea in bed was magic. "Good night last night," remarked Archie.

"Yes," yawned David not quite awake.

"For those who remember," chipped in Tom.

"I remember everything," Archie went on.

"Oh, do you. You remember David and I putting you to bed? I suppose you know exactly where you put your unfinished cigar?" challenged Tom.

"What? Well....Come on Tom, where did you put it?"

"So you don't remember. Admit it," Tom continued.

"Ok, ok. I don't remember a thing. But come on, Tom, where's the rest of my cigar?" he asked pleadingly.

"Under your clean shorts, if you care to look," came the response from Tom.

Archie dived into his wardrobe, turned over some shorts and there, to his great delight were the two remaining inches of his pride and joy.

At breakfast David had a pleasant surprise. Sitting at one of the tables having his breakfast was Alex. "Good god, Dave, fancy meeting you here. Great to see you."

He got up and shook hands. David introduced him to Tom and Archie and they joined him at his table. "How long have you been here, Alex?" David asked.

"Five days. When did you arrive?"

"Yesterday evening," responded David. "Great place by the look of things."

"Excellent. But I want to see a bit of the country. Maybe get up to Nairobi. I hope to hitch hike. Want to join me?" offered Alex.

Over cornflakes, bacon and egg, toast and coffee, Alex told them of his plans. He wanted to see some animals and in particular Mount Kenya. David was not very keen as he preferred a beach holiday and a rest. His stay in the Arabian mountains was quite enough adventure for the time being. Tom and Archie were also not very keen so it looked as if Alex would be going on his own. Breakfast became a lively affair with David telling some of his adventures, and even the taciturn Archie cracked a few jokes. They all agreed to meet down on the beach later that morning.

The beach was really lovely: miles and miles of white sand with palm trees in some places coming right down to the water's edge. Half a mile out there was a coral reef, which created a safe lagoon of crystal-clear green-blue water, depending how the light struck it. The white surf could be seen breaking over the coral, and apparently, sharks would not come beyond this surf unless they were washed over in a rough sea, so the swimming was very safe. There was a hazard, however, and that was the sea urchin. Unlike the United Kingdom where they are the size of a golf ball, and usually confined to rocky areas, at Nayali, they were about four inches across with long black spines. If you happened to tread on one, the spines break off into your foot and even if removed, and that is difficult, the place goes septic. They were warned to wear flip-flops or trainers in the water.

About three hundred yards from the beach was a diving platform where the good swimmer could dive or just laze in the sun. There were sailboats for hire, and a speedboat for those who wanted to water ski. The young man who ran the beach recreation turned out to be a National Serviceman. What a posting! Some people had all the luck. On the sandy beach were sunshades made of palm branches and numerous sun-loungers available free of charge. Archie, Tom, David and Alex met on the beach and settled under a sunshade. Having come from the

Middle East all of them had good tans, but they rubbed in sun-cream just the same. Many of the other visitors were very white and David assumed that they had flown from Europe, Germany perhaps.

David had brought a book with him and Alex had a newspaper. Archie dozed mostly and Tom kept up a flow of comment about nothing in particular. There was a stall just by where they had entered the beach selling cold drinks, so they were well catered for. Alex was wearing the very small white bikini he had worn in Aden and David felt it suited him perfectly. He really did look like some Greek god. Archie wore tight dark green beach shorts and Tom wore the same design in blue. Both had quite good physiques but unfortunately they were developing 'love handles' round the waist. David wore a new pair of skimpy green trunks that he had bought in Spain on the last holiday with his parents. He wondered if they were too brief, but when he looked at Alex and his brief he did not feel so bad.

Within a half hour they were all in the sea enjoying the warm, clear water. It was quite difficult at first swimming with plimsoles on the feet, as they tended to make you feel as if you were wearing deep-sea diving boots. After a while you got used to it. Surprisingly, Tom and Archie were not such good swimmers for people who confessed to being beach addicts. They could swim but not well. Archie still kept his head and face out of the water, restricting his movements and quickly making him tired. Tom was a little better. Alex was an excellent swimmer, though, as was David, and they showed off unmercifully in front of the others. Alex challenged David to a race out to the raft. They both set of at speed but soon slowed as the distance took its toll. It looked closer than it actually was.

They raced neck-and-neck and Alex got there slightly before David. He had very powerful shoulders to give him that extra pull. They flopped on the matting covering the wooden structure like tired seals, panting from the excursion. The raft was unoccupied and David supposed that few were capable of swimming that far as the tide was in and the raft was at its maximum from the beach. "You're.... a good ......swimmer,.... Dave," Archie panted.

"So are you."

"It was a near thing. Beat you by a neck."

"What a life," David muttered stretching out and lying on his back looking up into the cloudless sky. To just lie here and take in the sun is perfect."

Alex had been sitting looking at David but he too rolled onto his back. "As you say, Dave, what a life."

"Mmm," said David dreamily. "The sun feels wonderful......And that water....so clear."

"Paradise and all free," observed Alex.

"Lovely. I can't believe the colonel actually arranged this for me."

"Really?"

"Yes," went on David. "He said I deserved a rest before I went to the Life Guards and was entitled to leave."

"Sounds a good guy."

"He is. Unfortunately I can't stay with him. Posted to Little Aden. The Life Guards."

"Wow. I'm told they're very particular. All spit and polish."

"Don't let's talk about back there, Alex. Let's pretend we're not servicemen," suggested David. "Millionaires on vacation in paradise."

They lazed in the sun as the water gently lapped at the side of the raft. It was so quiet with the sound of the surf a hundred yards or so away, the gentle ripple of water on the raft sides and an occasional cry of a gull. As David lay on his back looking upwards he heard Alex say, "You look fantastic Dave in those swimming trunks. Suits your body. And what a body you have. So slim and muscular"

"Thanks Alex." David was flattered. "I must say that swim suit of yours is great. It really shows you off to perfection. A little bit brief for me though."

"I like my swimwear brief. The problem is when you have an erection." There was silence. Then he remarked, "Like now."

David looked sideways. Sure enough Alex had an erection. His brief was so small that it was showing through the side of them. He made no attempt to cover it "Huh, nowhere to hid eh!" David laughed.

"Do you know why, Dave?" he asked.

"What?" David asked not really understanding.

"Why I've got an erection," Alex said.

"No,"

"You,"

"Me? What have I got to do with it?" asked David.

"You turn me on. Just like that day in Aden when I rubbed sun oil into you. I get hard looking at you."

"Oh!"

"Does it bother you?"

David thought for a while. "No."

There was another silence. Alex still continued to overflow his swimwear and David could feel something stir inside his swimming trunks. He began to bulge although he fought against it. The next instant Alex leaned over onto his side and put his hand right on David's mounting erection. "That is wonderful, David. So big...... Does that mean you feel something for me?" he said softly.

David was confused. He thought Alex was very handsome. He had thought so the very first time they met at the RAF swimming pool. He had fought certain urges knowing them to be wrong. Men did not get excited about each other.

"I think...you are...very handsome....Alex," he whispered in shame. He moved away from Alex. "But it's wrong for us to be like this."

David did not know what to do. He liked Alex very much and did not want to hurt his feelings. If Alex had only touched his body it would not have been bad but to.... He quickly rolled over into the water to hide his embarrassment and his own erection. Alex followed. They were on the opposite side to the beach and as soon as his head surfaced Alex kissed him and thrust his hand between his legs. "No Alex, no," he spluttered. "You mustn't do this," and David pulled away.

Alex followed. "Ok Dave. But I love you. I've loved you from the first day we met. You are so perfect, so beautiful, and a lovely person."

"Alex, please," David pleaded. "I like you too. You're an Adonis but to.... Doing what you did... is wrong. I don't understand what I feel. I want to.....but it's wrong."

"Fair enough, Dave. But I want to be with you always. I can't stop thinking about you. Come with me up to Mombassa. I want to sleep with you. Cuddle you."

"No Alex," that's the 'last time you ever touch me." With that David struck out for the beach using a fast crawl. He did not look back. He knew Alex was not following as there was no sound of a swimmer in the water.

Alex left for Mombassa the following morning without saying a word to David. Archie had met him having an early breakfast when he collected the morning tea. It was weeks later, at Steamer Point, when David bumped into him. David bore him no grudge, but Alex behaved like a jilted female. He was very formal, polite but cold. There was no warmth in his greeting, no sparkle in his eyes, and he took his leave quite quickly. He had reached Nairobi, been to the Mount Kenya National Park and seen elephants. David never saw Alex again but often thought about him and what might have been.

Every evening David visited the Recreation Center where he would either read, watch the advertised movie, or just talk to the two Australian ladies who ran the center. Both were attractive and in their early fifties. It transpired that thy were friends who had lost their husbands within a couple of years of each other, and with money and time on their hands, they had decided to work their way round the world as is the custom of many Australians. Dolly had dark curly hair that framed her handsome face, whilst Annie had fair hair that she wore rather short giving her a little-girl look. They were both vivacious and real characters, almost like film representations of Australian women. They had opened a dress shop in Mombassa, which was very successful, and they used three evenings of their leisure time to staff the Recreation Center. David found that they were well educated and well informed. Dolly had been a dress designer and Annie had owned a flower shop. They were very smart, always looking chic and cool. David enjoyed their company and they his.

Some evenings Tom and Archie would join them, but mostly David had the ladies to himself. Most guests at the Center went into town for the evening, not necessarily for evil intent, but often to drink in the many bars. This is what Archie and Tom said they were doing, but David wondered. It was not for him to make judgments. David had been sitting in an arm chair on his own in a corner reading on the second evening when Dolly had walked over to him. "You new here, young man?" she asked smiling down at him. David began to rise from his chair. "Don't get up," she said.

"Yes, I came yesterday," David responded getting up from his chair. He liked good manners and was embarrassed not to rise when a lady greeted him.

"I'm Dolly and over at the counter is Annie." They shook hands. "We run the Center three evenings a week. If you want to know anything then just ask."

"Thanks," David smiled. "I'm David, David Earl."

"Where are you from?" asked Dolly sitting in the chair next to him.

"England, Leicester."

"You've got a wonderful tan. Leicester's not a hot place. You can't have been in England for a while. My friend, Annie said to me. 'Who's the handsome young man with the tan. Go and talk to him.' So here I am."

"I'm serving with the RAMC in Aden. National Service. I've been up country quite a while so one gets tanned. I like the sun and sea so I swim when I can."

"You're certainly a 'dishy' young man. If I were a few years younger I'd....."

David blushed. First the lady on the train, then Frank and Alex, and now this rather attractive middle-aged lady. And so the friendship began and David enjoyed their company, the stories about Australia and their loud sense of humor. They too wanted to know about England, as the only place they had visited was London. There was much in 'the old

177

country', as they called it, that they wanted to know about.

It was strange but David had no wish to go into Mombassa in the evening. He had been in one afternoon on an organized trip, but that was enough for him. It had been interesting as towns go. He was more attracted by the countryside than buildings, the port and shops. One evening the center was deserted and David commented on this.

"The boys have better things to do in town than we can provide here," drawled Annie.

"Boys will be boys," remarked Dolly.

"Say, Dave, why don't you go to town in the evenings?" asked Annie.

"Come on Annie," smiled Dolly. "David is a nice boy. He knows exactly what goes on in town. He drinks little and doesn't want to catch you-know-what"

"Got some sense then, our Dave," observed Annie.

"What does interest you, David?" asked Dolly.

"I suppose I'm not really a town boy. I was brought up in the countryside. We live in a village outside Leicester. I like to shop occasionally but really I like nature, gardening, wildlife."

"You like the beach, of course," responded Annie.

"Yes. My mother always says I was born Mediterranean and not English. I love the sea and the beach."

"Much more healthy," commented Annie.

David thought for a while. Alex had put an idea into his head. A safari. Why not try to go on safari and see the wild animals of Africa whilst he was here? Perhaps he would never get another opportunity. He voiced his idea with Annie and Dolly.

"We don't do any safaris from here. They can be booked in town but I think they are quite expensive," pondered Dolly.

"What about that...... You know, Dolly, that man who came in some time ago. Didn't he say he runs a private safari?" reflected Annie.

"Yees. Now what was his name? I can't remember...."

"He gave us his card. It's at home somewhere," went on Annie excitedly. "I'll look it out David and give him a ring.

"That's fine. Thanks," replied David. "Maybe I can get a group together and we can divide the cost."

Annie was as good as her word. She arranged for the man to come into the center a few evenings later to meet David. Jim Macdonald had been born in Kenya of Scottish parents and he earned a living as a tourist guide. He was about forty, tall and broad-shouldered with a rugged suntanned face and red hair. David had spoken to Tom and

Archie about a possible trip and they had collected another young man, Ben, who said he was interested. They all wanted to discuss the trip and talk with Jim, so there was an eager group ready to meet him.

Cost was a limiting factor as none of them had a lot of spare money. Jim explained that they could go down to Mount Kilimanjaro, (2) spend the first night at an hotel on its slopes and hope to see the three peaks of the world's second highest mountain, move on to Moshi and Arusha in Tanzania, see Masai people, (3) spend a second night in the same hotel and then back to Mombassa. On the way they would be traveling through two National Parks and were certain to see animals. He could not guarantee lions and elephants, but they might be lucky. When dividing his all-in price, which included transport, equipment, hotel and food, between four, it worked out within the budget of everyone. They agreed to start two days later.

Chapter 14

Jim Macdonald arrived at the Center, in a large Jeep with his African assistant, at five in the morning, to collect the four excited young men who were assembled outside the Recreation Center. They had arranged an early breakfast as the cook came on duty at four thirty. Dolly and Annie had got up early to see them start off on their trip. It was kind of them, and the boys appreciated it by kissing and hugging them. They packed their kit, which had to be kept to a minimum as space was at a premium, onto a roof rack on the top of the vehicle, eased themselves into their seats, waved goodbye and were off. They drove down the main drive to the road outside. It was still dark, lovely and cool, and the air was full of anticipation and the scent of tropical flowers.

The route took them round the outskirts of Mombassa and by this time dawn had broken and the sun was coming up. Crowds of men were waiting for ramshackle buses to take them to work in Mombassa. Many were walking, as they could not afford the fair. This was how the ordinary African lived away from the opulence of the tourist areas. It was quite a shock. Life was harsh away from the tourist areas, and poverty abounded. There were acres of tin shacks, and huts made of palm branches. Water was from a communal tap, and had to be carried, often long distances. Sanitation was minimal. Open drains were everywhere. Children played in the dirty water, and chickens pecked the effluent. The smell was bad then, but David suspected that as the heat of the day increased the smell would be intolerable.

Not many miles outside the city the metaled road turned into a track of baked red earth. Jim explained that in the rainy season, which would commence within a few weeks, the roads were just washed away in the torrents of water and keeping roads in good condition was almost impossible. The tracks would be a sea of mud, and their position changed depending on the flow of rainwater. Usually people traveled in pairs of vehicles with four-wheel drives. If one got stuck then the other vehicle would pull them out.

After about twenty miles of driving, the lush vegetation of the coastal plane thinned out and the landscape became more barren, with vast areas of grassland as far as the eye could see with the occasional thorny tree. Going was quite slow as the road was uneven and had large potholes in places. The sun was hot by now and they were all thankful for the solid roof of the Jeep. There were canvas sides to roll down, should it rain, but now they were up to provide cool and give maximum viewing.

Around ten thirty they stopped at an inn for coffee. It was a wooden one-storey building surrounded by a low fence of bamboo branches. There was a large parking area of red sun-baked earth, and a small green patch of grass with six tables and umbrellas for shade. The proprietor, a fat man of about sixty, who seemed to know Jim, brought coffee and biscuits and sat on one of the chairs to talk.

"Where ye takin' em lads Jim?" he enquired.

"Down to Kilimanjaro and then on to look for Masai," Jim replied.

"Long journey. Where you from, lads?" he asked.

They told him.

"Want to see animals?" he enquired.

"Yes," they responded and told him the many kinds they hoped to see.

"Elephant," he remarked, "may not be about. They're on their travels by now as the rains will be coming. Could be lucky though."

"Any snakes around?" asked Ben the new lad.

"Like 'em?" asked the proprietor.

"Not really, but I'd like to see one for real."

"Plenty round here in the rainy season. They come in where it's dry. This 'ere place is higher than most of the area and we gets a lot of snakes."

"Are they poisonous?" asked David rather nervously.

"Some are, some aren't. There's one bad one in particular, the spitting cobra – six to ten feet long – stands on its tail and spits at the eyes. Can spit four or five feet. Very nasty," the proprietor told them.

They all shuddered. Jim decided this was a good time to get them moving again.

Lunch came out of a huge picnic hamper that Jim carried. There was cold beer from a cold box, chicken, salad, chunks of fresh bread and butter and fruit to follow. They ate with their fingers from paper plates and drank out of paper cups. It all tasted excellent and there was more than enough for everyone. There was a slight breeze in the heat of the day and the shade of a huge acacia tree made a pleasant resting place. After food they stretched out on the mats that Jim had put down and rested while, Imran, Jim's assistant cleared up and put things back in the vehicle. After about an hour they were off again.

During the afternoon, they spotted a heard of wildebeest. They were rather like gray-black cows with scraggy beards and broad shoulders reminiscent of an over-developed bodybuilder. There must have been several hundred of them. They tended to be rather nervous and would kick and jump without warning. However, it was possible to get up quite close, and they all had a chance to use their cameras. Some time later they saw a herd of beautiful gazelle, but they were nervous and it was difficult to get near. They moved at huge speeds at the slightest movement, and even with his telephoto lens, David found that a good shot was almost impossible. David now knew why the nature photographers seen in the National Geographic Magazine (1) had such enormous lenses on their cameras.

They ran after giraffe, oblivious of the danger of snakes, to get good pictures and were amazed how fast such an ungainly creature could run. At one point they came to a tree with hundreds of hanging nests made by little yellow weaver birds. The noise of the birds was deafening. These small birds literally weave a pear-shaped nest from grass and feathers, suspended from a twig, with the entrance almost on the underside. This is intended to stop tree snakes and monkeys from stealing their eggs and chicks. It was easy to get photographs as the birds took no notice of them.

It was just getting dusk when the party turned into the gate of the "Hotel Kilimanjaro". The mountain, shrouded in mist, had been in sight for an hour or two as they climbed into the foothills. The vegetation had become more luscious and the road had begun to wind instead of being straight as it was on the plane. The hotel was surrounded by a high wall and its main gate was about eight feet high. Jim told them that this was to keep out the wild animals as they were in the heart of the jungle.

Reception was a long, low building which also contained the dining room and the kitchens. A series of thatched bungalows were dotted about a garden, which contained poinsettias, some twelve feet high and in full flower, hibiscus, and beds of red and yellow cannas. It looked really magnificent. These poinsettias were a far cry from the ones bought in pots for Christmas in England.

David was to share with Ben. They were just beginning to unpack when Jim rushed in exclaiming, "Come quickly. The mist has cleared from the mountain. The peaks are visible." They rushed outside with cameras at the ready, and sure enough the setting sun was reflected on the peaks of the mountain that were clear of cloud. They glowed gold and orange. Yet, within minutes it was all over. The sun had sunk behind the mountain and all was dusk. "You're lucky," remarked Jim. "The cloud rarely moves from the peaks. I've brought many visitors here and they saw nothing. "You're in favor lads. It's supposed to be a good omen if you see the peaks." David hoped it would be and set the standard for the rest of the trip.

The food at the hotel was simple but good. The lads tucked in with enthusiasm to steak and kidney pie and apple tart. After the meal, they sat outside on the veranda steps of the main building with Jim and

Imran who told them stories about big game hunts that they had taken part in. Kenya was a different world for the boys, and they were spellbound by the story of the hunt. By nine-thirty Jim suggested they retired to bed as they would be up at six-thirty for an early start.

The ringing of his alarm clock awoke David from a dream: he could not remember what it was about, but it must have been pleasant as he had slept soundly. Ben was still asleep and no amount of shouting would wake him so David had to go across to his bed and shake him. He blinked at David. "It's six-thirty, Ben," David told him. "Time to get up if you want breakfast."

"Uh, no breakfast, Dave. Bring me a cup of tea please. I need another half hour." With that he turned over and went back to sleep.

David showered in cold water, shaved and went off to breakfast. As he crossed the lawn to the main building, he looked up at the mountain and there it was, displaying its peaks with wisps of mist curling round the lower slopes like some artful woman revealing her nakedness. It was so beautiful. 'Another good omen,' he thought.

When Jim heard that Ben was still in bed he excused himself saying, "Nobody is late on my safaris." Within ten minutes he was back with a rather surly Ben, who looked as if he had been pulled out of bed by the hair. Ben ate in silence while the others chattered away quite oblivious to his mood, or seemingly so. He told David later that Jim had stormed into the room crying "Out, out lazy bones" and literally heaved him out of bed. He explained that they could not wait for him as there was a tight schedule and he would be left behind. He insisted on waiting until Ben had put some clothes on and then accompanied him to breakfast. "He's exactly like my father," moaned Ben.

Ben soon came round as they drove down the slopes of Kilimanjaro onto the planes. He was a little miffed when he found that the mountain had revealed herself once more and he had missed it. That day they hoped to see elephants, but as they found the water holes were dry, the herds had possibly moved on so their expectations were not high. However, the main point of their day was to visit Moshi and Arusha on the borders of Tanzania and places where the Masai people could be seen.

The Masai are warriors and cattle herders. These tall people, all over six feet and many nearly seven, are handsome, proud, fierce and immensely strong. As young men, to prove their manhood, they had to go out and kill a lion with just a spear. With a shortage of lions and under government protection that practice had stopped, except in rare illegal cases. They still drink the blood of their cattle as part of their diet and often eat the meat raw. Jim warned them that taking photographs of a Masai could be difficult as they believed that a photograph somehow sapped their strength. Permission was required and that could prove difficult.

Moshi was a small town of mainly wooden buildings and thatched huts with one main street and a white-painted hotel. It reminded David of the sort of town featured in American westerns and he quite expected to see a gunslinger riding down the center of the street. Instead, whilst they were buying toffees at one of the little shops, they were confronted by an ancient Englishman wearing a solar tope and looking like a character from a nineteenth century novel about Africa.

"Where are you from?" he enquired in a decidedly upper-crust accent." Politely they told him and where they were going. Jim kept quiet. "Good show," he responded. By this time his black servant had returned with something in a brown bag. There was a discourse in some African language. The African did not look happy. "I told you not to bring that, boy," shouted the man in front of them. The 'boy' was at least forty years of age. He raised his cane and gave the African an almighty whack on the back. "Take it back boy!" he yelled.

The group was horrified and nobody moved except Jim. He sprang forward and grabbed the cane out of the hands of the Englishman, who had clearly not expected such activity. Jim smashed the cane across his knee and it broke into pieces. "Don't ever do that to an African again," he shouted at the man. "Who the bloody hell do you think you are?"

"I.....I.....," spluttered the man quite amazed at the rebuke.

"Africans are people, not animals to be beaten like dogs," Jim went on very loudly as people began to appear. "We live in the twentieth century not the eighteenth." With that he turned on his heels and the lads followed him back to the Jeep where Imran was waiting.

There was silence for a while. Everyone was shocked. Shocked by what they had seen, and shocked by the ferocity with which Jim had defended the African. At last Jim said, "I hate that bloody type. Old colonials. Time has stood still for them. They still think they are in charge and can treat people as they want."

"Good for you," offered David. "I couldn't believe what I saw."

"Old bastard," remarked Archie. "I bet he's a retired colonel or something."

"Maybe a civil servant," added Ben.

"Or an air marshal," laughed Tony. They all laughed and the tension eased.

"Whatever he was or is," went on Jim in a more rational vain, "there's no need to treat people the way he did whatever the color of their skin."

After another picnic lunch they arrived in Arusha, which was a much bigger town than Moshi, but still reminded David of a western film set. To the south of the town was a huge market selling everything from plastic buckets and beads to dried fish and bananas. The Masai were easily seen because of their height, both men and women. The women had large gold hooped ear-rings which, because of their weight and over time, had pulled their pierced ear lobes down almost onto their shoulders. Their many neck rings tended to make their necks look very long. They were strikingly beautiful in their early years but quite ugly in old age. Both male and female had very black skins that shone like polished ebony. Neither wore much clothing. The men had a cloth hung over one shoulder that covered their essentials and the women wore a loin cloth of bright material and many strings of beads over their bare breasts. The young women had firm, pointed breasts, but the breasts of the older ones drooped nearly to their wastes. Nakedness was no problem for them. The children were as God made them and looked so wonderful with their chubby limbs and rather fat bellies. David felt that it was a pity that Christianity had made nakedness a sin. What was wrong with the human body? It was quite beautiful and in Africa, because of the heat, it was silly to wrap it up like a parcel.

Jim bought a huge branch of bananas from an old Masai woman who was part of a group of women selling vegetables. He asked if they would allow photographs to be taken. They declined, putting their hands over their faces. The boys had their cameras poised and the women began to get nasty calling for their menfolk. Jim decided to leave, quickly, before trouble started and revved up the Jeep, screeching its wheels as it tore from what was beginning to be a nasty situation.

David, seeing the negative response of the women, had climbed onto the roof of the vehicle and lay flat amongst their luggage and unseen. He took a number of photographs before the Jeep moved off at speed, and just managed to hold on with his fingertips. He had taken some close-ups with his telephoto lens. The risk was worth it, as he was to find later.

On their way back to the hotel, just as it was getting dusk and unsuitable for photographs, a lioness wandered across their track. She was a lovely cream color with touches of orange-brown where the muscles rippled along her lean body. Jim slowed the Jeep down but was ready to move fast if she should come too close. With open sides in the Jeep they were completely unprotected and only speed could get them out of a difficult situation. Jim whispered that they were to stay still and silent.

The lioness stopped, looked at them for a while, sniffed the air, and then continued on her way. They were all amazed how large she was and how close they had been. Jim explained that perhaps she had fed and as she did not feel threatened went on her way. "However, you never know with lions," he said. "Unpredictable." And added with a smile that crinkled his face, "Like women generally!"

Kilimanjaro was invisible that night and the following morning. They did not mind as they had been privileged the day before, and in any case they were tired after a long day. By nine o'clock and after a good meal, they were ready for bed, satisfied by an exciting and interesting day. Tomorrow they would have a last look at animals and be returning to the Leave Center in Mombassa. David hoped that Ben would not try lingering in bed. Strangely, as he said his prayers. he thought about Alex and his trip to Nairobi. It was risky hitching his way and he said a prayer to ask for his protection. Would he ever get there and would he see a lion or elephants? Maybe.

As the alarm clock rang, Tom walked through the door and yelled at Ben that it was time to get up. "Can't have the Brylcream Boys (2) being disgraced by the Pongos," he yelled. "Sorry, Dave," he apologized, "but you're not a typical pongo. A Brylcream Boy by adoption."

"Sticks and stones.....," David replied laughing at Tom's genuine anguish at the unconsidered slight.

"It just came out, David. No offence meant."

Ben, by this time was sitting on the side of his bed, yawning. "You're up too early for your own good, Tom," he quipped.

"Archie and I thought of giving you a cold shower.....," offered Tom.

"So where is Archie?" asked Ben.

"Still in bed....sleeping," grinned Tom.

"So what are we waiting for?" asked David. "A cold shower for Archie then."

With that all three ran across to Archie's room but only to find he was not there. He was having a cold shower!

The day went all too quickly. After breakfast they said farewell to the proprietor and his staff, and they were off down the mountain and once more onto the plane of the Tsavo National Park. It was hot and dusty and they stopped a couple of times to drink water and watch the herds of animals roaming the vast plane. Here and there were thorn trees and acacia, shaped like huge umbrellas from the constant nibbling of the giraffe. There were huge herds of deer of various kinds, wildebeest, giraffe, zebra and down by the river they had an opportunity to see hippos wallowing. But there was not an elephant to be seen, which disappointed them. In the late afternoon, some distance from where they were, vultures could be seen circling high in the sky. Jim told them that possibly there had been a kill, or there was a wounded animal and that the vultures would move in when the killer moved off, or the animal died.

It all came to an end with a bit of an anti-climax. The sun had begun to set and they were all tired. David nodded off. Suddenly the Jeep stopped with a jerk and they were back again at the Leave Camp.

"Wake up, David, Archie," cried Jim getting out onto the brown earth in front of reception. "You're home."

David rubbed his eyes and looked around. The others were looking sleepy too but Jim and Imran were bright eyed and bushy tailed. They all got out of the Jeep rather slowly as the long journey had numbed their limbs.

"Thanks, Jim, for a great journey," Tom said offering his hand to Jim.

"Don't mention it, Tom. A pleasure. Glad you had a good time."

"Me too, Jim," added Archie. "Absolutely great. Thanks."

"And me," offered Ben. "Sorry about over sleeping."

"No problem, Ben," smiled Jim. "You can sleep in every day now that uncle Jim is not around."

David offered his hand. "What can I say, Jim?" he said. "The trip has been perfect. A trip of a lifetime. Sorry you couldn't magic some elephants for us, but we can't have everything. Anyhow, the trip and your company is much appreciated."

They said their goodbyes to Imran who was visibly moved by their camaraderie. With that, Jim and Imran got into the Jeep and moved off down the drive with the boys waving as they went.

"There goes an A-one bloke," remarked Tom and it summed it up for all of them.

The holiday was coming to an end with only four days left. One afternoon, as was their custom, David, Archie and Tom were right down along the beach at a favorite spot where they could sunbathe and swim naked without interruption. These were lazy afternoons when they read, swam, slept but talked very little. There was little need to talk and the place, beautiful and peaceful, induced silence. If they were quiet, monkeys would come and play on the white sand close to them. David could watch them for hours as their antics were so amusing.

Tom, quite unusually, broke the silence that afternoon. Archie had gone off into the water by himself. Tom suddenly said, "Archie and I would like you to go into town with us tonight, Dave. What about it?"

David was quite surprised, as they knew his views on the delights of

Mombassa. "Well, I'm not....."

"Oh come on Dave. We only have a few more days left and we'd like to take you for a drink."

David did not want to offend them, as they had been such good companions, so he agreed.

That night they dressed up in slacks and shirt and ate dinner early so they could take the bus into town. Dolly and Annie were quite surprised to see David passing the center without coming in. All three were dressed to kill. David had been given strict instructions to look good for his visit to town, as it was to be special. David felt good in white slacks and a black and white silk shirt. He had sprayed himself with cologne and smelled a million dollars. Archie and Tom were equally smart, and as Archie had craftily said, "Good enough for any old tart."

The bar they took him to, the 'Pink Elephant', was small and clean. The bar was at one end of the room with high stools where they sat. It was all mirrors and pink lights. The rest of the room was dimly lit, and in the shadows were six or seven tables where customers could sit with their drinks and talk. Soft music was playing in the background and the pink glow of the lights gave a rather comfortable atmosphere. The barman, a small, slim African, greeted Archie and Tom like long lost brothers. "So this is your friend, man?" he remarked to Tom and indicating David with an inclination of his head.

Tom introduced David to Pete, the barman. Drinks were ordered. David had a chance to look around the bar. It was not very busy. Two of the tables were occupied with European men and African girls. At the opposite end of the bar itself, a man of about sixty sat with a young black girl. He was far from clean and could have been a merchant seaman. She was making a fuss of him, and he occasionally patted her bottom and said something that made her shriek with laughter.

David was no fool. Innocent yes, but quite able to realize that the girls were there to entertain the customers and that the bar was a picking-up spot. He realized he had been set up when a tall black girls emerged from a curtained opening near the bar and joined them. She obviously knew Tom and Archie and kissed each one on the cheek. She was introduced by Tom as Anna-Mary and sat herself next to David. Archie bought her a beer. "Wa you from?" she asked David.

"England," replied David. "Like Tom and Archie."

"I likes Englishmen," she said rolling her eyes, "so sexy."

"Oh, David's sexy all right, Anna-Mary," Tom told her with a nod towards his crutch. "Handsome too."

"He very ansome," she smiled putting her hand on David's leg.

"She's a nice girl, Dave?" offered Archie.

188

David was not too sure. "Mm....quite nice."

"You like me?" enquired Anna-Mary.

"Of course he does," responded Archie. "Best girl in town."

David smiled and Anna-Mary smiled back. He did not want to be rude.

The old man at the end of the bar had obviously been drinking quite a while as his movements were unsteady and his inhibitions were gone. He was groping the black girl's breasts without shame, and occasionally his hand went up her leg under her skirt. She just giggled and rolled her enormous eyes. Eventually David heard the girl whisper loudly enough for all to hear. "Let's be off to my place, darling." With that the man stood up, waving around like a cornfield on a breezy afternoon, put his arm round the shoulders of the girl, and tottered very unsteadily out into the night.

David was horrified by what he had seen. Suppose Anna-Mary had been with such a scruffy old man before him? It was obvious what Tom and Archie intended. Anna-Mary was to take him to her place for sex. She was quite an attractive girl but........ Did he really want sex with her? Sex with anyone other than your wife was wrong. What if he caught some terrible disease? Maybe someone like that horrible old man had passed the disease to Anna-Mary and she didn't realize. She would pass it to him. However could he hold his head up if he had.....

"I'm just going for a piss," said a female voice. It was Anna-Mary excusing herself in the most polite way she knew. Probably an expression learned from one of her rough clients, maybe even the old seaman.

That decided David. As soon as she had gone, after giving his crutch a grope in a supposed slip, he decided to leave too. "I'm going," he said to Tom and Archie. "Now."

"Hey, what's up, Dave?" asked Tom.

"I don't want her. I know what goes on here, so I'm leaving." He got up and quickly left the bar. It was ill-mannered he knew, but he just had to get out of the situation.

Within minutes Archie and Tom joined him.

"What's the matter, Dave?" Archie asked.

"You set me up," was all David could say fighting back tears.

"We thought you'd like a bit of skirt," Archie observed.

"Sorry," said Tom. "We though you would appreciate .....a little fun."

"It's not my idea of fun, Tom," David responded angrily. "There's nothing wrong with the girl. But....well it's not right."

"Ok, Dave," responded Tom trying to mend fences. "What about going to another bar?"

"No, Tom." David responded quickly. "I don't want sex." He turned to go.

"Wait, Dave." Tom looked troubled. "Don't go. We wanted this to be your night out. Give us a chance. We'll take you to another bar. If you don't like it just leave." He put out his hand. "No hard feelings?"

David took his hand. How could there be any ill will? They had tried to give him a good time. But to him, taking a prostitute was not a good time. Sex was part of love and having sex without love was wrong.

"Where are you taking us?" asked Archie.

"To the Star Bar," responded Tom. Maybe he'll like that." David did not see the wink he gave Archie.

The Star Bar was a huge place and very noisy. It was packed with humanity both male and female, European, African and Asian of all ages. There were few tables so everyone was standing around or dancing to music on a small dance floor. The waitresses were mostly Eurasian and very beautiful. They had the fine features of the European, the dark hair of Asia and a skin soft and golden. Their figures were perfect and their tight dresses showed every curve of their body. There were a few beautiful African girls. David suspected that they had mixed blood as they did not have the big features of the African.

Archie bought David a glass of beer and had to fight his way to the bar to get served. The place was dimly lit, but a huge mirrored rotating globe in the middle of the room sent flashes of light around the room, so that some part of the bar was illuminated at any one time to give a snapshot of the clientele. It was obviously a popular spot as there was little room to move, and little chance to hold a conversation. A juke box played popular discs and everyone was shouting to attempt to be heard over the top of the music. It was like Bedlam, David supposed. He would have liked to have talked but it was too much of an effort. The only way to communicate with Tom or Archie was to get close to their ear and shout. It was not his kind of venue but to please his friends he tolerated it.

After a while of parodying conversation, Archie indicated that he was going to the toilet. He disappeared through a door near the entrance. He obviously had been to the bar before, as the way to the bathroom was not obvious. David noticed that many of the waitresses, as they passed a young man, would touch his crotch or stroke his bottom and smile. The young men in question did not seem to mind, but responded with what David could discern as a cheeky remark. There were giggles from both parties and the girl would go on her way.

After about a half hour Tom began to get restless as Archie had not returned. "Find Archie," he managed to shout at David. With that he disappeared through the same door. David was now alone and after ten minutes he was rather fed up and wondering whether to leave. A hand suddenly came on his shoulder and a voice said in his ear, "Alone?" David looked round to see an African smiling at him. The man was perhaps thirty, broad shouldered, medium height, muscular and quite handsome. His cream shirt was open to the waist and David could see his well-developed pectoral muscles and a chest covered with curly black hair. His slacks were dark green and tight fitting and revealed muscular legs. He had great big brown eyes that sparkled as he looked at David. His lips were full like most Africans and his smile, enhanced by perfect white teeth, was electric.

"Well...I came...with...two friends," he tried to say. "But they...have...gone...somewhere." Shouting was difficult.

Pointing to an open French window the man motioned "Terrace" and for David to follow.

Outside it was cooler and certainly quieter. "I'm Jacob," he told David. "I'm South African but I'm here on business for a few days."

"David Earl from England," was the response and they shook hands. "I'm here on holiday."

"You can't talk in there. Too much noise. Better out here," pointed out Jacob.

"It's terrible in there," responded David. "Impossible to hold a conversation. I didn't know there was a terrace or I would have come out here before."

"Are you alone?" asked Jacob.

"Not really. I'm with two friends. One went to the toilet and didn't come back and the other's gone to look for him. Now he's not come back."

"Ooo," responded Jacob and rolled his eyes knowingly. "They'll not be back."

"No? Why?" asked David innocently.

"Your first time at the Star Bar?" he asked.

"Yes."

"You don't know about this place then?"

"Know?.....What should I know?"

Jacob looked in amazement at David and then smiled. "Let me ask you something," he said. "Did you notice the beautiful waitresses?"

"Yes."

"Well.....they are boys and not girls. What they call in the Far East lady-boys."(3)

191

David was amazed. He could not believe what he was hearing. "But... they looked like girls, beautiful girls. They were dressed as girls....they had....breasts.....they talked and moved like girls."

"Yes, yes and yes," responded Jacob. "But they had a cock between their legs if you will excuse the common expression. Had you cared to look or asked to see, they would have obliged you." He smiled at David and took a swig of his drink. "How old are you David?"

"Twenty-one."

"Never been to a gay bar before?"

"No but..." He did not know what to say. Gay bar. It couldn't be. "It can't be," he offered. "There are lots of women here."

"Yes, of course. Some of the men here swing both ways. They like boys and girls. Some of the girls like each other." Jacob smiled at David again. "I take it that you're not gay, David?"

"No.....no, not at all. Well I don't think I am."

"But you like me? I can see by the way you look at me."

David did not know what to say. Yes, he thought Jacob very handsome just as he though Alex was very handsome. "I think you...are very....handsome, Jacob but...."

"But what?"

"But that is as far as it goes."

Jacob smiled again. "You know, David, you are one of the most beautiful guys in this bar. Everyone wants to know who you are. There are so many guys here hot for you."

Fear suddenly rose up in David. He was in a gay bar, wanted apparently by many of the guys here, just as Alex had wanted him, and he felt sure Jacob wanted him too. What could he do if they....

Jacob could see the fear on David's face. He put his hand on David's arm. "Don't worry David. Nobody is going rape you."

He didn't want to run but he had to do something. "Look Jacob," he said. "I appreciate your honesty. There are times when I have feelings for..... But I know it is wrong. I'm going to be a priest. I'm going to university in London quite soon. I put God first."

Jacob smiled again and put a hand once more on David's arm as if to reassure him. "There are a lot of gay priests, David. I wouldn't be surprised if there aren't two or three here tonight." He smiled with those big brown eyes again. "I wouldn't be honest, David, if I said I was not attracted to you. You are very beautiful with your blond hair, slim figure and golden tan. Just the kind of guy I like. But I respect your position. If you say you are not gay, or you don't like me, then that is fine by me. We gays are not monsters. Most of us respect a person's wishes."

David looked at Jacob whose face really reflected the sincerity of his words. The man was honest and he was certainly attractive. "I don't want to be rude Jacob. You are a lovely guy but I must go. I'm in the wrong place. My friends fixed me up with a female prostitute and that was wrong too. I like you but as a friend…not as …….."

Jacob looked very solemn and quite disappointed. "I'm sorry, David, that you friends put you in this position. Please forgive me if I have embarrassed you. Can I see you again….just as a friend?"

David thought quickly. He would make a true friend he was sure but….. "Sorry, Jacob, but nothing could come of it. I leave in two days and we may never meet again. You're a lovely guy. If I were gay, you would be just the kind of person I would want as a lover. But I'm not gay"

They smiled at each other, shook hands and David left.

As he went through the French window back into the noise and out into the street he heard Jacob shout, "But I still think you are. You're too nice a guy."

Tom and Archie were not in bed when David awoke and did not return the following morning. It was the day before they were due to leave that Tom arrived in the early morning, wearing a T-shirt and boxer shorts only. "I met a girl when I left you Dave. I shacked up with her but the police raided her place. I had to run over the rooftops to get away and I left my trousers. There was quite a lot of money in my wallet, but no identification. I don't carry anything incriminating when I'm…" he explained. David made no comment. He wondered if the 'girl' was really a boy. Possibly Tom and Archie were gay. He would have loved to have seen Tom in full flight across the roofs of a shanty settlement, naked as the day, and pulling on his shorts and T-shirt.

Archie arrived that evening and explained that he had spent the last two days with a girl who had given him a good time for free. David did not believe him, but as with Tom, he said nothing and went along with the story. Tom was quite livid, as not only did he pay the girl but lost the money in his wallet, which he assumed the girl would take. David did not tell them of his conversation with Jacob. 'Let them assume I came home a few minutes after they left. What good would it do to reveal I know about the Star Bar,' he thought to himself. Anyhow, a number of strange incidents with Tom and Archie had now fallen into place and were no longer a mystery. They had been good holiday companions, and even if they were gay, they had not bothered him. Looking back, they had tried to give him signals. 'Was he that innocent or just stupid?' he reflected.

Chapter 15

Little Aden is some ten miles round the bay from Steamer Point and is the home to a vast oil refinery. Its silver cracking towers and huge storage tanks can be see miles away. A flame of burning waste gas, the myriad of lights illuminating all the installations, make it look like some futuristic city at night. It is a vast complex and strategically important. It has its own deep-water dock for delivery of crude oil from the Gulf region, and loading facilities for refined fuel to be shipped to the United Kingdom.

Beyond the refinery, along the coast, are bungalows where the refinery staff live, shops, cinema, churches, a community center, a club and beach. The Life Guards and the Prince of Wales Own Regiment live in single storey accommodation abutting the civilian development but not nearly as grand. It is to the main guardhouse of the Life Guards that David reported one hot, sunny morning. He was in fear and trepidation. This was the senior regiment in the British Army and Her Majesty the Queen's personal bodyguard. What would he find? How would he be treated?

"You can get those shortened, sonny," the sergeant major snapped, pointing to Davis's regulation length shorts.

David had tried to look immaculate for the Life Guards as he had heard they were fussy about dress. Shorts had to be regulation length of three fingers below the knee, according to military regulations. They looked stupid, but that was the rule, and here was the sergeant major complaining.

"Yes, sir," David responded feeling that things could not be that bad when shorts were no longer left to look stupid. He was to learn later that the Life Guards are a law unto themselves.

"Ask the other blokes about length, corporal. They'll tell you what and where to find the tailor. As you're a medic, you're allowed to wear black shoes. Surgeon Major's orders. Corporal Watts will take you over to the medical center and hand you over to Major Benton."

"Thank you, sir," David responded.

Corporal Watts appeared from an inner office, smiled at David and said, "Ok corporal you're sharing a room with another medic. We'll take your kit over and then we'll go see Major Benton."

As they walked between the various buildings, David had the chance to study corporal Watts. He was in his thirties, tall and well built with short brown hair and deep blue eyes. It was his eyes that made him attractive as they lit up his face like a gentle tropical sea lapping a deserted beach. He exuded calmness.

David's room was deserted when they arrived as the other occupant was on duty. It was next to the telephone exchange, and approached through another room occupied by two of the telephone operators. Corporal Watts introduced David to a young broad shouldered six-footer called Rob who worked in the exchange and was having his break. On looking round David found the usual iron bedsteads and wooden lockers. Rob said his kit would be safe while he went to see the major.

The Medical Center was a long, low building with a waiting room, treatment area and Major Benton's office. Behind it was accommodation where two trouper medical assistants lived. As it was nearly mid-day there were no patients and the MO was working at his desk, obviously getting ahead with his paperwork. An RAMC sergeant called Henton took over from corporal Watts and ushered David into the Office.

The major was in his forties, short and stocky with a small gray moustache. He got up from his chair as David saluted. "Ah, corporal Earl, at last we've hooked you. Elusive chap you know. Levy's didn't want to part with you, eh?" He shook David's hand, which surprised him. "Bit of leave as well. Good time?"

"Yes, sir. Thank you, sir." David responded.

"Not been to Kenya. See some lions?"

"Yes, sir."

"My kids will like to hear about that. Two - boy and a girl. Now corporal Earl, we're a medical unit so I keep the military part down to a minimum. Short sleeved shirt, shorts, socks and shoes. You can't work in a treatment room in boots and heavy kit. Sergeant Henton is your senior in everything other than medical as you have your C344. However, he's seen quite a lot of active service. I don't expect any problems. You each will be in charge of a shift as we are on call twenty-four hours a day. Work out the schedules together. Any comments sergeant?"

"No, sir," replied the sergeant.

"Corporal?"

"No, sir," David responded.

"Ok, then. You two get to know each other. Sergeant Henton will introduce you to the other staff. I'll be off home now, sergeant. See you in the morning."

David and sergeant Henton came to attention. The Major waved his hand in a kind of salute and was gone.

"Coffee?" asked sergeant Henton.

195

"Please," David replied. "I've drunk nothing since breakfast and I'm really thirsty."

They wandered over to a nearby building which was the mess hut. David noticed that everything was of the best that the army could supply, and all well painted and clean.

"Charlie," yelled the sergeant. "Any coffee going?"

A pale Catering Corps private appeared. "There's always coffee for you mate." He looked at David. "Two cups with milk and sugar?"

"This is the new medic, Charlie. Corporal Earl. Can't keep saying that. What do we call you?" He looked at David.

"David, Dave....I've been called plenty of other things," smiled David.

"Join the club," observed Charlie. "My boss calls me......no, I won't embarrass you at this stage. Good to meet you Dave. Any time you want anything just ask." With that he was off to get the coffees.

"We have a good relationship with the cooks," sergeant Henton told David. "We do lots of little things for them and they respond by giving us little perks, like coffee. In fact, everyone is the medic's friend on this camp. We're well respected. It's partly due to the MO. He's such a decent chap and really cares about the guys."

"I got good vibes from him," David observed. "He's not really military in his approach."

"No, not at all. He's really a G.P. in Windsor and just puts on a uniform when the regiment needs him. His wife and children are out here as well."

"So he said. Seems his kids like animals."

"And water. Do you swim?"

"Ye..s....?" David was perplexed.

"If you do you'll be their friend for life. They are both like water babies. Swim like fish. Bags of energy. You'll meet them on the beach. Officers have their own beach but the major's kids are everywhere."

"Sounds like one big family," David observed.

"It is," offered sergeant Henton. "The Life Guards are a wonderful mob. Basically, it's run by the senior NCO's, who are excellent. The officers are just around to look pretty."

And sergeant Henton was correct. The Life Guards got on with the job without banging about and saluting, except when it was absolutely necessary. They were highly efficient. Officers were rarely seen except on parades or on some other formal occasion. Many of them were too busy playing polo. An armoured regiment in the time of conflict, they undertook royal ceremonial duties on all the great state occasions in the UK and could be seen mounted on horses in their white pants, red jackets, gleaming breastplates and plumed helmets. Many of the officers had titles and all came from the top wealthy families in the country, as apparently, mess fees were exorbitant. Some had even brought their polo ponies over to Aden and most afternoons had a match.

David's roommate was an elderly private soldier who had been in the RAMC since the Second World War, had got promoted as far as sergeant, and been 'busted' a number of times down to private. He was a drunk and most nights went into Aden to get high and 'laid'. Pop, as everyone called him, was an untidy disgrace but there was little one could do about his dirty habits, except yell occasionally. He kept his clean clothes as well as his dirty attire in the same part of his locker, as well as half-eaten packets of biscuits. Consequently, when he opened his locker door, cockroaches scattered everywhere. David sprayed frequently and yelled frequently but to no avail.

Now cockroaches in Aden are a breed apart. They reach two inches in length with another two inches of feelers and are significantly tame. The accommodation was infested with them and no amount of spraying seemed to drive them away. It could be quite disconcerting at night when you went to the bathroom, switched on the light, and six or eight of these monsters confronted you. They scuttled away and then watched from a strategic point where they knew they were safe from your shoe. After a while you became immune to them and took their interest in you ablutions for granted, but nevertheless, David hated the ones emerging from Pop's locker.

His companions in the medical center were decent guys. Lance Corporal Harper worked with Sergeant Henton. He was a tall, willowy individual who seemed never to have been out in the sun as he was as pale as if he had just arrived from England. In fact, he did not like any physical activity and lay on his bed when he was not on duty. Apparently, he was an excellent curry cook and was often invited into the officers' mess when it was a curry evening to prepare the side dishes. Most people called him 'Harpic' after the cleansing fluid, as they were convinced that he was 'clean round the bend' when there was a full moon. He was easy going and did not mind the title.

The third individual in the team was Trouper Peters, who was a Life Guard loaned to the MO, as he was some distant relation doing his National Service. He had dark auburn hair, freckles, large brown eyes with long lashes and rather feminine features and was always dressed very smartly. His friend, Trouper Ellis, was another Life Guard, tall, dark with an excellent physique. They shared the accommodation behind the medical center. Everyone regarded them as gay and at times

197

they came in for quite a lot of ragging. David could not care less. Both were delightful individuals, hard-working, reliable and very polite, and what they did in their spare time was none of his business.

Of course, David got landed with 'Pop', but he was a good medic and stood no nonsense. He liked to go off in the evening, and so when David's team was on duty he did the afternoon session, while David went on the beach, and David did the evening treatments with Troupers Ellis and Peters. It worked beautifully and Major Benton's only concern was that the work was done well and that someone was on call at any time of the day or night. As Troupers Peters and Ellis shared a room actually in the medical center complex there was always someone there, and they would fetch either David or Sergeant Henton in an emergency.

As Major Benton promised, he introduced David to his children whom he brought with him one morning. They were both blond, slim and full of energy. The boy, Ben, was eight and his sister, Sally, seven. David took them to the NAAFI for a lemonade, while the MO got on with the sick parade, and told them all about his trip to Kenya. When they found David was a keen swimmer, they took to him immediately, and promised to meet him on the beach that afternoon.

Now the Bureka Club was exclusively for the families of the oil company employees, but within walking distance of the military compound. The Club House was luxuriously appointed with garden, umbrellas, changing rooms, a bar and restaurant. There was a huge beach and swimming area formed by two rock walls built out into the sea in the form of an L. A metal netting and posts joined one wall to the beach, so that the sea could enter the area, and swimmers were protected from the many sharks found in Aden waters. The beach itself was divided into two parts, one for families and officers in front of the club itself, and the other smaller area for other ranks. A wire mesh fence separated the two parts of the beach. There was no segregation in the actual water but the beaches were exclusive and any soldier breaking the rules was punished. David could understand how the blacks of South Africa must have felt when 'the haves' were provided with every comfort and the 'have-not blacks' had nothing. Great Britain might be a democratic country but in Aden there was no democracy. The Bureka Club was out-of-bounds as well as all the hotels in Aden itself.

Ben and Sally arrived with their father who waved to David through the wire. The children were soon round to his part of the beach and pulling him into the water.

"Come on uncle David," they cried. "Race you to the raft." With that they were in the water and splashing out to a diving board right out in the deep water. David went after them. Gosh, they could swim. Like two little fish. They all got to the raft together and climbed on board. It was rather unsteady but the children seemed to like it. "Dive, uncle," they yelled and in they went. David followed. It was good fun but they eventually got tired and lay panting in the sun.

After a while the children regained their energy. "Throw me," requested Ben.

"Pardon?" David asked.

"Throw me into the water. Daddy does it all the time."

"And me," Sally joined in. "Please throw us uncle David."

David looked across at the beach. Major Benton was chatting to friends and quite unconcerned about his children.

"Please throw us," Ben requested again. "Daddy won't mind."

David picked the boy up in his arms and threw him into the water. He went in with a huge splash, disappeared below the surface, and came up a few feet away with a wide grin on his face.

"Now me," said Sally jumping up and down. "Me, me."

David picked her up. She weighed so little and he threw her just as he had done her brother. Splash. Down she went and up she came spitting water and grinning like a Cheshire cat. By this time Ben was back on the raft wanting to be thrown again.

After some time of this sport David began to feel tired. The children were still full of energy. Out of the corner of his eye he could see Major Benton waving. "Come on Ben, Sally your father seems to want you. Race you back to the beach." He dived into the water and was off with the children chasing him with noisy comments and lots of splashing. The children returned to their beach and their father with so much to tell him, whilst David returned to the segregated area. Major Benton waved as did the children and then they were off into the clubhouse.

"Got yourself a job as nursemaid," a soldier next to him commented.

David looked at the man who had a smile on his face and obviously meant no harm. "Seems like it," David replied. "I don't mind. They're lovely kids."

"They obviously enjoyed it," the soldier commented. "My kids would. They're lucky. Father an officer?"

"Yes, he's my boss," David replied. "Great guy, so I don't mind. You a married man then?"

"Yes. Two kids just about the same age. Would love to have them out here. It's ok for officers, they get all the privileges but .... My wife and kids are in army accommodation in Aldershot." (1)

"You in the Prince of Wales Own Regiment then?" asked David.

"Yes. Not a bad mob. Driver. Signed on for nine years. No job in civvy street, so I stayed on after National Service. Officers not too good though. You Life Guards?"

"I'm a medic attached to the Life Guards," David responded.

"Good mob, seems to me."

"Well, this is my third day with them and they seem ok," David observed.

"What do you think to this bloody segregation on the beach?"

"To tell you the truth, it rather shocked me," David responded truthfully. "I thought this sort of thing only happened in South Africa."

"We're still a class-ridden society in spite of all the claptrap we hear from politicians. The working man gave his life in the War for what? A better deal we were told. Greater equality and we get this." He waved his arms at the wire divider.

David pondered a while. He had found a different world since he started his National Service. It was not a world he was used to. Nowhere had he come across such an emphasis on privilege and class as in the military, and it was alien to him. "In some ways I can see the reason for this segregation as some of our lads can get pretty rough but.....well, there are other ways of ensuring good behaviour. My eyes have certainly been opened since I joined the military."

"The military are still living in the bloody middle ages. Officers are everything and we are shit," observed the soldier. "They're supposed to be intelligent but some of ours are as thick as pig shit."

"Well.....maybe you're right. Some are not fit to be officers. I don't know how they get through the selection process," remarked David.

"Influence. They have a relative who is or was an officer. Maybe went to the right school. Me, I went to the local Secondary Modern. What about you?"

"I went to Grammar School,"

"Got 'O' levels then?"

"Yes, ten and three 'A' levels," David told him as fact and without pride.

"Wow! Some of our officers don't even have 'A' levels."

"One unit I was with," responded David, "a lieutenant came one evening for an aspirin as he had a bad headache. I asked what caused the headache. He told me he had been studying 'O' level maths. If he passed he would have two 'O' levels."

"Blimey, I've got four 'O' levels. D'ye think I could be an officer?" asked the soldier.

David thought for a while. Perhaps the man would make a good officer but.... "They'll not accept you. You don't have the right accent, you've not been to the right school, and you eat peas with a knife." He smiled. "That seems to sum up selection criteria."

On the first Sunday in Little Aden, David went to morning service at the wooden church near the family compound. It was painted white, had a small bell-tower from which the sound of a peal of bells was coming – obviously a recording. Quite a crowd of people was entering the building, mostly families, but David noticed one or two officers dressed in civilian clothes, and a few soldiers dressed likewise. There seemed to be no segregation here.

It was a simple place with rows of wooden chairs and an altar at the east end with a simple altar cloth and a brass cross and two candlesticks. An upright piano was against the south wall and recorded organ music was playing quietly in the background. The whole place had a nice welcoming feeling about it. A few minutes before ten-thirty the vicar, a young man in his thirties in a black cassock, came out of the vestry and lit the candles. The lady pianist commenced the first hymn, 'All people that on earth do dwell...' which the congregation took up determined to have a good sing, and the vicar entered to kneel at his lectern. For David, who had been used to a Sung Eucharist at his parish church with great pomp and smells and bells, Matins was a beautiful reminder of what Anglicanism (2) can be. The service was simple with rousing hymns, a short sermon about fishermen directed at the children in the congregation, and prayers presented in a way that did not bore even the most inattentive member of the congregation. Before the blessing, the vicar announced that there would be coffee and biscuits served behind the vestry for anyone who wished to stay.

David was rather swept along by the congregation and he found himself under a canvas awning being handed a cup of coffee with two biscuits in the saucer by a small, slim, dark-haired lady who said her name was Irene.

"You're new aren't you?" she asked.

"Yes," David replied.

"When I've finished serving I'll come and talk to you. Now don't go away," she said flashing a smile at him and off she went to help distribute more coffees.

David looked around and saw the vicar coming towards him. He was in his black cassock. There was a smile of greeting on his face. "Hi, I'm Jerry," he said shaking David's hand. "My wife is over there....in the blue suit talking to Irene. I believe you've already met her?"

"Yes sir, she made me very welcome," David responded. "She said she'd be back to talk."

"And she will," laughed the vicar. "A real bundle of energy is Irene.

I don't know where she gets it from. She keeps all of us on our toes."

"I got the impression when she spoke to me briefly that she had bundles of energy."

"Makes me tired to watch her," laughed the vicar. "Wonderful person. That's her husband over there – Eric. He runs the refinery. Top man and all that. Been in the oil business many years....Iran I think." He took David's cup and gave it to a passing lady with a tray. "Now, what about you? Tell me something about yourself."

"I'm David Earl from Leicester, twenty years of age, doing my National Service with the RAMC and now attached to the Life Guards. I've been in Little Aden just five days and in the Protectorate for six months."

"Where were you before?" asked the vicar.

David replied slowly: "I was with the York and Lancs until they went home, then in the RAF Hospital for a week, and then the Aden Protectorate Levies for three months. Before that I trained at the Queen Elizabeth Hospital in London."

"You were well trained then, David," the vicar observed.

David looked amazed. How could he know about Millbank?

The vicar smiled. "Don't look so amazed. As well as being vicar of this church I'm also an army chaplain to both the Life Guards and the Prince of Wales Own. Call me vicar, David. I prefer it. My military rank is unimportant."

"Yes, sir." David responded.

"Yes, vicar. Only sir me, David, if I happen to be in uniform. That keeps the military happy. I'm your vicar."

"Where did you go to church at Khormakser?" he asked.

"At the RAF church."

"I know the church. The padre is a good man. He's gone back to the UK, now."

"Oh, I'm sorry," remarked David and then added as he thought his remark rather selfish, "Sorry he's gone home as he was excellent and very kind to me, but delighted he's back in the U.K."

Suddenly Irene was by his arm with the vicar's wife. She was tall and heavily pregnant, with a round face that radiated happiness. David had never seen two women before who emitted such bonhomie. "This is Mandy, Jerry's wife," said Irene. "We were trying to guess where you came from and what you are doing here."

"I think," Mandy said looking straight at David that you are Jerry's new curate." She smiled. "No?

"No," responded Irene with a twinkle in her eye. "He's the twin of the Angel Gabriel come down to earth. He's so blond and healthy."

They both laughed. "He's so handsome Jerry," went on Irene. "We were considering ditching our husbands and marrying him."

David blushed.

"You wicked women," cautioned Jerry. "Don't take any notice of them David. You'll find that they both have a rather over developed sense of humour."

"No, really, we both think you are National Service," added Mandy and you are very welcome. I hope we'll see a lot more of you."

"Now that's enough you two. You're obviously a great hit David. He is National Service, a medic serving with the Life Guards."

"We were right," Irene and Mandy laughed and jumped around like a couple of school girls.

"It's not hard to get right. He's either military or oil and Irene would have known about a new addition to that community. Take no notice David. These two are great teasers."

"I don't mind getting my leg pulled," responded David, "particularly by such attractive ladies."

Mandy and Irene giggled like two teenagers.

"Watch it ladies," Jerry laughed, "I've a feeling David can give as good as he gets."

Jerry and Mandy excused themselves as the piano player wanted to discuss the evening hymns. Irene took David over to where her husband, Eric, was talking to a rather military looking man who took his leave as David and Irene neared. Eric was in his fifties, slim, medium height and graying at the temples. After David was introduced and they had shaken hands Eric said, "Do you know the man I was talking to, David?"

"No, sir."

"He's only been here five days Eric," Irene chipped in. "He can hardly be expected to know everybody."

"Ah. He won't know then," Eric responded. That's the colonel of the Life Guards. He's your commanding officer. He pushed off a bit sharpish. I suppose he saw you coming. Didn't want to talk to an other rank." He turned to Irene. "You know Irene, I hate all this class distinction and in God's House as well."

Irene looked up at him, as she was quite small compared to Eric, and flashed a loving smile at him and squeezed his hand. "It's the way the world is, dear. If Our Lord couldn't change it I'm afraid you won't."

"But such un-Christian behaviour makes me wild," he responded.

David was quite taken aback. Here was a man who actually voiced his belief in equality.

Irene linked her arm through her husband's as if to give him comfort

"Never mind love. One day society will change and class divisions will no longer matter. With God's help."

"I pray it will," offered Eric looking down at her with such devotion. There was a pause and then Eric said, "Now David, will you be coming to Evening Service?"

"Yes, sir. I'm not on duty tonight."

"Good," he replied. "After service come back home and have a little supper with us. All right with you, Irene?"

She flashed him a wonderfully adoring smile, "That will be lovely, dear. Only a simple cold supper, David, but you are most welcome."

With that they shook hands and Eric and Irene wandered over to the car park by the side of the church.

David walked slowly back to the Life Guard's camp thinking over the events of the morning. He liked Jerry and his wife. There was something very natural and sincere about them. They were certainly not stuffy like many clergy. And Irene and Eric? It was very clear that they were in love by the way they looked at each other. Had they children? He would find out that evening. It was good to see affection being shown. Something his father had never done to his mother. Yes, he liked Eric and Irene a lot. They were real, genuine, Christian people with warm hearts. David thought that the essence of Christianity was love and that love should be practiced. He had no time for repressed religion. Christianity is what you do every day to each other and to your neighbor, a dynamic practical belief being lived day-by-day.

Just as morning service had been aimed at families and children, evening service was more for adults and the vicar's sermon was more theological and yet still down to earth. It was on the subject of suffering. The reading from the gospel had been from John's Gospel, Chapter 12 about the healing of Lazarus. Jerry spoke about how faith could help in the healing process. He did not delve into mysticism and miracles but explained that conviction in the healing power of God somehow gives the body extra strength to fight illness. He quoted a case of a terminal cancer patient who because of her faith lived so much longer than expected, and a wounded soldier who insisted on helping his fellows even though he was seriously wounded. "Faith can move mountains," he said. David was glad that he kept away from miracle cures where there was so much cant and little positive proof. It was an excellent service that certainly uplifted David, and judging by the attentiveness by which the congregation listened, many others found real comfort too.

Eric and Irene were sitting near the front of the congregation and after the service waved to indicate for him to wait for them at the entrance. Jerry met his congregation as they left and had a word with each one. "We should talk, David, as you are new here," he said as David left the church. "I'll try to pop into the medical center tomorrow if that is convenient?"

"Yes, sir...er...vicar," David responded.

"Good lad. Hope you enjoyed the service?"

At that moment Irene was at his side. She and Eric must have left by the vestry door.

"We're off to a little supper, Jerry," she told him.

"Lucky you, David. Irene is an excellent cook. Enjoy your evening."

Then Irene bustled David to the car park where a white Mercedes was awaiting them with Eric in the driving seat.

The drive to the house took only a few minutes. Although Eric was the chief of the refinery, he lived in the same style of house as everyone else. They were bungalows made of wood and plaster, each in a little garden of its own. Eric's house did have a larger garden than the others, but it was three bedrooms and two bathrooms like all the other families. Eric drove through the gates and parked the car in the car-port while Irene took David in through the front door. The lights were all on and an Indian maid met them in the hall. "Thank you for waiting, Aisha," she said. "I'll see you in the morning." The maid smiled and disappeared. "Aisha stayed so that everything was ready when we came from church," offered Irene. "Her husband works in the refinery and I employ her to keep the house tidy. Been with us since our days in Iran."

Irene sat David in a large, comfortable armchair in the L-shaped living room. It was very comfortably furnished with two huge settees and four armchairs in the main part of the room, and a dining table, six chairs and a sideboard in the smaller part. There were inlaid side tables, lamps of different sizes and paintings on the wall. The room was quite feminine and obviously contained treasures that had been collected during their travels. By this time Eric had arrived and offered David a drink. "Well, sir, I do drink a little. My father let us have a sherry or a glass of wine with our meal. Sherry would be lovely"

"Sherry it is David. What about you Irene?" Eric asked.

"I'll have sherry as well, dear," she responded as she bustled about bringing food from the kitchen and placing it on a low table between them. It was quite a feast for David after over a year on army rations.

"We always have a cold buffet on Sundays, like this," Irene told him. "Informal and easy."

Soon they were tucking in to cold chicken and ham, salad and warm buttered rolls washed down with delicious red wine. There was cheese and biscuits and fresh fruit to follow and a delicious coffee that Eric said he had sent from Holland.

They talked about mundane things at first and then Eric asked about David and his family. David told him of his family and about his desire to be a priest and his acceptance at King's College, London University. "Does Jerry know about this?" Eric asked.

"No. He is coming to see me tomorrow and I'll tell him then."

"He'll be delighted, David," Irene added. "Jerry works terribly hard. He's our vicar as well as the chaplain to two regiments and he takes his work very seriously. If you could give him some help on Sundays, I'm sure he would be grateful."

"I helped the RAF padre at communion whenever I was free," David offered.

"Good man," Eric chipped in. "Regard us as your family while you are here."

"Our teenage daughter will be home from school in England soon and she will love to have a handsome escort," added Irene.

"You just have a daughter then?" asked David. They looked at each other and David thought he had made some kind of error. He quickly added, "I didn't want to pry."

"It's not that, David," Eric said looking at Irene. "Yes, we have only one child, Andrea, and she is just sixteen. You see Irene cannot have any more children." There was sadness in the eyes of them both.

David understood more than they were telling by the look on their faces. Irene must have had major surgery for some reason. David hoped it was not cancer. "I understand," he said. "Please forgive me for causing you any pain."

"You were not to know, dear," Irene responded in her bubbly way. "We have a lovely daughter who is our pride and joy. When you meet her you'll see why."

The evening was quite wonderful but David made his excuses when he looked at his watch and found it was ten o'clock. What a delightful couple they were. He felt so relaxed in their presence, and they had talked non-stop all evening. He offered to help Irene with the dishes but she told him she would put the food away and Aisha would clear up in the morning. He took his leave and thanked them for the hospitality.

"Now remember what I said, David," Eric reminded him. "While you are in Aden regard us as your family. Come any time. If you don't I shall come and get you." Irene nodded in agreement and David shook hands, waved goodbye from the gate, and walked back to camp.

David had not been with the Life Guards more than a month when he and the other junior NCOs were invited to a party in the senior NCO's mess. "Better get plenty of food inside you before we go," advised Lance Corporal Harper. "They tend to be very boozy do's."

"Oh!" was all David could say.

"You do drink, don't you?" Harper asked.

"Well....yes....but not much," David replied.

"Suppose I'll have to carry you home," commented Harper.

David looked at Harper and smiled. He was so tall and skinny that he wondered how he actually managed to walk around. "What about you?" he asked.

"I'll be fine. Been to a party before. No trouble. I can hold my liquor."

The party was a great affair. All the junior NCOs had been invited and the sergeants and warrant officers were excellent company. Everyone was relaxed and friendly. There was a huge buffet supper with every dish imaginable, including smoked salmon. Waiters wandered around with trays of red and white wine, and as Corporal Harper had promised, it was a boozy affair. David chatted to a great many people in the course of the evening. Corporal Watts from the office was very attentive and hovered around David. He really was very handsome. In some ways he was like Frank. He told David that he was married with three children and lived in Windsor.

Corporal Harper slid to David's side. "He's got a crush on you, Dave," he whispered.

"Go on!" There was a pause while he sipped his wine. Then David asked, "How do you know?"

'Harpic' looked at him in amazement. "You mean you don't know? The whole camp knows. It's common knowledge. Can't you see from the way he looks at you? I thought you knew. You are an innocent Dave. Why do you think he comes and chats almost every afternoon?"

"But 'Harpic'," offered David, "he's a married man with children."

"So what?" questioned Corporal Harper. "A man can love another man. There's nothing physical, is there?"

"No, of course not," David replied quickly. Now he was embarrassed.

"What's the problem then?" enquired Corporal Harper.

"It's just that everyone knows. How can I hold my head up?"

"Easily," grinned 'Harpic'. "Just stretch your neck a little and stick out you jaw."

David had to laugh. So Corporal Harper did not seem to mind, maybe nobody else did. Everyone had been very kind to him. Oh well, he supposed he should be flattered having a handsome older man as an admirer.

He was deep in thought when the Sergeant Major grabbed one of his arms and a big, burly sergeant the other. "Now Corporal Earl," the Sergeant Major yelled. "Your time has come."

David wondered what was going on. They frog-marched him into the bar area where a huge crowd had assembled. Someone banged on the table and demanded quiet.

The Sergeant Major spoke: "Lads, as you all know very well, we have our customs in the Life Guards."

Somebody yelled, "Get on with it sarge."

"Belt up and listen," yelled another.

"If I can have the floor," the Sergeant Major yelled in his best parade ground voice.

"Take all the bloody planks you like," offered another wag to a peel of laughter.

"It is our custom," went on the Sergeant Major, unperturbed by the comments, "that newcomers have to undertake a forfeit."

There were shouts and whistles. "Get him to drop his pants. Let's see what he's made of."

"We, the senior NCOs, have decided that Corporal Earl must drink a Mickey Finn," went on the Sergeant Major.

"What the hell's that?" asked someone loudly.

"Barman," commanded the Sergeant Major, "take one of those pint glasses and put a little of everything from your shelves in it."

The barman did as he was bid. A little Drambuie, Vodka, Gin, Quantreau, Parfait Amour...and so it went on until the glass was almost full. The contents changed colour umpteen times as different liqueurs were poured into the glass until it ended up a dark brown like muddy water.

"On your knees," the Sergeant Major commanded David.

David got down on the floor and the glass was handed him. "Now drink," he was told.

He did drink. The stuff tasted quite pleasant. Slowly he got it down amidst cheers and catcalls.

"Who's taking him home," somebody shouted.

"Bet he has a head in the morning."

"Get it down lad. It'll come up later," someone yelled to hoots of laughter.

"He's a doc, he'll give himself something," yelled another.

After he'd drained the glass, strong arms raised him to his feet and his hand was shaken by numerous individuals who welcomed him to the regiment. For David, it was all a haze. He was not used to strong drink, and that was strong. Perhaps 'Harpic' was right and he would have to carry him back to his room. Fortunately, it was not far. He was offered more drink by grinning well-wishers but he declined with an equally mischievous grin.

Corporal Harper approached. He was not too steady on his feet and his speech was not quite right. Or was this due to David's state of probable intoxication. By now he was really feeling quite happy. "How yer feel, Dave?" 'Harpic' asked doing a little dance in front of David.

"Better than you look," David replied.

"I'm fine, Dave," 'Harpic replied blinking his eyes and moving like the Eiffel Tower in a wind. "I'll take you home....before you pass out. You've had too much to drink"

David did not argue as he too was feeling a little.....no, not drunk..... yet. Best to get home while he was ok.

"Right, 'Harpic', let's go." They waved goodbye and went through the door into the dark night.

They had not been out in the fresh air for two or three minutes before 'Harpic' almost fell over. David managed to catch him, in a fashion, and the two just avoided crashing to the ground. "I feel terrible," moaned 'Harpic'.

"You're drunk, "observed David. He too was a little hazy but he could stand, see and control his movements. 'Harpic' was quite gone. David got one of 'Harpic's arms round his shoulders and almost dragged him to his room. He rolled him into bed, loosened his shirt and belt and left him snoring happily.

He remembered getting back to his room and rolling into bed, having taken off his shoes and socks but nothing else. 'Pop' as usual was snoring like a steam train and nothing would wake him until morning. David felt slightly sick. That was all he remembered until he awoke the following morning with the father and mother of a headache.

Chapter 16

During the Second World War, the British built gun emplacements on the tops of hills around the large bay that is the port of Aden. One of these gun emplacements is on a hill between a little bay, holding the refinery port, and the next little bay around, holding the hospital and dwellings. A series of over three hundred steps takes you up to the top where there is now no gun, but a fantastic view around the series of small bays that make up Little Aden. The water is so clear that large fish, like shark, can easily be seen. In fact, the waters around Aden are so full of sharks, that everyone is warned not to swim outside the shark nets. Also to be seen from this high spot, are giant rays, some eighteen to twenty feet in length, looking like huge underwater birds flapping their immense wings gently as they glide through the clear sea, and large silver shoals of fish jumping out of the sea trying to escape the jaws of larger fish. The shoals are so big at time it looks like silver rain descending from above.

The effort to reach the top in the heat of the day is immense, as David and his companions found, but the view is worth it. To one's left is the oil refinery with its silver towers and storage tanks, and the huge breakwater, built of granite boulders, with pipes snaking from the refinery to the docking area where, if lucky, a huge tanker may be seen disgorging crude oil, or taking on refined fuel for a western port. To one's right and below, is the hospital at the foot of the hill, and further on little bungalows, rather like homes for dolls than for humans, set out in a regular pattern with their fenced gardens, and the other community buildings. Beyond this are the buildings used by the military. On the beach further to the right, is the Bureka Club and its partitioned beach.

In the distance, further to the right, are a number of other small bays, only frequented by the hardy as the only way to get to them is by a sort of goat track tramped by a succession of soldiers, who tended to be fed up with partitioned swimming, and wanted something they could call their own. Of course, there were sharks in the water, but that did not seem to deter the hardy. It was to these beaches that David and his friends went. Of course, David still frolicked with Major Benton's children, but they did not go to the beach every afternoon.

It was very hot walking, perhaps 43 Celsius, and one slid on the volcanic scree that made up most of the hills around Little Aden. It was worth it as the beaches were usually deserted and the water fabulous. Those who accompanied David were generally free spirits, and bathing naked came to be a symbol of freedom that these young men had lost when they were recruited. There was nobody to bother them, and in any case the odd inquisitive person could be seen coming along the narrow path, and bathers quickly donned something to cover their nakedness. It was ideal as they relaxed and laughed, read if they were so inclined, swam in the shallow water, talk endlessly, and slept in the shade of a rock, or just enjoyed the sun.

One afternoon, David and his single companion, Paul, found that during the course of their siesta some Arab fishermen had arrived unnoticed in their dugout canoes: huge logs hewn out and trimmed into shape. It was very rare to see anybody but even more unusual to see Arabs. They put on their bathers and walked down to the other end of the beach to see what they were doing, and to have a word with them. As they approached, they could see six huge black sharks lying side-by-side on the sand.

"*Salaam alicum*," David greeted them.

They responded, "*Alicum salaam*," and smiled at the two white men showing rather dirty, broken teeth.

David pointed at the sharks and made a gesture to ask where they had caught them. One of the Arabs pointed to the bay indicating an area quite close to where they were. Paul tried to ask them when they had caught them by pointing to his watch. One Arab took Paul's wrist and indicated about two o'clock that afternoon. Both Paul and David were amazed as they just did not believe sharks could be in their bay. They had not even been aware of the fishermen on the water. But that was not so strange, as both of them had been snoozing.

After walking around the sharks and noticing their huge jaws and sharp teeth, they made their farewells and walked back to where they had left their clothes. Neither said a word. It was quite a shock. They had been warned about sharks, but not really believed that they would be in their bay. Yes, they had seen some in deeper water from the hilltop, but never expected them in the water where it was comparatively shallow. "I wondered why the bay was so quiet this afternoon," Paul remarked. "If you think back, there were no sea birds resting on the water like they usually do. Not even fish jumping."

"It's a good thing we only go on the edge and don't really swim," responded David. "Let it be a lesson to us."

"We'll come to the beaches but be extra careful, Dave. I like the peace and freedom we have here," noted Paul, "but the risk is too great to swim properly. We'll leave that to the regular beach.

"Ok," agreed David, "but we don't come alone. If we do then we don't go into the water, or we go to the little place further round where there are safe rock pools to cool off in."

Not long after this incident, David found that he had no companion for his afternoon trip to the beach. Paul had a guard duty and his other friends were too lazy that afternoon to go to the beach and wanted to sleep on their beds in air-conditioned luxury. David decided to go on his own and to visit a small rocky area where there were lovely rock pools. It was a little further on, but he had time and energy. It was an exquisite place, secluded and peaceful. It was really a flat area of lava from the ancient volcanic flow, sticking out into the sea. Waves splashed over the lava to make warm pools that one could lie in and be showered when a wave came in. There were other flat place where one could sunbathe in seclusion.

It took him forty minutes to get there and he was hot and sweaty when he arrived. He put his towel on a smooth area, stripped off, and immersed himself in a rock pool. Really it was perfect. After a while, he lay on his towel, opened his book and began to read. Some time later, he went in again and splash about in the pool in order to cool off, and then he returned to his towel for a little snooze. There was no sound only the splashing of waves against the rocks. Sleep came easily

He did not know what awoke him, but when he looked around there was a young Arab, perhaps a little older than himself, squatting about ten feet from him. David greeted him in Arabic, smiled, turned to his book and commenced reading. He was not in the mood to attempt holding a conversation in halting Arabic, or even halting English. If he ignored the young man then, perhaps, he would go away. But he did not. He came closer on David's left side and squatted about three feet away. David looked at him again and the young man smiled and stared at him. Then David noticed something else. The Arab was wearing the usual piece of cloth round his waist and a shirt but in squatting the cloth had run up his legs so that from where David was lying he could see right up his legs. He was not wearing underwear and there was something sticking out at right angles to his body. When the Arab sensed that David could see his erection, he waggled it and looked David right in the eye. It was a challenge. 'What are you going to do about this?'

David did not know what to do. If he turned on his back then that might be seen as an invitation to the Arab. He had been warned about Arab customs. They were rather partial to European bottoms. Best not turn over. That really would be courting trouble. What if he got an erection? The Arab would see it immediately and it could be a come on for him. What could he do? Shout at the young man and tell him to go away? If he was unpleasant, the Arab might turn nasty. Many of then had a knife around their person. He decided he would ignore the young

212

man and read his book. Maybe he would get bored and go away.

After about twenty minutes, the young man got up and walked away. David thought that was the last of him. But no it was not. The Arab took off all his clothes and lay down on his back in the shade of a large rock. Give him his due, he had a lovely body, but his huge erect penis stuck up like a radio mast. David tried not to look but the Arab kept stroking it so it kept erect. He kept looking over at David. He tried to read and ignore the man, but it was difficult. The Arab was certainly very handsome with an unblemished brown skin and a nicely muscled body. He had no pubic hairs. David knew that it is the custom in Islam to shave that area. His penis was very large and David could not help being fascinated.

He knew that his interest was wrong and yet something kept making him have a look over the top of his book. He could not concentrate. He felt his own considerable organ begin to swell. No, he must go before things got out of hand. He got up suddenly, put on his underwear and shorts, grabbed his towel, shirt and book and almost ran from the beach along the track to where it joined the main road. He did not look back. He never went to that beach again for fear of meeting the Arab. But there was another reason. He had been attracted to the Arab, he knew it. He wanted look at him more, and even to touch his lovely brown body. David knew that such feelings and thoughts were wrong and he had to take control of himself.

Two or three evenings a week, David would visit the home of Irene and Eric. He always looked forward to these visits as they were so friendly and he relaxed completely. Sometimes they talked, or played card games, and once in a while he was taken for dinner at the Bureka Club, although David explained that it was out-of-bounds. Eric just waved off any objection and said that he was with him as his guest. It was not that David imposed himself on them. When he did not contact then after the first visit, Eric rang the camp on the fourth day to asked what the problem was and insisted that he visited whenever he could.

One morning, after a visit to the Club the previous evening, David was summoned by the Sergeant Major. It was an informal meeting but he was warned, on the orders of the Colonel, that he must not go to the Bureka Club and that if he did then he would be charged with disobeying an order. David explained that he was a guest and had told his host the ruling, but the host had ignored it. It put David in a difficult situation. He was fearful of what the military might do to him.

Some weeks later, Eric suggested that they go to the club on the coming Saturday to celebrate their wedding anniversary. It was a difficult situation for David. He could invent some excuse, but to tell a lie was not in his nature so he explained to Eric and Irene what had transpired between him and the Sergeant Major.

"Do you mean to say, David," exclaimed Eric looking rather dismayed, "that the Colonel communicated this through one of his NCOs?"

"The Sergeant Major was very nice, but he warned me in no uncertain fashion and said that the order came directly from the Colonel," David related.

"Did you explain that you were my guest?" Eric asked.

"Yes. I said I was a guest."

"What was his comment about that?" asked Eric.

"He said it didn't matter whose guest I was. I was not to go there."

"And he made a threat?" chipped in Irene.

"Well, yes. He said I would be put on a charge for disobeying orders if I went there again."

By this time Eric was getting angry. He got up from his seat and went over to the telephone.

David was not sure what he intended to do, but when he heard the opening remark he was left in no doubt.

"Give me the Colonel," Eric said very firmly to the person on the other end of the phone. There was some kind of reply and then Eric said, "Then put me through to his home." Obviously the telephone operator declined. "This is Eric Roberts, Head of the Refinery, and I want to speak to the Colonel urgently." There was a pause whilst the operator contacted the Colonel's home. David felt very apprehensive, but things were out of his hands now. He had only spoken the truth.

"Colonel, Eric Roberts here. Sorry to ring your home, but I have a rather serious matter that I would like cleared up immediately." There was a pause while the Colonel said something to Eric. Eric went on. "I have a young man here, a friend of the family, who is one of your soldiers. He accompanies my wife and I to the Club on frequent occasions as our guest............Name? .....Corporal David Earl....... It's my wedding anniversary on Saturday and I invited him to dinner at the Club. He tells me he is forbidden to go." There was a pause while the Colonel must have explained the rule about Other Ranks not entering the Club. "Yes, Colonel," continued Eric. "I quite understand the reason for your rule. But surely there are exceptions?" There was another pause and David could see that Eric was getting angry.

At last the Colonel stopped and Eric replied in a quiet but firm voice. "Let me remind you Colonel that the Club belongs to my company and I am its head in Aden. I decide who visits it, not the Colonel of the Life Guards. There are times when your officers are a

214

disgrace and should not be members. This young man has far better manners than most of your officer. And lastly, he is my guest. You insult my wife and I by not allowing us to bring our guest into our Club. Corporal Earl will be our guest on Saturday and if any action is taken against him, I will ban all officers of the Life Guards from the Club. I hope that is understood...... Good night." And with that he carefully put down the phone.

There was silence in the room. Eric looked at Irene and said, "I don't know who that fellow thinks he is. He talks as if the Club was his. Cheek. God, these Life Guard fellows are so arrogant."

Irene smiled sweetly at her husband. "So we go on Saturday?"

Eric broke into a smile. "We do. David, put on you best shirt and slacks, and make a show of it. If anyone, and I mean anyone, tries to threaten you in the slightest, I want to know. I'd love to ban these fellows. Some of them have the manners of apes."

Saturday evening went off beautifully. What Irene did not know was that many of her friends had been invited, including Jerry and Mandy, and a group of thirty sat down to an excellent dinner. Not a word was ever said again to David about his presence in the Bureka Club.

One afternoon when David was with Major Benton's children on the diving board in the center of the swimming area, they were joined by a rather wiry young man in his twenties. He was not thin exactly, but delicately muscled so that his body looked like that of a prize racehorse. He had black curly hair, a pleasant face and masses of energy. He was what you might call a 'pretty boy'. Everything about him was delicate and yet he was obviously very strong as he was a wonderful diver. The children loved his antics. David had never learnt to dive, or to swim for that matter. It just came naturally to him. He just did it and improved as he went along. His diving was courageous, but poor, while this young man's dives were things of beauty. He introduced himself as Peppino, from Italy, and said that his father worked in the refinery and he was home from university in Italy. His English was good, with a most charming accent, and he sat with them on the diving raft and talked, occasionally flashing a smile at David with his big brown eyes. He was great fun and they all laughed a lot.

Peppino joined them on quite a few afternoons and began to teach David and the children how to dive properly. He was a real athlete, and once astonished them by diving from a high rock on the far side of the swimming area into quite shallow water. He just glided along the surface of the water rather than going deep. In fact, he was a real daredevil, and a good teacher. The children improved so much that Major Benton mentioned it one morning at sick parade. Peppino soon became a friend and made it very clear that David was someone special. They would meet most afternoons and dive and swim. There were always squeals of laughter from the children.

One afternoon, when the children were not present, Peppino had suggested that they go fishing. They walked to one of the rocky outcrops some distance from the swimming area. Peppino had brought two spear guns and masks. He explained that one set belonged to his older brother. The water was so clear that fish could be seen, even at a great depth. David had never really noticed the different kinds of fish in these waters until Peppino pointed them out. There were large green, blue and yellow parrot fish two feet in length, so called because of their color; triangular angel fish with their yellow and black stripes; red fish some eighteen inches long with poisoned dorsal fins; fish of every color and size, hundreds of them. The sea off these particular rocks was teeming with sea life.

David decided not to snorkel as he could not bear covering his nose and mouth and so let Peppino do the fishing while he watched. Peppino wore a tiny white thong that hardy covered anything, a webbing belt with a knife attached to it, rubber diving boots, a pair of goggles and a snorkel on his head. David thought he looked a little like Tarzan crossed with a spaceman with his muscular body, brief cover and diving apparatus. As a new type of fish was speared, Peppino threw it onto the rocks for David to see and take a photograph. He then threw it back into the water. Peppino caught two huge green-black crayfish, which he said his mother would cook. They had bodies eighteen inches in length and huge claws, and whiskers that made them appear enormous. It was a perfect afternoon. After fishing, they stretched out in the sunshine and talked and laughed.

That evening David was invited to Peppino's home to sample the crayfish. The family lived in a company bungalow just the same as Eric and Irene, but much closer to the refinery. His mother was very Italian, large and gray haired and spoke very little English. His brother was well-built, handsome and darkly Italian with his black hair and swarthy skin. David could see that in later years he would become fat like his mother. Peppino was like his father, slim and energetic. The three menfolk spoke quite good English so the conversation was not a strain. They wanted to know about David's family and about England as well as his military service. Both Peppino and his brother had escaped service in Italy up to the present, but would have to do it eventually.

The crayfish was excellent: cooked in a sauce which David guessed was like that used with lobster thermadore, which he had eaten only once before. It was eaten with an excellent green salad and washed down with neat whisky. David wondered why whisky and not wine, but was too polite to ask. The main course was followed with cheese and fruit and excellent coffee. By the time the meal was over, David was feeling quite 'heady' and was glad when Peppino suggested he walk back to the camp with him.

It was a lovely evening with a clear sky and full moon. The towers of the refinery reflected some of the moonlight making the place seem like some enchanted city. There was a warm breeze and the sea could be heard lapping up onto the beach.

"Let's go sit on the beach, Davy," Peppino suggested. "It too nice go in."

"Ok," agreed David. "It is a lovely evening."

"I want talk Davy," Peppino revealed.

"Oh!" David was quite surprised.

They wandered down to the next beach from the Club, where soft music floated over the jeweled sea. They sat on the soft sand, silent at first, and throwing pebbles into the shallow water with a distant plop.

For a long while Peppino said nothing as if miles away in thought. David had his own thoughts. They stretched out on their backs and looked up at the moon. The night was so peaceful that there did not seem to be a need for conversation. In the distance, a ship's bell rang, and the music from the Club continued to float towards them. Small waves lapped gently on the beach. Over the water from the direction of Steamer Point, lights of vessels could be seen. They were obviously waiting to unload their cargoes in the absence of a proper dock in the port of Aden. (1) And yet, David felt that there was a tension between the two of them. Peppino had something to say, but would only say it when he was good and ready.

After a while Peppino sat up and looked down at David. "I want talk Dave. I not know how to begin," he said.

"Just say what you want," David replied. "Whatever it is cannot be that bad."

The next instant David felt his hand being taken by Peppino and put to his lips.

"Carro, Davie. Carro, Davie," he kept saying.

David was not sure what he was saying. He did not mind what he was doing. He did not pull away. He found that it was quite acceptable from Peppino.

Still holding his hand, Peppino said, "I love you. I never before loved a man but..." David was going to reply when Peppino cut in, "No, not speak, Davie. I want explain. I know men not supposed to love each other, but I no help it. Before, I have no courage to speak on

217

raft. I just watched you each day. My desire get stronger and stronger. At last I get courage to speak. We friends and my love greater and greater. I have to tell this now or maybe I burst. I want touch you, kiss you and ...."

This really did not come as a surprise to David. He had noticed the way Peppino looked at him sometimes. Those big, brown eyes said so much. David sat up, took Peppino's other hand and kissed it. "You not angry.....or unhappy, Davie?" he said in a quiet voice.

"David kissed his hand again. "No, of course not. I'm not even surprised. I've noticed the way you look at me for weeks now."

There was a sigh of contentment from Peppino and David could see a tear fall down his cheek. And then a smile formed that lit up his charming Italian face. He bent over and kissed David on the forehead. "Oh, Davie, I been so anxious. Maybe if I say my true feelings friendship become bad. Is wonderful you understand."

The next moment Peppino had pushed David onto his back, moved so that he lay across David's chest and was kissing his face and neck with such passion. David surprised himself. He did not mind in the least, in fact he rather liked it and lay there quite passively. "Oh, Davie carro mio," Peppino kept saying. "I love you, I love you."

David found that he was sexually aroused, but strangely he didn't care. Peppino was such a lovely person, beautiful in his muscularity, his smile and his laughing eyes. He could feel Peppino's arousal as he lay clasped in his arms. It did not seem to matter. Maybe the whisky had relaxed him but now he was kissing Peppino's face, throat, arms and chest through his open shirt.

He was not aware how long they had been lying there, and that they were almost naked, until voices came out of the darkness some way off. They stopped, peered into the darkness whilst buttoning up their shirts. "Shush, be still," cautioned David. "Better go when people have passed by. We don't want to be caught kissing." They waited in silence until whoever it was had progressed along the road and there was silence again.

"You ok?" Peppino asked.

"Fine. I liked what we did."

"You let me love you?" Peppino asked.

"Yes, of course. I've never kissed a male before, but it's better than kissing my girl."

"I never kissed a man before," Peppino offered. "But is better than kissing my girl." He giggled.

"We meet tomorrow?"

"Of course, Peppino."

They wandered along the beach towards the gates of the camp where they shook hands and said 'Chow'. David watched Peppino walk off into the night and then turned and strode towards his barrack room. He was elated and yet confused. Elated that such a beautiful person as Peppino should fall in love with him, and elated by the kissing which had been far better than he had ever achieved with his girlfriend back in the UK. He was confused because he did not understand his emotions. Jesus had loved his disciples, but did that mean he kissed them? No, surely not. You could love a man without being physical. But he had kissed Peppino, and fondled his body. That was physical. He had enjoyed it and been aroused by it, as was Peppino. What did it all mean?

David and Peppino saw each other when it was at all possible. Some afternoons and evenings David was on duty, or he would visit Irene and Eric, but where possible he would meet Peppino at the beach, and together with Major Benton's children, they would swim and dive. Some afternoons Irene would swim out to the raft and join in the fun. She was not a good swimmer, but loved to sunbathe on the raft while Peppino, David and the children did their silly dives. One afternoon Irene said, "You know David you ought to be a teacher as well as a priest. You are so good with the children and they love you so."

"Priests are teachers," David replied. "That's part of their job."

Yes, but I mean in a school," went on Irene. "You can be a priest and a schoolmaster, you know."

"Maybe," responded David. "I don't know what the Lord has in mind for me."

Later Peppino questioned David about the conversation. "You going to be priest, Davie?" he asked.

"Yes. Is there a problem?"

"I make love, Davie. Only special person become priest. I know you good man. Maybe wrong for me to love"

"Are you unhappy about what we do together? I'm not. I have thought about this a lot and prayed to God to guide me. Jesus loved his disciples and He taught us to love others as ourselves. We kiss. Yes. We cuddle. That is all. I know you get aroused sexually but that is all. We are not bad, in fact, I think we are better people for knowing how to love."

Peppino thought for a while. "I not unhappy. I love you. I want kiss and hold you. My priest in Italy, he tell me that kissing and holding a man is wrong. But I know many priests who touches boys. We do no wrong. I not touch you....."

"Fine, Peppino. I love you too. I have to tell you that I love your body and would like to touch, but I know it is wrong."

"Me too, Davie. I like to kiss all over, but is wrong."

"Then we both know the limits to our love, Peppino, and providing we keep to those limits, for me, we do no wrong."

David's fine ideals never wavered with Peppino, but only once did he do something that caused him a great deal of pain afterwards. One morning Major Benton asked David if he was interested in going into Steamer Point to do some shopping. Once a week military trucks took soldier into town for shopping, but other than that a taxi had to be paid for and it was quite expensive. David jumped at the chance as he wanted a new pair of swimming trunks and had found nothing suitable locally.

Steamer Point had quite a few excellent shops where many European as well as Indian brands could be purchased. One shop, Bikergee and Cowasgee, was an outfitters of distinction. David knew that they sold Janzen swimwear, which is expensive, but a quality all on its own. In the window of the double-fronted shop was a pair of bright red trunks, cut quite briefly, so they fitted the hips tightly. He went inside.

The assistant behind the counter was an Indian of about David's age. He was tall, nicely built and very handsome with flashing white teeth. David pointed to the swim trunks in the window and asked if they had a pair to fit him. The assistant smiled broadly and brought out a box containing about two-dozen pairs. "What waist are you?" asked the assistant.

"Twenty-eight," David told him.

"That would be a small, sir, "the assistant replied. "You have a lovely slim waist and yet quite broad shoulders."

"That's because I swim a lot and do gymnastics," David told him.

The assistant looked through the garments. "Ah yes, sir. We have a red and there is a dark blue your size."

"I like the red," David told him.

"I think you better try them on, sir, just to make sure they are the right size."

"Ok," David agreed.

With that, the assistant led him into a changing area at the back of the shop. The cubicle had a curtain that the assistant drew across the entrance and then he left David to try them on.

David was in shirt and shorts so it was easy to try the trunks on. He slipped down his shorts, took of his underwear and put on the trunks. They fitted him perfectly as the material was stretchable and it showed his figure to perfection. He took off his shirt to see how he looked in the mirror.

Quietly the curtain was drawn aside, and the assistant stepped into the cubicle. "Wow, they do look fine on you sir," the assistant observed. "Your narrow waist complements those shoulders of yours, sir." He put his hands on David's shoulders while facing him and started to feel his muscles. "You have super muscles, sir."

David quite liked his body being praised and was quite flattered. "I try to keep in good shape."

"You have wonderful pectorals," said the assistant stroking David's chest and giving a nipple a tweek.

By this time David was beginning to get a little erect. "And sir had another large muscle," said the assistant putting his hand on David's growing bulge. "Gosh, it's huge."

With that, before David could resist, he pulled down David's trunks and was handling his large erection. David found that what he was doing was rather pleasing. It felt...., well he didn't know what it felt like. Like what they used to do in the showers at school.

"Sir, you have everything," said the assistant stroking him, "perfect waist, broad shoulders, handsome face and this

Suddenly David realized what the assistant was doing and he pulled away. "Please don't," he said. "It's wrong."

"Sorry, sir," responded the assistant, "but I thought you liked me?"

David quickly put on his underwear, shirt and shorts and carried the trunks out into the body of the shop where the assistant, not at all flustered, put them into a bag while David paid. "Please come and see me again. If I can do anything for you......," the assistant said flashing a smile at him as he opened the door.

David really felt bad about what he had allowed to be done. It should not have happened. Why was it that everywhere he went males made passes at him? It had happened at school. Boys and even one teacher had played with him. His physical education teacher could not keep his hands off him. In the army in the UK, there had been a number of incidents where other soldiers had suggested things to him. Now out here in Aden, actual physical things had happened to him. A young officer from one of the tankers had groped him in the water and asked him to spend the night with him. He even offered money when David refused. What was going on?

He had never given any indication that he liked that sort of thing as he had seen other servicemen do. He was certainly not effeminate. Handsome? He could not see it, but others were convinced of his good looks. He often looked at his reflection in shop windows, and wondered what all the fuss was about. At school he had been driven by the belief that he was quite ugly with his spotty face and skinny body. Maybe he had changed like the ugly duckling (2) in the Hands Anderson story. He could not see it. He was flattered that someone like Peppino loved him, and even to some extent, flattered by the attentions of the Indian shop assistant.

Most young men were easily aroused sexually. Just brushing against someone, or the tight fit of one's trousers, could make one hard. At school, in spite of his spotty face and lean figure, he had been popular because of his huge organ. So many boys envied him and wanted to see it in the showers. Even in training, the other recruits had wanted to have a look. Again he was flattered, as he was considered by his peers to be very masculine with such a large appendage.

But that did not explain his own feelings. He liked to have an erection, even if it was embarrassing at times, as it could not be hidden. It felt good. He liked the admiration of his peers. He liked to be cuddled and yet he knew it to be wrong. He had to admit also that he admired the male body and was aroused when he viewed male nakedness. The human body was a thing of beauty, not of shame. Of the female body, he had seen little, except on the beach, but the male form was familiar to him from school and now in the army. In his mind, a seed of worry was beginning to grow. Do other men have the same feelings? If not, was there something wrong with him?

Chapter 17

The pursuit of pleasure in Little Aden is limited to outdoor activities like tennis and volleyball, if it is not too hot, and water activities like swimming and sailing, although sailing can be very dangerous if you fall overboard. The Bureka Club and the NAAFI have snooker tables and the Life Guards officers have their polo ponies. The one open-air cinema operates three times a week. Apart from drinking, which is limited to the NAAFI and Bureka Club there is nothing else to do. It was possible to go shopping at Steamer Point but taxis are expensive, even when the cost is shared.

Many soldiers played cards at night, usually for beer, and some played for money. It was easy to lose your week's wages at the turn of a card. Playing for money was not really allowed, but barrack rooms could not be policed all the time, and in any case card schools always had lookouts. Apart from that, you could read, chat to your friends or just lie on your bed and vegetate. David read a great deal, swam in the afternoons, and in the evening frequently went to the home of Irene and Eric, or with them to a restaurant at Steamer Point. It was quite a happy life for him. Some of the lads were bored and got drunk or went off to the brighter lights of Ma'alla or Steamer Point.

On a Saturday evening around seven o'clock, two or three open military lorries would travel the long distance round the Bay of Aden and take their occupants to Ma'alla and Steamer Point. Arriving about eight o'clock, there was time for two hour's shopping, or a cinema visit, and any other activities up to ten thirty when the lorries left promptly. Some frustrated soldiers would be dropped off in the district of Ma'alla between Steamer Point and the RAF camp at Khormaksar. There were lots of dirty, little shops but the big attraction were the numerous brothels.

Ma'alla Mary was a famed 'madame' and became the symbol for 'a good time'. "Oh, you've been to see Ma'alla Mary have you?" became a frequent question to soldiers who arrived at the medical center with the 'clap'. She was supposed to be a huge black Somali woman with breasts as big as melons and an appetite for sex to match her 'melons'. This was by reputation, but those who had visited Ma'alla had never actually come in contact with her.

'Pop', who shared a room with David, was reputed to visit Ma'alla Mary once a week, but he certainly did not catch the 'clap'. Maybe he just drank at the seedy bars in Ma'alla and fondled the girls there. Nobody knew as he was a loner. Anyhow, the trucks were always full.

Those who went on to Steamer Point just had time to visit the cinema, but were not allowed to frequent the few hotels. Many tended to saunter round the little shops in the alleys that cris-cross the area behind the seafront at Steamer Point. One can buy anything there quite cheaply as it is a 'free port' with no tax on any item. From Rolex watches, Pentax cameras, jade, ivory, silver, to cheap clothes, towels and plastic items, all could be purchased in a myriad of little businesses. Bartering was the accepted method and an entertaining evening could be achieved, and maybe a bargain, with a little skill.

At times when the wooden dhows from Africa came across the water to bring their wares, they also brought 'grass' or "khat". Khat is a native plant from Ethiopia, a semi-narcotic, and looks a little like a tea plant or privet. It is grown in huge quantities in Kenya and exported to the Arab world where it is chewed to produce a semi-intoxicated state. Many shopkeepers in Aden use it when it is available, the first forty-eight hours of freshness producing the best results. They become intoxicated. At such times a real bargain may be negotiated. Frequently the shopkeeper will be so 'happy' that he lets an item go at a 'rock bottom' price. David actually got a lens- hood for his camera for nothing from one befuddled shopkeeper who spun a coin to complete the deal.

On another occasion, David was passing a little shop that sold wicker baskets, amongst other things. The owner and some of his friends were sitting outside chewing 'grass'. As he went past the lid of a basket flew open and a huge cobra waved its fanged head. David yelled with surprise and shot like a rocket up the street. He hated snakes. The Arabs outside the shop threw themselves about with laughter. David's companions, who were behind him and saw the incident, told him that the lid of the basket was raised by pulling a piece of string, and the snake was made of rubber and on a spring. They laughed as much as the Arabs, but David has quite a shocked and did not see the funny side until much later.

The back streets were an experience in themselves. They were narrow, busy, smelly and exciting. Goats wandered amongst potential customers, flies were everywhere, filthy stalls offered glasses of tea and Arab delicacies, and traders shouted out the superiority of their wares. A few Arab women, dressed in black from head to foot with their faces covered, would subserviently accompany their husbands. One never knew what was to be found in each shop as they sold almost everything all jumbled together. A shop could have a tray of expensive watches and cameras alongside cheap plastic buckets and jugs, children's toys and male and female underwear. To purchase something, one had to go from shop to shop, ask for the item, compare prices, and then return to where you wanted to make the purchase in the hope that the shopkeeper would keep his word. Shopping took time and patience.

Shopkeepers could be very insistent, and unless you were quite tough, browbeat you into their shop to sell you something you did not want. At first David was too polite and was hauled into the shop to find it difficult to extricate himself. Over time, he learnt to be firm and sometimes rude when a trader would not take no for an answer. There were, of course, the young boys who tried to be helpful in order to earn a few coins. Others offered their sisters for sex. "You like my sister?"

"No, *imshi – go away.*"

"You like me?"

There were also the beggars. Begging is a 'profession' in that part of the world and parents often mutilate their children so they have a profession in life. Many beggars have twisted limbs, unnaturally contorted to arouse pity. The military authorities told the troops not to give to beggars as it only encouraged the practice.

Most Saturday evenings David was on duty in the medical center. Sergeant Henton and he usually alternated with Saturday evenings as they both were no bothered by weekends. As Sergeant Henton once observed, "When your family is not with you, every day is like the next." As was usual, 'Pop' had gone to visit Ma'alla Mary and the others were off duty doing their own thing. It was David's turn to be on duty overnight, and so he had brought his book to help the night along. Treatments had been few. Trouper Peters had popped in for a chat and then was collected by his friend and they had gone off to the cinema. The cinema was showing James Dean in 'Rebel without a Cause' (1) and half the camp seemed to be going to see it.

Generally, the men of the Life Guards were fit and well. They all lived in air-conditioned accommodation, unlike the York and Lancs, and so the ills of the intense heat rarely got to them. The senior NCOs, who ran the regiment, looked after their men and made sure discipline was sensible. There were parades, usually early in the morning when it was cooler, so heatstroke and prickly heat was rare.

David rarely did a parade. Somehow his name was missed off the parade list. He suspected that his friend, Corporal Watts in the COs office, had a lapse of memory on parade days. However, he had done one parade, taken by a major, a belted Earl who was reputed to be a close friend of the Queen and Prince Philip. The parade would remain in his memory for the rest of his life, for he had never heard such foul language used by a person before. Here was a Peer of the Realm with a vocabulary that would make a stevedore (2) blush. As David realized early in his military career, obscene language was a way of life, but the obscenities used by this 'gentleman' were beyond belief. It was all said in an 'upper crust' voice with the venom of a rattle-snake. The trouper in the telephone exchange next to David's room said that the officer and his wife spoke to each other with obscenities as well. So much for the aristocracy!

Another officer, a twenty-one year old Lord and a platoon commander, was as nutty as a fruitcake. It was said that daddy was rich and influential in top circles so that his eccentric son obtained a commission. On patrol this tall, willowy officer would wear his revolver low-slung on his hips like a cowboy. When the sergeant bellowed, "In'juns about, sir," he would spin his revolver on a finger like a cowboy and take aim. To add to this, he was seen about the camp wearing a shirt and Arab *futta* - a sort of skirt – a red Egyptian fez and dragging a monkey on a piece of string.

One Saturday evening, an evening that David would never forget, he was quietly sat reading when one of the regimental police brought an Arab civilian to him. It was just after eleven, as he had glanced at his watch a few minutes before to see if it was time for his coffee break. The man, dressed in western clothes, was obviously agitated. "Accident. Bad. Come," was all he could say.

"Where?" asked David.

"Road.....truck," was said in broken English. "Come..... car ....outside."

"It's at the gate," the regimental policeman offered.

David asked the regimental policeman to contact Corporal Harper and to inform the MO. "Get Corporal Harper to come with an ambulance."

He grabbed his emergency bag, a large electric torch and ran with the Arab to his Toyota and they were off at breakneck speed.

David wondered if he would arrive at the accident in one piece as the man drove so fast. Once the refinery with all its lights was passed, it was pitch black. It was a dark night and there were no moon. One each side of them was blackness: the desert sands stretching relentlessly into the distance. Luckily there was no oncoming traffic and so the headlights lit the road adequately.

Suddenly a light appeared in the distance, a faint light. As they got closer, David could see it was a person holding a torch and waving it to signal them to stop. When he got out of the car he could see little until his eyes adjusted to the darkness. A northern voice asked, "Are you the doctor?"

"No, I'm a medic," David replied. "The doctor and an ambulance are on their way."

By now David could see that there was a military truck overturned on the sand at the side of the road. It was clear that this was the 'late truck', the last of the three that picked up the stragglers. The other two must have been back at camp. "Is anyone trapped?" David asked the man who turned out to be a sergeant from the Prince of Wales Own Regiment.

"No, but there are a number of casualties. We've not moved anyone."

"You OK?" asked David.

"Scratches and bruises, nothing much."

"Right. Can you get someone to come with me and hold my torch?" suggested David. In the meantime can you round up those wandering about and keep them together, sergeant? Have a look at them all and get any injuries ready for me to deal with."

David had little time to assess the situation. He could see figures lying on the ground and a group sitting on the edge of the road while the rest of the occupants of the lorry wandered around aimlessly, obviously in shock.

The sergeant designated a soldier who was not injured to go with him and hold his torch. It was a great shock to both of them when the light fell on the smashed face of the first figure emerging from the darkness. The jaw was dislocated and probably broken, there was a three-inch gash across his forehead and blood was everywhere. The man opened his eyes as the light fell on his face, seemed to try to move his mouth to say something, and then passed out. David was immediately worried about the reaction of his helper as he did not want him passing out. "Ok mate?" he asked.

"Ok doc. Don't worry about me," came the response.

David turned the man onto his side and made sure the windpipe could not be blocked from his tongue. He gave the man a shot of morphine to help with the pain and hastily tied a label (3) round his neck from the emergency pack he carried on his jacket. He scrawled a large M on the label. And before he moved on to the next shadowy figure, he got an uninjured soldier to stay with him.

There was a groan from the next figure before David even got close. Obviously the man was in pain. His flashlight revealed that the man had been badly scalded. He must be the driver. His clothes were wet and sticking to his flesh. Blisters were beginning to form on his face and the backs of his hands. There was little David could do except make him comfortable and reduce the pain. The clothes would have to be carefully cut away in hospital and specialist treatment given. He

227

administered morphine and labeled him, spoke quietly to the man to reassure him, put a folded jacket under his head and directed an uninjured soldier to stay with him.

The third figure he saw had a badly fractured leg. It looked as if the thigh was shattered from the way the leg was sitting. David gave the man a morphine shot to kill the pain then strapped his injured leg to his good leg to immobilize it ready for transportation in the ambulance. There was little he could do in the field. It was another hospital case. This time he wrote a large M on the man's forehead, made him comfortable and posted another soldier, who was only suffering from cuts and bruises, by his side.

He had just finished with the fracture case when the MO arrived in his car, followed by the ambulance and Corporal Harper. David reported what he had done. The MO then took charge and directed Corporal Harper to look at the sitting injured.

"Right Corporal," he said, "let's look at the serious cases."

When he saw the soldier with the smashed jaw he immediately ordered him taken to the ambulance. "Nasty," was his comment. "You did right to make sure his air passage was kept clear and to put someone with him. If they turn over it can be fatal. We'll get him to hospital as fast as we can."

He then went with David to see the scalded soldier. "Not much to be done here, corporal. The hospital will have to carefully remove his clothes and find the extent of the burns. Right, get him into the ambulance." Corporal Harper then reported that there were two with broken arms and one soldier with a sprained ankle. The rest had a few cuts and bruises but nothing serious. "OK, we'll have a look at the fractured thigh and get him into the ambulance and the two with broken arms can go too. You go with the ambulance Corporal Earl and I'll follow when I've checked the rest of the fellows."

David was amazed when he looked at his watch that the whole operation from his arrival at the scene to the departure of the ambulance had taken about a half hour only. From what he could learn from the slightly injured soldiers he had talked to, was that the driver had been blinded by an oncoming car's headlights and swerved off the road. The rough terrain at the side of the road had caused the vehicle to turn over, and because it had no canopy, to throw the occupants out. The driver had crawled from his cab scalded by the hot water from the engine.

Now military ambulances are made for rough terrain in warfare and not sprung very well. Hence, the journey to the Refinery Hospital in Little Aden was not a pleasant one. It was hot, as there was no air conditioning and the ventilation openings were small. It was rather bumpy, even though the roads were smooth. The soldier with the fractured pelvis found the journey very painful as the broken bones touched each other at every bump. David had to apply traction by pulling gently on the foot to stop the bones from coming together. It was the only solution and reduced the groans of the patient. The other patients were either suitably sedated or stoically accepting their lot.

The hospital emergency staff were ready when the ambulance arrived. They had been alerted in advance by telephone before the MO left his home. He did not know the extent of the accident but understood there were casualties. There was no phone out there in the desert so he had to anticipate the possibilities. It was a relief for David to hand over the responsibility to others, and for the first time the enormity of the situation hit him and he began to shake and feel sick. The ambulance driver, a soldier in the Prince of Wales Own Regiment, a man in his forties, must have seen David's sudden change and asked, "Are you all right mate?"

"I....well....I feel a little sick," David responded.

"Shock mate. Just come over you, 'as it?"

"Mm...I suddenly realized what has happened. It was all a blur while I was working but now..." he observed quietly.

The man put his arm round David's shoulder. "Sit down, mate. I'll get us a cup of tea. Made me feel queer too." With that he was away to scrounge some tea.

He was soon returned with two mugs of sweet tea. "Here, drink that mate," he said handing David the steaming brew. "Got friends here.....make excellent tea." He smiled. "Come here quite often to see my girl. Nurse here."

David drank the tea and slowly he began to feel better. What a night it had been. For the last hour he had been under such pressure without really realizing it. Adrenalin had been pumping around his veins and all he thought about were the injured soldiers and what he could do to help them. Now his nervous system had had time to adjust and there was a contrary reaction.

His thoughts were broken by the ambulance driver. "You did a good job, mate. Got it sorted out mostly before your MO arrived. Nice work. Easy to panic but you didn't."

"I didn't have time to think, let alone panic," was David's response. "After seeing that smashed face, I was just driven on by..... I don't know what. Training? Empathy? Maybe anger that such a thing could happen."

"You did well lad," came the reassurance. "How old are you?"

"Not quite twenty-one," David told him.

"Twenty. You're very cool for one so young."

"I was then, but not so cool now," was David's response.

'That's natural. I've seen lots of horrible things being an ambulance driver, but it still gets to me."

"Did what you saw tonight affect you then?" David asked innocently.

"So, so....." the ambulance driver replied waving his hand from side to side. "You'll be fine after a good night's sleep."

And so he was. The ambulance dropped him at the guardhouse around four o'clock in the morning and after a quick word with the guard commander, David crept into bed without waking 'Pop' who was snoring enough to rattle the shutters. His snoring did not keep David awake long. He was so tired that not even memories of the evening kept him awake. It wasn't until 'Pop' brought him a mug of tea before he went on duty that he saw the light of day. "Sergeant Henton says to sleep in, Dave. I understand you had a rough night." With that he was off to the medical center leaving David to go back to sleep.

Around midday, after he had showered and shaved and was almost ready to report for duty, Major Benton appeared in his room with Sergeantl Henton. David stood to attention. He must have looked worried as the first thing the MO said was, "Well don't look so anxious corporal, we're not here to reprimand you. Just the opposite. We've come see you're all right and to say well done."

"Thank you, sir," David replied relaxing a little.

"I also want to pass on the appreciation of the colonel of the Prince of Wales Own as the men involved were his."

David could not believe it. The colonel of a regiment sending personal thanks.

"What you did last night was very prompt and very effective. I had little to do after your good works."

Sergeant Henton chipped in, "What you did was in the real spirit of the RAMC corporal."

David did not know what to say as his thoughts were in turmoil. He thought of the injured men. "What about the badly injured, sir?"

"I understand the burns case and the facial injury are to be flown back to the UK sometime tomorrow as they need specialist treatment. The fractures all will be fine."

"That's good news, sir," David offered with a smile.

"Well, young man," the MO beamed, "you did a great job. Well done." He turned to go and then stopped at the door. "My two monsters want to know if uncle will be at the beach this afternoon." He paused and looked at David. "Will you?"

David broke into a broad grin. "Of course, sir. Can't let the monsters down, can I?"

David saw Eric and Irene at church that evening and they had heard about his exploits. "I understand you did a great job, David," Eric observed shaking his hand enthusiastically. Irene kissed him on both cheeks. "It's exactly what I expected of you. You're Aires, capable and giving."

David was embarrassed by all this praise but intrigued how the news had crept out. "How did you know?" he asked.

"Eric has his spies," giggled Irene and winked.

"Remember the man who raised the alarm and took you in his car...?"

"Yes."

"He works in administration at the refinery. He rang me this morning. I tend to hear most things that are remotely to do with the refinery."

"He drives like a maniac," David observed, "but he helped to save life by his generous action. Please thank him for me."

"I'll certainly do that," promised Eric. "Now young man, as a reward, what about a trip round the refinery?"

"That would be super Eric," David responded. He had wanted to have a look round for a long time being Aires and inquisitive he could have reminded Irene.

"That's fixed then. What about Tuesday morning, say ten o'clock?" Eric enquired.

"I'm not on duty that morning but I'll check with Major Benton to see if he approves." David did not want to tread on any toes by accepting Eric's generous offer.

Eric collected David in his car. The refinery was only about a quarter of a mile from the camp, but it was far too hot to walk. They were waved through the gate, although Eric had to sign David in as a guest. "Can't be too careful," Eric explained. "Everyone keeps to the rules including me. Colonel Nasser is breeding discontent everywhere in the Arab world and a refinery is a legitimate target. That's why you people are here." He glanced at David. "Although some of your officers think they're here to play polo." He winked.

"The senior NCOs won't let you down, Eric. They're an excellent mob." David was always supportive of the Life Guard's senior NCOs as they were impressive, efficient and fair.

"From the ones I've met – the ones who go to church – I think you're right, David."

"You don't seem to have much time for the officers, Eric?" David observed.

"Not really. They mix very little in the Club. Their manners at times have much to be desired. I'm sure they think they are slumming at the Club. Keep to their own kind. Most of the refinery personnel didn't go to the right school."

"Or speak with the right accent," David added.

"True lad," Eric replied with a broad Yorkshire twang.

"You know, Eric, before I did my service I had never really came across snobbery. Oh, there are one or two my mother came in contact with on the Conservative committee who had airs and graces, but basically they were just unsure of themselves and pretended to be superior. When you got to know them they were ok."

"Not so sure that's the case with your chaps," Eric observed with serious look on his face. "They really do think they're superior. Dinosaurs really. The world is changing. They'll be left behind eventually."

Eric parked the care alongside a number of others. "No reserved space, Eric - for the boss?" David asked mischievously.

"No. We're all equal citizens here," he laughed. "There's plenty of parking so why pull rank?"

They walked across from the office block to an area that consisted of various widths of metal pipe all painted silver and twisting and turning in all directions. There were huge valves here and there and some valves emitted a little steam. Eric suggested that they climb up one of the adjoining 'cracking' tower (4) so they could get a 'birds eye' view and then he could point out the various parts of the huge complex. He handed David a pair of cotton gloved that he had in his pocket. "Wear these, David, as the metal handrail as we go up is likely to be hot from the sun."

There were hundreds of metals steps winding up the tower and it was true, the handrail was hot. David could feel it through the gloves. By the time they got to the top, both of them were hot and breathless. However, there was a little shade from some large pipes and they welcomed it. They must have been sixty feet up and a gentle breeze also helped them cool off.

The view was fantastic. One could see three hundred and sixty degrees across the bay to Steamer Point, around the many little bays that formed Little Aden, and right across miles and miles of desert sand. They were silent for a while as David took in the vista. At his feet was the sprawling refinery and the tanker harbor. To the left, at the foot of the hill David and his friends had trundled up to get a good view, was the hospital. The hill seemed just a pimple and the hospital a child's toy. Further round were the homes of employees, the regimental accommodation, the cinema and churches, and on the beach the Bureka Club with a tiny fenced beach area. It was all in miniature.

David turned to Eric. "It looks like Lilliput appeared to Gulliver." (5)

"I've never thought of that, David. You're right. It's a fantastic view though?"

"Fantastic."

"Now let me explain what you see," Eric began. "The dock is obvious. When a tanker with crude oil arrives – that is the thick oil out of the ground – it is pumped into those storage tanks you see on the left of you. It's held there until we are ready to 'crack' it, that is, break it down into a usable form. That is done by using heat in a sort of distillation process. In the center, behind the office block is the power plant generating electricity to work the pumps and provide energy for the whole process. It's the key to everything. It generates enough electricity to provide for a medium-sized town.

"So you have four 'cracking' towers?" David asked.

"Yes, but they are not all in use at once. We tend to use two at any given time, unless there is a demand for maximum capacity. Waste gases are burnt over there to your extreme right. You can see the flame atop the tower – very hot and fierce. We have our own fire service, although the plant is fitted everywhere with a safety foam system."

"The firemen have a good job," joked David. "Not much to do."

Eric smiled. "In fact, they're kept very busy. They are our safety people too and are constantly inspecting the plant. If they do their job properly we should have no accidents. Any problem and it is immediately put right. A serious problem and we close down a section. That's why we generally only have two towers in production at any one time. We can switch very quickly. Everything is monitored in the main control room as well. That's the place that stands on its own on the very far left. It's a safety measure in case of fire."

"What happens to your new product?" David asked.

"See those tanks on the dock?" Eric pointed.

"Yes, the four big silver ones?"

"The refined oil is stored there ready for pumping onto tankers that take it to Europe," Eric told David.

"It's quite a process."

They came down from the tower quicker than they went up and certainly were not so breathless. Eric took David into his office in the administration block and his secretary brought them each a glass of ice cold Coka-Cola. The room was large and air-conditioned with a view across to the dock. There were three easy chairs around a coffee table, a large desk with two phones and an 'in' and 'out' trays, and in one corner a long table with ten chairs round it. They sat in the easy chairs and drank their cold drink.

"Your office looks cosy with its easy chairs and coffee table," observed David.

"I find talking to people in an informal way makes better relationships. Yes, I'm the boss but we're all part of a team. There is no need to thrust status down an employee's throat. Sitting behind a big desk produces a barrier," Eric offered.

"I wish some military officers had that view. They just thrust their superior status down your throat at every opportunity," David complained. "You know, Eric, the best officer I ever had was a Major with the York and Lancs. I met him up country. Everyone respected him as he was informal and fair. We called him 'Ken' when nobody was around but 'Major' when brother officers were about. Nobody took advantage and everybody worked their socks off for him."

"Exactly, David. You earn respect, the sort of respect that lasts. You can force it through pulling rank and through fear, but it is only a temporary condition." There was silence for a while and then Eric went on: "Being a boss is not easy. If you are too informal it is often interpreted as weakness and taken advantage of, on the other hand, if you are too formal and strict you lose the confidence of your workers and they tell you little of what they actually think. Good communication is essential."

"I wish you'd tell that to our bishop," was David's response.

Eric's had a puzzled expression on his face. "Why, David? I thought bishops were approachable and kind."

"They should be," David offered. "Our bishop likes to be called 'My Lord' and we ordinands are terrified of him."

"You surprise me, David."

"No kidding, Eric. He doesn't seem to have much charity in his nature. Even our Director of Ordinands bows and scrapes to him."

"What's his background?" enquired Eric.

"I believe he was the principal of a theological college before he became a bishop."

"An academic rather than a pastor. Someone who has had very little pastoral experience. A politician," David nodded.

"There are too many like that in the Church. That's one of the reasons why people are leaving the Church," Eric offered. "Not leaders of men but bullies of men."

There was a silence while David mulled over Eric's comments and

234

then he asked. " Are leaders born to lead or can they be trained?"

Eric was somewhat surprised. "Wow, David, what a question. He thought for a while and looked out towards the sea. He then turned to David and explained. "There are some people who are born leaders. Churchill, for instance, Gandhi who led from the front, Alexander the Great who must have had great charisma, and... it may be bold to say it, but even Hitler."

David raised his eyebrows.

"Yes, Hitler, although it may surprise you. But he used his talent, his charisma, for evil purposes. These leaders have what we call 'charisma' or special personalities that cause people to follow them. There are others kinds of leaders who have technical abilities like Henry Ford or Frank Whittle.(6) Other leaders like your bishop or the Queen are appointed for other reasons and they have to take on the leadership mantle."

"So there are a number of different kinds of leader," David suggested

"Yes. Just as there are many styles of leadership. Most people learn to lead, either through experience or by being trained. In the armed forces they have leadership courses and likewise in industry and commerce. There are psychological tests to help assess leadership qualities. I prefer the practical approach. The man or woman who serves his time and rises up the organization through sheer ability."

"Can you spot people with leadership qualities then?"

"Yes," Eric replied. I think you can recognize a good leader quite early on in a person's career. They become good leaders if they recognize their mistakes and learn from them."

"I'll remember that," David laughed, "as I make plenty of mistakes."

"Do you want to lead, David?"

That was a difficult question to ask and David thought for a while. "Well," he said, "I don't exactly lust to be a leader as some people do, but as a priest you automatically become a leader. You are thrust into it whether you like it or not. I would like to think I cared about the people in my parish and set an example, if that is what you call leadership. Like the famous Father Potter of Peckham. (7) You know, he actually turned down becoming a bishop as he wanted to stay close to his parishoners."

"Interesting. I've not heard of Father Potter," noted Eric.

"There's a small book about him in SPCK. (8) He died a little while ago."

"Mm," Eric said thoughtfully. "I'll try to get the book." He looked at his watch. "Gosh, it's two o'clock. Time I got you back to camp."

Chapter 18

Early in July David found on Orders that he was to travel home the following month on a troopship in preparation for demobilization. His time in Aden seemed to have gone so quickly when he compared it to training and his sojourn in London. Two years of enforced slavery were nearly over.

Some of his friends warned him that life on a troopship was not really a pleasant one. Apparently, the accommodation was cramped, the food bad, and the discipline very 'military'. It would be quite a shock after the excellent treatment he had been given with the Life Guards. However, the day after his name had appeared on Orders his friend, Corporal Watts, visited him as was his custom, but opened up about his impending return to England. "I saw Orders, David, and apparently you are to return home by troopship. How do you feel about it?"

"I've no option, Derek," observed David. "That's what Orders say."

"Would you like to fly home?" Corporal Watts asked.

"Fly?" David was quite dumbfounded.

"Yes. I think I can fiddle you a flight. There are lots of flights to the UK from Khormaksar and I'm sure I could get you one."

"But how? asked David.

"Well, the Life Guards are always sending someone or other by air to the UK. Nobody asks any question when we arrange a seat. I'm sure I can fix it."

"That would be wonderful," David responded, not quite able to believe was he had been told. "But won't you get into trouble if you're found out?"

"No," Derek replied. "Most days the colonel just signs what I give him. Some days I just forge his signature."

"But...doesn't he know?" asked David incredulously.

"Oh, yes. But frequently the call of polo is stronger than signing bits of paper."

Corporal Watts was as good as his word. Orders showed a few days later that David was to fly home on 29th July. When Derek Watts came to visit David the next time, he was thanked warmly for his action. "No problem, David," he smiled. "You've been a good friend to me. It's the least I can do."

"But I've done nothing, Derek. You come regularly to visit me in my room. Sometimes I've been to your room. We've talked. But we've never been out together, although I've tried to persuade you to come with me to the beach."

"You've listened to my ramblings about my family, David," Derek pointed out. "Besides you are a lovely person and I enjoy your company."

David could feel himself blush. He said nothing.

"You know, David," Derek Watts went on, "you are very handsome and have a super physique. I've just enjoyed looking at you. Maybe my son will turn out like you when he grows up."

They smiled at each other. Did Derek Watts know that David knew of his love. Maybe, but he was not going to admit it. "Derek," David said most sincerely, "I think you are very handsome too and I have enjoyed our conversations. I shall miss you."

They agreed to write and exchanged addresses. David never heard from Corporal Derek Watts again, although he wrote to him a couple of times.

The last few days with the Life Guards, before his departure, became a whirl of activity. There were all kinds of administrative things he had to complete before his departure and then he had to say goodbye to his friends.

Irene and Eric gave a little dinner party for him and invited the Padre and his wife. It was a lovely evening but deep emotions lurked behind their jollity. Irene cried when he said his final goodbye, and David fought hard to hold back the tears. He actually kept in contact with Irene and Eric for many years until one day he received a letter from their daughter, now married, to say that Irene had died of cancer and Eric had gone to work in Iran. David cried bitterly for they had been true friends. Later in life, he often wondered what happened to Eric. They were two people he would keep locked in his affections forever.

It was with a heavy heart that he told Peppino of his impending flight home. He arranged that he would tell him on the beach in the exact spot where they had revealed their love some many months before. Peppino knew that at some time David would leave the army and go on to university, but did not expect it quite so soon,

"Davie, oh Davie," was all he could say as tears streamed down his face. "I know you must go but....." He could not go on as huge sobs shook his body.

David cried too. He loved Peppino. He never realized how much. He would truly miss him. His smile, those flashing eyes, his sense of humor, his vitality, and that lovely muscular body like a sensuous cat. His sobs cut like a knife into David's heart. Nobody had ever cared for him like this. He put his arms around him and hugged him tightly until eventually his sobs subsided. "Peppino," offered David, "we are so young and have a whole lifetime ahead. What we have had here is wonderful, but it can't go on forever. I'm to be a priest and you will get married. Let us always savor the memory of our relationship in our hearts."

"Davie you right. I never forget you. You write me sometime?"

"Of course, Peppino carro," David gently responded.

They wandered back along the beach after kissing each other with passion. Now they were both calm and reconciled to their parting. Neither looked back when they got to the camp's main gate. David and Peppino did write for a number of years. They even met in Rimini when David was on holiday in Italy. But the letters became infrequent and the last thing David heard was that Peppino was working for an airline and had been moved to Egypt. He wondered if Peppino ever married?

David's fellow NCOs in the Life Guards gave him a farewell party in the NAAFI the night before his departure. It was a boisterous affair and the beer flowed. David was careful not to drink too much as he had to be up early the next morning, and he didn't want to have a hangover. He joined in with the singing, and took part in the conga around the NAAFI, and at ten thirty when it closed, he went to his room and lay down on his bed and listened to 'Pop' snoring for the last time.

On the morning of his departure, David was up early and breakfasted in the cookhouse. The duty cook had insisted that David have a good breakfast. The cooks were always up early anyhow and an early breakfast was no problem. He was happy that he had no hangover from the party the previous evening, and two mugs of steaming tea, bacon and egg and toast prepared him for the journey.

A Land-Rover was waiting for him at the guardhouse and he was soon on his way the ten miles round the bay. Nobody else from the Life Guards was joining the flight. However, when he got to the airport, he found that there were quite a few people waiting for the flight. His leave orders were checked and his kitbag taken from him. He looked around and found that they were mostly families returning to the U.K., but amongst them were eight or nine senior officers who kept together in an exclusive group. He found that the only other junior personnel on the flight were two RAF corporals. He found they were from Singapore and had been posted back to Britain. They were very friendly and David did not feel quite so out-of-place.

"You're lucky," the RAF corporal, called John, told him.

"Why?" David asked.

"You don't know?" John was quite amazed. "We're on a Comet."(1)

"It took the Duke of Gloucester out to Singapore on some official visit and instead of returning empty it picked up a few favored individuals," the other RAF corporal, called Patrick, told David.

"Wow! I'm impressed," David observed. He had heard of the Comet, the latest subsonic airliner that could fly high over the clouds. The newspapers had been full of information.

"I believe we are privileged. See that group over there?" Patrick pointed to the officers. "They're 'top brass', probably Ministry men and the rest are the families of officers returning to the U.K."

"How come you managed this privilege, David?" John asked.

David pretended ignorance. "Don't really know. But when you serve with the Life Guards anything is possible.

John and Patrick looked at each other in a knowing way. "Senior British Regiment and all that?" observed Patrick.

"Suppose so," commented David and left it at that.

After a while they were politely asked to walk out onto the tarmac and identify their baggage, which had been placed in two rows some distance from the plane. Dawn was just coming up and the plane could be seen clearly. It was beautiful with sleek lines and the RAF insignia on the tail fin. Its engines were already humming. Of course, the officers went first, then the families, and last the three 'misfits' on the privileged flight.

The Comet was quite wonderful. David thought it was the most beautiful aeroplane he had ever seen. Its sleek form and white paint with the RAF insignia made it so different, and it had jet engines rather than propellers. Propellers, David thought, made a plane look ugly. They walked up the steps to the doorway near the nose of the plane and were greeted by an RAF steward who showed them to their seats. The senior officers were already seated and studied the three juniors somewhat suspiciously. The families were noisily and chaotically settling down in their seats and fastening their seat belts. There must have been about thirty passengers, although David calculated it could hold three times that figure. They were privileged.

The cabin door was closed, the cabin staff, four stewards, took their seats and the plane taxied onto the runway. With an immense thrust the plane took off. It did not seem to need much runway and climbed almost vertically into the air. They were above the barren rocks of Aden quickly and heading out to sea. David caught a glimpse of the storage tanks at Little Aden, reflecting the rising sun as if they were made of silver, and then they were gone. Would he ever see Aden again? No, perhaps not. Would he see his many friends again? He hoped so.

The Comet flew high above the clouds so there was little to see.

David had been given a window seat and had hoped to get a view of Africa as they flew north but it was not to be. He did, however, get a wonderful view of the curvature of the earth as they flew over the desert region of North Africa. There were the cotton wool clouds below, and above, a darkness almost like a black fog, and to his left, an orange haze from the sun, and then the curved surface of the earth. It was quite amazing and something he had read about in books but never thought he would actually see.

Breakfast was served at around eight o'clock. It was excellent. Tea or coffee, cornflakes, scrambled egg and toast and marmalade. Everyone seemed to have the same. No first class discrimination here. After breakfast David dozed. It had taken him an age to get to sleep the previous night. It was partly due he supposed to being 'hyper' after the party and partly because of the excitement of actually going home. Home......home to his family...to his mother's love, and cooking....to his friends......to university.......even his father's negative attitude to him did not seem so bad.

He was awakened by the pilot's voice over the intercom saying that they would be landing at El Adam Air Base in Libya in a half hour for refueling. They would have lunch there. They were half way home.

Coming in to land, David could see that the airbase was right in the middle of the desert. It was a basic place with a runway, airport buildings, a control tower, fuel storage tanks, some hangers, and a little way off some tiny houses and other buildings. When he came down the steps from the plane, he could see that everything was much larger than it seemed. They were shepherded across the tarmac of the runway and into the terminal building where they were divided into two groups. There was no passport control as the airbase was nominally British territory. The officers and families went in two buses to the officers' mess. David and the two others were driven in a Jeep to the NCO's mess.

After being shown the bathroom, they were escorted to a table set for three. Lunch was collected from a large serving hatch and there was a good choice. It was clear that the RAF looked after their personnel in the middle of the desert. After tomato soup, meat pie and chips, jam sponge and custard follow by coffee, David was satiated and ready for a good sleep. It was not to be. They were summoned to leave and the Jeep took them back to the aeroplane. It had taken just two hours and they were off again.

David slept all the way to Britain and was awakened by one of the stewards telling him they would be landing in ten minutes and to make sure his seat belt was fastened. He glanced out of the window. It was dark and lights on the ground were twinkling. He hardly felt them land. The plane was like a bird that drops out of the sky and gently paddles along the ground. He was home, or at least back in Britain, and soon to be released from his bonds.

There were formalities at RAF Lynham where they had landed. Passports were checked and customs awaited like vultures pouncing on easy prey. It took an age. The senior officers and families came in for intense scrutiny and had to open all their luggage. When it got to the three boys, they were let through without a comment. David reasoned that the customs had earned their quota from the officers and families. He assumed, perhaps rightly, that they thought the other ranks were so poorly paid that they could not afford to bring much back of value.

When he got through all the formalities, the RAF boys said goodbye and reported to the RAF authorities. David reported to a military policeman, who checked his travel documents and phoned for transport to take him to the RAMC Depot at Crookham. While he was waiting, he managed to get a coffee and doughnut at a coffee bar at the terminal run by the NAAFI. Good old NAFFI: they were always there when they were needed.

It was nearly midnight when the Land-Rover deposited him at Headquarters Company office. The vehicle had come all the way from the Depot to collect him, and the cheery private driving had chattered all the way. David appreciated his talk as he did not want to arrive half asleep, even though he felt tired. The main guardhouse waved them through and the duty corporal in the office put David into an empty barrack room just round the corner. It struck David as rather strange that the room was empty, but he was so tired he threw the sheets and blankets on the bed and was sleeping like a baby within minutes.

He woke late but nobody seemed to mind. After a leisurely breakfast, he reported at the HQ office. Sure enough his old friend Sergeant York was still handling the paperwork for those going abroad and returning home. He was delighted to see David and greeted him like a long-lost brother. On examining his orders, all he could say was, "You're early."

David explained that the Life Guards had sent him home for demobilization. Sergeant York took him to see the Duty Officer who commented, "Who are we to contradict the Life Guards?' and signed to send him on leave the following day. He argued that he was due some leave anyway and there was nothing to do at the camp. "We've just taking in our last intakes," he told David. "The government had stopped National Service." (2)

The empty barrack room then fitted into the picture.

242

David phoned his parents. They were so surprised and very pleased. His mother shed a few tears as she snuffled down the phone. "We'll drive down and pick you up, David," his father said. "I expect you have all your kit with you and it's heavy to lug from one train to another, particularly when you have to cross London. We'll be there in the late afternoon."

And so, the following afternoon, a Saturday afternoon, a large, new MG Magnet saloon in two-tone gray with gray leather upholstery and walnut facia drew up at the guardhouse to collect 933 Corporal David Earl, RAMC. A phone call had informed him of their arrival and David emerged, broad shouldered, bronzed, fit and with a greater confidence, dressed in his green tweed jacket, cavalry-twill trousers and green trilby. They were the same clothes he had worn when he joined up, but now they were tighter across the shoulders: it was not the same David Earl, however, who had entered those gates two years earlier.

Chapter 19

Trafalgar Square in London is known the world over. Its huge obelisk topped by a statue of Admiral Horatio Nelson has been photographed by millions of tourists. The column was erected by a grateful people after the Battle of Trafalgar, which provides the name to the square. At its feet are enormous lions, and nearby are fountains, that have given many a reveler a drenching. Thousands of pigeons assemble every day in the square, hoping that the unwary visitor will provide a meal, and are equally as famous as the square itself. To the back of the square is the imposing façade of the National Portrait Gallery, to the left the church of St Martins in the Fields, and to the right is Admiralty Arch. Through the Arch is the Mall leading to Buckingham Palace, standing in majestic splendor. In front of the visitor is Whitehall, which contains the various imposing buildings of government, and down this wide road is the Cenotaph, a memorial to the fallen in two World Wars. Further on to the right is Downing Street, (1) where the official home of the Prime Minister is found, and at the end of this great thoroughfare are the Houses of Parliament and Westminster Abbey.

This is Central London and among this collection of historic buildings is Kings College. It is situated at the far end of the Strand, which is one of the roads that radiates on the left from Trafalgar Square. It is a busy street of shops and offices, and contains the famous Savoy Hotel and Savoy Theatre where W.S. Gilbert and Arthur Sullivan performed their comic operas. The street is intersected at right angles by Vauxhall Bridge Road, and some three hundred yards after this intersection is the archway leading to Kings. It is right next to the imposing Somerset House – once the London home of the Dukes of Somerset but now the depository of the nation's records of births, deaths and marriages. One could quite easily miss King's College as the gilded nameplate is high above the gate, beyond the normal vision of the pedestrian.

David would have missed the college had it not been for his recognition, from a previous visit, of the church of St Mary Le Strand in the center of the busy road and almost opposite, Kings, and Thresher and Glenny, the expensive outfitters, right by the entrance. He turned into the entrance with many other students one Monday morning ready to begin his first term at the college. On the left of the large courtyard were the steps up to the imposing main entrance. Inside and opposite was a large assembly hall and on each side marble steps taking him up to the college chapel and the office of the Dean. Registration was in the main entrance and through the doors of the great hall David could see that many tables had been set out to provide information to freshmen about the various clubs and societies Kings had to offer.

His demobilization had been quite painless. After just over a month's holiday, he had returned to Crookham for two days to go through the formalities of his release from Military service. He handed in his kit and in return was provided with his paybook, duly stamped, and showing a final wage of two pounds fifteen shillings per week. A travel warrant was issued to him to Leicester.

During the long journey home, it was as if layers of heavy stone were being peeled off his shoulders. Away from the RAMC Depot for the last time, never to see it again, if he could help it, made him feel less tense. London was seen with different eyes when he crossed it to get to St Pancras Railway Station. Now he was not under the endless pressure of the military hospital and its regime, ridiculous discipline, work, study and parades. Another layer of tension was peeled away. He actually looked forward to university in London and exploring the city, something he had never had time for during military service. By the time he got to Leicester, he felt quite light-headed. He wanted to jump up and down and yell, "I'm free, free, free, free..."

Now here he was starting a new chapter in his life. He was staying in lodgings at Turnham Green on the District Line of the London Underground. Turnham Green is an area of large houses, some obviously fading, built at the turn of the century. William Morris, (2) a famous Edwardian designer had designed some of the houses and they were listed as buildings of historic interest. The one he lodged in with the Wentworth sisters was a fine example of the Morris style. It had three floors, a small front garden and a larger back garden and, in a way, was quite attractive, if you subscribed to that style of architecture.

David's parents had driven him down from Leicester. His father had had some difficulty in finding the house and in the end hired a taxi, which they followed through a maze of streets. The lodgings were recommended by the college as the sisters' father had been a priest and the household were regular churchgoers. The local church, St Stephens, was very High Church, and only a hundred yards away from the house. The two sisters and their elderly bedridden mother, as David was to find, were devoted to their religion and their church.

The elder sister, Clair, was about sixty, small and energetic with a mass of gray hair around her wrinkled face. She welcomed David with a smile and a hug. He liked her immediately. At the end of the long, narrow hall with its brown linoleum covering was a winding staircase leading to the other two floors. Just by the staircase was the door to the kitchen. To the right of the hall were two doors, one into a long dining room where he would have his meals with the rest of the household, and the other was that of their private family sitting room.

Up the stairs on the first floor was his room. It was quite small with a window looking over the rear of the house. It was very old fashioned with an iron bedstead, large mahogany wardrobe, writing table and chair, and in the wall a small Victorian iron fireplace in which had been fitted a gas fire. A coin gas meter would fuel the fire on cold evenings. The bathroom, equally archaic, was nearby. This was to be his world for two years. It was comfortable, friendly, and more important, private. A far cry from the military accommodation he had experienced over the past two years.

His mother fussed around and helped him unpack while his father sat on the bed and criticized the untidy gardens he could see from the window. Houses and gardens were back-to-back and a number of gardens were visible, all in need of some hard work. At five o'clock Clair knocked on the door to see if they would like some tea. It was to be served in the dining room. They went down stairs.

The dining room was a long room with a huge polished dining table and eight chairs, a big old-fashioned sideboard, ancient sepia pictures in heavy frames on the walls, a television set on a table and two easy chairs at the side of a fireplace. The room looked over the little front garden where there was a low privet hedge sheltering it from the street. In one of the armchairs was a huge black cat. "That's Nimbus," Clair told them. "He's twelve and very lazy." She picked him up. "Who's a sleepy boy, then?" she enquired of the cat and took him out to her sitting room.

"Can't stand cats," David's father whispered just before Clair returned.

The tea was set out on the dining table. Silver teapot, sugar and cream. Victorian and possibly quite valuable. The bone china tea service had little violets on the sides of cups, saucers and plates, and the spoons were solid silver. There were little homemade cakes on a cake stand. David's mother looked across at him as if to indicate her approval. His mother had been a nanny in London when she was young in the house of the First Sea Lord so she knew how things should be done.

After tea and pleasantries, David's parents left for the long drive home in the certainty that their son would be well looked after. At dinner that evening, David was introduced to the other sister, Patsy, who was much younger and rather severe in her manner. She had worked at the Bank of England, but now retired, she gave her time to the Girls' Friendly Society, a Church of England sponsored youth movement for girls.

The sisters took in three student lodgers, one being their nephew, Martin, who was an architectural student. He was just eighteen and straight from Rugby School. (3) Martin was of medium height, curly haired, bespectacled and had a great sense of humor. His glasses seemed to be always slipping off the end of his nose, and he seemed to be perpetually pushing them back. He talked very quickly and had a slight stutter. David liked the way he referred to his Aunt Patsy's job as working at the 'Friendly Girls' Society.

The third student David met at dinner was Ken Roberts. He was twenty-six years of age, of medium height and thin, with a pale, round face and fine mousy hair. He was commencing his second year at Kings on the Bachelor of Divinity course. David soon found out that he had served in the RAF and was rather contemptuous of the army. He came from Chorley in Lancashire and spoke with a pronounced Lancashire accent. It was quite clear that he was full of himself, and David wondered what sort of priest he would make.

Dinner was a formal affair. A bell was rung in the hall to summon everyone into the dining room. The polished table was laid with solid silver cutlery, as were the two cruet sets, and there was a silver candelabra in the center of the table. Everyone had their own napkin to be held in a silver ring. Grace was said by Patsy, who served from the sideboard, while Clair scurried back and forth to the kitchen. There was oxtail soup to start, roast beef with horseradish sauce, roast and boiled potatoes and buttered cabbage. It really was very good. To follow was jam sponge and custard. Clair was an excellent cook and David felt that he would be well fed.

Martin, David and Ken sat in the dining room after dinner and talked generally in an unconscious attempt to get to know each other. The time went quickly. Suddenly, the bell was rung at ten o'clock to signify evening tea before retiring to bed. The students were invited into the sisters' sitting room. It was comfortably furnished with two huge settees and three easy chairs. There were family photographs on the shelf over the fireplace as well as on a sideboard. The bay window was curtained rather luxuriously. Some ancient oil paintings, depicting religious themes, hung on the walls. Nimbus was dozing on Patsy's lap. Tea was served from a low table in front of the blue and white tiled fireplace, which had black fire irons, a brass poker and a miniature shovel on the tiled hearth. They all chattered about the day's events before David made his exit, wishing them 'good night' and went off to bed. He slept like a log.

David was awoken by Martin banging on his door. "David. If you want to go to communion at eight, the bathroom is free."

It was seven thirty and Sunday morning. "Ok Martin," David yelled rather sleepily through the door. "Thanks. I'll be down in ten minutes."

And so he was. Army training had taught him to complete his ablutions quickly. He had shaved the night before as he knew he would be going to church early. Martin was waiting for him in the hall but there was no sign of Ken

"I must buy an alarm clock, Martin," David commented as they went through the front door.

Saint Stephen's Church was a barn of a place. It was genuine William Morris and unusually, had its chancel and choir raised four steps up above the nave. There was no screen, only a low wall and so the congregation had an excellent view of the service. The choir stalls were painted a light green with darker green embellishments and there was a low pink marble balustrade between the choir and sanctuary. The altar had an ornate green frontal embroidered with INRI in gold thread (4) and the reredos (5) was of the same pink marble with the crucified Christ, angels and saints in relief. There were six gilt candle-holders on the altar holding very tall candles and a huge gold and jeweled crucifix. The stained-glass window behind the altar had the figures of Adam, Abraham, and Moses in the glass. This was the only colored window in the church; the others were clear glass. David wondered if this was intentional or due to lack of funds. He later learned that all the windows were blown out during the war, and this was the only window they could afford to restore

The walls of the church were green tiled to a height of about five feet and the rest of the wall was white. Above the tiled panels, all around the walls, were colored ceramic Stations of the Cross, (6) more than likely designed by Morris, as part of the ambiance of the church. At the west end were large double oak doors, to one side of which was the font for baptisms and on the other side a bookstall. The congregation entered from a side door where there was a ceramic angel holding a bowl of holy water. There were no pews, only rows of chairs each with a petit point kneeler. The whole place smelt of incense.

At each side of the chancel was a side chapel at nave level. One was dedicated to the Virgin Mary where there was a Reserved Sacrament in a safe (7) on the right side with a little red light glowing. The flags of the Mothers' Union and Girl Guides were in holders on the wall at the left hand side of the altar. The other altar was dedicated to Saint Stephen. The boy scouts had placed their flag against the wall at the left side of the altar.

It was to the chapel of the Virgin to which Martin and David made their way. The six candles on the altar were already burning and about a dozen people were already down on their knees in silent prayer. As they knelt down Martin whispered to David, "When Clair and Patsy arrive, don't say anything to them. They like to be silent until mass is over."

"Ok," David whispered back.

Martin gave him a sidelong smile and pushed back his glasses, "They take their religion very seriously."

Within minutes, David saw out of the corner of his eye, that Clair and Patsy were sliding into a pew behind them.

Whilst saying his prayers, David heard a small bell ring and a server in a white alb appeared out of a side door preceded by the Celebrant in white alb with a green stole, maniple and chasuble. (8) He carried a gold chalice. The two genuflected at the altar steps. The server went to kneel at the right step, whist the Celebrant placed the chalice in the center of the altar. He genuflected again and turned to the kneeling congregation with arms raised. "The Lord be with you," he greeted his fellows.

"And with thy Spirit," the congregation replied.

And so the service began with The Lord's Prayer and the beautiful Collect, "Almighty God unto whom all hearts be open, all desires known, and from whom no secrets are hid...." The words of the 1662 Prayer Book were so simple and uplifting. And so the Communion began, the server waiting on the Celebrant smoothly and efficiently.

At the consecration of the bread and wine the server rang a three-toned bell. David had not come across this except in the Roman Church. It was clear that St. Stephen's was going to be 'spiky'. He did not mind as long as the pomp did not interfere with the spirituality of the service. In fact, there were few congregational responses at a mass: they had a little part to play and to take this away and give it to a choir, as some churches did, made the service a priestly performance only.

Turning to the congregation the Celebrant, holding a tray of wafers, said, "Draw near and receive the Body of our Lord Jesus Christ which was given for you, and His Blood which was shed for you......." This was the signal for the congregation to file to the altar rail and receive communion. The Celebrant gave communion to the server first by popping the wafer in his mouth. Then he came to the altar rail where the supplicants waited, and he popped the wafer in their mouths. Usually, in most Anglican churches, the wafer is placed into the crossed palms of the supplicant, who sucks it into his mouth. Not in this case. It was like a mother bird feeding her chicks. David had heard about this practice before but this was the first time he had experienced it. It was based on a theological argument that hands may drop the wafer on the floor, or remnants may remain on the hands. In this way Christ's Sacred Body would be defiled. The Celebrant then came round with the chalice and gave a sip of wine to each supplicant.

It all depended on how you considered the bread and wine of the communion service. The theological argument was controversial. The doctrine of transubstantiation held that the bread and wine actually became the body and blood of Christ. It was a doctrine fundamental to the Roman Catholic branch of Christianity, some Orthodox Churches and High Church members of the Anglican Church. It was one of the tenets of the Oxford Movement and David felt that Patsy and Clair would be believers in this doctrine.

An alternative doctrine was that of consubstantiation. This held that the bread and wine were symbols of the body and blood of Christ. Protestants and the majority of Anglican members held this belief. David was no theologian but he felt that the bread and wine were symbols. He had read enough about pagan religions to recognize that shedding blood and drinking blood, sacrifice of humans or animals, were themes that ran through many of them. It was natural that such a theme should run through Christianity, but as a symbol only. After all, early medicine thought that the blood was the stuff of life. Why not the early church? But in the twentieth century, pagan beliefs were no longer relevant. Perhaps transubstantiation was pagan, and no longer relevant in a world where superstition was waning? He had come to university to sort these things out and he would make up his mind when he knew more. What was important to him was that whatever belief enhanced the persons' spiritual condition, and enabled them to be a better person, was acceptable.

After the faithful had received communion, the Celebrant completed his ablutions, said his final prayers, and was gone with a swirl of green and white. The small congregation chattered to each other as they left the church. It was a comparatively elderly group. David and Martin seemed to be the youngest. They all knew each other for Patsy and Clair greeted a number of people as they left rather speedily. "They've gone to get breakfast," Martin observed. "I'm starving. I hope that big, black monster has not been thieving."

"Black monster?" enquired David not really following Martin's thought process.

"Nimbus. He's the biggest thief in the business."

"Do they allow him near the table then?" David asked innocently.

"They allow him everywhere. Clair dotes on his. He's like her baby. She talks to him like a baby and pretends he replies."

"Oh!" David responded. "I'll have to watch my step, I'm not too fond of cats."

"Me too," Martin told David. "Give him a good kick. I do."

They had reached 'home' and the front door was slightly ajar. When they got into the hall they were met by Patsy. "Morning boys," she greeted them with a smile. "Leave the door slightly open, will you, so that Father Bebe can get in? He's bringing the sacrament to mother. Breakfast is ready in the kitchen."

David and Marin went directly into the large kitchen. It had a huge table in the center where breakfast was laid out on a white tablecloth. There was an Aga cooker on one wall where the bacon and eggs were being kept warm. On another wall was a window looking out onto the garden and on a third wall was a door leading to a scullery where the dishes were washed. There was a lovely smell of toast and freshly brewed coffee. Nimbus was on a chair near the Aga licking his chops. "I've had a lovely breakfast. Fish," said Clair.

David didn't quite understand until Martin gave him a wink.

"Did you give him a good kick too, Aunty Clair?" he asked quietly laughing.

"Oh, Martin," responded Clair quite serious. "How could you be so cruel?"

"Easily," laughed Martin. "Great, fat, idle lump."

"He's only teasing you Clair," Patsy explained to her sister.

Clair broke into a smile. David soon found that Clair had a really sunny disposition. "He's the one who needs a good kick, isn't he Nimbus my love." And she gave the cat a stroke.

The four of then sat down to breakfast. "Where's Ken?" David asked innocently.

"Doesn't eat breakfast," Patsy responded rather scathingly.

"That boy doesn't eat enough at all," Clair offered. "He'll be ill if he's not careful.

"Never mind, Aunty Clair, Nimbus will eat his share," Martin responded determined to provoke his aunt.

"Thank you, uncle Martin," Clair responded in her Nimbus voice.

They all laughed.

"Judges a person by their appetite," Martin said. "The more you eat the more dear you are to her."

"Then you should be my favorite nephew," Clair replied laughing.

"Then David will be your favorite student," giggled Martin. "I watched how much he ate last night."

"Martin!" Patsy pretended to be shocked. "How rude."

"Not at all." Clair defended her favorite nephew. "I watched David enjoy his food last night and I was very happy."

David felt that he was turning rather pink but said nothing.

High Mass at St. Stephens was quite something. David was used to 'smells and bells' at his own church in Leicester but St. Stephens was way over the top. Martin declined church again but Clair and Patsy took David and Ken along to sing in the choir. David had the feeling that Martin was his own man and was not going to be bullied by his aunts. Ken had been lodging with them from the previous term. His other lodgings had been a disaster, and so the college had persuaded the Wentworth sisters to take him in. He had a good tenor voice and enjoyed singing so he was soon pressed into the choir. David also loved singing and was pleased to be invited.

Father Bebe was a rotund, jovial priest who shook David by the hand and slapped Ken on the back. "Good to see you both," he said as he hurried out of the choir vestry. "I must dash and check the organist has got the list of hymns right."

"What a huge vestry," David observed as he though of the tiny place in his own church at home.

"The clergy vestry is just as big," one of the choir members informed him. It has wonderful storage places for all the vestments, clergy and servers.

"Reputedly all designed by William Morris," somebody else added.

The choir had ten men, five ladies and twenty choirboys. David was told that choir practice was Friday night at seven, but most of the men and ladies were sight-readers and rather busy, so they did not attend. However, the sound they made was quite pleasing.

The service was spectacular. Apparently, Morning Service was said at ten thirty and the High Mass, the center of the Sunday worship, was at eleven. The congregation was quite large and for David it was good to see so many young families. They processed from the rear of the church down the nave and up the four steps to their appropriate places. Father Bebe in Green cope with two servers carrying candles, a thurifer and a master of ceremonies went into the sanctuary. The choir sang , the organ peeled and the congregation joined in. There was much splashing of holy water, and the thurifer swung his thurible creating enough smoke to fetch out the London Fire Brigade. The ritual was a little 'over the top' but David felt uplifted and he did enjoy the Stainer (9) mass that was being sung. It was simple music but effective. There was a good selection of appropriate hymns so the congregation was not left out in the cold.

At the end of the service Father Bebe put his head round the door to thank them for their singing. "Lovely," he said beaming. "The anthem was particularly good. The best yet. Thank you." And then he was off.

"Abba Bebe is like a whirlwind," observed Ken.

"Abba Bebe?" questioned David.

"Oh, I forgot," responded Ken. "You don't know any Hebrew.

"No," David offered honestly. He suspected Ken wanted to be superior. "I've just got here, remember?"

Ken smirked with satisfaction. "'Abba' means 'father' in Hebrew so I christened him Abba Bebe".

"It fits him beautifully," David agreed. "He has a little of the Old Testament prophet about him." And so the parish priest of St. Stephen's, Turnham Green, was known as Abba Bebe.

And so, on the first Monday of the new term David was ascending the stairs to the Dean's office as part of the registration process . Ken had declined to come with him saying that he would pay his fees at some later date when his grant came through.

The faculty office was next to the Dean's room on the right at the top of the stairs. Miss Prentice, the Dean's secretary of many years, and who behaved as if she were the dean herself, was in her office. She was about sixty, gray haired and walked with a limp. David did not know whether it was from an accident or birth defect. She reminded David of his great aunt, well-spoken, well-mannered and imperious. He liked her, but many students went in fear.

"Ah, David Earl," greeted Miss Prentice. "Welcome, and how is civilian life?"

David was quite surprised she remembered him as he had only been once before for his interview. "Wonderful, Miss Prentice, thank you."

"How are your lodgings?" she asked.

"Really fine. I'm sure I'm going to be very happy there."

"Give Clair and Patsy my regards will you?" Miss Prentice went on. "I asked them to take you, you know. They've been friends of mine for years. Their father was a very famous priest in London years ago. He and my father were friends."

"I'll certainly do that, Miss Prentice." David smiled. The world was such a small place really.

"Now, David," Miss Prentice continued getting more serious. "I've got some bad news."

David's heart fell. He obviously showed it in his face. "Don't look so worried," she said. "It's just a change of direction."

"Oh!"

"While you were away in the army and after your interview and acceptance, the university changed some of its regulations. They now regard two of your 'A' levels as the same – biology and zoology – and

253

this means you cannot register for the Bachelor of Divinity degree as now they regard you as having only two 'A' levels."

"Oh!" David really looked crestfallen. "The syllabi were not the same."

"It's not the end of the world, David," went on Miss Prentice. "You can study for the AKC degree. It is a special King's College degree for the priesthood. A BD is rather heavyweight."

"If I'd know about these changes I could have done another 'A' level in the army," offered David.

"There wasn't time, David. The changes were quite recent. Anyhow, the Dean wants to talk to you about it. I'll tell him you're here." With that she went through a door at the side of her desk into the Dean's study.

Within a few minutes David was being ushered into the Dean's study. The Reverend Eric Price-Jones was in his early fifties, dark hair, sharp features, tall, slim and elegant in his black suit and immaculate shirt and silk tie. "David," he said with genuine delight shaking hands with him. "Welcome. You're looking very fit and well. The army must have agreed with you."

"Thank you, Dean. Yes, I am fit but I'm glad to get out and have some freedom," responded David with a smile on his face.

"Your letters made it sound quite grim at times," the Dean observed. "Particularly when you first went to Aden."

The Dean had written to David a few times while he was in the forces. David marveled that such a busy man should have the time to write to him. "Thank you for your letters, Dean. I really appreciated them."

The Dean smiled and his face lit up. It was a kindly face. "Don't mention it David. Some of you lads are stretched too far by the military. They don't seem to have much sense at times."

"I certainly was stretched at Millbank, Dean." David laughed, "But I survived."

"And you'll survive here, David. I'm sorry about those changes in course requirements, but there was nothing I could do. It was a university council decision. You are just as well off with the AKC. Trust me."

And David did. This was a good man. He could sense it. There was something about him that he liked. "I'll take your advice, Dean. Thank you."

"You can register downstairs. Miss Prentice will tell you what to do." He shook hands again. "Lectures commence on Wednesday. All the best for your first term."

Miss Prentice explained the procedure and David registered without any problem. His fees were to be paid by the Leicestershire Education Committee and all the rest would be funded by his father, who had agreed to give him a termly allowance. When he had finished he went to have a look at the freshman's exhibition in the main hall.

There must have been sixty or seventy stalls providing information on everything from the Students Union to the Dramatic Society. He had a good look round and finally joined the Rowing Club. He had always wanted to learn to row and one of the students on the stall said he was a theological student in his third year and so persuaded him. While passing the Cross-Country Society, he was accosted by a young man of around his own age. The stall was not getting much attention. "Hey, you look fit," the man said. "The right build for a runner?"

"I do run, " David told him, "But not for the last year. I was in Arabia and it was too hot."

"Thought you'd been abroad. Good tan. Didn't get it round here. So....what about joining us?"

"I don't know whether I'm good enough," David responded. "I ran at school and then in the army." He failed to tell the young man that he had come in first in training.

"Don't worry, we'll be the judge of that." He looked at his colleague who nodded in approval. "Sign your name, faculty and London address in this book, please."

He slid a book across to David. It had three names only above his. "Looks as if you need the lame and blind as well," he laughed.

"It's quality we've got not quantity," the other student laughed. "Can you make it Saturday?" David nodded. "Be downstairs by two o'clock. We have a match with the Bank of England. We'll show you how to get to our club at Mitcham."

"I'll be there," David promised.

As he turned away from the stall he bumped into a rather plump, pale-faced young man who had been standing behind him obviously listening to the conversation.

"Sorry," David said. "I didn't see you there."

"My fault," replied the fellow. "I'm afraid I was listening to your conversation. Sorry."

"No problem," David offered. "Were you thinking of joining? They're short of members."

"No way," responded the student. "No way. Rather you than me. Running.?. Look at me. I find it difficult to run for a bus." He held out his hand. "I'm Tom, Tom Bowers. Just registered in the theology faculty. AKC course."

They shook hands warmly. "David Earl, and I've just registered on the AKC course as well."

"What a coincidence," laughed Tom. "Have you finished here, or is there some other society you want to join? Like mountain climbing or bungee jumping? If not, let's go for a coffee. There's a Lyons just along the Strand."

David chuckled. This guy had a sense of humor. "No, I've done here. What about you?" asked David.

"Me? I'm too lazy. Besides I have a girlfriend and she wants to see me most weekends."

They wandered out of King's, through the arch, turned left, past Thresher and Glenny's, and the Lyon's Coffee House was just beyond. It was obviously a favorite haunt of students as quite a few were drinking, eating and chatting. "You get a table," suggested Tom, "and I'll get the coffees." David found a table for two by the wall.

Tom arrived with two large coffees and two jam donuts. "Thought you might be hungry," he explained. "I get famished around eleven."

"Thanks," David responded.

They drank their coffee and munched their donut in silence for a while. Tom ate ravenously and slurped his coffee. "My mum," observed Tom with his mouth full, "says I eat too much. Maybe. She says I'm overweight. But my girlfriend doesn't seem to mind."

David made no comment, but agreed with Tom's mum.

"Where are you from?" Tom asked putting down his empty coffee cup.

"Leicester. But I was born in Yorkshire."

"Oh. You don't speak like a Yorkshireman," Tom observed.

David could see that Tom had no guile. He was direct and honest. He liked that. "We don't all work down the pit Tom."

"Sorry," Tom apologized. "My mum says I'm too direct. I don't mean to be rude."

"No need to apologies, Tom. I like a straight talker. Now where were we? I live in a village just outside Leicester, have one brother who's at Nottingham University, I went to Grammar School and I've just finished National Service in the RAMC."

"I've just completed National Service too. Served with the Royal Horse Artillery in Germany. Spent my time as a batman cleaning belts and boots," responded Tom with great candor.

"I have two younger brothers and an older step brother and step sister. My father's first wife died so he married again. He died two years ago. I went to Charterhouse school where I learnt nothing except how to be a gentleman. Full stop." Tom stopped for breath.

"Where's home then?" David asked with genuine interest.

"Frensham in Surrey," was the reply. David was quite unaware of the location of Frensham, but said nothing as he did not wish to divulge his ignorance.

The two talked for about an hour and agreed to meet the following day when they would collect their lecture schedule and book list. Money did not seem a problem for Tom as he suggested they went to buy their gowns and some essential books. David had a cheque from his father and a little money of his own that he had saved from his meager pay, so he could spend a little. He liked Tom, who told him he could have gone for a commission, but wanted to be an ordinary soldier. He seemed to be a socialist in many of his views, and a capitalist in his lifestyle as the cut of his clothes was expensive. Tom was not pretentious. He could have been with his Charterhouse background but he was not. Yes, he liked Tom just as he liked the Dean and Clair and Martin. He was happy.

After breakfast the following morning he called in at the Midland Bank on the Strand and opened a Student Account with the cheque his father had given him. His other money was in a Post Office account. Tom was waiting for him at the same table and insisted in getting the coffees again. "You can't keep doing this," was David's challenge to Tom.

"Oh yes I can," was his reply, plonking his bulk opposite David.

Tom was an organizer. "Now," he said, "after we've collected out book lists, and lecture schedule from Miss Prentice, I suggest we then go to the Chesham and acquire a locker."

"Chesham?" David enquired.

"That's the Students' Union Building behind the college. It's in Chesham Street that runs down the side of the college, hence Chesham."

"How do you know these things, Tom?" David was puzzled. Tom was new to the college too.

"Oh, I know one or two of the second and third year guys."

They collected their paperwork from the office, obtained a locker in the Chesham for a five pound deposit, and tried gowns at Thresher and Glenny. It was the rule of the theological faculty that a black undergraduate gown should be worn at all times around the college and for short visits along the Strand. They were marked men. Everyone knew to which faculty they belonged and the Dean considered that as they were begowned their behavior would be appropriate. At first David felt quite self-conscious but it soon became second nature. It was a sort of uniform just as he had worn a uniform in the army.

Wednesday morning saw the first of the lectures. It was New Testament Studies given by a Professor Tucker in the main lecture theatre. The place was quite full. There were students from the Kings faculty, but also students had come from other colleges in the University of London. The lecture theatre, much like a Roman auditorium with tiers of seats and a balcony, had a raised area at one end. On it was a lonely lectern and at precisely ten o'clock the begowned professor ambled on stage. He was about sixty with pure white hair, tall and with a distinct belly that his well-cut suit could not disguise. He looked directly at his audience. "Good morning gentlemen," he said without emotion. "Welcome to new members of the faculty. Today I am going to talk about the Synoptic Problem." (10) He took out a pair of spectacles, carefully placed them on his nose, put his head down and began to read his notes.

The lecture droned on for one hour exactly. A printed register on a board was passed round to sign in to the lecture and David noticed that one or two wags had signed their name and written "Yawn, yawn" by the side of it. They were right. The professor's voice was low and uninspiring, so that after the first ten minutes you lost the thread of his arguments about the authors of the gospels. All David got was 'proto Mark' and the rest was a blur. He and Tom stayed the course, but only just. At the end of an hour Professor Tucker looked up, took off his glasses, said "Thank you, gentlemen" and walked off the platform.

"What a prat," Tom said as they reached the bottom of the main stairs. "I've never been so bored in all my life. Never looked up once."

"Could you understand what he said?" David asked.

"I couldn't even hear the old codger," was Tom's reply.

"He did mumble."

"They should retire him, fellows past it," observed Tom.

By this time they were at Lyons Coffee Shop to where a lot of the students from the lecture had dispersed. It was busy and they had to share a table. This time David bought the coffee at his insistence, and by the time he got back to the table Tom was in conversation with its two other occupants. "They were bored like us," Tom observed. "From New College – not theologs – subsidiary for a history degree."

David greeted them with a smile and the four of then chattered. Apparently, Professor Tucker was famous for being a bore, and usually after the first week or two, students just cut his lectures. They made up for it by reading his books. "We'll go to the college bookshop and buy two copies of 'The Synoptic Problem,' suggested Tom. "That's the only way we're going to understand the old fool."

Lunch was eaten at the Chesham and the afternoon was free as

Wednesday afternoons could be spent in sporting activities. On Thursday morning there was a lecture given by Dr Evans who was a renowned philosopher. Unlike Professor Tucker, he really knew how to fascinate his students, although his subject was far from easy. He introduced himself to the assembled students, and just as the lecture started in one of the small lecture rooms on the third floor near the Library, a student slid into a space next to David. He was quite breathless and whispered, "Sorry, missed the tube. Walter's the name. Walter Denton."

"David Earl." David nodded and smiled.

Walter must have been in his mid-twenties, tall, elegantly dressed, round faced, short-cropped black hair, and eyes that seemed to be coming out of their sockets. He smelled of expensive after-shave.

"There's a lion in that corner," Dr Evans began in his singsong Welsh accent and pointed to a corner of the room near the door.

"He's mad," Tom whispered. "There's no bloody lion."

"I know what you're all saying," Dr Evans went on. "What are you saying?" He stopped and looked around. Obviously he wanted comments.

"There's no lion," came a comment from somewhere at the back.

"Can't see a lion," someone else yelled.

"Can't touch it. Not that I'd want to."

"Where's the smell, the roar?"

"He's quite mad," another honest voice offered.

The whole room roared with laughter, including Dr Evans. He was obviously having a good time and could take a joke against himself.

"But there is still a lion in the corner," the singsong voice argued. "You have said to me that you can't see it, touch it, hear it..." and with a twinkle in his eye, "smell it. But that does not prove it's not there. I say it's there, and you....," he waved his arms around the lecture room," say it's not. Who is right? Who would like to prove it's not there without using your sense experience?" There was silence. Nobody dare take up the challenge.

"What I'm trying to show," he went on, "is that our senses cannot always be relied on to give us accurate information. I'm sure all of you can give examples of how your senses can deceive you. The mirage for instance is the most obvious. The sea can look higher than the land if you are on a level with the beach. How do we know that air surrounds us? We breath it and our respiratory system moves because of it, but we can't taste, smell, see, touch it. But we know air exists; we know the sea is lower than the land or it would swamp it; we know that a mirage of water is an illusion when we get close.

259

"I know the toilets at the Chesham smell. My senses don't deceive me," a wag observed to the loud laughter of the assembled students.

"That's not air," laughed Dr Evans, "that's pure student." The students went wild and clapped in appreciation.

Dr Evans waited for silence and then went on. "In my mind I know the lion is present. I can THINK it. The human brain has the ability to THINK and to create. When I mention the word 'dragon' you can all picture one, I'm sure. But you have never actually seen a real one. You THINK it. The eighteenth century French philosopher Descartes locked himself in a heated room, so he would not be disturbed, and used his thought processes and tried to consider what it was we actually KNOW."

"I bet he could still smell the Chesham bog," came the comment to peels of laughter.

Dr Evans did not mind. He was getting over his point. His students were spellbound and the amusing comments indicated that they were following his every word. "Descartes came up with the famous phrase 'Cogito ergo sum' – for the non-Latin students – 'I think, therefore I am'. What he was suggesting is that the only things we can be sure of are those things that the mind, thought process, can define. If we can think of it then it must be."

There was stunned silence. From that point onwards there was a too and fro between students and lecturer. Dr Evans actually encouraged it. David found it intensely stimulating as did Tom, who kept nudging David and whispering "Why didn't I think of that?" The hour soon came to a close and as Dr Evans left the students stood and clapped. The little Welshman seemed to be quite embarrassed and scurried away down the corridor. "What if all the lectures were like that," remarked Tom as they began to leave the room.

"Tucker will never be," commented the late student, Walter. He introduced himself to Tom. "I saw you both there this morning."

"Coffee?" suggested David.

They walked down the stairs, into the courtyard, through the arch and into the Strand with gowns blowing in the breeze like three gigantic beetles.

Now coffee and a large cream cake is not good for the figure but David and Walter had no choice as Tom insisted on doing the honors. He just did not care how rotund he was. While Tom was getting the coffees, David asked something that had been puzzling him. "Walter," he began, "as we left Dr Evan's lecture you seemed to intimate that you've heard Professor Tucker before?"

"Yes, I have," came the reply. "You see, I was here two years ago and completed two terms and then I became unwell."

"Oh, I'm sorry," David replied, genuinely concerned.

"The Dean suggested that I have a year off and work somewhere and then, if I still wanted to be a priest, to start the first year again. So here I am."

"Did you do your military service before that then?"enquired David.

"Two years in the RAF, nearly a year here and then a year and a half in the steel works in Sheffield."

David was amazed. "I was born in Sheffield," he told him with pride. "We lived at Beauchief until I was twelve and then moved to Leicester."

"I know Beauchief - Millhouses Lane and Beauchief Abbey – lovely," was Walter's response.

Tom returned with the tea and cakes. David did not say anything about Walter being at Kings before but said, "Walter knows Sheffield where I was born, even the district where I lived."

Tom smiled mischievously, "We've two eh-by-gums now have we?"

"I must warn you Walter," David laughed, "Tom is obsessed with the Yorkshire accent. Can't wait to get his tongue round those hard vowels."

Tom threw his trilby at David, but missed.

"And I thought Tom came from Birmingham," added Walter, "by the way he speaks."

"Peace," said Tom raising his hands in supplication. "I'm not going to win with you two around. "That's the last time I mention accents. I mean it." And it was.

Chapter 20

The Thursday afternoon Church History lecture was cancelled. Dr Parish had not returned yet from a study visit to the Holy Land. David saw from the notice board that Friday was used to see tutors and he was scheduled to meet his tutor in the afternoon. He had been allocated to the Chaplain of Kings College, the Reverend Jack Westmore. He decided to spend the morning doing some sight seeing as the weather was so good. It was what is commonly called 'an Indian Summer'

He alighted from the underground at Green Park Station and walked round the lake in the nearby park. It was a fresh, sunny morning and the autumn tints were just beginning to parade the trees in their Autumn glory. The good weather had brought many of the ducks onto the grassy bank of the lake where they were sunning themselves, standing on one leg appearing to sleep. Others were preening their feathers and London brown sparrows hopped amongst them. With the towers of Horse Guards Parade and Whitehall in the background, the park looked more like a Disney film set.

Emerging up the slope at the far end of the park, David had a wonderful view of Buckingham Palace. He joined the many tourists on the outside railings and was just in time to see the last ten minutes of the Changing of the Guard. (1) It was his first time but not his last. He walked up the side of the Palace wall along Grosvenor Place, past St George's Hospital, (2) across the road and into Hyde Park. There he sat on a seat amongst the flower beds in order to rest his feet and watched the tourists as they wandered about.

He had lunch at the main Lyon's Corner House on Oxford Street, having walked through the park to Hyde Park Corner. He caught a bus, as walking in London is very deceiving, and as there is so much to see, you forgets how far you have walked until weighed down by tiredness. After a reasonably priced lunch of soup and chicken salad, he took the underground at Oxford Circus and arrived at the Chaplain's door exactly on time.

His knock summoned a rather croaky, "Come." Jack Westmore was standing at the side of his desk beaming as David entered. "Ah, David," he greeted him as if they had known each other for years. They shook hands. "Come and sit down and tell me all about yourself," he croaked indicating one of two comfortable chairs near his desk. They sat. David felt that the Chaplain already knew all about him as his piercing blue eyes penetrated into him. There was silence. David felt uncomfortable. What was he supposed to say?

"Not long out of the army, eh?" the Chaplain squawked.

"Yes, Chaplain. Three weeks."

"Good, good," the voice said. There was silence again.

David wondered what he wanted to know. "I...served in Aden with the Life Guards. RAMC really, but attached."

"Good, good," the squeaky voice responded.

The man was quite unnerving as he looked through you with those eyes. David wondered what he could see. Maybe all his dark secrets. There was another silence.

"Married?" came the question out of the blue.

"Er...No, Chaplain." David wondered how old he thought he was.

"Good, good." There was another silence. "Engaged."

"Er..." David wondered what he should tell him. "Er, no."

"Girlfriend?"

"N..no, not at the moment. I haven't been back in England very long."

"Good, good," came the squeaky reply. There was another silence and more of the piercing eyes. "I'm to be your tutor for this first year. We'll meet every Friday. Sometimes I'll see you individually as today, and other times we'll meet as a group of five. Any problems?"

"No, Chaplain."

"Good, good. Lodgings all right?"

"Very comfortable, thank you Chaplain."

"Good, good. We'll meet next week. Watch the notice board for the time. I shall be teaching you New Testament Greek as well." With that he got up, shook hands and showed David to the door.

When he got outside he felt drained. The man was like a leech sucked things out of you. Yet..... He felt a kindness there. Those piercing eyes that saw everything were kindly eyes as well. He had a crumpled face, sort of lined, and yet a lovely smile. Maybe he would turn out to be better at a second meeting.

As he went down the stairs he saw Walter coming the other way. "You look a little wan," was Walter's opening remark.

"I've just had an interview with my tutor."

"Who is it?" Walter asked.

"The Chaplain."

"Now I know why you look so drained. Did he ask you about your sex life?

David was quite surprised. "No....but he did ask me if I had a girlfriend."

"What did you tell him?" Walter asked.

"I told him not at present. Why?"

"He's obsessed with sex," Walter reported. "It's reputed that when he counts he says 'one, two, three, four, five, sex....'" They both laughed.

Walter looked at his watch. "I'm late for my tutor – Miss Henshaw ....historian...a pushover....big tits....if you like that sort of thing" and he was off running up the stairs.

On Saturday afternoon David met the cross-country runners as agreed. There were three of them waiting, the two he had met previously and a freshman, like himself, named Richard who was in the engineering department. They caught a bus on the Vauxhall Bridge Road that took them all the way to Mitcham High Street and walked the quarter of the mile to the College sports complex. In the main changing room they met up with about forty other runners. Some were from the Bank of England Club and others from various other colleges within the university. David changed and noticed that the runners seemed to wear all kinds of smart shorts, vests and footwear. It seemed to depend on personal taste and comfort. One runner from the Bank's team wore a pair of the shortest shorts David had ever seen. He showed part of his bottom and a band of his jock strap. He had a fine pair of legs and thus David felt he could carry off such skimpy kit. His own strip was positively old-fashioned. He had used it at school, so he determined to get a more modern strip for the next time.

They were all briefed by a steward using a large map to show them the course. It was an eight mile long course, mainly across fields, but at one place they had to run some way along a main road. There would be markers along the way to give directions where the course was difficult to follow. Stewards would monitor traffic along the main road. Soon they were outside and lined up on the rugby pitch. Someone shouted go, a stop-watch was clicked and they were off, making for the exit, across the tarred main road, and into the fields. David's policy was to keep a steady, constant pace. Some went very speedily to get in front, but that did not mean they could keep it up. Winning in fine, but for David the pure joy of the physical exertion and fresh air, was quite enough

It was not long before the runners thinned out: the faster ones were ahead and quite a few were behind. David felt comfortable with his pace, and after the first three miles a little stomach cramp came and went. He was now functioning well and increased his pace. At the four-mile marker, he entered the main road where the traffic was being slowed down by a police motorcyclist, who waved him on cheerily. He could not see the front runners, but he knew he was not last, as he had overtaken quite a few others. The route then veered to the right off the road and onto fields and lanes again. He recognized that he was on familiar ground that he had already covered and was on his way home. Soon the gate of the complex loomed ahead. He was through, onto the field and the finishing flags were ahead of him. Panting, he gave his name and college. He was quite surprised how fresh he felt really, as he had not done any serious running for over a year. He easily found his way again to the changing room where he could have a hot shower.

The changing room was large and had two rows of ten showers. In a separate room, it also had a great big bathtub. After washing the mud from his body, he followed some of the others to the great white-tiled bath. It must have been eight feet square and two feed deep and full of lovely hot water. The room was so steamy it was difficult to see who was in the water. Putting his towel on a hook on the wall, he entered the bath naked. It was easy to slip over the side into the water. He sat with his back to the bath's wall. The water came right up to his chin. It was wonderful and just what his aching muscles needed. A shower was fine to get rid of the dirt but wallowing up to your chin in warm water was a luxury.

Through the steam he could see that there were about five others in the bath. One runner was the man in the short shorts. After a while, he slid across and sat next to David introducing himself as Roger from the Bank of England.

"Where did you come?" he asked.

"Eighth," David replied. "Where did you come?"

"Third."

"That was excellent," David responded enthusiastically. "I noticed you before we set off. I thought you'd do well as you have very powerful legs."

"And you couldn't fail to miss my bright red shorts?" he laughed. "My wife bought them for me and insisted I wear them. All the boys have been ragging me."

"Well I must admit," David told him, "You can't really miss them – bright red and very short. Mind you, you've got the right legs for them. Your wife chose well."

"They'd suit you," Roger observed. "You have a fine pair of legs too." He put his hand on David's thigh, gave it a squeeze. He did not withdraw his hand.

David did not know what to do. Was he just being friendly? He said nothing.

"Your first time here?"

David nodded.

"What did you think to the course?" Roger asked, smiling at David and with his hand still on his thigh.

"Good, a little muddy here and there but fine. I'm glad the police were at the main road."

"You should see some of the courses we run sometimes," Roger told him. "Terrible. Mostly road. It's heavy on the ankles."

David could feel his hand begin to move. He was terrified. He was also getting excited.

"I only joined our club on Monday so I'm not familiar with... the ...other ....." He gulped. The man had put his hand on his developing arousal. David moved away slightly and took Roger's hand and pushed it away.

"You don't like that?" Roger asked quite unconcerned and smiling at him.

"No."

"You were very excited. Pity. You're a big boy and very handsome."

"I'm not like that," David told him.

"No hard feelings?" Roger asked.

"No."

They chatted for a few more minutes before Roger said , "Cheers. I'm sure we shall me again at another meeting," and moved into the steam to the side of the bath where presumably he would make a suggestive move on somebody else. He appeared to be quite unconcerned at what he had done. David was alarmed and confused. Roger was married but..... He had been aroused by the fondling of his leg. Was that normal? There were boys at school who became easily aroused. Perhaps his reaction had been normal, a bodily function, but no way could Roger's part be normal or acceptable. As a boy at school, things had happened in the showers. Now he was a man and Roger was married. Such things should have been left behind.

Over the weekend David worried over the incident with Roger but by the time he met up with Walter and Tom his worries were forgotten. Monday morning's subject was New Testament Greek. It was quite different to the Greek language of today. The Gospels, originally written in Aramaic, the language of the Holy Land, had very early on been translated into Greek and to understand that language gave a better insight into their true meaning than in English. Hence all theological students had to study the Gospels in Greek. All three of them had studied some Greek before, but were not looking forward to the course.

The Reverend Jack Westmore, Chaplain of King's College, was a double first in mathematics from Cambridge University and clearly had an excellent brain. He was an enthusiastic lecturer but his problem was that he assumed everyone could grasp things as quickly as he could. At the end of the session many students, including David, were unhappy about their grasp of the language. "May God help us," was David's initial comment. "I certainly need Him. I've never been good at languages and this morning confirms my view."

"He's exactly the same as he was two years ago," complained Walter. "Doesn't seem to appreciate we're mortal."

Tom, ever direct, observed, "Well we've just got to do it, so no use moaning. What about working together?"

They all agreed that they would meet at Walter's room at the Theological Hostel in Vincent Square on Wednesday afternoon when they were free.

The afternoon lecture was down as 'Speech' and given by a Miss Audrey Bull. When Walter was asked about the course and the lecturer he just put a finger to the side of his nose and said, "Mum's the word. Wait and see."

Miss Bull was a large lady in every respect. She had a large personality for a start and called everybody, "Deeah". Walter informed them in a whisper that she taught at the Royal Academy of Dramatic Art. (3) That explained why she was so theatrical. She was six feet tall, rather stout with a large bosom, a big backside in her trousers, and she wore what seemed to be a man's dark green velvet jacket over her white blouse. Maybe she was in her late fifties. It was hard to tell. Her voice carried right to the back of the lecture room and it was exquisitely modulated but not 'posh'. David suspected she had had a northern upbringing like his own as her vowels were clear.

"Now deeahs," she began after she had introduced herself. "You are my children and I am your mother. My job is to help you to speak so that you are clearly understood like any good mother would do. You are going to be clergymen, preachers, so you have to be able to speak clearly. There is no point in addressing your congregations if they don't understand you. You may as well talk to them in Russian."

A student at the back put up his hand. "Yes, deeah?" came the response.

"But Miss, we may have a parish in Russia so it's no use speaking in English." A general titter went through the assembled group.

Miss Bullard was unperturbed. "Ah, I see we have a joker in our midst. What's your name young man.?"

"Ashley,"

"Just Ashley?" came the response from Miss Bull.

"No, Miss. My first name is Ashley. Ashley Cole."

"Oh, I see deeah. What a splendid name. Ashley Cole. More like the name of a dress designer than a clergyman." There was a titter from the students. "Anyhow, Ashley Cole, come down to the front and help mother with her demonstration."

Ashley Cole was tall, willowy and weedy looking. It was clear that he was a bit of a fool by just looking at him. Tom whispered to David, "His father is chairman of an oil company. Very influential." David wondered if he had asked the question in all seriousness. However, he was soon to find out that you don't mess with Audrey.

"Now, deeah," she said smiling at him once he stood before her. I want you to demonstrate some breathing exercises for me. Ashley looked at her as if he wanted to say, 'But Miss I can already breathe' but he kept mum. "Now take off your jacket, deeah, and put it on that chair. We can't breathe properly wearing a tight jacket, can we?"

Ashley took off his jacket and faced the students. He really was thin. "Now, deeah, put your hands on your hips."

Ashley did so but not to Miss Bullard's requirements. She moved his hands so that he stood in a rather effeminate pose. There was another titter amongst the students. "That's better, deeah," she said. "Now bend your knees. Further, deeah, further," she coaxed.

By this time he had his knees half bent and was wobbling a little. "Breathe in, deeah," Audrey commanded. "Now out." He wobbled and fell over. There was a huge round of applause and great guffaws of laughter from the assembled students. Ashley Cole had been made to look an utter fool. He would not try to upstage Audrey again.

"You'll never be able to preach unless you can do that, deeah," was Miss Bull's comment as Ashley retrieved his jacked and walked back to his place, flushed with shame and the realization that he'd been 'had'. "Now, deeahs," Audrey continued, "let me show you the right way. Breathing is essential to good speaking as is posture....." And so the lecture continued. It was excellent and the students clapped and cheered as Miss Bull left the lecture room waving her hand like the Queen herself and blowing kisses.

"That was really something," David observed as they went down the stairs. "It was....."

"A performance," cut in Walter. "She's a clever lecturer and a brilliant speech teacher. The guys mess around sometimes .... in some ways she asks for it....but you never win."

"We're lucky, then," Tom added. "I suspect teaching speech to a group of lively young men is not easy, particularly for a woman. She really impressed me. Speaks beautifully...every word can be heard....but she doesn't have the affectation of some debutants (4) I know."

Walter and David looked at each other.

"Debutants?" Tom. "Really. I thought that had all been stopped."

"Yes, it has but they still have their parties. It's like going to buy a car. Deciding which one is the most serviceable." He grinned.

"You been to one of these do's then, Tom?" Walter asked.

"Yes, my girlfriend took me. Her sister's a top model and she gets invited to that sort of thing. I go for the beer," Tom admitted with a twinkle in his eye.

And so the week continued. Tuesday morning was Old Testament studies given by Professor Ulrich Simmonds. He was reputed to be a German Jew who had accepted Christianity. He spoke with a broken East European accent, and when he spoke the Hebrew name for God, *Yahweh,* one could imagine him with long hair and a cloak receiving the tablets of stone on Mount Sinai. (5) He oozed the spirit of the Old Testament and fascinated his students. In consequence, one always had to get to his lectures early in order to get a seat.

David felt that generally they were very lucky at Kings in the quality of their lecturers. The Liturgy lecturer, the Rev. Dr Styles, was quite fascinating. Liturgy interested both he and Walter as it traced the development of the symbolism within the worship of the church. The course was to cover the Eastern as well as the Western Christian community. Tom said he was not bothered much about what the priest wore, but the course would be much more than that, as David was to find out.

On Wednesday afternoon, just before three thirty, David went to meet Walter at the third year hostel in Vincent Square as had been arranged. He wondered how Walter had managed to obtain a room there when he was only a first year student. He would ask him. The hostel, an imposing stone-built building on two floors, stood behind low railings and an expanse of manicured lawn at one end of Vincent Square. It was approached through substantial iron gates. There was a wide paved pathway leading to a huge wooden front door. At the side of the door, mounted in the stonework, was a large bell-push. David rang the bell, which echoed through the building. A maid in green uniform answered the door.

"Yes, sir?" she asked.

"Mr Walter Denton, please," David informed her. "He's expecting me."

"Yes, sir. Please go up the stairs on the right and his room is number sixty-one."

David thanked her and climbed the stairs.

When he got to the top of the stairs Walter was waiting for him. "I heard the bell. I knew it was you as my room overlooks the main entrance and I saw you come through the gate. Come along to my room." He led David half way along the corridor and entered a room on the right. It was quite small but very comfortable. Walter closed the door and waved David to a rather fine armchair upholstered in green velvet. There was a bed along the wall covered with a green brocade cover, a dark green rug on the floor and gold velvet curtains. On the wall was a print of some cathedral or other and in one corner a large Victorian wardrobe.

"It's very comfortable, Walter," David said appreciatively. "Are all the rooms the same?"

"Good Lord, no," Walter replied. "These are all my things except that terrible wardrobe and the bed. They were too big and heavy for me to remove." "Well, it's lovely. Home."

"Glad you like it," beamed Walter. "I like nice things."

"Tell, me Walter.....I hope you don't mind? How did you manage to get a room here in your first year? I thought it was a third year hostel."

"Well, David....," started Walter. "If I tell you my story will you say nothing to anyone?"

"Of course, Walter." David was mystified. "But if you prefer not to tell then it all right with me."

No, David. I want to be frank with you. I hope we can be friends and so I want to be honest with you."

Walter was brought up by an uncle and aunt. He had never really known his parents as they were killed in the blitz over London in the Second World War. They were kind to him, but being rather elderly, they were not good at communicating with him, and he became rather solitary. When he was eighteen he went in the RAF to do his National Service, and there he managed to get two 'A' levels as he had wasted his time at school and left without any qualification. After service, he worked as an assistant in a large store in South London and attended the local church. It was at this stage that he decided to become a priest. "I came for an interview at King's and was offered a place the following year. Well I came. Everything was fine at first and then my problem began to impose itself on me."

David waited.

"You see, David," Walter said looking directly at him, "I'm gay, a homosexual."

There was no reaction from David.

"You're not shocked?" Walter asked.

"No, why should I be Walter? We are all as God made us."

There was a look of relief on Walter's face. I'll not go into details, but I found out about myself in the RAF, and later working in the shop, opportunities just flowed. At Kings I became more and more depressed as my sexual inclination imposed itself on me. My studies suffered so I went to see the Dean."

"That was a brave thing to do, Walter," David pointed out.

Walter smiled awkwardly. "I was desperate. At one stage I felt like ending my life. Anyhow, I went to see the Dean. You know, David there is far more to the Dean than people suspect. That man has so much compassion."

"I suspected that, Walter. I don't know him well but there is something about him"

"Well, he was very understanding," continued Walter. He saw that I was in a state and used to see me every day for about six weeks. You know how busy he is but he gave up his precious time for me. I shall always treasure his sacrifice. Well, to cut a long story short, he suggested I left the college mid-term and get a job for a year. I could then work out my sexuality and whether I really wanted to be a priest, and, he would leave a place open for me if I still wanted to return."

Walter sat back in his chair. It obviously had been a strain to tell his story. "So," he continued, "I went to work in a steel works in Sheffield. The Dean actually got me the job and I lived in a clergy house in Attercliffe. A contact he had who was very caring and helped me a lot."

"Tough?" was David's response. "It's one of the worst parts of Sheffield. By the way, what did you do in the steel works? Work in the office?"

"No way. I was given a job in the pipe shop cleaning the cast pipes once they had come from the foundry."

"Dirty work." David commented.

"In more senses than one," Walter replied with a grin. "There was just as much gay sex going on amongst the steel workers as there was in London."

"You amaze me."

"Bend down and they were behind you. Those young apprentices…..I could tell you some stories but I won't embarrass you."

"So while you were in Sheffield you sorted things out?" David asked.

Yes, kind of. I still wanted to be a priest. I knew I could not give up sex. I'm made that way. Somehow, I had to reconcile the priesthood with my sexuality. Working in the steel works made me see that sexual orientation was not black and white but all colors of the rainbow. There were gays, like me, there were bisexuals, as were many of the married men in the works, and there were others who were just opportunists who exercised their dicks in any way when the opportunity arose. I learned that morality is something one has to sort out for oneself. I also learnt that what the Church says and actually does are two different things. I'm gay, and as long as my partner is willing, and I don't do anyone any harm, where is the wrong? It's far better than creating an unwanted baby."

David was just going to quote St Paul (6) when Walter stopped him. "Don't quote St Paul and *'arsenikes'* because that is the view of one person, and generally refers to a specific act only. It does not refer to homosexuality proper, as the Church would have us believe. Perhaps St.Paul suffered from homophobia, the extreme dislike of homosexuality, as he saw it in himself and tried to suppress it. It's a very common cause of homophobia. In any case, did not Christ Himself surround Himself with males? He loved James and John who put their heads on His breast." He stopped, looked at his watch. "Wow, look at the time. Time for tea and there's no Tom and we've done no Greek."

"Never mind," David responded. "We've used the time to get to know each other and that's important. Plenty of time for Greek. Don't know where Tom's got to."

At this Walter plugged in his electric kettle, went to his wardrobe where he assembled two china cups, teapot, milk and sugar on a tray. He even had some delicious-looking chocolate cake. "To get to your question, David," he eventually continued as he brewed the tea, "the Dean put me here, I suppose, so that he can keep an eye on me."

"It's a nice place to lodge," David suggested.

"Y..es," Walter responded, "but it does limit your freedom." He smiled. "I suppose that was another reason why he put me here."

The tea was excellent. Walter explained that he put a little Earl Grey with Lipton's tea. While they were having tea, Walter suddenly asked, "Are you gay David?"

David was taken off balance and spluttered over his tea. What should he say? Was he? He thought for a while.

"Hope I've not offended you David, but I hope we can be honest with each other."

"To tell you the truth, Walter, I don't really know," was David's response. "What makes you think that I might be?"

Walter thought for a while and looked directly at David. "I just have a feeling. You're very handsome, too good-looking to be straight. You're always immaculately turned out, even if you are in jeans, and you have a sensitivity that is quite rare."

"Oh! And that's an indicator is it?"

"Can be. Have you ever.....?" and Walter stopped without finishing his question.

"Ever what?" David asked anticipating Walter's next comment.

"Been in love, had a special friend?"

David pondered on some of the things that had happened to him. "I have had lots of people who have made passes at me. The only person I can say I loved was an Italian boy in Aden. He was very special. I also met a beautiful guy from South Africa that I liked immensely, but nothing else."

"You've never....." Now it was Walter's turn to be embarrassed. "You know...been to bed, played?"

"Well...." David told him about the incident at the King's sports complex.

"Well in London there are guys who are always making passes. A handsome guy like you will have to get used to it. But tell me, did you get.... excited?" Walter asked.

"Was I aroused. Yes. I think most men who get their thighs fondled by male or female will get an arousal."

"And what did you feel about .....your...'state'?"

David was not sure. "I felt ......excited, but...... I also felt guilty. Males shouldn't do that sort of thing. It's a sin."

"Tell me, David," Walter asked. "Which do you prefer, the male or the female body?"

This came right out of the blue. Here was the big question and he knew the answer. It was something he had been fighting against since he started grammar school. He had always pushed such feelings down into his sub-conscious and here was Walter making him face the truth.

David looked at Walter. There were tears in his eyes. "I think the male body is so beautiful."

Walter came across to him and put an arm round his shoulder. "That doesn't mean you're gay, David. I'm sorry if I've made you consider things that you have tried to forget. You are confused at present as I was. Keep an open mind. Be yourself and it will all become clear in God's time."

Walter's invitation to tea had been far more than David expected. He had been forced to consider things about himself that perhaps cowardice had made him push into the back of his mind. Some females had lovely bodies, but for him the male physique was exceptional. He had never wanted to really fondle a woman's body, but there were a number of males he would have loved to fondle. Christianity told him it was wrong for a male to love a male, or a female to lover her kind. But why? Love was the foundation stone of Christianity. It is that which

273

made it different to all other religions. Love God, and love thy neighbor as thyself. That was the essence of Christian teaching.

His memory of the afternoon chat with Walter remained with him for many days. It worried him. Was he homosexual like Walter? No, surely not. OK he didn't go a lot for women but he was a sportsman and certainly not effeminate. Tom had told him that he lodged at the University Chaplaincy House in Camden Hill Square and when he invited him for tea on Sunday afternoon he readily accepted. Maybe he would get the opportunity to approach the subject with the Chaplain himself.

Camden Hill Square is near the northern end of Hyde Park, off the Bayswater Road. It is an avenue of large houses on a hillside and the Chaplaincy House is just on the bend as the road heads down the hill. It is a large building with four floors, the upper floors being rented to students and the ground floor being an office and an apartment for the London University Chaplain.

David rang the bell and the door was opened by a tall figure in a black cassock.

"Oh," David said. He was expecting Tom to be at the door as he was exactly on time.

"You're David," stated the figure. "Tom told me you were coming. He's going to be late. Girlfriend trouble. I'm Father Ivor, University Chaplain. Come in."

He opened the door wider, shook hands with David and led him into his own sitting room on the ground floor.

"I'm sorry to be a nuisance....," began David but was cut off by Father Ivor.

"No problem at all. In fact, it will be nice to chat before Tom arrives. He's told me so much about you."

"I hope it's not all bad," David laughed.

"He has great respect for you. Maybe I'm not supposed to tell you, but Tom is just a little boy really and I hope you can be a good influence on him."

"All I know is that he's very unreliable," David observed. "He was supposed to work on some Greek with Walter and I on Wednesday and didn't turn up. Girlfriend problem again."

"Have you met Ziph ...Elizabeth...but that's what he calls her?" Father Ivor asked.

"No. He's always talking about her. Seems to be in love with her."

"Lovely girl, possibly prettier than her sister but a real spitfire. Red hair and all that."

"You've met her then?" David asked.

"He brought her here a couple of times. I've seen pictures of her sister in the newspapers. She calls herself Fiona Lunt-Roberts."

There was a silence while they studied each other. Father Ivor was not European, maybe Indian originally as he had a lovely brown skin and black straight hair swept back from his face. He must have been six feet two inches in height. His English was perfect and beautifully modulated as is the case with many ex-patriots. It was clear to David that he could not open up about his problem when he was being asked to support Tom.

"Tom needs a close friend, David," Father Ivor told him. "Someone who is stable and reliable. He has moods and fits of melancholy. I hope you will give him that stability as he's a great person really."

"I don't know him so well really, Father," David explained. "Nearly three weeks. We get on well. But he does keep changing his mind about his girlfriend. Some days he says he's going to throw her over and the next day he says he loves her."

"Exactly, David. I hope you'll help to keep him on the right track." There was a loud crash of the front door. "And if I'm not mistaken that's Tom now. He never closes a door. Rushes through like a bull in a china shop and slams it.

"We're in here, Tom," Father Ivor shouted.

Tom appeared at the door ruddy faced and breathless. "Sorry David. Thanks father for holding the fort. Ziph was having one of her little moments. She'll make a good actress. I sorted her out."

"You both need sorting out," laughed Father Ivor. "Go on, have your tea and you both can accompany me to the University Church tonight as a penance."

Chapter 21

Once immersed into the routine of lectures, tutorials, library research and meeting essay deadlines, it was surprising how time flew. Before David knew it, Christmas had arrived with all the glitter that London could offer. He had been aware that cards and bunting had been on sale in many shops since October, and had been thinking about Christmas presents, but it was not until the huge Christmas tree in Trafalgar Square went up, and the windows of the big stores twinkled with lights, that he got into the spirit.

The famous Harrod's Store in Knightsbridge was a joy to wander round. It was like an Aladdin's cave and the main exhibition hall on the ground floor was a fantasy for every child, small and big. Harrods catered for the wealthy and one could buy anything from a diamond tiara to an elephant. Poor students like David and Walter could only walk round and look, but this year David decided he would buy his presents from Harrods. He had been careful with his money and something small with a Harrods label he was sure would be welcome.

In Oxford Street the windows of Selfridge's Store were magnificent. The store, instead of displaying merchandise in its windows, provided a scene from a different children's story. In each window were life-size figures, many of which were mechanical and moved. Parents brought their children especially into town to traverse the windows and watch the display. At night the windows were lit like a theatre set, and the whole building was covered in lights. David found it fascinating. There was some advantage of living in the capital city, even if you were poor.

Over the weeks since college had commenced David, Tom and Walter had become great pals, although Walter and David tended to socialize more together as Tom spent most weekends with his girlfriend. David had met her once when they had lunch together at Lyon's Corner House in Oxford Street. She certainly was a beautiful looking girl but, like most redheads, had a quick temper. It was clear that they both doted on each other.

Both had distinct personalities and clashes were inevitable.

On some Saturday mornings he and Walter would go to Fortnum and Mason's, the famous grocers to the Queen, in Piccadilly for coffee. They usually dressed up for the occasion as it was a very smart shop. David had bought a dark brown suit from Walter, who had got too large for it, and it really suited him. Fortnum's was expensive and they could not really afford, but Walter liked the good life. He met up with friends he called 'the queens'. They tended to be wealthy men from many walks of life who liked to be seen at the best places. One man David was introduced to turned out to be a bishop and his very handsome companion was his chaplain. How Walter knew them David never asked. "It's best to know the right people, David," he advised. "If you don't know them then go where they are. It'll get you on in the world."

It was clear that a number were homosexual, though not all. Some were very obvious but their wealth gave their eccentricity a certain immunity from ridicule. One morning they found a very strange 'man' sitting at one of the tables with a group of Walter's acquaintances. He must have been around fifty, wore makeup, and clothes that made 'flamboyant' an understatement. He had many rings on his fingers and bangles on his arms. On his head was a floppy fedora. He was holding forth and waving his arms about in a rather effeminate way.

Walter stopped at the table and was introduced to the figure. He inclined his head to one side to be kissed on both cheeks. David stood some way away, quite embarrassed, and not really wanting to get involved. "That's Quentin Crisp," (1) Walter told him when they had found a table. David was none the wiser. "He's very famous in London."

"I'm sure he is," David responded, "looking like that."

On another occasion Walter persuaded David to go to the Royal Opera House in Covent Garden to see a production of 'Swan Lake'. "It's Fonteyne," he remarked with great enthusiasm." David had never been to the ballet before and was quite thrilled. He liked the theatre and music so this would be an experience. He did not like to ask who Fonteyne was in case he looked stupid. Anyhow, he would eventually find out.

They managed to get tickets for the gallery, which was all they could afford, and then David thought it was expensive. There were endless steps to climb and he found the seats were hard benches right at the back and very high up. The rake of the gallery to the stage was so steep that he felt as if he would fall. The 'gods', as everyone called them, were full, mostly with young people, but there were one or two older men with younger companions. It was quite hot too but nobody seemed to mind. Below him David could see red-plush seats, gilt plasterwork and candelabras with little pink shades, and an audience of well-dressed balletomanes. It was a wonderful sight and enhanced the excitement of the evening.

Without being aware of it, the orchestra had entered the orchestra pit. There was applause for the conductor, who raised his baton, and the show began. After two or three minutes of the overture, lights were dimmed, and then the red and gold curtains of the Royal Opera House slid silently open. Another world of make-belief unfolded.

For David the evening was magical. He had never seen such grace. These were humans on stage behaving as if they were fragile flowers floating on air. The story was of a swan who takes on human form and falls in love with a human, only to die as a result of a curse. The whole effect of music, movement, costumes, and scenic beauty transported him into another world. With the entrance of the leading ballerina there was a great cheer, particularly from the gallery. Now David knew the identity of Fonteyne.

In the interval they bought coffee from the coffee bar on the floor below. The only thing that marred the evening was someone stroking David's bottom while they were in the crush to get coffee. When David told Walter as they took their seat for the last Act, his only comment was, "Well you do have a nice bottom." It was clear that supporters of ballet did not only have ballet on their minds. However, the incident was soon forgotten and David wanted to weep when the mystic swan died. He wondered how any human being could perform movements so delicate. It must have taken a lifetime of discipline, and the strength of a gymnast, to dance in the way he had witnessed that evening. He left the theatre elated and determined to make a return visit when funds allowed.

Rowing was a disaster. David had joined the club because he thought it might be a good sport, but after the second visit to the boathouse at Chiswick on the River Thames, he packed it in. They had practiced rowing strokes in a practice boat inside the boathouse. It was dark, wet and very cold. He had never felt so cold in all his life. Everyone was very friendly, but, David had to admit that he did not enjoy the sport, and so with regret he discontinued his rowing.

Running was still enjoyable and he had matches nearly every other Saturday. Sometimes it was a home fixture, and sometimes it was away at another club. He often ran on Wednesday afternoons, just for the pleasure of it, now that he was not rowing. The weather had become cold, but he did not mind as a good run was exhilarating, and he could do some serious thinking. There were things he was hearing in his lectures that worried him. Christianity was not as clear-cut as he had been led to believe.

One Wednesday afternoon, not long after his first match at Mitcham, he was running on his own and somehow or other took a wrong turn. Perhaps he had been pondering some difficult Christian concept. He suddenly found himself on Mitcham High Street amongst the many shoppers. He felt quite embarrassed in his new short shorts asking a group of beefy housewives the way back to the sports ground.

Their looks seemed to undressed him. With a little light banter, they sent him in the right direction.

Term was soon due to end and David was to travel up to Leicester; Walter was going to Sheffield to stay with a family who had befriended him; Tom was going home but said he would spend Boxing Day with Ziph who lived quite near. There had been a Carol Service in the College Chapel and David had sung in a makeshift choir. Ken, who rarely appeared in the College Chapel, actually sang in the choir as well. Both Walter and Tom declined to sing as they said that the local tomcat could make a better sound. It brought back memories of his childhood singing carols around his neighborhood in Leicester.

While in rehearsal with the college organist, he met the College Sacristan and his deputy. The deputy was a second year student called Martin, whom David knew slightly, and the Sacristan was a lively and very amusing third year student called Rupert. The job of Sacristan was a Dean's appointment. Nobody knew how the post was filled but there was some kind of selection procedure based on a notion that the student had promise of going far in the hierarchy of the Church of England. It was a responsible post as they had to prepare the chapel for daily morning and evening service, as well as the sung Eucharist on Friday morning.

David loved the Eucharist at King's for its pure simplicity. It was usually celebrated by the Dean, assisted by the Chaplain and one or two of the ordained lecturers. There was no excess ritual and the Dean's celebration was perfection. The two Sacristans, dressed in white albs, acted as servers and nothing ever interrupted the smooth and gentle flow of the liturgy. It was such a contrast to St. Stephen's. The celebration at King's was 'over-the-counter', a new innovation in liturgical circles, where the celebrant faced the congregation from behind the altar. With its huge un-cluttered, bowed sanctuary, King's College Chapel was a perfect setting for this new liturgical innovation.

The Eucharist (2) on Fridays was well attended and many students from other faculties and other colleges came. Morning service with hymns was every day at nine o'clock and every theological student was obliged to attend. But as the term progressed, David saw that fewer and fewer of his fellow students were present. A few students said Compline at five fifteen. They tended to be those who stayed late for a lecture, tutorial or to work in the library. For David it was nice to end the day saying this office if he happened to be around.

It was a great shock for David towards the end of term when he found how little the beautiful college chapel was frequented. The theological faculty was organizing a Day of Prayer for the starving in

Africa. They had collected quite a lot of money, but it was felt that spiritual help, as well as practical, was required. A list was placed on the Chapel notice board dividing the day up into fifteen-minute slots, from ten o'clock after morning service to five fifteen, when it was planned to say evensong. After a week there were no more than a dozen names on the list. David was asked by the Sacristan if he could do extra slots to fill in the day. Tom and Walter also agreed to give extra time. David could not believe that a theological faculty of some three hundred students could not support their chapel with fifteen minutes of their time. It really made him think, and Tom in his usual forthright way complained, "There's not much hope for the Church if its future priests won't give time to pray."

In early November, Clair and Patsy started singing the latest pop songs around the house. It was quite bizarre to hear two staid and elderly spinsters singing 'What do you want if you don't want money' or 'All I want is loving you, BABY' as they went about their chores in the house. "Pantomime," commented Martin one day to David. "Every year they co-write the Christmas pantomime for St. Stephens. They're trying out the songs they might use."

And so one evening, whilst they were having their nightly cup of tea in the sister's sitting room, Martin raised the issue. "Tell me aunt Clair and aunt Patsy what is the pantomime to be this year?"

Clair and Patsy looked at each other. "How do you know we're planning a pantomime?" asked Patsy.

"Well the two of you have been going around like stage-struck youngsters for a few weeks now singings all kinds of pop songs. Not really in character is it? And in any case dad told me all about your thespian activities," offered Martin.

The two sisters smiled at each other. "You liked our songs?" asked Clair. "We've been trying them out."

"Mm....too many BABIES for my liking. So what is it to be?" Martin innocently enquired.

"Cinderella," they said in a chorus.

"And who's playing the ugly sisters?" asked Martin with an evil grin on his face and looking directly at his two aunts.

"Oh, Martin," Patsy smiled looking at her sister, "you are so evil."

"So?" insisted Martin.

"We are, dear," Clair owned up with a satisfied smile on her face. "We knew what you would say."

"But wait," chipped in Patsy, "the best comes next. Who is going to play Simple Simon?" They both looked at Martin.

"No way," grinned Martin.

"If we're to play the ugly sisters, then you have to play Simple Simon," Clair responded. She looked directly at him. "You'd be perfect."

"Wouldn't have to act either," said Patsy putting in the boot.

Martin knew he was beaten.

Martin was not going to let the rest of the household get away. "So what is David playing?" he asked giving David a hefty nudge.

"Oh, the wicked baron," Clair giggled.

"But why?" asked Martin. "I thought David might play the prince. Oh, they didn't tell you David, at St Stephens they don't have a principal boy."

"Why?" David asked innocently.

"They're all so old nobody has a decent pair of legs." Martin rushed over the comment with a side grin to his aunts.

"Martin, you continue to be evil," remonstrated Patsy, "that's not true. There are lots of girls who could do it."

"What about you auntie Patsy?" Martin asked with that twinkle in his eye again.

"If I were twenty years younger Martin Easterbrook I would have done it. I've still got good legs I'll have you know."

Martin and the others tried to stifle giggles. "Yes, aunt Patsy," Martin just managed to say.

"It's tradition, Martin. Didn't your father tell you? We've always had a male hero and a female heroine."

"Ok then," Martin went on. "Who is going to play the prince?"

"Ron," Clair replied and the three boys almost fell off their seats laughing.

"Ron?" they asked in chorus. "Ron, the head verger. But he's.........old."

"We decided we'd have a mature prince this time. In any case, Ron is quite good looking and has acted in our pantomimes before."

"Mmm," the boys murmered.

It transpired that Ken was to play Dandini and a rather cute blond girl, new to the parish who sang in the choir, had agreed to play Cinderella.

And so the oddest production of "Cinderella" that has ever graced the London stage, be it amateur or professional, was performed in St Stephen's Parish Hall ten days before Christmas. It was a resounding success in spite of the fact that Ron could not remember his lines and ad-libbed to the consternation of the rest of the cast. He was also a practical joker and stood on David's cloak so that he could not make an exit. The audience loved it. And the Wentworth sister, as the ugly

281

sisters? They were a sensation. They had gone over the top with their costumes and makeup and their ball gowns would have made Norman Harnall, the Queen's dressmaker, green with envy. They were really very good and David admired them for their willingness to be ridiculed in front of an audience who knew them so well. Father Bebe echoed this in his warm appreciation to the cast at the end of the show. "When we can present ourselves for a little ridicule for the Glory of God and the entertainment of our neighbors in a true spirit of love and friendship," he said, "we can say Christmas has come."

And so, with his head full of new knowledge and his heart full of love for those who has provided such a perfect first term, David traveled up to Leicester by British Rail and to the family home for what was to be the last Christmas in the house where he had spent so many years.

The Earl family had lived in 'Tudor Cottage' the mock-Tudor residence in an acre of pristine gardens, since he was eleven. His parents had moved from Sheffield, his birthplace, to a village outside Leicester, as Leicester had a very active business community, and was in the center of England, giving easy access to other business communities. Much had been done to the house over the years, but his father liked roaring, open fires and central heating was never installed. The kitchen was warm as it had a Potterton boiler for hot water, but David found the rest of the house rather cold in winter. It had oak floors, oak doors, oak beams, mullioned windows, and a winding staircase that looked down from the landing into the hall. His mother, with little help, found the house very hard work and often complained, but she in her way loved the place.

And so, after lunch on Christmas Day, when they were all relaxing beside a roaring log fire, and after he and his brother had helped their mother wash the dishes, and before the Queen's Speech, his parents made an announcement. They had bought some land in Sheffield and would be moving back. "You see," his mother explained, "you boys won't be long before you leave us. John will probably be getting married next year and you David, well it won't be long before you're off somewhere."

"We decided that we'd go back to Sheffield," his father told them, "where we have brothers and sisters, rather than being here on our own. I can manage to do business from there. So, we bought some land at Ecclesall some months ago and we've commissioned an architect and builder to build a house."

"My dream house," beamed his mother. "And it will have central heating," she said looking at her husband."

"It will have central heating," confirmed his father.

David and his brother were delighted with the idea of a new house for their parents. They deserved it as both had worked hard all their lives. Both he and his brother would miss their old home, but both were to start out on a new phase in their lives. Why not his parents?

Chapter 22

The new term commenced at the beginning of January and ended just before Easter. It would be the last Easter celebration at his parish church as his parents were planning to move into their new home by December so that they would have had around a year for completion. His father was a man of set habits and once he fixed on a date then there was no changing it. So December 19th was sacrosanct.

Whilst he was at home during Easter Week, David arranged to do a postal round with another local student for the duration of his summer vacation. David's father had always encouraged his boys to take on some form of work in their long vacations. The local postmaster was a friend of his parents and always had difficulty in finding relief postmen during July and August, so since the boys had been seventeen, they had helped out and taken on a postal round between them. This enabled the regular men to have their vacation and provided money for David and his brother. This year his brother would be commencing a job after doing his finals, so David was to work with somebody new. The area was rural and the isolated farms and hamlets took some finding, but having lived in the area so long, location and distance was no problem.

David always found the Easter celebrations in church lovely, perhaps just as impressive as Christmas. The pageantry of Maundy Thursday and the symbolic washing of feet, was in stark contrast to Good Friday with the black-draped crucifix on the altar. Holy Saturday with its candlelight service heralding in the gold and white of Easter Sunday, was something that always delighted him. And the Easter hymns were so lovely too. He felt rather sad that this would be his last Easter on familiar ground; an old parish church that had become so dear and friendly. A part of his growing adulthood, the friends and acquaintances that had molded his adolescence were to be mere memories.

In David's mind, looking back with nostalgia was not something to which he subscribed: looking to the future having learnt from the past was much more important. What he was experiencing at King's College was to formulate his life from this point onwards and lead him to the priesthood. Yet, at the back of his mind doubts began to stir. They were intellectual, organizational, and a growing personal awareness.

One afternoon sitting on a park bench in the Spring sunshine, he and Tom were mulling over a lecture they had just attended on St Mark's gospel. "It's clear from internal evidence that the Gospels according to Mark and Luke were written by more than one writer," David noted.

"The writers were presenting a compilation of eye witness accounts and oral tradition under an editor. We might call Luke and Mark editors. There's nothing wrong in that. The editor wanted to provide as complete a picture as possible of the life and teachings of Jesus. There is also evidence that Luke and Matthew 'borrowed' from each other or used the same sources. I can accept this. Oral tradition comes before a written tradition. Memory becomes hazy and fact gets embellished. But why are there only four gospels included in the canon of accepted texts and not more, as there are other gospels of equal merit?"

"Because they fit a pattern," Tom admitted. "That pattern was in line with what early Christianity knew and accepted about Jesus."

"But," went on David. "that means these writers were sort of playing politics. They were picking out those writings that fitted their particular concepts of what Christ preached and the way he lived. It's like........a newspaper just reporting the events that fit the editor's prejudices."

"No, you've got it wrong, David." Tom was quite exasperated. "The early church included those writings in the canon that they deemed the truth. Some of the rejected gospels are really fanciful - angels, spirits and people flying through the air, much like Mohammad did."

"But Tom," went on David. "The synoptic gospels, (1) Matthew, Mark, and Luke, are also full of fantasy. Virgin birth, miracles like feeding five thousand people, water into wine, raising the dead, angels paying visits and even the resurrection itself. And John's gospel? It even begins in fantasy. *En harke ho logos – in the beginning was the word*. What is meant by 'the word'? It means 'spirit' or 'power' or God. It's mystic. "

"They fitted the message, David, that Jesus was the Son of God, was killed and resurrected from the dead," Tom pointed out.

"But, Tom," David was now becoming emboldened, "can't you see that the mystic parts of the gospels are not new. There are many earlier religions that are full of angels, people rising from the dead, blood and sacrifice. Such concepts in religion are not new. Might the writers not have drawn on these concepts? What if the writers of the canonical gospels were selected as orthodox just because they chose the blend fact and the mystical to get over a powerful point – a new, different point – the divinity of Jesus." He stopped and thought for a while. "The fact that the central character, the Son of God, could overcome death has huge pulling power."

"Wow, David, that slaps at blasphemy," was Tom's amazed response.

"What if Jesus was just a man, an Essene, (2) who presented to the world a philosophy of life based on love and....and...." David stopped at the thought of the enormity of his supposition. "was not divine?"

"Phew," uttered Tom. :Now stop, David, your thinking is too radical."

"But Tom, we have brains in order to reason. I want to get to the truth. It seems to me that nobody has yet answered my various questions. All they say is that I need faith. Faith, faith....For every difficult problem they quote faith, like they did in hospital when the child with cancer died. It's a copout. You can have faith in anything." He looked at Tom, gave him a push so he slid off the end of the bench. "Faith that you and Ziph will one day stop arguing and get married."

It broke the tension. David ran with Tom chasing after him. "You wait 'till I get hold of you," he yelled, but was too fat and too unfit to catch up.

There were in the theological faculty a number of students whose fathers were rich and famous. One parent was a well-known merchant banker, another a captain of industry, and another a member of parliament. There were many other students whose parents were 'well heeled' and possibly two-thirds had been to an English public school. Tom joined David one morning breathing fire. "I can't believe what I've just heard. The bastards." They had both been in the services and the habit of foul language unfortunately still existed.

"Calm down, Tom," David said putting his arms round his friend's shoulder. "It can't be all that bad. Now tell."

Tom was still angry. "I've just come up from the Chesham. A group of our charming colleagues – would-be priests – took me on one side and asked me to support them to get all the grammar school boys out of college office. They knew I went to Charterhouse and assumed I was one of them."

David was amazed. "One of them? What do you mean?"

"A public school boy with prejudices."

"What did you say?" David calmly asked.

"I told them to sod off in no uncertain terms. Bastards. Who do they think they are? I told them that high office should be based on merit and not on money, family and school. To get off their idle backsides."

"But why, Tom?" David asked innocently. "Why should they want to do this?"

Tom looked at David with such compassion. "Oh, David, you're such an innocent. You can only see the good in people. These guys feel threatened. They regard themselves as top people, leaders, and want the top jobs. They think it's their right."

"But Tom, we're living in the twentieth century. There's been a

286

world war and privilege has been turned upside down."

"So we...you, like to think," Tom pointed out. "In reality nothing much has changed. The top people will allow the masses to think they are in charge, but in reality they will be pulling the strings. I know, my family is part of it." He thought for a while, his anger decreasing. "Tell me, David, the name of a bishop in the Church of England who is the product of a state school."

David could not think of one. "I think the Dean went to a state school," David observed.

"But he's not a bishop and probably never will be," Tom suggested. The Church of England is dominated by privilege. Bishops are lords and sit in the glory and pomp of the House of Lords, with no mandate from the people, like all the hereditary peers. Just because your forefathers pleased a king, or your great, great, great grandmother slept with a person of importance, or you're a so called 'prince of the church', why should you wield such power?"

"If you come from these kinds of people, Tom, why are you in a different camp?" was David's innocent question.

"Because I believe in merit. I believe England has to change, David. If we don't change our attitudes and the way we do things, we'll become an anomaly, in a different world and be left behind. And because, like you, I'm a radical at heart."

One afternoon over tea Walter raised something else that David had never considered before. They somehow got into the controversial issue of Church and State, the question of disestablishment that a Sunday newspaper had been suggesting in a series of articles. "My dear," he said in his inimical style of address, "we're no longer a predominantly Anglican country. We're Roman Catholics, Protestants of various sorts, Jews, Muslims, Buddhists. Why should Anglican bishops be appointed by the Prime Minister and sit in the legislature?"

"Bishops appointed by the Prime Minister?" David repeated.

"Yes, weren't you aware of it? It's a farce really. You get the cathedral clergy praying for guidance on who to select for their bishop while Downing Street is making the selection. They are state nominees. It's a mockery!"

"Seems like it," David observed. He was quite shocked as he thought bishops were elected by the clergy after guidance through prayer.

"Think of it, my dear," went on Walter, a Protestant or Jewish Prime Minister selects our Archbishop of Canterbury. They're political appointments. Men who will say what the establishment wants to hear and won't rock the boat."

"I have to say," David responded, "that my only experience of a bishop – our own in Leicester – was not a happy one. He's very much the lord."

"Exactly. Most of them are. They forget who they really are. They are puffed up by being number one, a member of the House of Lords. They forget that they are the heirs of simple men chosen to carry out the work of teaching by a simple carpenter. So many are career clergy, saying the right thing, being in the right place, meeting the right people."

"Like going to Fortnum and Masons?" David smiled at Walter.

"Like going to Fortnum and Masons, David. You're learning."

"So you want to get to the top then, Walter?"

"Oh, I don't want to be a bishop or a dean but I do want to get a good living in an exciting parish. I don't want to be pushed into a back street in a mining town. Remember that bishop I introduced you to in Fortnum's?"

"Yes, the one from some diocese in Africa. The one with the very handsome chaplain?" David confirmed.

"The same, my dear," Walter responded. "Well, his chaplain is his boyfriend. I've known him for three years. He was determined to have an easy ride in the church and found his bishop to give it him."

David was dumbfounded. "A gay bishop and a gay chaplain!"

Walter laughed. "Dear David, you're so innocent. Where have you been all these years?"

"Tom says I'm innocent too," remarked David.

"And Tom's right," smiled Walter. "And we love you for it."

"What are you doing for half term, David?" Tom asked David one morning in May as they sat having coffee at Lyon's.

"Going up to Leicester to the folks, I suppose Tom."

"What about spending the long-weekend with me at Westwick? My mother is always suggesting I bring you for a visit," he informed David.

"You've told your mother about me?"

"I tell her about all my friends. She'd love to meet you. Honest."

"That would be super, Tom. Sure it won't put your mother to any inconvenience?" David asked knowing how pushed mothers could be with guests in the house.

"No, problem. I'll go down this weekend, borrow my mother's car, and we can travel down in style."

David's parents were a little disappointed when he phoned them to tell them the news. His mother was concerned at the extra work he would give Mrs. Bowers and asked him to be sure to offer some help.

Tom was as good as his word and on a lovely sunny Friday morning appeared early after lunch at his lodgings in Turnham Green in a maroon Riley. It was a small car but very well equipped and quite nippy. After putting their luggage in the boot, they were waved off by Clair, and then they were heading out of London towards Guildford.

The traffic was quite heavy and David left the navigation to Tom as he did not like back-seat drivers. He had no clue as to where he was going. Some village or other called Frensham, near Farnham, was all he had been told. Tom drove well and obviously knew the way as he chattered all the time and pointed various landmarks out. "We're on the Hogs Back now," Tom told him at one point. "It gets very busy and there are lots of accidents in the winter when it's foggy up here." The road traversed a ridge and the countryside fell away on each side. The view was perfect. "That's Guildford over there in the distance," Tom pointed out. "You can see the new cathedral on the hill." And so you could. David could just make out a pristine neo-Gothic building.

"Very different to Coventry Cathedral," David told him. "Coventry is very modern, all concrete and colored glass. I'd rather go for you Gothic, Tom. Much more romantic."

After about three hours of driving the scenery changed to fields, farms and woodland. The lanes were quite narrow and bends had to be taken judiciously. They passed through the village of Frensham, which was larger than David had expected, and seemed to be a rather wealthy community by the number of large houses that stood back from the road in their own grounds. "Commuter area for London," Tom offered. "They make their pile by day in the big city and invest it down here in property and high living. The present Lord Mayor of London lives in the village as does Sir Miles Thomas, chairman of the British Overseas Airways Corporation."

David was impressed. He had heard of Sir Miles. Who had not? He was always in the newspapers pushing the success of BOAC.

Once through the village they continued along narrow lanes. There were fields on either side with cows grazing, an occasional farmhouse and copses of trees breaking up the pastureland. It was lovely. The sun was still quite high in the sky and the smell of moan grass and cattle made it feel really rural. Quite suddenly Tom swerved left, through some large iron gates that were standing wide open and down a drive that David could only gape at. On each side of the drive was one of the most perfect herbaceous borders that he had ever seen. It was sheltered at its rear by an eight-foot ancient brick wall. They had a small border at home but nothing like this. It must have been seven feet wide and stretched on and on. He did not know how long it was. There was everything arranged in perfect height and color: delphiniums of various shades of blue from deep to pale, even pink, standing like sentinels at the rear of the bed; shrub roses in many different colors; phlox in white, red, pink and salmon; huge daisies in varieties he had not seen before; peonies in red and white; dahlias of all shapes and sizes; hostas and much more. It was perfection. "What a wonderful border," David gasped.

"You like gardening?" he asked.

"Certainly do. We have an herbaceous border at home but it's nothing compared to this."

"It's my mum's pride and joy. She only lets the gardener touch it when she can keep her eye on him," Tom remarked. "If you like gardening you and mum will get on fine."

They came to the end of the four hundred yard border and pulled up on a gravel drive.

David was shocked, speechless, when he looked around. They were parked in front of a Palladian mansion with pillared portico and great windows on two floors along the front. It was not old. In front of the house, at the far side of the very wide gravel drive, was a huge lake with a pristine grassy bank going down to the water where there were water lilies and ducks. "We're home," said Tom jumping out of the car. David sat there just taking it all in. "Come on idiot," shouted Tom as he headed away from the car. "I want you to meet mum."

From across an immense lawn came a lady of about fifty, slim and graying in a faded print dress, battered old shoes, and wearing gardening gloves. She was trying to remove one of the gloves at the same time as she was holding a pair of secateurs. On her head was an ancient straw hat. "Tom, darling," she said with a look of delight on her face. Tom kissed his mother on both cheeks. She then turned her lovely blue eyes on David. "And this is you friend, David?"

"This is David, mum." Tom told her. "My best friend at college. And far too handsome for his own good."

Mrs. Bowers laughed. "Trust you to embarrass him. Welcome David to Westwick."

"Thank you, Mrs. Bowers. It's good of you to invite me." David responded rather over awed by the whole scene.

"He's just been admiring you border, mum. Says he likes gardening. Can't think why."

"Then we'll go and have a look at it right away," she said. And with that she took David's arm and led him away. "Get someone to take the bags up, Tom." She then turned her gaze on David. "We'll leave Tom, he's a Philistine, and I can get to know you, David." And off they walked down the drive, companions with a compelling interest.

Mrs. Bowers was such an easy person to get on with David found. She was very informal and talking to her felt like talking to his own mother. She obviously loved gardening and was a mine of information. She certainly was proud of her herbaceous border and she should have been as it was truly splendid.

As they chatted she asked him about his parents, brother, school and future plans and she told him a little about Westwick and herself. "My husband built this house in 1935 just before the war as a bit of fun. He pulled down the old farmhouse and built what you see. We were newly married. I was his second wife; his first had died. Tom and his two brothers have a step-brother and sister who are more my age. My husband died five years ago so I was left to run the estate. I love it here but the house will be too large when the boys are gone. I'll build a smaller house on the estate and sell this one."

"You'll miss your garden," David observed.

"Yes," she sighed. Then she brightened up and smiled at David. "But I'll have the pleasure of creating a new one."

"My parents are going to move in December," David told her.

"Oh, where too?" she asked with interest.

"Back to Sheffield where they were born. They think they'll be lonely once my brother and I have left home."

"Very wise," Mrs. Bowers commented. "But won't it be cold up there?"

"I suppose so but my mother has been promised her dream – a house with central heating. My father is going to do something a little like your husband, build a dream home for my mother. Though not on such a grand scale," he added.

After viewing the wonderful border, Mrs. Bowers took David past the main entrance and down the side of the house where there were sweeping lawns, great trees, by this time casting long shadows, and more beautiful borders. There was a walled kitchen garden beyond. An old man with a wheelbarrow was working near the entrance to the kitchen garden and David assumed this was the gardener. Laid out on a small table surrounded by three chairs was tea. A lady was hovering in the background and Tom was tucking into scones, jam and cream. "I'm famished," he said. "Cook makes the best scones in the county and our cows produce the best cream."

"You'll have to excuse Tom," Mrs. Bowers said shaking her head. "I paid a fortune for my son's schooling and what happens? They forgot to teach him any manners."

"But mum," groaned Tom, "I was hungry and in any case David's family and so I don't have to put on airs and graces."

Mrs. Bowers smiled at David. "I expect you've got used to Tom's blunt ways, David?"

"That's his....er 'charm'," David explained looking at Tom having picked his words carefully. "Tom is always honest, even if it hurts sometime. That's why we get on so well. I admire honesty."

"He's too honest mum," Tom observed nodding towards David and with his mouth full of jam and cream scone. "Innocent as well."

"That's not such a bad trait Tom Bowers," his mother scolded. "Now David, sit yourself down and let's have some tea. As Tom says, you're one of the family so we can all be informal." With that she turned to the lady hovering in the background. "Oh, Miss Bane, this is David, Tom's college friend. You have his room ready?"

"Yes, madam," she responded. "Pleased to meet you, sir."

"Bane's a winner, David," Tom remarked much to the pleasure of Miss Bane who smiled with pride. "She can always be relied upon to provide a snack when the going gets tough."

David's room was enormous and looked out over the garden. It was as big as the sitting room at his home in Leicester and it had a dressing room and a bathroom en suite. He had only once had something like this before when he stayed with his parents in a very exclusive hotel in Sienna in Italy. His suitcase had been brought up by someone, and towels were set out in the bathroom. There was a huge marble bath, washbowl in marble, a toilet and bidet. The bathroom itself was as large as his room in Turnham Green. He just could not believe that Tom lived on such a grand scale. He had mentioned the name of the house, but not that it stood in eight hundred acres, had a lake, its own farm and a first-class shoot. Tom was so.......unassuming. But that was what made Tom such a good friend. He was honest, direct, rudely blunt at times, but he was also loyal, cheery, and never arrogant. His word was his bond and his simplicity his charm.

David had been 'instructed', yes, that was the right word, 'instructed' by Tom to meet him in the hall downstairs at six-thirty. "We don't dress up for dinner, David, so you'll only need a wash," Tom commented. "Tradition of the house that I take you to meet Billy the bull and our farm manager, Joe. If they approve, you're 'in'," he smiled. David wondered what would happen if he was 'out'. And so David appeared in the hall as instructed and they walked to the farm buildings, which were just over the road from the main house.

The Home Farm, as it was called, was quite large and had a variety of buildings around a central courtyard. Tom did not make for there but walked a little down the road that was separated from the farm by a low wall. Suddenly Tom stopped, scrambled up the wall and sat sideways on it. "Hey, Billy," he said as if talking to an old friend, "I've brought someone to see you. Give him the once-over." With that he signaled to David to have a look over the wall. David was taller than Tom so there was no problem. What he saw startled him.

Not more than ten feet away and making its way towards them was a huge Hereford bull. It was massive, with gigantic shoulders, a great head and standing nearly as high as the wall. There was a ring through his nose. It was certainly male and could have weighed a ton. It obviously recognized Tom's voice as it made straight for him. It ambled in a friendly way. Now David had been told stories about bulls and how dangerous they were and here was this monster coming towards them. Tom put out his hand, quite fearless and the bull nuzzled it. "What you been up to my old fruit," he asked of the bull. "I bet you've had a good time since I've been away?" Billy snorted and let Tom scratch his head. "Come on, David, just let him smell your hand like I did."

"You sure he won't bite it off?" David asked.

"Might," grinned Tom, "but you won't know until you try."

David tentatively put his left hand over the wall just above the bull's nose. The bull sniffed it and did nothing. "Now scratch his nose as I did." David did so and Billy closed his eyes in ecstasy. "He likes you," Tom beamed.

"It's not often Billy accepts strangers," a voice said behind them and they both turned to see a tall, ruddy-faced man in his late fifties standing in the road. This clearly was Joe.

Tom jumped off the wall and shook his hand while David turned to face him. "Good to see you, Joe. This is my college friend, David Earl."

"Pleased to meet you, sir," Joe said. His brown eyes were roofed with thick, black eyebrows and looked David up and down. "He seems a darn site fitter than you Master Tom, if I may say so." There was a twinkle in his eye.

"You're just influenced by his good looks, Joe, that's all," was Tom's quick response. "You don't recognize a good waistline when you see one."

Joe looked David up and down a second time. "Billy 'ere like him. Putty in his hands. Not the same with all your friends. Went mad with that Rupert something or other. Nearly broke the wall down."

Tom laughed. "I forgot about him, but I knew he would like David."

Joe turned to David. "Welcome to Westwick, sir. Now that bull is more sensible than most humans. Can tell what a person is like at a glance."

"But he seemed to know Tom like a long lost friend," observed David.

"Well, they was young'uns together weren't they? Billy was a baby when Tom was a nipper and they were inseparable. Bond between them."

"I understand now why Tom has such an appetite," David smiled and winked at Joe. "He and Billy are trying to compete as to who has the biggest waistline."

Dinner was served in the huge dining room on the right hand side of the entrance hall. It was half-paneled in oak and had a beautifully carved fireplace in the same wood with green marble insets and hearth. The huge windows were curtained in rich cream brocade and there were two brass chandeliers to shed light. The three of them seemed to be lost in such a vast room as Miss Bane served them from a sideboard near the door. David had never seen so much food. He ate well at home but at Westwick it seemed like a feast. There was a huge steak pie, boiled potatoes, carrots, peas and broccoli and to follow apple pie and fresh cream from their own cows. Mrs. Bowers explained that most things were produced on the estate, even the steak for the pie. "Cook is a wonder," she explained, "and bottles and jams when things are in season so we buy very little. She lives in the village and comes in every day."

"How does she make such wonderful gravy as we had in the steak pie?" David asked. "It really was so delicious – sort of black and nutty?"

"Ah, that's a real secret," Mrs. Bowers laughed. "Shall we tell him, Tom?"

Tom nodded. "She adds a bottle of milk stout."

David was amazed. "But I had stout once and I hated it. But in the pie....wow!"

"So you do like food," Tom commented.

"I do, Tom. We get very well fed by the Wentworth sisters. Clair is an excellent cook," he said. "But I have to be careful eating out – small grant and careful father."

"That's one way of reducing your waist line Tom Bowers," his mother offered. "I'll reduce your allowance and you can eat carefully with David."

Tom looked at David, grimaced, scratched his nose and said, "See what a fine mess you've got me into Stanley."(3)

Miss Bane brought David a cup of tea at eight o'clock the following morning, and informed him that breakfast was at nine in the main kitchen. She asked if she might draw his bath. David declined her offer and thanked her for the tea. Tea in bed. It was something he had always felt was the height of luxury. Miss Bane had drawn his curtains so he could see out over the garden and towards the wooded rising ground. To think it all belonged to Tom's family. In his wildest dreams, he had never thought that one day he would stay in such a place. And here he was, David Earl, poor theological student, sitting in bed drinking excellent tea and gazing out over the grounds of an incredible mansion.

He had just dressed in jeans and a sweater when there was a crash at the door, and "Are you up you lazy blighter?" when Tom burst into the room with energy worthy of the rugby field rather than the bedroom. "Mum said you were to be left to sleep in this morning or I'd have been here before. I'm famished. Are you ready?"

"You're too energetic for me in the morning, Tom," David told him.

"That's because me and Billy have lots of stored energy," he remarked slapping his waistline. "Come. I'll show you the way."

They went down the main staircase, across the hall past the butler's pantry, and through a door that led along a small corridor. On the left was a sunny sitting room that Tom explained his mother used for sowing and writing letters. "When she wants to get away from us she comes here. We know then to respect her privacy." At the end of the corridor was the door leading into a spacious kitchen.

In the center of the kitchen was a large table covered with a white linen cloth. It was set for two. Opposite the window that looked over the garden was an Aga Cooker and there was another door leading to an outer kitchen and other offices. On a big Welsh dresser was a collection of blue and white Delft pottery and hung on one wall a copper warming pan. The whole ambiance of the kitchen was of quiet comfort. Mrs. Bowers bustled in. "Good morning, David. I hope you'll excuse me but I had my breakfast earlier. Tom will see to you. I've got to dash as I have to go to Guildford this morning."

David gave his greeting and wished Mrs. Bowers a safe drive. A rather rotund, jolly woman came in from the outer kitchen.

"This is Mrs. Ash, David. She will look after your hunger." She smiled at the cook, pecked Tom on the cheek and was off leaving behind the fragrance of French perfume.

"Now, Master Tom, do you want me to serve you or will you help yourselves?" Mrs. Ash asked.

"We'll help ourselves cookie," Tom replied with a knowing twinkle in his eye.

"Right you are, sir," Mrs. Ash responded obviously wise to Tom's strategy. "The bacon is keeping warm on the Aga. Enjoy your breakfasts." And with a smile she was off back into her domain.

"Best help ourselves," Tom said quietly. "We can eat more that way."

And so they ate a hearty breakfast as newspapers are reputed to say about condemned men.

After breakfast Tom took David round the farm. It had been a dairy farm in his father's time but latterly the production of milk had become less profitable. His mother had decided to go in for beef production with a fine herd of Herefords. It was less labor intensive, but more capital intensive. David assumed that finance was no problem. "My mother has gone to see the trustees of the estate this morning. That's why she's gone to Guildford. Quarterly meeting or something. My youngest brother, Minimus, wants to run the estate when he leaves school, and my middle brother, Jonathan, intends to become a banker. He's at a crammers' school at present hoping to get admitted to the London School of Economics next year. You'll meet them on another occasion when their terms end."

For the rest of the morning they wandered around the estate. There were acres of woodland as well as pasture. The herds of Herefords were in excellent shape and made a wonderful picture on the rich pastureland. Tom told David that in the spring the woods were carpeted with bluebells and the hedgerows with primroses. David could see wild roses in flower here and there in the hedgerows. "My father was a nature lover. When he bought this estate it had been badly managed and many of the wild flower had died out because of the use of chemical sprays. He was one of the first to introduce organic methods and so slowly over the years the estate has returned to its former glory. Now we have a full-time forester and game expert. My mother rents out the shoot in the autumn. It brings in quite a lot of money and pays for the forestry management. She has also replanted some woodland for future income. You must come and stay when we have a shoot."

"That would be lovely but ....."

"You don't like to shoot the birds?" chipped in Tom.

"Yes, sort of."

"Soft hearted?"

"I suppose so." David though for a while. "When I was about twelve my father gave my brother and I an air-rife for a present. We use to shoot darts at a paper target and occasionally we would go in the garden and shoot apples or plums out of the trees. It was great fun. One day, I got bold and shot at a blue-tit. It fell from the tree in a splutter of feathers and lay at my feet quite dead. It was so small and defenseless. From that moment on I vowed I would never kill a bird again."

"But you didn't mind killing humans if the need arose in the army?"

Tom asked quite seriously.

"I did mind, Tom. But we had to kill or be killed. That's why I joined the RAMC, because there would be less chance of me being required to kill." There was silence. "I also wanted to know how to heal." David added.

"You know, David, you're difficult to work out. You're so ordered and self controlled, an athlete, an excellent brain, and yet you have a soft, innocent center that sometime astounds me."

"What about you, Tom?" David asked. "Could you kill another human being?"

Without hesitating Tom said, "Yes, of course. If someone threatens me, my family or my country, I'll kill."

"But what about the command of Jesus 'Thou shalt not kill' and 'to turn the other cheek'?"

"I anticipated you'd raise that issue," Tom replied. "I've thought a lot about it. It may have been right for Jesus but not for me. In war it's kill or be killed. The strongest overcome the weak."

After an excellent cold lunch cook had left on the kitchen table, Tom suggested they walk the lanes into Frensham, visit the church, and call on the vicar. "Your mother asked me to remind you that the Mortons are here to dinner this evening, Master Tom. Seven-thirty for eight. Tie and jacket."

"Thanks Miss Bane. I quite forgot. We won't need any tea. I'll cadge some from the vicar." He turned to David. "Lenny's always good for a free tea."

As they walked along the narrow lane that led towards Frensham, they met the occasional car that Tom greeted with a wave or stopped for a brief chat. He was obviously well-known and well-liked. In between these interruptions, he told David a little about the dinner guests. "You'll see their house as we get nearer the village. It's modern and stands above the road. There are two brothers and a sister. None of them are married. Retired now but have lived fascinating lives. The elder brother was a diplomat and served all over the world. His brother was a journalist and historian. He's very bright and has written several books. Their sister was a senior civil servant in London until she retired about four years ago. They decided to live together and built a very comfortable home that they can manage financially and with minimal help. They have been friends of mothers ever since they arrived here. Keen gardeners and you can assume the rest knowing mother. They come to dinner about once a month or mother goes there. If I'm at home, or my brothers, the invitation is open. We all enjoy their company. I'm sure you will too."

The Morton's house stood high about two hundreds yards back from the road, a driveway winding its way up the hill through a neat shrubbery. David could see that the whole plot of maybe two acres was beautifully planted and lovingly tended. Somebody waved from the garden, a lady, and Tom waved back indicating they were walking to the village. "They do most of the gardening themselves," he told David. "Have a man in two days a week to do the heavy work." It certainly was a lovely spot. Not really isolated but private, with what looked to be spectacular views towards the village. "Their parents had an estate somewhere around here. They sold it after the war when upkeep got expensive."

The village of Frensham was really lovely and David enjoyed looking round. Wealth was obvious. There were many large houses with extensive gardens as well as more modest homes, but all were well kept. In the drives of some of the larger houses very expensive cars were parked. In one home, a gentleman was cleaning his Bentley. He waved and Tom waved back. "Sir Miles Thomas," Tom reported without comment

The church was quite large, stone-built and nestled in a neat churchyard. There was nothing unusual about it and it could have been the village church for any of Britain's thousands of villages. Now there is something about a village church. Timelessness is one thing, security in its ancient walls is another, but David felt that it represented a simple faith in God that transcended the religious divide. Many churches had withstood the excesses of Henry VIII's changes, the rise of Lutheran Protestantism, war, famine and pestilence and maintained a belief in God that could not be shaken. When he was in such a place there were no doubts, but away from such security, David was not sure that his faith was strong enough to withstand the battering that life had opened up to him.

A large vicarage stood close to the church. It was well maintained as was its garden. David felt that Frensham was possibly one of those plum livings that were handed out still by rich benefactors. This was the sort of living for which so many clergy in Jane Austen's novels were always looking. As they opened the gate of the shady drive, a figure emerged from the shrubbery. He must have been around sixty, wiry, bald-headed with a surround of gray hair, dressed in old gray-flannel trousers, striped shirt with sleeves rolled up and a panama hat on his head. "Tom," he greeted them. "Good to see you. When did you arrive?" His twinkling gray eyes looked at David. "You've brought a friend with you?"

"My best friend from college, David Earl. Another trainee bible basher, vicar."

"It's good to see you both." He shook hands with David. "Excuse the dirty hands but I've been trying to sort out this shrubbery."

"Everyone seems to be keen gardeners in Frensham," David observed to the vicar. "The gardens are lovely."

"Suppose we are really," he replied. Then he looked at Tom and smiled. "We get into trouble with Tom's mother if we lapse, eh Tom?"

"Mum's a bit fierce when she sees a decrease in effort, I suppose."

"Even Tom's been known to succumb to her overtures," he said and winked at David.

"She nags me, David, until I go and help some old biddy dig her vegetable garden, or prune her roses," admitted Tom.

"Not true, Tom," the vicar said turning to David. "He's being modest. His mother just mentions somebody needs help and he's there in minutes is our Tom." Poor Tom did not know what to say. His lazy façade had been exploded.

"Now what can I do for you gentlemen?" the vicar asked.

"We thought we'd come for a free tea, vicar," Tom explained, ever truthful.

"Thought that was the case," he laughed. "You don't change. Except you waistline which gets larger by the year."

"Let's go and find Helen and see what she's got."

There was tea, scones and chocolate cake on the table in the big kitchen. "Thought it was you, Tom Bowers, talking to Lenny so I got the tea ready." She looked at David, smiled and shook hands. "If Tom calls around five you can bet he wants some tea."

"You make it sound as if I only come for a free tea. I suppose next you'll be saying I only come to church for the free communion wine."

The vicar laughed. "Well don't you?" He winked at David. "No, on consideration there's not enough wine to get you out of bed."

And so the tea went on in the same vain. The vicar and his wife were so jolly that David found it hard to believe that he was having tea in a vicarage. It was as if they were some fun-loving aunt and uncle receiving their favorite nephew. They certainly thought a great deal of Tom. David had not come across clergy like this before. Most of them he knew were a little severe, even his own parish priest. His heart went out to them. This was how Christians should be to one another.

David had little time to wash and put on a clean shirt and tie before he heard a car on the drive. The vicar had brought them home in his car, and with a little mild scolding from Tom's mother they both went their separate ways to get ready for dinner. He just got to the bottom of the stairs as Tom appeared from another direction. "We made it," he said.

299

"This collar is killing me."

The doorbell rang and Miss Bane went to answer the door. "Good evening madam and sirs," she said and led the Mortons into the saloon where David and Tom had slipped and were awaiting their guests. The Morton men were both tall, rather skinny, probably over seventy and looked very distinguished. Their sister, now in her early sixties, must have been very pretty in her younger days; she was still quite a looker, tall like her brothers and elegant. Tom shook hands and introduced David. "I saw you with Tom this afternoon," she remarked. "I wondered who the handsome young man was."

David blushed. He just could not get used to being given compliments. "We were off to look round the village and then to see Lenny," Tom informed them.

"For a good tea, if I know you," said one of the brothers, "or my name's not Frank Morton."

"Why does everyone imagine I only think of food," laughed Tom.

"Because you do," chipped in the other Morton brother whose name turned out to be William.

At that precise moment Mrs. Bowers entered the saloon. "Do I hear you mention food?" she asked. "I'm sorry not to have met you at the door but cook had a little crisis with the salmon. Don't worry all is well." She beamed at everyone. Miss Bane then arrived with a silver drinks tray and everyone was served with an aperitif of their choice. David chose sherry and as he sipped it he had a chance to look round the room. He had not visited the saloon before. It was opposite the dining room and the same size. Six huge windows looked out over the garden, but now they were draped with lovely pale green brocade curtains. The walls were covered in what looked to be delicate lemon watered silk. The four huge settees and six easy chairs were covered in dark green brocade, and the many cushions in the chairs were of lemon watered silk. Between the curtained windows were huge mirrors that made the room look even larger and on the opposite wall were a number of oil paintings of country scenes. A fireplace in dark green marble was at one end and at the other another window that looked out over the front entrance. On the oak polished floor were lovely Turkish rugs in various shades of green. There were many tables, some finely inlaid, with large lamps on them and smaller tables dotted around on which to place one's drinks. It was truly a beautiful room.

It really was a lovely evening. The conversation was sparkling and very interesting. David found that Frank Morton had briefly visited Aden and so they swapped lively comments about the place. The dinner of real oxtail soup, salmon, salad and boiled potatoes with a béchamel sauce, strawberries and cream was lovely. There was an excellent hoc with the food and after dinner, coffee and a liqueur in the saloon David felt quite sleepy. The evening seemed to be over before he even realized it. When he looked at his watch it was eleven thirty and the visitors were saying their departing goodbyes and issuing a return invitation.

When Tom and his mother returned from seeing their guests to their car, David thanked them for a wonderful evening.

"I'm glad you enjoyed our friends, David," Mrs. Bowers said. "They are the sort of people I like, no airs and graces. They have led such interesting lives. Believe me, in Frensham there are some awful people who just play a part all the time. I can't stand that."

"The Mortons are great," Tom piped in. "They like you. Told me to take you along any time."

"That will be lovely, dear," Mrs. Bowers told Tom. "You'll like their house, it's so interesting. It has wonderful things they've collected from all over the world." She looked at the two boys who were showing visible signs of being tired. "Right, you too. Off to bed. I assume you're going to early communion tomorrow morning?"

Tom and David looked at each other. "Yes," Tom said, "unless the flesh is weak."

The flesh was not weak and they made the back pews just as the vicar entered in green chasuble with a server in black cassock and white surplus. No high church vestments here. There must have been forty people at the service and it took quite a while to administer the sacrament. The vicar met everyone in the church porch and shook hands. "Breakfast now, is it?" he said to Tom with a twinkle in his eye. "See you at morning service."

Mrs. Bowers decided to go with them to church. She had already had her breakfast and went out to do a little weeding before church. Tom and David washed the dishes as cook and Miss Bain did not come in on Sundays. By ten-fifteen everything was ship shape and Tom went to call his mother while David returned to his room to spruce himself for morning service. At his church in Leicester everyone arrived in their Sunday best and David assumed the same would apply to Frensham, maybe more so. It was that sort of place where many people go to church on a Sunday morning to be seen.

At a twenty-to-eleven they sauntered out to the car, which Tom had parked opposite the front door. Mrs. Bowers was nowhere to be seen. "Had to drag her in from the garden," Tom explained. "A bit of a rush." Seconds later Mrs. Bowers appeared dressed in a wonderful beige lace dress, with a brown handbag, brown gloves that she carried as well as a large brown straw hat. She looked wonderful. "Come on mum, we'll be late," Tom yelled. "You go in the back."

David held the door for her and as she got in the car she cried, "Oh, I've not changed my shoes. They're my old ones I use in the garden."

"Oh, mum," Tom said, I don't think you'll have time to change them unless you want to be late."

She looked at Tom with a lovely smile on her face. "Nobody will look at my feet, dear, will they? I'm sure the Lord won't mind."

And so they set off to church.

It was exactly as David had anticipated. The church was packed with worthy members of the community and they just managed to squeeze into a pew at the back. The road outside the church was bumper to bumper with expensive cars. As David looked round the congregation, he could see that the ladies were fashionably dressed and the men were in well-cut suits. Rather than smelling of incense, the church smelled of expensive perfume. David wondered if God would be impressed.

The congregation sang sedately as if to let rip in ecstatic joy was not quite the thing. He did not know whether Tom did it out of bloody mindedness or pure joy but he sang lustily and so David joined him. Tom's mother had a wry smile on her face as she watched the two young men as if to say, 'they're up to something'. The vicar's sermon, based on the gospel text of the day, was simple, brief and to the point. "Lenny sometimes goes on for ages," Tom whispered, "but today he's behaving himself." The final hymn, 'Fight the good fight with all thy might...' roused the seemingly over-fed and over-indulged congregation so that as they left the church people become quite animated.

A large number of people came up to Mrs. Bowers and Tom and paid their respects. David watched it all with quiet interest. Some were obviously workers on their estate but others belonged to the well-heeled burgers of Frensham. It was clear that the Bowers family was well-known and respected. The vicar and his wife had a word with them. "My Tom," he said, "you and David really did lead the singing this morning."

"You heard us vicar?" Tom asked rather craftily. He smiled sweetly, "About time Heaven heard us in Frensham. They forget the Lord can be deaf at times."

At the door they emerged from the shady interior of the church to the bright sunlight outside. It really was a lovely day. David reflected on the service he had just attended and the great services that took place in cathedrals across the country. Somehow he felt nearer to God in a village church than in the grandeur of a cathedral.

After lunch and completion of their chores, as Tom and David insisted on washing up, they read the Sunday papers in the saloon and snoozed a little. "What about a picnic?" Mrs. Bowers suggested. "It's so lovely. We could walk up to the woodland pool and have it there." Tom immediately agreed and while his mother packed a hamper, he explained to David where they were going. "When father bought the estate he wanted to keep deer in the woodland as well as breed pheasants. Unfortunately, there was no stream up on the hill so he had a pool constructed so that the deer had a place to drink. It's really lovely. As children, we would go up there to picnic and swim and if we were lucky and quiet - we weren't usually – deer would come down and drink. You'll love it."

They climbed the hill behind Home Farm, Tom and David carrying a picnic basket between them. The fields were gloriously green, 'mown' to perfection by the cattle that grazed them. Through a gate in a hedge, they entered a woodland of beech and elder, a bridle path winding its way amongst shade and golden sunlight. Birds fluttered in the branches and the distinctive sound of a pheasant could be heard some distance away. After about twenty minutes the path opened out into a vast clearing where water sparkled in the afternoon light. It was a magical place.

The pond was more like a small lake, perhaps an acre in area. It had some gently sloping grassy banks and in other places huge rhododendron bushes swept right down to the water. Wild yellow iris wallowed at the water's edge and there were clumps of water blobs with their lily-like leaves. A fish jumped occasionally and dragon flies skimmed the surface. David just stopped and stared. "It's beautiful," was all he could say.

"I thought you'd like it," Mrs. Bowers smiled delightedly.

"This is my most favorite picnic spot in all the world," Tom told them as he spread out a groundsheet and slumped onto it. "There's no other spot that reminds me of such happy times."

"That's what your father wanted, a place for deer to drink and a secret family spot where everyone could forget the world outside."

"And he achieved it," David told them. "I can't think of a more perfect place."

"Sometimes we come up here on Boxing Morning with coffee and mince pies. Of course the trees have lost their leaves and it's quite cold, but even then there is something wonderful about it."

David could see that that was not the only reason. There was a tremor in her voice. It reminded her of her husband and Tom of his

303

father. It was a special family place and he was privileged to have been allowed to enter their private world.

They returned to Westwick just as it was getting dark, tired by the walk and satisfied by their magical experience. They all agreed to eat in the kitchen and Mrs. Bowers gave the boys each a task in the preparation of a cold meal. It was another feast, particularly the crusty bread, home-produced butter and ham. In fact, they remained in the kitchen for the whole evening taking time over their food, enjoying each other's company, and eventually dealing with the dirty dishes. The warmth of the Aga and the soporific effect of good food made them too lazy to move further. At ten o'clock Mrs. Bowers made them all Horlicks and they went off to their several rooms. It had been another lovely day and David fell fast asleep as soon as his head touched the pillow.

When Miss Bane brought David his morning tea and drew his curtains, he found it was raining. It was typical of England. A couple of sunny days and then down comes the rain. David supposed that was what made England so green and beautiful and its gardens so fertile. From his travels he knew that the British had some of the finest gardens in the world. What was it in the British mentality that made them create a garden, no matter where they landed, be it dessert or tropical isle? It was not just the thought of 'home'. Maybe the love of plants and color came from the rather dull and wet climate that predominated in the British Isles. Perhaps it really was an attempt to bring color into what might have been a dull, gray life. He looked at the garden at Westwick again. It was not quite so magical, now dripping and wan, but it was still very beautiful.

After breakfast they decided to set off for London around midday when the heavy commuter traffic had got away. Tom knew of a good motel on the Hog's Back where they could get lunch and they would arrive in London before the rush hour. It all seemed very sensible, although David was not keen to leave the peace of Westwick for the bustle of London. Their cases packed and stowed in the car, David said au revoir to Mrs. Bowers who kissed him on both cheeks.

"Now, David," she said, "you can come and stay any time you like. No need to accompany Tom, as I know," looking Tom in the eye, "he has other diversions in London. Just telephone and I'll send Joe in the Land-Rover to collect you at the station."

"Hm," Tom commented. "I don't know what you mean by a 'diversion'. I'll tell Ziph her new name."

They all laughed, the car moved off, and they waved and they sped down the drive between the herbaceous border that looked a little bedraggled in the continuing rain.

"Westwick is heaven Tom," David told his friend. Tom nodded in agreement.

Chapter 23

Exams were over and they were all awaiting the results with trepidation. The three-hour papers had not been easy. David felt that he had not done very well in Greek. However, God willing, he hoped he passed and could undertake another year at the college. He was not sure that he really liked London. It had been fun at first but it was beginning to get to him. The weekend at Tom's home had unsettled him. It was not the luxury - one would be foolish not to like it - but the freedom from tension that the countryside brought. He realized he was not a town person, but a countryman at heart. London had been fine for a while but its busy pavements, endless traffic, noise and pollution began to turn David away from it. He longed for a little greenery, and so he tended to visit the vast expanse of Hyde Park more and more when he had free time.

The weather in June was very warm and he had spent many hours in the park reading and revising for his exams. Now that they were over, he tended to sunbathe on good days, read a little and sleep a little. There was a spot just opposite the entrance to the bathing area beside the lake that he found. It was a long grassy bank that sloped down to a path where park visitors ambled. It was a popular place for sun-worshippers and David found the spot quite easy to get to from the underground.

One afternoon, after a quick lunch in the Chesham, he settled in his usual spot having changed into the red bathing costume he had bought in Aden. He was still tanned and the June sun had helped a little. As was his custom, he always brought a book to read. It tended to be a novel or thriller, not theological as he got a little fed up with constantly being fed religion. 'Man must not live by bread alone' was his motto and so Rudyard Kipling's "Kim" was his present reading material. He had started it at school and for some reason never got very far. Now he was wrapped with interest in India and the developing career as a spy of the book's main character.

He had not been there long when out of the corner of his eye he noticed someone walking up the bank towards him. He really did not take all that much notice as people did tend to wander all over the grass, except that the man was rather striking in appearance. He was immaculately dressed in cream trousers that hugged his fine legs, and he wore a dark brown, half-sleeve, linen shirt that enhanced his broad shoulders. Across one shoulder he carried a brown leather duffle bag. David continued reading, but became aware that the man had taken a towel from his duffle bag and placed it quite near to where he was settled. He removed his shirt and trousers to reveal a rather brief pair of white bathing trunks. Now the man was rather hairy. Black hair from chest to navel, and the white trunks made him look especially dark.

David carried on reading but glanced up from time to time. The man lay on his back. He certainly had a wonderful body, fine pectoral muscles, washboard stomach and great muscular legs. He wondered if he was a model as his face was finely chiseled and handsome. David knew that frequently famous people could be seen in the park. On one occasion he had seen Sir Malcolm Sergeant, the famous orchestral conductor, walking in close conversation with a young lady.

For about a half hour the man lay in the sun and then suddenly sat up, rummaged in his bag and got out a bottle of sun oil. He looked over at David and smiled. "Sorry to interrupt your reading but would you mind rubbing some sun oil on my back?"

David did mind a little as he was at an interesting point in his book, but obliged anyhow.

The man's back was very firm and muscular and David worked hard rubbing in the oil as he flexing his muscles against David's fingers. When he had finished and handed the bottle back, the man introduced himself. "Robert Wade" and held out his hand.

"David Earl."

"You a student?" Robert asked.

"Yes, first year at King's College."

"I've seen you here before," Robert said.

"Yes, when it's a lovely day like today I prefer to be outdoors than stuck in my room."

"In lodgings?" Robert asked.

"Turnham Green. Do you know it?" David asked.

"Been there once. Chiswick way isn't it? Not far from the river."

"Yes."

There was a lull in the conversation while Robert put the bottle of oil back in his bag and David began to read again. "I live in Earl's Court," offered Robert.

"Not too far from the park then," David responded. It was clear that Robert wanted to talk so David put down his book. "You're not a Londoner," David observed.

"How can you tell?" Robert asked.

"Your accent – Midlands somewhere," David offered.

"Birmingham. Now where do you come from? You don't really have an accent."

"Leicester, but I was born in Yorkshire," David informed him.

Robert smiled. He had a really beautiful smile that made his face even more handsome. "We're neighbors then."

"I hope you don't mind me asking, Robert, but are you working in London?"

"No problem," Robert responded. "I'm in construction. Been here for two years."

"I thought perhaps you were a model or something as you dress so well, and have a super body."

"Thanks, that's quite a compliment. No afraid not. I do work out though and look after my body. You've a good body yourself."

"Well, I was in the forces – the army – not so long ago and I run twice a week so I suppose I keep fit as well," David told him.

"I like your bathers," Robert said giving David another broad smile. "The red suits your coloring. You fill them very well."

David did not know what to make of that. "Did you buy your briefs in London," he asked Robert as they looked very smart. "They're very nice. I tried to get a pair like yours and couldn't find any."

"Carnaby Street," Robert offered.

"Oh, where's that?"

"You mean to say you've never been to Carnaby Street – the center of world fashion?"

"No," David felt quite stupid.

"It's behind Regent Street. Very trendy. It's the Mecca for modern fashion. People come from all over the world to shop there," Robert told him. "I'll have to take you."

"Tell you what. Tomorrow is Saturday. Come round to my place in Earl's Court. You can try these of mine on, and if you like them, we can go up to Carnaby Street and buy a pair. What about that?"

"Sounds great," David agreed.

Robert gave David his phone number and they agreed to liaise the following day. Later they walked up to Knightsbridge Underground Station where they got a Piccadilly Line train. Robert left the underground at Earl's Court and David changed to the District Line and headed for Turnham Green.

A phone call on Saturday morning settled the arrangement to meet. Robert gave David his address in Earl's Court and David arrived at Burlington Mansions a little after three o'clock. The apartment block was quite old but well maintained and when David rang the bell and spoke to Robert through an intercom, he was invited to the third floor. The lock on the main door clicked and David went down the hall to the lift. The lift gates reminded him of an animal's cage, but it was efficient and took him to where Robert was waiting. Ever immaculate, he was in tight pale blue jeans that showed every ripple in his legs, and a white T-shirt. "Gosh, you look really……" David was at a loss for words.

"Sexy?" offered Robert.

"Yes. You do. Like you see in those expensive magazines – model wearing some Italian designer's latest creation."

"Glad you approve. You don't look so bad yourself. In any case, David, you're so good looking I suspect you look good in pretty well anything."

He led David through into his apartment, which looked out onto the tree-lined street outside. It was quite small but very nicely furnished. "Did you do the furnishings?" David asked quite impressed.

"Yes," Robert replied. "I quite like interior design."

"Very masculine, browns, creams and a dash of orange. I particularly like your rugs. Afgan?" David commented.

"Yes, I've collected things over the past two years. I don't like to rush. Started with that folding bed over there and an easy chair. A bit primitive at first."

Robert showed David the small kitchen and even smaller bathroom. Everything was neat and tastefully done. "You have really good taste, Robert," David told him.

"Thanks."

Robert made a pot of tea and offered a slice of Madeira cake. They talked about London for a while and David told him about National Service.

"I did mine in the Royal Navy nine years ago. I signed on for three years."

"So you're twenty-nine?" David asked.

"Yes. Is that old?"

"No." David looked at the man sitting opposite him. He really was most striking. Possibly the most handsome man he had ever met, except for the South African, Jacob, he met on holiday in Mombassa. He smiled shyly at Robert. "I think you are the most handsome person I have ever met."

"If you ever look in the mirror, David," Robert told him, "you would also see a very beautiful face on a perfect body."

David still did not think he was good looking. "I'm too skinny," he said.

"You're perfect. I love a slim, muscular body. Now, to talk of bodies, you might as well try on my bathers to see how they fit. That was the purpose of our meeting wasn't it?" He looked directly at David.

Robert had put the bathing briefs out on the bed settee. They looked very small and David wondered how he was going to get into them.

"They're very good quality," he said as he took of his socks and shoes and dropped his trousers, which he folded carefully and hung on a chair. He left his shirt on. He took off his underpants and put on the swimming briefs. They fitted beautifully, and in spite of his large equipment, everything fitted in. They were really comfortable.

"Take your shirt off and look in the mirror to see the effect," Robert told him as he opened a wardrobe door to reveal a full-length mirror.

The effect was stunning. David wondered who this bronzed Adonis was. He really did have quite a nice shape and the swimwear really enhanced it. A voice behind him said, "Satisfied?" and he could see Robert standing close behind him eyeing the whole effect.

He came closer, put his arms round David's chest, and whispered into his hair, "You really are the most beautiful young man I've ever seen."

David could feel his arousal pressing into him but he didn't mind. To have Robert's strong arms around him gave him a wonderful sensation. But...what was he doing allowing this man to get so close and to get sexually aroused? It was wrong really but...... Oh, it felt so wonderful.

Before he knew what was happening, Robert had spun him round and was showering his face and neck with kisses. Peppino and he had done the same in Aden, but this was far more wonderful. They had been boys in love in a way only boys could know how. Here was a twenty-nine year old man, with all his maturity, kissing as if there was no tomorrow. David responded. He never thought of the implications. He just wanted to show Robert how he felt about him. He stood there and let Robert kiss every part of his body, slowly and passionately. Oh, the ecstasy of it all.

Eventually Robert lowered him gently onto the bed and removed the white swimming brief that had started the activity. David did not try to hide his nakedness or the way he was reacting. Robert looked down at David with gentle eyes, smiling, his whit teeth glistening in that wonderful face of his. "God, you're beautiful David. I could stand and just look at you all day." He began to remove his clothes. His jeans were removed first to reveal his wonderful legs, then his T-shirt. His hairy chest glistened with perspiration from his furious activity, and there he was naked, except for an expanding pair of white briefs. He took those off to reveal the extent of his nakedness. Instead of being embarrassed, David was fascinated. What a wonderful body he had. "You look...," his strangled words sounded strange, "...like Michelangelo's David, except you have a hairy chest."

Robert bent down and kissed David full on the lips. "If I'm that

David then you're the biblical David, the strong youth who killed Goliath with a stone." With that he gently lowered himself on the top of David so their bodies touched and their excitement was communicated. For the next hour they explored each other with lips and hands. David never knew that lips and tongue could be so exciting. Robert was a master at excitement and David could not get enough. However, they eventually relaxed and lay side-by-side holding hands and occasionally kissing. "Is this.....your....first time?" Robert asked.

"Yes," David turned to him and smiled.

"I thought so."

"How could you tell? Am I so obvious?" David asked.

"Afraid so. You've never been to bed like this before, then?"

"No," David responded.

"How do you feel now that.....?" Robert asked.

David thought for a while. He did not feel dirty as he had expected. He did not know what he felt. "I don't really know, Robert, to be honest. I don't feel guilty, if that's what you're asking?"

"You don't hate me for what happened?"

"Why should I? I let it happen, I enjoyed it. I think you are fantastic," David responded.

Robert looked at him with those wonderful eyes. "Do you think you could love me, David? Do you think we could do this again and again?"

David was taken aback by the intensity of Robert's questions. Here was a beautiful, mature man asking him, David Earl, a mere boy to be his lover. He liked Robert very much but did he 'love' him? Love was a special word. He looked at his Adonis. He really was so super. "I like you very much, Robert, but I don't know if I love you. To love somebody is very special. We have only met once. If you like to see me more I'm very willing. You are very special to me and I feel flattered over what you have said."

Robert looked at him with such fondness. "Not only are you beautiful. David, but you're honest. I like that. I hope that as we get to know each other you will come to love me."

They talked for a while longer and then Robert took David to the shower and they showered together. It was getting on towards six o'clock by this time and Robert said he had an evening appointment. He walked with David to Earl's Court Underground and put him on the train. They promised to phone. As Robert walked away from David, he looked back and waved. David felt comfortable with his new friend.

Images of the afternoon haunted David as he, Martin and Ken watched television on the black and white set in the dining room. It was 'Saturday Night at the London Palladium' and very good, but David

311

kept wandering. By doing what he had with Robert, did that mean he was homosexual? Was it wrong to be homosexual? The Church said it was. Society was ambivalent. What would people say if they found out about him? Could he still be a priest and be gay?

He slept badly, and after church and lunch, he decided to phone Walter and hopefully discuss it with him. "My dear, of course you can come to tea. I'll be delighted. No, I shall be on my own. No visitors, alas." Walter had the good sense not to pry but could recognize an urgency in David's voice.

It was Walter who opened the main door. "Saw you coming. You're always on time, David, so I sat in the hall and looked out of the window. Come along up, the tea is already brewed." Walter's room was warm and friendly, the Earl Grey tea excellent and his fruit cake scrumptious. They chatted about mundane things until David plucked up enough courage and asked, "How do you know if you're homosexual or not, Walter."

Walter stopped in his tracks, a slice of cake hovering before his lips. He put the cake down, and looked at David. "Coming from you, that's an amazing question, David. What brought it on?"

David told him the whole story and about Peppino, his meeting with Jacob in Mombassa, about Robert and the feelings he had for these men. He omitted nothing. For a while Walter just sat and thought, closing his eyes and clasping his hands. At last he said, "Thanks for being so honest David, and for trusting me. Before giving you a definitive answer let me tell you one or two things. First of all, we males all have in our psyche the ability to love another male. Sigmund Freud said that all males are naturally bisexual. In the animal world there is also homosexuality. Jesus loved his disciples and the gospels tell us that He loved James and John more intensely than the others. Male bonding, the desire of males to do things with other males, like the rugby club, or the motor club, is a natural instinct and part of that love we have. In adolescence, the great majority of males have a physical homosexual relationship, but they cross over at some stage to become heterosexual. It's natural. However, some males stay homosexual for one reason or another. If you read the research evidence, ten per cent of males are homosexual, some overt but the majority are covert."

Walter took a swig of tea and then continued. " Sexuality is not black and white, gay or hetero, it's a continuum with various traits in between. If I can give you examples. There's the bisexual who likes both men and women, although many gays who get married pretend to be bisexual. There is the effeminate man who may be gay or he may not. There is the man with a male body, the transsexual, who thinks like a woman and wants to be a woman. Some have an operation and change sex, some just live very unhappy lives pretending to be what they are not. There is the transvestite, who love dressing as a woman, but likes sex with females. These are often the ones who wear their wife's knickers and in extreme cases share her dresses."

David began to laugh. "It's true," Walter went on. "I know of a very famous London barrister who wears a pair of his wife's red knickers when he goes into court. His colleagues call him 'the knickers lady'.

David could not believe what he was hearing. "You're having me on, Walter."

"No, it's all perfectly true," Walter admitted. "When you have time sit in the library and read the literature as I have done. Believe me, David, when I found I was gay, I made it my duty to read everything." He stopped, drank some more tea, had another bite at his cake and continued. "So, sexuality is not one thing or the other, just as gayness is not one thing or the other. We are spread between rather masculine individuals like you, for instance, and screaming 'queens' who wear makeup and walk around in drag. It takes all sorts to make a world. Neither is homosexuality exclusive to social class or intelligence. There are gay laborers, doctors, barristers as I have mentioned, clergy, tycoons, army officers and.....the man who cleans the drains. Did you know that one of the greatest generals the world has ever known, Alexander the Great, was openly homosexual.; Leonardo da Vinci, perhaps one of the great geniuses this world has ever known, artist, engineers, poets, philosophers, was also openly gay. In the Bible, the Book of Samuel tells of King David's love for Jonathan. Because you are gay does not mean you are stupid or useless, although many in the Church would have us believe that."

"The Church, that is the people who administer Christianity, have been wrong time, after time, after time. They cast out lepers from society; burnt so-called witches; tortured those thinkers who would not tow the party line; put to death one of the world's greatest thinkers, Galileo; alienated Jews; pilloried scientists; were intolerant, immoral and cruel; and stigmatize homosexuals, because they don't understand." He said the last phrase slowly as to emphasize a point. "The Christian Church has been wrong so many times. It has so much to answer for, and yet it sets itself up as a moral guardian. They call homosexuality a sin against the flesh, but how many church leaders in the Second World War actually came out against Hitler's concentration camps and branded them as sinful and a crime against humanity. The Roman Catholic Church vehemently condemns homosexuality, but was silent in the war over the treatment of Jews. It's easy to castigate a minority." He stopped suddenly, looked up and smiled at David. "Sorry to get so carried away, but some things about the Church make me very angry."

"But why, Walter, are we so different? Why should a minority be homosexual and the majority not?" It was David's turn in the puzzle.

Walter thought for a while, got up and walked round his room and then sat on the windowsill looking down at David. "I can't tell you why for each individual. Why some are gay and some are not. Only God knows that. What I do know from my reading is that it's partly genetic, partly to do with neuron patterns in the brain, and partly environmental. As I mentioned earlier, all males have a genetic inclination to other males. It's an established psychological fact. The majority move on but some are left. When we are in the womb we all begin as female but some developed into males. It's something to do with the amount of testosterone that is secreted. There is a growing body of research from America that indicates that a particular gene plays a role as well as our sex endocrines, and the environment. A body of opinion believes that parental relationships have an influence. What is not agreed is in what proportion these things operate. Some young men are 'pushed' into homosexual activity by the friends they keep and the lifestyle they adopt. Others have no choice as they just are not attracted at all sexually by women. That's me. I like women as friends, but I have no inclination to have sex with them."

David now got to the million dollar question. "What about me?" he asked.

Walter looked at him with such empathy. "David, David, David," was all he could say. He sighed. "David I've always known you were gay, although you did not know it your self, or at least would not admit it. I suspected it's in your genes, that you have always looked at the male body and longed to touch."

David nodded his head in affirmation.

"You lingered in the gym at school in order to watch the older boys. You were fascinated by their developing masculinity. But you repressed your desires, except with one or two special friends. You told nobody and you felt that you were the only one. You felt dirty. You tried hard to like girls, went out with one or two, but found you had no desire for them?"

A tear fell onto David's cheek. All that Walter was describing was true. For years he felt he was odd, different, unclean. "I was so terrified, ashamed," he admitted, tears now streamed down his face. "Even in Aden when I so loved Peppino I felt….." He broke down and sobbed. "Why should it be me, Walter? Why can't I be normal?"

314

Walter came over, sat on the arms of David's chair and put his arm round David's shoulders. "Because you are you, David. What is normal, anyway? You are normal, because that's the way God made you. He has a plan for you. Because..." and he stopped abruptly and lifted David's tear-stained face up to the light. "Because you are beautiful, sensitive, honest, intelligent....because God gave you these gifts and the sensitivity that goes with homosexuality to use for His greater glory. That's why you're homosexual. You'd be surprised, David, but you are really loved by many. Not in the sexual sense, but deep down in the heart. These are people who could not care less if you are gay. Their love is real."

It took a while for David to calm down . Walter's words were swimming in his head. He was homosexual. But he had always known it in his heart of hearts. Now it was out. What was he to do about the priesthood? Water's words came to him. 'Because God gave you the sensitivity of homosexuality'. He looked directly at Walter now. "And what about the priesthood, Walter?"

Walter smiled. "A good question. Well, what about it? My belief is that God made us what we are and if He in His wisdom will have us as priests, so be it."

"You don't think we are.....immoral if we love someone....physically?"

Walter waited a while thinking. "No matter what some people in the Church may say, I don't regard the expression of love in a sexual act as wrong. I've thought a lot about this, David. It's why I had a year off and went to Sheffield. I've also discussed it with the Dean. Think of it this way. Do we judge a married man by his activities in bed? No, we don't even ask. Then why should gays be judged by their bedtime activities?"

"What does the Dean believe?" David asked quite intrigued.

"Oh, he takes the party line. It's to be expected, really in his position. He's not against homosexuality per se, but against sexual acts. 'Bend you love outwards' he says. You know how smoothly he talks and waves his hands around." They both laughed. "But I suspect that in private, off the record, he's quite tolerant. There's so much more to our Dean than people think."

"So what do you think I should do?" David asked.

"My dear, do nothing," was Walter's reply. "Enjoy your man. He sounds a dish. Whether you love him or not you will find out. But take my advice, the word 'love' in the gay world is thrown around and to most means very little. Don't rush things. Enjoy the experience. You know, David, most of us, including me, don't know what real love is.

And that goes for heterosexuals as well as homosexuals. It's something special. I've only seen it once or twice between people. When you have it then it transcends everything else. I think that when Jesus speaks of 'love' He is trying to convey this deeper emotion. One day, God willing, we'll find it." (1)

David rang Clair Wentworth to tell her he would not be able to make supper. She kindly promised to leave him a cold plate on the sideboard in the dining room. He and Walter went to the church of All Saints Margaret Street up near the BBC. The church was famous for its anglo-catholic liturgy and frequented by writers and artists, who seemed to prefer color and ritual in their worship. Evening service was no exception and David found it a little over the top, but he enjoyed Walter's company. He would be ever grateful for the honest advice he had given. His prayers were for all gays everywhere. They were a group that needed prayer as they were mainly misunderstood and frequently abused. Many lived under terrible emotional pressures, just as he had been doing. Yes, Walter would make a good priest. He had empathy and an honesty that accepted all men and women for themselves. He felt better now, reconciled, and for the first time in years ready to hold his head high and accept his destiny.

David rang Robert on Monday afternoon and arranged to see him on Wednesday instead of going for his usual run. "What about meeting for lunch?" Robert suggested. "I'll see you at Harrods in the banking hall at one o'clock."

Now the restaurant at Harrods is not special in its décor, but is a meeting place for the wealthy and famous. David did not want to embarrass Robert by wearing his usual jeans and sweater so he wore his best suit. He had bought the suit, French blue with a narrow lighter blue stripe, from the Savoy Tailor's Guild on the Strand a few weeks earlier. It had cost an arm and a leg but he realized that there were many social events associated with the theological faculty that needed a decent personal presentation. Hence, the suit. He argued that, given the quality and cut, it would last him many years, provided that his waistline remained reasonably slim.

His lecture had finished at twelve and Harrods was easy to get to by underground. "We're on a special date?" beamed Walter winking at David. "I like the suit, you look good enough to eat."

Even Tom, not known for his sartorial interest, had to agree that he looked smart. "You'll have to wear it to impress the natives at Frensham Parish Church, David," he observed.

Even the Chaplain, meeting David on the stairs as he descended from his New Testament lecture, complimented him on his attire.

"David," he squeaked, "Like your suit. Something special today?"

"Yes, Chaplain. I've been invited to Harrods for lunch," he said. He smiled mischievously and added, "Thought I'd better not look like a penniless student."

"You certainly aren't dressed like that," the Chaplain beamed. "Good, good. Enjoy your lunch." And with a wave of the hand he was off up the stairs.

David was early and hung around the entrance to the banking hall in expectation. Robert suddenly appeared from nowhere. David's heart took an extra beat when he saw him. He was dressed in a gray-flannel suit that had a feint darker gray stripe in it. Single breasted with narrow lapels it made him appear to have very broad shoulders and a narrow waist and his muscular legs filled his pants. He was certainly quite something. A few heads turned as he shook hands with David. "Been waiting long, David?" he asked.

"No, not really. I like to watch people and certainly people are interesting at Harrods," David told him. "They represent so many nationalities."

"That' because its summer and the tourists are about," Robert told him as they made their way to the lifts. "Although, it doesn't matter when you come here, there seem to be tourists. Even in the winter."

"I like the suit," Robert told him. "You look.....great. I'd like to give you a hug and a kiss but we'll get arrested." They laughed as the lift took them to the restaurant. Robert had managed to get a quiet table to one side so they could talk. The food was excellent and lunch was a great success.

After lunch they wandered around Harrods. Robert seemed to know it well and took him to see the zoo. David never realized how big the store was. It was huge and seemed to cover acres. Around three o'clock Robert suggested they went back to his apartment for "Tea and something." He winked at David so he was clear about the 'something'. The Underground took them to Earl's Court and before long they were drinking tea and chatting. David told Robert that term was at an end and he would be going home for the summer holidays. This news upset Robert for a while and he went quiet. "I forgot it's June and students have summer holidays," he said. "Can't you stay in London, David?" he asked.

David explained that his father expected him to work as he was paying quite a large proportion of his university expenses. "I've arranged to be relief postman for six weeks. If I don't turn up the regular men will not get a vacation," he explained.

Robert came over to where he was sitting a knelt beside him. "I'll miss you, David," he said. "It's only a few days since we met, although quite a while since I first saw you. I was attracted to you all that time ago and wanted to speak to you but didn't know how." He kissed David on the lips and then on the neck. "Let's go to bed," he suggested.

David hoped he would suggest it. He was frantic to get Robert naked again. And so, the two made love.

Their parting was quite emotional on Robert's part. He took David to the Underground, shook hands and kissed him, continental fashion, on both cheeks. "Telephone me David," he asked. "I shall await your every call. You're my special guy." He turned on his heels and was gone and did not look back. David's feelings were mixed. Yes, he would miss Robert very much. Seeing him was so wonderful, but being back at home with his parents and brother was also important to him. His brother was to get married just before next term commenced and he was to be best man. He had an obligation to the postmen. And more important than that, he realized that no matter how much he enjoyed sex with Robert, it must not get out of proportion. Did he love Robert? What was love? Robert said he 'loved' him but how can you love somebody when you have only known them a few days. 'Like', 'admire', 'be attracted to', yes, but 'love' was something else. It was with these thoughts that he left Robert, returned to Turnham Green and later to his home in Leicester.

Chapter 24

Now a postman's life is not easy. Delivering letters and small parcels in a rural area on the outskirts of Leicester had its drawbacks. Sometimes, when David knew he had to visit a farm he took the communal postal bicycle, but other times he walked, and walked and walked. There were evil-tempered dogs to deal with, and quite frequently evil- tempered customers who blamed the postman for an un-received letter. Then there was the weather. Hot summer days were exhausting, and cold rainy day were uncomfortable. It is said that England does not have a particular climate, just weather. Certainly the weather could make a day pleasant or downright miserable.

David soldiered on in spite of the drawbacks of the job. The pay was quite good after his earnings as a soldier, and there were days when he really enjoyed himself. He and his colleague shared the round and the wage was split equally. They had roughly the same area to cover and were allocated plenty of time, so there was time to chat and to receive a cup of tea when it was offered. The vast majority of people were kind and friendly and generally David enjoyed his days.

He got into a routine of phoning Robert. He found that Robert was out on many evenings but that Mondays and Fridays were his nights in. They talked for about a half hour and said how much they missed each other, and that the time would pass, and talked of their next meeting. Generally, he phoned from a call box as he knew his father would complain about long and expensive telephone calls. His father had a thing about phones. They were to be used sparingly and you got over your communication as quickly as possible. Gossip was out.

Despite being bound up with his family and his brother's forthcoming wedding, David though a lot about Robert. In fact, his image was in his memory all the time as he trudged on his postal round. His wonderful smile, perfect body and gentle touch impinged on other thoughts. To be fair, he was not obsessed with the image of Robert, as he thought of Tom and Westwick, Mrs. Bowers in her old shoes pruning roses, Walter in bleak Sheffield. He wondered if Walter had managed to get a job as he intended. He could not phone Walter as his friends had no telephone, but he did phone Tom who sounded very relaxed but had had another row with Ziph. "She says I don't spend enough time with her, David. But mum is on her own at present as Min is holidaying in Greece with his Charterhouse friends, and Jonathan is in Scotland staying with a wealthy college friend." Poor Tom, his love life was so frequently in turmoil. David thought of his love life and smiled.

David did not commence his postal job until July and one weekend in the spare days of June his father and mother drove him up to Sheffield to see the progress of the new house. His father had just bought an Armstrong Sidley Saphire, a real luxury car of distinction, so the journey up to Yorkshire was most pleasant, particularly as they followed the old Roman Foss Way as far as they could. It was a leisurely journey and they stopped in Warwick and Stratford-on-Avon to do a little sight seeing. His father had booked them in at the Peacock Inn in Baslow for the night so there was no rush.

After breakfast the following morning, they drove from Baslow to Totley on the outskirts of Sheffield and then to Broad Elms Lane in Eccelsall, a rather smart district on the edge of the city. There his father had purchased an acre of land on which to build his house. The land had been a prosperous nursery garden until the death of the owner whose sons had sold it off in plots at an enormous profit to themselves. Land in Eccelsall was at a premium as it was a prime residential area where the wealthy of this steel and cutlery town built their mansions. Broad Elms lane was no exception, except that it was not fully built up, and after the nursery plots there were only fields.

The house was built up to and including the roof. David was impressed as it was constructed of honey-colored Portland stone and roofed in dark brown, antique tiles. There was a deep loggia at the front door, which led to a square entrance hall, and on the right of it was the dining room with the kitchen and laundry room behind. On the left as you entered was the sitting room that ran the whole length of the building. Upstairs would be three bedrooms and two bathrooms, however they had to look through rafters as the stairs and wooden floors were not yet fitted. His mother explained that they were having stained glass windows fitted. One would stretch down the length of a curved staircase. It all sounded very splendid and both his parents were excited.

The land his father had purchased was long and narrow. He had decided that at the front there would be a semi-circular drive with entrance and exit gates. The builders were already working on the walls when they arrived. Behind the house a ten foot wide terrace right along the rear of the house was being constructed . His father explained that as the land sloped downwards towards the end of his holdings, steps would go down onto a lawn and then there would be a series of smaller gardens wandering into each other, each hidden from the other by yew hedges. At the end would be a kitchen garden and greenhouse. He mentioned a rose garden as roses grew exceptionally well in the polluted air of Sheffield and the possibility of a rose garden with a lily pond.

When the architect arrived his father went off with him to discuss various points. With his father being in the stone, granite and marble business, he knew where he could get all kinds of unusual things for the house and needed to inform the builder. "Do you like it?" his mother asked.

David looked at his mother with such affection. Life with his father had not been easy. If it were not for himself and his brother, he suspected there would have been a divorce years ago. But his mother was a home-maker and believed in family and so she had put up with a great deal. "The question is mother," he said, "do you like it?"

"It's what I've always wanted, dear. We've lived in nice houses, but they have been such hard work. Your father never understood. We've not always been well off and....." She broke off as memories came rushing back.

David put his arm round her. "I'm glad for you, mum. I hope this gives father a new interest in life and that being nearer to the family will bring its rewards."

They spent about two hours at the house and after a ploughman's lunch at a local pub his father suggested that they visit Chatsworth Park before heading home. Chatsworth is one of the Stately Homes of the Dukes of Devonshire, (1) set in many thousands of acres of park with its own village for estate workers. It had been open to the public since after the First World War. The good burgers of Sheffield and their Derbyshire colleagues had adopted it as their own and many thousands visited the grounds for free every year. On certain days the house opens to visitors, and David had happy memories as a child of walking round the State Rooms of the 'Palace of the Peaks' as it is called.

The weather was lovely and after parking the car they all three walked down by the river and sat on a bridge looking towards the magnificent house. The surrounding parkland, hosting deer and cattle, was as if a lawnmower had cut the grass, it was so short. Behind the immense mansion and its formal gardens, where a twenty-foot fountain burst into the air, was a forested hillside on top of which, poking through the trees, was the top of a hunting tower. It was, perhaps, one of the most magnificent of views of any mansion in the country.

David was reminded of Tom's home and found that he was telling his parents all about it. He had not said much about Westwick before but his memory was pricked into action. "Of course," David added, "Westwick is nothing like Chatsworth. This is a Stately Home in the grand style, a palace, to impress the rich and powerful in the land, while

Tom' home is home. It's small in comparison but equally impressive."

"What did his father do to have that sort of money?" his father asked, ever conscious of wealth.

"I'm not really sure," David told them honestly. "I didn't like to ask. I think it was something in the City, publishing, a newspaper or something. But it certainly is a lovely house and estate."

"It sounds to me," his mother remarked that you're rather in love with the place, David. I've never heard you enthuse about a house so much."

"Maybe mum," David chuckled. "I certainly found it lovely and relaxing. And Mrs. Bowers and Tom made me so welcome."

"I'm glad for you, David." His mother put her hand on his arm. "Life has not been easy for you these last few years."

"Humph," his father retorted and got up. "National Service did him good. Made a man out of him." He walked off. "Come on, let's get moving," he shouted.

David's mother looked at her son with such pride. He was a man now, no longer a boy. He was so handsome. Yes, the army had done him good in some ways but he was still the sensitive, loving David she had always known.

The wedding of David's brother was a splendid affair and took place in the local parish church where both boys had been servers. The bride, a local girl that his brother had met at the church youth club, looked stunning, and David did his job as best man and guardian of the ring. The reception was at the Belvoir Hotel in Leicester from where the bride and groom went for a honeymoon in Majorca. On their return, his brother was to take up a post in Cardiff with an international company. David' father had given them a down-payment on a house as a wedding present and they were to move in on their return.

David's last few days at home before returned to college were rather quiet without his brother and the added excitement of a wedding. It would be hard on his mother as for twenty-two years she had had her 'babies' around her. David felt for her and tried to spend as much time with her as possible. However, the time swiftly arrived when he had to say his farewells to his parents, his friends, and to Tudor Cottage, his home of so many years. The new house in Sheffield would be waiting for a Christmas entry. A new term was about to begin. He was a second year student and expected to chaperone the freshmen in the faculty. And then there was Robert.

On the evening David arrived at his lodgings there was a call from Robert. He was eager for them to meet that night but David was tired with the journey and so they arranged to have tea in the open-air restaurant in Hyde Park. He was uncertain whether he had a lecture or not but did not want to screw things up by making arrangements he could not keep. As it turned out, there were no lectures until the following day and so he went to the park early as the September sun was so lovely. There were a lot of people walking around the Serpentine Lake and David joined them. Ducks swaggered on the grassy banks and the London pigeons challenged them for a place in the sun. Autumn tints were just coming into the trees and David thought how lovely the park would look with its oranges, reds and yellows in another month. Passing the Peter Pan statue, (2) it reminded him of J.M. Barrie's story of childhood innocence and the subjugation of evil by love and a little magic. If only life was like that? Reality was much harder.

Robert looked well. He was sitting at a table looking like an advert for Vogue Magazine. He wore tight white trousers and a black sweater that showed off his distinctive chest and the summer weather in London had obviously been good as he had acquired an excellent tan. "You look wonderful, David," he said flashing a smile at David. "Being a postman obviously suits you."

"You look super also," David responded shaking his hand. "I thought you were just sitting here posing for a fashion magazine. Hey, you've got a wonderful tan."

"Wait 'till you see more of it," Robert said with a wink.

"I've thought so much about you these past few months, Robert. I really missed you."

"And me you," Robert responded. "Let's have tea and then......" He looked at David and smiled slyly. "....maybe we can be more....informal."

And so they ended up after tea at Burlington Mansions, Earl's Court.

David found when he returned to his lodgings in Turnham Green that Ken had gone into the Theological Hostel in Vincent Square, as he was now a third year student, and a fresher from Newark in Nottinghamshire, had arrived to take his place. Ian was twenty-nine, had served in the RAF in Singapore, and on demobilization took a job as a mechanic for seven years. He had studied at night to gain two 'A' levels so that he could read theology at King's. He was engaged to a mathematics teacher and they intended to get married as soon as he was ordained. He was tall and thin, very laid back, and found it hard to get up in the mornings. He had two alarm clocks in his room. One, on his bedside table, would ring at seven and he would stretch and switch it off. He would then go back to sleep. The second clock, on a chest of drawers at the other side of his room, would ring at seven-fifteen. He would get out of bed, switch the alarm off, re-enter his bed and fall asleep again. After a number of late entries to breakfast and to college, David took it on himself to thump on his door until he opened it and spoke. That seemed the only way Ian could arise on time. David wondered how he had managed in the RAF and in his job. Maybe he had a minder there too. Anyhow, Ian was a most agreeable person and David did not mind.

After lunch one wet Sunday afternoon, Ian and David were browsing the Sunday papers as was their habit if there was nothing else to do. David came across an article in the 'Sunday Times Magazine' section about ectopic pregnancies. He found it fascinating as he had not known such a thing possible. The article suggested that perhaps the birth of Jesus might have been ectopic and that could explain the doctrine of virgin birth. "Hey, Ian, did you read that article in the 'Sunday Times' about ectopic pregnancies?" he asked.

Ian looked up from his reading. "No, tell me."

David read him the whole article, which was quite short. "It makes you think," David commented as he ended.

"In what way, David?"

"Well," David began, "I've always been skeptical about Mary's pregnancy. Women can have 'false pregnancies' where they produce the symptoms – stomach increases in size as do the breasts, but they don't produce a child. It's a psychosomatic condition. A woman can become pregnant some time after menstruation because a sperm has remained in the vagina. But for a woman who has never been touched by a man to produce a child, well....?"

Ian was quiet. At last he spoke very carefully. "Are you questioning the gospel story that an angel somehow gave Mary her child? That Mary was not a virgin?"

"I suppose I am," David admitted. "Oh, there are plenty of stories in the Hindu and other religions about virgin birth. If I read the commentators correctly, they attribute it to the desire that a god should be perfect and not tainted. I accept that. How can the god be perfect if he, she, it is the result of an ordinary union? But there are some things associated with the birth of Jesus that don't ring true."

Ian sat up in his chair. "Such as?"

"Well, for one thing, if Mary was having a child outside wedlock, then why was she not stoned to death as was, and still is, the practice in some places, in the Middle East."

"That's easy," Ian replied. "Joseph married her before her pregnancy became obvious."

"But it would be easy to do a calculation and deduce they were not married when she became pregnant," David offered.

"Well they went from their home town of Nazareth to the new town of Bethlehem to be counted because of taxation. Nobody knew," Ian counter suggested.

"Exactly," David pounced. "It's far too convenient. It just happened at the right time. The time when Joseph wanted a cover-up. In any case, Mary must have been showing her pregnancy before they left for Bethlehem."

"There's another problem," David continued. "The normal Arab male, and remember that Joseph was an Arab and a Jew, shunned any girl who might have had previous sexual relations. It was a matter of family pride at all levels of society. In fact, they go to great lengths to show their respective families that the girl was a virgin. The women folk follow the bride and groom to the nuptial bedroom right after the marriage ceremony. The door to the bedroom is closed while the women wait outside. When the act is done, the bloodstained bedsheet is given to the assembled women, who with whoops of delight display it for all to see. Would Joseph not comply with tradition? Would he fake the act?"

Ian was dumbfounded. "I just don't know what to say, David. I've always accepted the story, virgin birth, Joseph's love for Mary and the move to be taxed and then the flight into Egypt. It's a wonderfully romantic story."

"I agree with you, Ian," David said. "It is a romantic story. But is it true?"

"OK," Ian responded, "what's your explanation?"

Now David was put on the spot. He was being asked to propound an idea that had been running around in his head for quite some time. "Let me ask you something first, Ian," he said, "before I put my head on the chopping block. If there was no virgin birth and Jesus was born of woman, what are the implications for the Christian message?"

Ian laughed, not in amusement, but in sheer panic. "Wow, you do ask some direct questions, David. Well....I suppose.....it..... I don't know what the implications are. You tell me."

"I can't tell you anything, Ian," David told him "All I can do is to make suggestions and get you to think. I feel we just accept things we are told at King's and we never think." There was a pause while David assembled his thoughts. "It seems to me that Christianity sets itself apart from all other religions because of two things. One, God sent His Son to earth and He became Man. Jesus is God and Man. As I've already suggested, in the eyes of the Church, if he was God then He

325

would also have to be Perfect Man. If He was born of a normal union then, according to the doctrine of original sin, He could not be perfect. If Jesus is man only, or tainted by man's sins as an accident of His normal birth, then the credibility of Jesus being the Son of God, the Messiah, is weakened. Hence, the importance of the concept of virgin birth. If Jesus is the Son of God, of the 'same stuff' as the Nicene Creed states, (3) then it follows that the Resurrection and Ascension are believable."

There was silence as David thought. "Secondly, the other central tenet of Christianity is love – love God and love thy neighbor. Didn't Jesus tell his disciples just this?"

Ian nodded. "I follow your argument."

"Now," went on David. "The loving part presents no problems, unless of course, you ask what is really meant by love. Then you have to look at the Greek of the gospels. Loving God and one's neighbor is really a simple concept." He smiled. "Though not always easy to put into practice. But if you understand the Greek word used in the Gospels then that love of God is something very special. That special love of God is strengthened if you accept the power of the Holy Spirit working through Jesus who is the Son of God."

"I have to admit," David told Ian, "that I am beginning to question a number of things we have been told. My schooling taught me to question. The first grammar school I went to in Sheffield just plied us with knowledge, facts, and we regurgitated them for exams. If you had a good memory you did well. The second grammar school I went to encouraged us to question and think things through for ourselves. I believe that is what we should be doing at university. But at King's......" He thought for a while looking for the right words. "I don't want to over influence you.....but at King's we are being brainwashed....our minds broken down and built up into a certain mould. We never discuss in New Testament lectures and where we could, with our tutors, controversy is avoided. It's common knowledge that in your exams Professor Tucker marks you down if you don't take his line."

Ian looked rather pained. "That may be fine with you, David, but I'm new here and I want a peaceful life. I'm quite prepared to be 'brainwashed', as you put it. I want to be a priest and I'm quite happy to take the Church of England line."

David felt he had been put down. Where was the desire for truth? Surely, a priest had to know in his heart that what he was preaching was the truth. If not, he was a charlatan, a mere politician presenting party doctrine. David and Ian never had a theological discussion after that. It was clear to David that Ian was to be a 'yes man.' He was a nice guy, but David couldn't see him burning with passion for what he believed and even giving his life for them.

The relationship with Robert got into a routine as did his college work. Much more time now was spent in the library researching for his various assignments as more rigorous demands were made on second year students. His problem was that his thoughts kept coming more and more back to Robert and it was difficult to keep his concentration. He only saw Robert now on Mondays and Fridays, but he found he was becoming more and more involved. He consulted Walter. "My dear, you have got it bad," was his comment. "You've just got to be strong and get focused. Keep your meetings to twice a week. Be strict. If the guy loves you he will understand. When you lose concentration walk around for a while and then go back to whatever you've been doing. You'll find it helps."

David was grateful for Walter's experience and his advice did work, but there was always that longing at the back of his mind. He was not sure whether it was love or lust. He did enjoy their play and he also enjoyed Robert's company. At one stage he asked Walter if he thought he was in love. Walter laughed. "Oh, David, you need a good shake at times. Only you can know if you are in love. It's in films that lovers walk around with 'cow eyes' for each other. Do you feel sick every time you see him?"

"No."

"Would you want to spend all your waking hours with him?" Walter asked.

David pondered that question for some time. Would he? At last he said, "No, not really. In fact, we don't have much in common except bed and looking good. I don't think he's much of an intellectual. Come to think of it, I've never seen a book anywhere in his apartment and we never discuss anything serious."

"There you are my dear," Walter said putting his arm over David's shoulder and giving him a hug. "You're not in love. Infatuated, maybe. Sex starved? Aren't we all, but not in love. Love is like a rainbow. It has many colors but real love is at the end of the rainbow. You'll know when you reach the end of the rainbow. Let me give you a little fatherly advice."

"Fatherly advice." David laughed. "And you all of twenty-eight and a woman hater at that."

Walter was not deterred. "Let me give you some advice. Don't be pushed into a relationship, David. It's too early. Play the field, get to know the gay world. Oh, enjoy your relationships but remember.....there are plenty of fish in the sea. When that special person comes along you will know without asking."

After Walter's interrogation and advice David felt better about his relationship. His concentration improved and he really began to enjoy the huge workload they had to undertake. Spending time in the library reading and reading was exacting but exciting. So many questions needed to be answered. They still made their trips to Lyon's for coffee in the morning where they engaged in theological discussion. But tea was usually not taken as they wanted to dash off home to work. Tom was seeing less and less of Ziph and she was complaining more and more.

"I've finished with her," Tom announced one morning as the three sat drinking coffee. "She's getting in the way. All we do is fight."

"But do you still love her?" David asked.

Tom thought for a time. "Yes, I suppose I do. But, David she just doesn't understand that I have a degree to get. It's all right for her working in an office from nine to four. Her evenings and weekends are free. Mine aren't"

"Have you talked to her?" Walter asked.

"I've tried, Walter," Tom explained painfully. "She just doesn't listen."

"I take it you shout at her and she shouts back. That's what you usually do Tom if you want to enforce a point," Walter pointed out.

With downcast eyes and a pained expression on his face Tom asked, "Do I really?"

Poor Tom. David felt sorry for him. Walter was being a little brutal but he was right. "Afraid so," David had to admit. "Look, Tom, just let it ride for a while. Give each other space and see how you feel in a few days."

Tom agreed.

But events took their own course. A couple of days later Ziph rang him at his lodgings and was in quite a state. She cried bitterly and said she loved Tom but he had thrown her over. David calmed her down and suggested they meet for lunch the following day at La Popot Restaurant just off Regent Street, a popular place amongst students and largely staffed by 'resting' actors.

Ziph was waiting for him at a corner table. He apologized for being late. There had been some sort of power failure on the Underground and he had to wait ages for a train. She looked very unhappy with black rings under her eyes, and David suspected tears were not far away. She really was a beautiful girl, even when she was troubled. Her red hair and green eyes were perfect. They ordered and David waited for her to open the conversation. "I'm sorry to involve you, David," she commenced. "Tom and I had a terrible row at the weekend. I wanted us to go to the cinema on Monday evening and Tom said he couldn't. You know how he is sometimes, he just said no? Well I accused him of not really caring about me and we ended up shouting. I slapped his face and he stormed out. The following day he rang me early to say our relationship was over. I didn't know what to do and then I thought of you, his best friend." She stopped and a tear dribbled down her cheek. David was a little concerned as he had no experience of crying females and had no idea what to do. Instinct made him lean over and put his hand on the back of hers. "Please don't be upset, Ziph. I'm sure Tom didn't mean it. You know what he's like. Quick to temper and quick to forgive."

Tearful eyes looked at him. "Do you think so, David? Do you really think he didn't mean it?"

"Tom may be all sorts of things, Ziph," David told her, "but I have never known him be angry for long. He has a forgiving nature and I'm sure he would never really hurt you. I know he loves you very deeply."

David was not great on women, but he could have put his arms round her and given her a hug. Her huge green eyes opened wide and a smile spread across her face like the rays of the sun emerging from behind a cloud. "You think so, David?" she asked. "Will you talk to him? Tell him I'm sorry. I know I react too quickly at times."

"Of course Ziph," David reassured her. "But there is something you should know. Tom is at university in his second year. Work pressures are greater this year and he is determined to get his degree and become a priest. You have to help him?"

"But how, David?" she innocently asked.

"You have to give him space, not pressurize him. Accept it when he says he's busy. I know he was worried the last few days about getting an essay in on time. You have to be supportive, even if it means just bringing him cups of tea while he studies."

"But he never said," Ziph pointed out.

"That's his problem and yours. You have to talk, not fight. When you're married you will have to talk."

The mention of marriage seemed to cheer her up. They ate their lunch amicably with Ziph telling David about her sister's new boyfriend, a famous racing driver. They parted and she kissed him gently on the cheek. "Thank you," she said, "Tom's friend."

She was one hell of a girl and was so in love with Tom.

That evening he phoned Tom at Camden Hill Square. At first Tom thought David wanted to discuss an assignment they had been given but when David told him he had been out with Ziph for lunch he went quiet. "Now listen, Tom, and don't say a word until I've finished," David ordered him. "She rang me last night in a state and I agreed to have lunch with her. We talked. You great inhuman brute, can't you understand that she's madly in love with you. I explained about your work and your worries over the essay. She didn't understand, Tom. Now she does. Ring her and make it up. If I had a girl like her – and I'm not into girls – I'd bag her right away."

There was silence for a while and then the voice of a little boy said, "I love her. I've been so unhappy, David, since…. Well you know what happened. I know I love her."

"Well get on that bloody phone and tell her," David responded forcefully. "Do it. See you in the morning."

Tom and Ziph were to have more fights because that was how they were made. Tom obviously sorted out his relationship with Ziph and all three of them bonded into something very special. Once when David challenged Tom over his rather masculine handling of his girlfriend, his comment was, "She loves it. If I didn't shout and she didn't slap me a little, she'd think I didn't love her." David felt that human relationships were unfathomable. He didn't want his relationship to be so traumatic, but, you never know how humans will act until one day they surprise you.

"Have you ever been to a gay pub?" Robert asked David quite out of the blue one afternoon.

"No, well not knowingly. I was once taken to a pub in Mombassa by some RAF friends and it turned out to be gay. I had no idea," David explained.

"Would you like to go?"

He considered the proposal. "Fine, no problem."

"Right, there are two famous ones in Earl's Court quirt near here. I'll meet you outside Earl's Court Underground Station at nine. Oh, jeans and top will be fine. They don't dress up at these places."

Robert may have said that they didn't 'dress up' but when he arrived to collect David at the station he looked…. He wore tight black leather trousers that showed everything he had. How he got into them David could not imagine. David's jeans were tight but Robert's pants had been painted on. His white polo-neck sweater was worn under a soft black leather jacket. He wore black cowboy boots. "How do I look," Robert asked enthusiastically.

"Marvelous," was all David could suggest. How could he tell him that he looked so sexy he felt like undressing him there and then and making love.

Robert took David's arm. "It's only a few minutes walk."

The 'Colehurn' Pub was on a corner with two entry doors, each in a different street. It was rather dowdy to look at with its name etched in large gold letters in the maroon painted glass windows and there was a dimly lit sign over each of the doors. It was heaving when they got inside. The atmosphere was hot and humid from the many sweaty bodies standing around. There were a few women but men of all ages predominated. Just about everyone was either dressed in jeans or in leather. Some characters wore leather chaps, cowboy style, over their jeans with just a leather jacket over their bare jewelry-adorned necks. Others were dripping in black leather: pants, jacket, cap and boots. A few wore dark glasses with their ensemble. The common drink seemed to be beer but a few were imbibing wine or gin and tonic.

David followed Robert as he wound his way to the bar. He was obviously well-known as he was greeted many times. "Hey, who's your friend, Robert?" or "You certainly know how to choose 'em, Robert," were yelled at him over the noise.

"Don't take any notice, David," Robert told him. "What are you drinking?"

David chose a half pint of lager and Robert had the same. Sipping his drink gave him the chance to look around. The clients of the pub seemed to be of a type, masculine and very much into dressing in leather or jeans. One or two looked quite fearsome with the peaks of their leather caps almost hiding their faces. Some of the men in jeans had tattoos on their arms and he noticed that, unlike his freshly pressed jeans, theirs were decidedly dirty and torn. In a few cases white flesh could be seen. He wondered if this was by design or due to poverty. Eventually, after seeing how much they spent on beer, he decided it was not poverty.

A newcomer, a big guy in leather, and denim jacket, wearing a black peeked cap, pushed his way to the bar. He was all of six foot two, broad shouldered and heavily mustached. David could not believe it when he asked for a drink. "Gin and tonic please," he said in a very feminine voice with a little lisp. David looked at Robert and wanted to laugh. Robert winked. It was clear that the 'butch', masculine image was all a big blind. The man was clearly quite feminine. David and Robert moved away so they could talk.

"Surprised, David?" Robert asked.

David smiled. "I thought he was such a masculine type......then when he asked for a gin and tonic......in that prissy voice, ...I just wanted to laugh."

"There are many like that here," Robert told him. "They live in a fantasy world, a world of image. Get them in bed and they are puppy dogs."

"So, this bar is like a fancy dress parade," David suggested where they can play out their fantasies. The effeminate can pretend to be masculine."

"Mm, I suppose so," Robert agreed. "But believe me there are some characters here who are tough, very tough."

"What about the girls?" David asked.

"Oh, some are lesbian and some just like to hang about with gay boys. They're safe. Finish your drink and I'll show you the other bar."

The 'Boltons' was almost in sight of the previous bar and of roughly the same style except it was not on a corner and had one door only. There must have been thirty or forty motorbikes parked outside. It was full when they got inside and they had to push and shove to get to the bar. This time David ordered lagers. The clientele was the same and yet different; they wore jeans and leather but also sported chains round their waist, on their caps, around their necks, seemingly everywhere. Many had pierced ears with large rings hanging and one or two sported studs in their noses. David noticed that some wore rings on most of their fingers. "Different?" Robert remarked as they placed themselves in a corner out of the pushing throng. "These guys are bikers, motor bike enthusiasts."

"You can't help notice their chains and rings," David pointed out. "Is there any significance?"

"It's part of their 'uniform'," Robert explained. "It sets them apart from the leather boys in the other pub. Many have rings through their tits though you can't see unless their shirt is open."

David shuddered. "Weird!"

"The leather boys in the other pub tend to like sex involving whips and pain while these guys just enjoy a romp," Robert told him.

"You mean to say," David observed, his eyes growing wider, that some of those leather boys like being abused and others like to abuse?"

"Yes."

"But that's ….." David could not finish.

"That's what?" asked Robert.

"It's not natural. To enjoy being beaten with a whip or to beat until you produce pain, is inhuman."

"I assure you it's not," Robert told him. There are men from all walks of life who like to be beaten. Masochists. Some heterosexual men like their female partner to beat them. Then there are those who get sexual arousal from doing the beating. They're called Sadists after

332

the French Marqui de Sade."

David was not happy. If Robert was right then it bore out what Walter had told him about there being a whole spectrum of sexual differences. He was not sure he wanted to be part of this world and he told Robert so.

David had been described by a number of people as being innocent. Now that his eyes were being opened as to sexual variation and the practices in the gay world, he wondered if it was not better to remain innocent. He had thought that sex and love were nearly the same thing. He was beginning to become aware that they were not. Sex was a bodily function. The Church said it was for pro-creation alone but he knew better than that. Sex for many was an exciting experience where you got rid of your frustrations. For others it was a game where you played out your fantasies. He knew that over the centuries the Church had professed one thing and done another. Popes were supposed to be celibate but many, like the Borgias, had families. Monks too were supposed to be celibate but it was common knowledge in the village of Buckfast in Devon, the home of Buckfast Abbey, that widows were befriended by some monks. And of course, there was child abuse among celibate priests. He came to see that for many men sex was a problem.

Sometime after the visit to the pubs in Earl's Court, Robert suggested that he take David to a gay club in the West End. "This kind of place will be more sophisticated, David, and I don't think you'll be so unhappy."

"It's part of my education," David told him with a smile.

One Friday night, suitably attired in smart suits, they visited the 'Blue Angel Cub' in Greek Street in London's Soho. The area is famous for its girly bars, pornographic book stores, and prostitution. Outwardly it seems quite ordinary with little shops selling bijou delicatessen, books, clothes, antiques and tourist items. Look more closely and the little adverts in many of the shop windows advertise sex in subtle wording. 'Model seeks light work', 'Massage given by oriental lady' or 'Comfort provided in discreet surroundings'.

The 'Blue Angel' was a smart, pale blue, painted doorway with heavy brass bell-push and a subtle neon sign above. There was no indication of the kind of place it was. It could have been an exclusive photographer's or the office of a film company.

Robert rang the bell and a voice asked, "Name, membership number?" Robert gave the appropriate information, there was a click of an electronic switch, and the door swung open. Inside was a short, narrow hallway with a staircase to the first floor at the end. On the walls were photographs of film stars, subtly lit from above, and an air of quiet opulence. It was such a contrast from the street outside. Classical music could be heard drifting down the rather steep stairs. At the top was a reception desk staffed by a handsome young man in a dinner jacket. "Robert, good to see you. How are you?" he said. Robert signed David's name in the visitor's book and made an introduction to the reception clerk. He appraised David with considered appreciation. "I hope you have a pleasant evening," he smiled.

From the small reception they entered through an arched doorway into a large bar area decorated very tastefully in blue and pink. It was such a contrast to the pubs in Earl's Court. The club must have stretched over two or three of the little shops below as there was lots of space even though there must have been about fifty people present. The bar was long and well appointed with dark blue velvet-covered stools, and behind it, glass shelves containing a myriad of bottles of drink. Their names were mainly foreign to David. There were three barmen, all extremely attractive, in white shirts and black bow ties. "Good evening, sir, what can I get you?" One of the barmen addressed David. David looked at Robert to see what he would like.

"I'll get them, David," he insisted. They had gin and tonic. When they sat down at one of the small tables near the bar on comfortable pink chairs, Robert said, "Drinks are very expensive here, David, almost three times the price as in a normal bar. You're a student and I know students don't have a lot of spare money."

"Thanks, Robert," David responded gratefully. "I had no idea about costs but really I prefer to pay my way."

"These places are exclusive, for the more wealthy gays and one has to pay for that exclusivity."

"It really is very nice here," David enthused. "Comfortable, relaxed."

"Don't be taken in by all this...." Robert waved his hand to indicate the bar. "The guys are much the same underneath. They may be wearing suits but they all have sexual intentions. That's why they come here, to make contact with a partner. Maybe they want some quick relief, or maybe they are looking for something more permanent. Some want a cuddle and kiss, others want to beat and be beaten. Clothes only dress, they don't indicate innermost desires."

David began to realize that frequently in life things often are not what they appear to be. Here were men of all ages, obviously well heeled, sitting around in elegant surroundings, soothed by classical music and sipping sophisticated drinks. An instant onlooker would never dream that this was a bar exclusively for gays. There were a few females, beautifully dressed, some with male escorts and some with a friend. There were no overt indications that sexual excitement was the motivating factor. As he and Robert chattered, he began to see covert signs of contact that the casual observer would miss: a raised eyebrow or the flash of eye contact, a hand on a knee, the offer of a drink to a newcomer, a lingering arm round a shoulder. It was all so subtle, but just as potent as the blatant sexual innuendo at the "Boltons' or 'Colehurn'.

A voice broke their tete-a-tete. "Robert, fancy seeing you here." They both looked up to see a handsome, stocky man of about thirty standing to one side of them.

Robert stood up and shook hands. "Mitch you son-of-a-bitch how are you?

"Fine, fine," he replied. "And who's your handsome friend?" He put his hand out to David who by this time had got to his feet. "I'm Mitch."

"David." They shook hands. Mitch gave David and appraising look as if to tell him that bed was his should he desire it.

Robert waved to the waiter and indicated another gin and tonic. Mitch drew up another chair and they sat down. It was clear they were old friends.

Mitch seemed to be very relaxed and talked excitedly about the musical 'Oliver' he had seen recently. He appeared to be a theatre buff as he knew the ins and outs of how the production worked. "The sets are an engineering wonder," he told them. "It's a new stage technique. None of this lowering the curtain while the scene is changed. One scene just dissolves into another as the show goes on. They obviously do it using a number of revolves and pieces of scenery on trucks. Fantastic. In the scene where Bill Sykes murders Nancy, it goes from a noisy pub to the misty River Thames before your eyes. The mist even comes out into the audience so you feel you're actually there."

"What about Lional Bart's score then?" Robert asked.

"Good, super songs," was all he could admit to.

"He goes to the theatre to watch the technical side only," Robert told David with a teasing glance at Mitch. "A musical philistine really."

"Not true, David," Mitch responded. "At least I go to the legitimate theatre, unlike Robert here who only frequents Raymond's Review Bar and sees mucky films at the Biograph." Robert looked decidedly uncomfortable but said nothing.

In the course of the evening, after another round of drinks, Mitch started to fondle David's knee under the table. David moved his chair a little but Mitch followed. Eventually, David discreetly moved his chair so that any hanky-panky was visible for all to see. The nonsense stopped. Mitch made it very clear with his charm and attentiveness that he was attracted to David. Looking at both Robert and Mitch, David knew that Robert was the one for him. His wonderful face, flashing eyes and electric smile, as well as that perfect body adorned by a smart suit was irresistible. Mitch was attractive and obviously had a good body, possibly more muscular than Robert, but he lacked something – perhaps it was a certain sensitivity. Anyhow, the evening was most enjoyable and David thanked Robert with a kiss and a hug as they left the club.

Chapter 25

Winter had come to Britain and London did not escape. The nights were drawing in and by five o'clock it was dark. It rained, sometimes for days on end and the climate was cold and unpleasant. The lights from the shop windows reflected on the wet pavements; taxis, buses and cars sprayed muddy water over unsuspecting pavement walkers; wet coats and umbrellas dripped onto each tightly packed passenger on bus and underground. Everyone was muffled against the cold and wet, and many sniveled openly, distressed by the annual epidemic of the common cold. Yet life went on and the frenetic rush of London dominated the lives of its inhabitants.

David was no exception. Flu struck without warning: one moment he was fit and well and the next he was confined to bed with Clair fussing over him, providing hot drinks and tempting snacks. Fortunately, he was strong and after three days he was back on his feet. It was strange but Robert had not phoned to enquire of his progress.

He phoned Robert as soon as he could. It took three separate calls to contact him. He seemed pleased to hear from David but....there was something not quite right. He could not put his finger on it but there was something. They agreed to meet on the following Friday at his flat in Burlington Mansions.

David rang the bell and a rather distorted voice, unlike Robert's, told him to come up. When the door of the flat was opened it was Mitch, not Robert, who stood there. "Come in, David," he said smiling pleasantly. "Robert won't be long. He had to go out."

Mitch waved David to a chair and then sat on the floor beside him. "Robert told me you've not been well. Flu?"

"Like a million others in London," David told him. "Being packed like sardines on the underground, you just can't get away from the bugs. It's inevitable really. Fortunately, I'm fit and threw it off in a few days."

Mitch put his hand on David's thigh and gave it a squeeze. "Mm, very muscular. You are fit." He looked David in the eye. "I'm a great one for legs."

David, a little disconcerted, suggested, "You've good legs yourself. Do you play football?"

"No, not much good," Mitch confessed. "I bodybuild. Go to the gym four times a week. It keeps me in good shape, and of course you can build your legs." Mitch looked directly at David and asked, "Would you like to see my body?"

Now David was tempted as he saw when they first met that Mitch had a good physique, although the track-suit bottom and sloppy sweater he was wearing did nothing to enhance his body. He also knew that Mitch liked him and he did not want to do anything to signal interest. He had no intention of being unfaithful to Robert. "It's good of you to offer, Mitch," he replied diplomatically. "I'm sure you have a super body, but Robert will be back soon and I don't want to cause anyone any problems."

Mitch laughed. "David," he said, "Robert has left us alone at my request. He knows I like you and though we should get to know each other. Now let me show you." With that he pulled off his sweater and lowered his track suit bottom. All he was wearing was a backless white brief that bulged in a way that showed his interest. He certainly had a wonderful body, hairless and muscular. "Now what about that?" he asked as he stood close in front of David.

David could not believe what he was hearing. Robert had sanctioned this meeting and gone out so they could..... Could what? Go to bed together? Surely not? It seemed unbelievable. How could he? What had gone wrong? Did he not care any more?

Mitch came closer, lifted David from the chair and began to fondle him. He pushed his bulging briefs into David. Given ordinary circumstances David may have liked this physical contact from a muscle man, but his emotions were whirling.

He pushed Mitch away. "Please don't, Mitch. It's not that I don't like you. You have a perfect body but....I'm in love with Robert." There, he had said it.

"Please won't you go to bed with me, David?" Mitch almost pleaded "I've thought so much about you since we met at the club. Pease."

"No, Mitch, it's not right. Robert and I are....lovers."

Mitch looked at him with a little pity on his face. "Lovers?" he asked in amazement. "Robert doesn't seem to think so. Sorry to disappoint you, David, but Robert has never considered himself your lover. Oh, you may have been to bed together and he's told you he loves you but that's Robert. He doesn't mean it."

"Are you saying," David began almost in tears, "that Robert has been playing with me? Using me for...enjoyment."

"I'm afraid so. You're very handsome, David, and very sexy but you're also naive. Robert and I have known each other for two years now. He's quite incapable of love. He loves himself and then sex, in that order."

What could David say? He felt dizzy and would have fallen if Mitch had not steered him into a chair. "Easy, David," he said holding his hand. "It wasn't supposed to happen this way. We planned it differently."

David went rigid. "We,…. you…...planned…….this?" he asked slowly.

Now Mitch was embarrassed. "Well not planned exactly. We talked about how I might get you interested into going to bed. He said you liked a good body. Robert said he didn't mind and he didn't think you'd mind."

"What does Robert think of me?" he asked out aloud without realizing it.

"He thinks you're beautiful and great sex. But he seems to want a change."

"Has he got someone else?" David asked.

Mitch pondered a moment. "Possibly, I'm not sure. He likes to keep changing."

'And that's all?" David asked.

"Look, David," Mitch said starting to become serious. "Robert is a machine, a sex machine. He can have it with anybody at any time. He has no moral qualms about it." He paused for a while as if considering his next move, and then went on. "You do know what he does for a living? Where all the money comes from?"

And so the truth about Robert came flooding out. It appeared that Mitch felt guilty causing David so much pain so he spilled the beans. Robert was part of a team of five men who provided a cabaret for wealthy gays in London. They were paid huge sums for attending private gatherings and stripping off their clothes. Three of the five men were gay, but the other two just did it for the money. "You see, David," Mitch told him, "they have sex with each other in front of their special audience. There's no love involved, just pure sex for entertainment."

David was disgusted. He was disgusted with Robert for using himself in such a way as it was pure prostitution, but he was even more disgusted with himself. To think, he had been making love with a…… prostitute. Yes, what he did for a living was prostitution. And he was to be a priest . That was even worse. He could morally justify to himself when sex was an expression of love, but what he had been doing with Robert was reprehensible.

Mitch offered to make him some tea but David wanted to get away from the place as soon as possible. It reminded him too much of his sin. Yes, he was a sinner. He felt that Mitch was a decent person at heart, but had become involved in a lifestyle that could not be justified. "I'm so sorry, David," were his parting words. "Robert has abused you. You're a very decent guy and this has come as a shock. Don't think too badly of me."

David said nothing and left without a word.

On the underground as he went back to his lodgings he sat in a corner and silent tears streamed down his face. What a fool he had been. He had trusted and been let down. He had fallen right into the pit. He felt dirty, humiliated and very low. "Are you all right, mate?" a London voice asked.

David looked up. A youth of about eighteen was standing over him with a concerned look on his face. He was the only other passenger in the carriage. "I'm all right now," he replied wiping his eyes with the back of his hand. "Someone just died (he lied) and I was a little overcome." He smiled weakly. "Thanks for your concern." He brightened a little. There were people in the world with a little decency.

How he got through the evening he just didn't know. By the time he reached Turnham Green his eyes were clearer and he managed to get through dinner with a minimum of discomfort. He pleaded a headache and retired to his room where he shed tears of humiliation and remorse. Eventually he drifted off to sleep, but Robert remained in his dreams – beautiful and deadly.

He was due to have coffee with Walter on the Saturday morning so he rang and tried to change the venue. "I need to talk, Walter," he told him. Walter, realizing something was not quite right, suggested he came to his room in Vincent Square. David could not face that. The theological hostel reminded him too much of his sin. They agreed to meet in the coffee shop at Selfridge's.

As ever, Walter was the good friend and waited until David had the courage to tell his story. David missed nothing out. He was calmer now after a good night's sleep, although as he got to the end of the saga he was close to tears. Walter listened without saying a word. When David had finished his story Walter leaned over and put his hand on top of David's. "You poor love," he said gently. "What a situation to find yourself in and you had such high hopes. What do you intend to do?"

David had thought his future actions out beforehand. "Nothing, Walter. I'm going to wait to see if he phones. If he does, but I don't think he will, I'll tell him I want nothing to do with him. I won't tell him what I know about his 'business' life as then he would realize Mitch had shopped him. I don't want to screw up whatever relationship he and Mitch might have."

"And how do you feel about yourself?" Walter asked.

"Dirty, let-down, a sinner," David responded thoughtfully.

"Well, let's look at these feelings, David," Walter suggested. "'Let-down' is a natural reaction. You trusted the guy and he destroyed that trust. It's no problem. Life is like that. Walter smiled at his as if to say that the problem was now resolved. "You say you feel dirty. Why?"

"Because I went with a prostitute," was David's automatic response

"But you didn't know he sold sex for money. You didn't pay for it, did you? It was a willing union between the two of you?"

"Yes," David admitted. He smiled for the first time for a while. "It was enjoyable."

"Well, then," challenged Walter, "why was it dirty. It was done for the best reason because you enjoyed each other." There was a pause and then he said, "Now the 'sin' bit."

"It's a sin to have sex just for pleasure," David pointed out.

"Oh, who says so?" Walter asked.

"The Pope for one," offered David.

"He'd deny an ice cream to a child if he thought the child was born out of wedlock," Walter responded viciously. "You know, David, the modern medical view of sex is that it is a healthy activity given that precautions are taken. It is psychologically healthy in that it reduces frustration, and physically healthy in that it assists the natural rhythms of the body. The Church, as usual, is out of tune with the present day world. So, sex is a good thing according to enlightened medical men."

David was amazed at Walter's knowledge. "But what I did was sinful because I did it with a person who sold sex."

"But he didn't sell it to you. You didn't know at the time he sold sex. There is a Christian doctrine called the 'Doctrine of Intention. It simply states that if your intentions are for good, and you are unaware something is sinful, then you cannot be blamed for committing that sin."

David looked at Walter with new eyes. From where did he get all this information? "How do you know all this?" he asked.

"Because I've been in a similar state as you and went to seek advice. That's the kind of advice I got. Don't worry, David, you're no different to anyone else. Most of us find out about life the hard way. What we have to do is pick ourselves up and carry on."

Picking oneself up is easier said that done and from time-to-time David had fits of doubt about the morality of his actions. What was now certain, and perhaps a positive result of his disastrous relationship with Robert, was his acceptance of his homosexuality. He was clear in his mind about his feelings. He also accepted the reason why he had such a cross to bear. It was inbuilt, whether a genetic defect or a special gift from nature, and there was nothing he could do about it. What God had given him was a gift that he could use for good or ill. However, he was not sure whether he could present himself for ordination. The

Church of England did not accept gay clergy, although there were many covert ones in orders. Some were married and some were not. He suspected that the married ones lived unhappy lives, and the unmarried ones were constantly under pressure in case they were found out. It was a dilemma that he was determined to resolve.

The Warden of the Vincent Square hostel, a tall, willowy, bespectacled priest, Father Sumner, was regarded by all the theological students who knew him as wise, empathetic and holy. He gave out some sort of vibration that endeared you to him. His whole demeanor was of calmness and love. David had met him once or twice when he visited the Hostel and had a high regard for him. He decided to make an appointment to see him and to confide in him.

Father Sumner met David at the Hostel door at their appointed time and took him to his room on the ground floor. It was sparsely furnished with an iron bed, wardrobe, writing desk and two easy chairs. There was a large crucifix on the wall, nothing else. Father Sumner waved him to a seat.

"Enjoying your studies, David?" he asked.

"Yes, father. I have some doubts here and there but generally things are fine," he replied.

"Of course you have doubts," Father Sumner observed with a smile. "That's partly why you are here. To work things out as well as increase your knowledge. As you progress through this year and next you'll get things sorted out in your own mind. Pray and all will be shown to you."

"Yes, thank you father."

"How do you like London?" he asked.

That was a million dollar question. "I enjoyed it at first, father," David told him honestly, "but I'm a country person at heart and I long for green fields."

"Let me see," Father Sumner said, "you come from somewhere outside Leicester. That's quite a big city."

"Yes, but I live in a village on the outskirts of the city – five miles away from the hustle and bustle. My parents are moving back to Sheffield where I was born though. Their house will be right on the edge of the city near green fields."

"So, you would prefer to be a country priest?" he asked.

Now this was the opening David had wanted to raise his doubts. "I don't know if I can become a priest, father."

Father Sumner seemed surprised. He looked directly at David. "Oh! Why do you say that?"

David waited a minute or two. His chance had arrived but should he take it? What if Father Sumner was disgusted by what he was to tell?

No, he was a priest and seemed to have an understanding of people. "Because I'm homosexual and homosexual priests are not encouraged by the Church." He rushed it all out. There, it was done. He could not retract now.

Father Sumner did not ask how he knew or whether he was sure. He looked at David with such compassion, such love and then he smiled as if what he had been told was the greatest gift he could be given. "But that's wonderful, David," he said. David could not believe his ears. "God has given you a special gift to serve Him. You are blessed." The expression on David's face must have been one of amazement as Father Sumner went on to explain. "When a married priest loves his wife he has to divide his love two ways. He loves God and he loves his spouse. It's often very difficult to keep the two in perspective. If you are homosexual all that love can be channeled to God. His will and His works profit. Do you understand, David?"

"Yes, father. Single-minded love can all be devoted to God." He thought for a moment. "But...."

"But what, David? Is there something else?" Father Sumner asked.

"But what about sex, father? I can understand your point about love but love and sex are two different things."

David was sure Father Sumner was startled by this observation. "What makes you say that, David?" he asked a little flustered.

"Well, sex is not just for procreation as parts of the Christian Church suggest. It's a bodily function that has a cycle and if reproduction was its only aim then the cycle would be infrequent. But it isn't. Some people are not bothered by their sexual feelings, others are. For some, celibacy is easy, but I guess for the majority it's hard."

"Oh, yes," admitted Father Sumner, "it's hard."

"For me," David admitted, "it's hard. I'm a very potent individual, very fit, and I need sex. I think I'm also a loving person. I need both to love and to have sex. How can I reconcile the two?"

"Sublimation is the word," Father Sumner told him. To be a priest and to convert your sexual energy into pure love means sublimation. It's hard but it's possible."

"So you don't consider homosexuality sinful then, father?" David asked him.

"No, David, not per se, but when it is practiced, when there is an act between two men, or two women for that matter, then it is a sin."

"What if two people live together openly but do not sin?" David asked.

"In the eyes of God there is no sin, but in the eyes of some churchmen and in the eyes of society it is likely to be seen as sinful."

Father Sumner responded. "Does that satisfy you David?"

"Yes and no."

"Tell me," Father Sumner requested.

"An unmarried priest is likely to fall to temptation," David suggested.

"So is a married priest," Father Sumner offered.

"But the married priest is less likely as his desires can be fulfilled. An unmarried priest with a partner can, at least, sublimate some of his sexual desires through tactile contact with a partner. A celibate priest has nothing only willpower and love of God. I don't think I have the will, father."

"My son," Father Sumner said getting up and clasping both of David's hands, "that is between you and God."

It was settled that Father Sumner should became David's spiritual guide and that they should meet regularly for confession and a discussion afterwards. Father Sumner explained that confession was a sacrament of the church, and if used wisely, could have a profound effect on reducing guilt and tension. David was not so sure. He had not been to confession before but was willing to try. He did feel tense from time to time about his homosexuality, as well as some of his doctrinal doubts, and maybe the sacrament would help. He still wanted to be ordained but not with unmanageable pressures on his shoulders. That was no way to perform a successful ministry.

Christmas once more ended the term and most students were ready for it. Not only had it been an emotional time for David but it had been hard intellectually. Greek was still giving him trouble and everyone found Professor Tucker's lectures boring. New Testament studies should have been fascinating. David found them tedious. There was no excitement, no link to the realities of history, just the comparison of various texts and sub texts within the synoptic gospels. Philosophy had been replaced by lectures in Comparative Religion and a new subject, Doctrine, given by the Dean, was placed on Friday mornings so tutorials had to be in the afternoon. Comparative religions was fascinating, particularly Buddhism, and David had spent a long time in the library reading around the subject.

Doctrine was based on an understanding of the ramifications of the Nicene Creed and knowledge and acceptance of the Thirty-nine Articles of the Church of England. The Articles expressed the fundamental adjuncts to the Creed: those beliefs that were special to the Church of England as opposed to the Roman Catholic Church or Methodism. The Dean made material that could have been tedious and legalistic quite interesting. Whilst the Dean always asked for questions at the end of his lectures, very few ever asked one. The reason probably was through the intimidating weight and importance of the particular article presented, or because students did not want to look foolish in front of the Dean. Most students, like Tom, Walter and David discussed things later over coffee.

"How can the Queen be the head of the Church of England?" Walter was saying. She is not ordained. She does not have apostolic legitimacy down the centuries through apostolic succession and the laying on of hands."

"So?" asked Tom. "She is and you have to accept it or become a Roman Catholic or...." and here he winked at David, "...a Baptist."

"I'd rather become a heathen than a Baptist," retorted Walter.

"Oh, come on Walter," David intervened, "it's better to be a Baptist and believe in God than a heathen who has no God."

"All right, all right," Walter agreed. "But you know what I mean. Have you considered," he asked looking first at David and then Walter, "that it would be quite possible for the Queen or the Prime Minister to be heathens?"

"But Walter..." David commenced and Walter stopped him.

"This is hypothetical but possible. The Queen could be Head of the Church and not really interested or even a Buddhist. The Prime Minister could appoint bishops and an archbishop with the express purpose of bringing about dissent or schism." They were silent. "And there's another thing," he went on, "the Queen is German and not English. (1) The family changed its name to Windsor after the First World War when there was so much anti-German feeling. The Head of the Church could be a German unbeliever."

David and Tom laughed. "Dear Walter," David giggled, "what are you trying to do, put yourself out of a job or appoint the Pope as head of the Church of England?"

"What I'm trying to do," laughed Walter is to show you two complacent would-be priests that things aren't so simple as you have been led to believe."

Walter was right in a way David felt. The Church of England had got itself into a real mess since Henry VIII had split from Rome over his divorce and re-marriage. Was it sex or politics that drove him to it? David gave him the benefit of the doubt and attributed his actions to his desire for a son and heir to rule England. And yet, it was his daughter, Elizabeth I, who ruled and became one of the greatest rulers England had ever known. It was ironic really. Now a new Elizabeth was Head of the Church. Not a descendant but from a family of Germans who had been in the right place at the right time. David felt that the Church should have separated a long while ago from the State and the monarchy. When you looked at Walter's argument, the situation was really laughable.

These things passed through his head as he traveled north by train to Sheffield and into the industrial heartland of the nation for the Christmas holiday. It was December 19th, the day his father had arranged to move into the new house. With luck, he would be there by teatime. He knew that his parents had left the day before and the removal van was expected around midday. Maybe they would be settled in by the time he arrived, if not, he was there to help.

The train was packed with people rushing home or to relatives to spend Christmas. He had to stand for the first half hour and then he managed to get a seat. He had brought a book to read but it did not hold him. The doctrine discussion buzzed around his consciousness as well as his worries about his homosexuality. Then there was no word from Robert. Surely he would have been put in the picture by Mitch. It hurt him deeply to leave the situation in the air without a word to each other. He resolved to phone him when he returned to London and say goodbye. Enmity was not part of his personality.

A taxi took him from the station to Broad Elms Lane. The huge furniture van was still there when he arrived. He immediately dumped his case in his new bedroom and joined the activity. The removers had met a lot of traffic and were late. His mother was well organized, having arranged for the whole house to be cleaned and new carpets and curtains to be fitted by a local store. Furniture just had to be placed and essential cartons unpacked and loaded into cupboards. His father, after getting the central heating going, stood around looking useless. He was not very domesticated so his mother had put him in charge of making cups of tea. Removal men always seemed to require endless cups of tea.

By six-thirty the van was emptied and the removers, having put all the inessential cartons in the garage, decided to move off and drive back through the night. They were a cheery bunch and David's father tipped them well. At last, the three of them sat down with a cup of tea and rested their aching limbs. In the bay window of the dining room his mother had placed a huge oak linen chest that had been a wedding present. In fact, during the war, when there was an air raid and his mother had been waiting for help to carry the two boys to the shelter, she had put her babied in there to give them protection in case a bomb dropped. "Where's the Christmas tree and decorations?" David suddenly asked.

"In the garage," his father told him. "The tree's in a long box and the decorations are in a carton. Why?"

"You may think I'm crazy," David told them, "but I'm going to put the tree up on that oak chest and decorate it."

To his surprise his parents beamed. "What a lovely idea, dear," his mother said. "It will be a sort of welcome to us."

"Come on then," his father said jumping up. "Let's get cracking."

And so the tree, decorations and lights went up that evening bringing Christmas cheer to the Earl family, and unknown to them, to their neighbors.

The house really was lovely and with David's help his mother got it all ready by Christmas Eve. Cards, not so many this year, as perhaps some had gone astray, were placed on window ledges and other flat surfaces; discreet holly and paper decorations were placed over pictures and the festive season was created. The central heating made all the difference, so that the family could go from room to room without feeling cold. Even his father, a supporter of the open fire, had to agree that it was a boon.

On Christmas Eve, just after dinner, as he and his mother were washing dishes, his father crept into the kitchen and put his finger to his lips to indicate quiet. He beckoned them into the hall. Through the front door they could hear, 'Noel, noel, born is the King of Israel.' Carol singers. It was lovely to hear them. After their carol there was a knock on the door. David's father opened it to reveal two ladies, two gentlemen and a youth of about eighteen. "A merry Christmas," a stout lady said. "We are your neighbors from across the road and we thought we'd greet you with a carol for Christmas."

"That's lovely," David's mother replied. "Come in out of the cold and have a warm drink."

"Or something stronger," David's father responded winking at the menfolk.

The assembled neighbors looked from one to the other, smiled and accepted. Everyone trooped into the dining room where the Christmas tree was twinkling away on the oak chest, shining its greeting out of the window into the world outside.

"That's the tree," laughed the stout lady. "We knew you would be nice people when the tree went up the day you moved in. I said to Nigel, my son," and she indicated the youth, "they take after us. It's exactly what we would have done."

There were introductions. The stout lady with her rather tiny gray-haired husband and the youth were called Nichols. The other two lived next door. They were younger, in their forties named Mitchel. He was stocky, gentle and wore glasses and was, he told David's father, the manager of Cole Brothers, the largest and most prestigious store in

Sheffield. He said his wife was a school doctor. The ladies drank coffee and the menfolk, except David and Nigel, opted for whisky and soda. David and Nigel deposited themselves in a corner while the oldies chattered.

Nigel was eighteen and had just begun to work for his father who had a small steel business making components for the electrical industry. He confessed that he really did not know what career to follow and was working for his father on a temporary basis. "I don't want to go into business," he confessed, although dad would like it. I'm not interested. Really I'd like to be a television cameraman but I don't know how to go about it."

David suggested he write to a tv company or just turn up on their doorstep and ask questions. "If you don't ask, you don't get," he said.

From across the room David heard, "Oh, and the vicar is going to call. He asked me to let you know. He wasn't sure when as Christmas is a busy time. Lovely man. You can rely on him."

David heard his mother say, "Oh, that will be nice. David will be so pleased. He's going to be a priest you know."

All eyes turned on David. He felt so embarrassed. It was just like his mother. Although she was not happy about him being ordained, she was very proud of him. He was her son, the weakest of the two, the one who had to have extra care. Her baby. He smiled at everyone and satisfied they went on with their talk.

"You going to be a priest then?" Nigel asked as if his mother's information was not convincing enough.

"If I get through my exams and if God is willing," David responded. "There's a lot of water to flow under the bridge yet."

"Our vicar as the Parish Church, the Rev. Billington, is excellent," Nigel enthused. "Quite young, late thirties, played cricket for Yorkshire for a while. His wife was an actress. Very good looker and smart. They often broadcast services from his church. He really works hard and if he says he's going to do something, he will."

"That's good," David responded. He's heard about these glitterati clergy and was skeptical, however this one sounded fine.

"I'm not all that interested in religion," Nigel continued, "but it makes mum happy if I go to church. But this guy I have time for."

Their neighbors stayed for about an hour. When they left the ladies promised to introduce his mother around, and the men offered to show father their country club where he could pay golf. David knew his father. He would not join as he neither liked golf nor social clubs, but he thanked them all the same. Nigel promised to call in after the Christmas festivities. And so, a Christmas tree placed in their window in the spirit of Christmas had engineered an introduction to their neighbors and heralded Christmas itself.

David got up early on Christmas morning to go to communion at the Parish Church. It was a bitterly cold morning with glittering frost covering the ground as if it had been sprinkled with powdered diamond. His parents were not churchgoers. The church was some way away and David's father loaned him the car. He drove very carefully as the side roads were slippery, but the main road had been salted and there was no problem.

Eccelsall Parish Church is a great barn of a place standing high up from the road above the tram terminal. David was surprised how big the congregation was when he got inside. There must have been well over a hundred people. It was warm inside also, surprise, surprise, as so many churches tended to be cold because of lack of funds for heating. The interior was brightly lit and there was a massive Christmas tree near the carved screen. Huge bowls of yellow and white chrysanthemums had been placed strategically, and red poinsettias were everywhere. The church really looked quite beautiful. 'This church has money,' David thought to himself.

The service was simple in the Anglican tradition. No smells and bells here. The festal vestments were simple and modern and the celebration of communion similar to that of King's. The vicar, assisted by two curates, had a wonderful voice and every word could be distinctly heard. David wondered if the vicar had been a pupil of Miss Bull. He could see why the BBC television used the church. It was an impressive place and its vicar a perfect television performer. They could obviously rely on a large congregation for their religious broadcasts. Fair enough, he did not object to the mass media presenting religion as long as it was well presented, honest, and the viewer had the option of switching off.

The vicar and the curates were at the main door of the church as the congregation left, shaking hands and wishing a happy Christmas. David was received by one of the curates, a deacon by the way he had been dressed at the service, a man not much older than himself. It was clear that congregations at this church were always large and the vicar needed help. David was surprised when the curate said, "Your first time here, isn't it? Welcome and a merry Christmas."

"Thank you," David replied.

"Are you just visiting or are you living here?" he asked.

"My parents and I have just moved here," David told him.

"Oh, where?"

"Broad Elms Lane," David informed the curate.

"Oh yes, I remember now," The curate told him. "The vicar did mention there were new people in Broad Elms. You live opposite the Nichols family?"

"Yes."

"I know the vicar intends to call on you," he told David.

"That would be fine," David smiled at him. "My parents and I look forward to meeting him." They shook hands and the curate moved on to shake more hands.

This was the first time that David had come across a parish run so efficiently. It must be run on business lines where the vicar has regular meetings with his staff, communicates and delegates. Usually, parishes just bumble along. He thought of St Stephen's in Turnham Green, and his previous parish. Having two curates helped. It must be an important church, and wealthy, to afford two curates. He would be interested in seeing how the parish was run. It could be useful in the future.

Christmas Day was pleasant. He had phoned Tom who was at Westwick with Ziph and his brothers and then he phoned Walter who was staying with a priest friend in London. He was out, so David left a message. He helped his mother prepare their traditional turkey lunch and even his father assisted in washing the dishes. His brother phoned during lunch. Typical. He was at the home of his in-laws in Leicester. They watched the Queen's speech on television and then his father nodded off in his chair. David and his mother went quietly into the kitchen to prepare tea.

For years, as far as he could remember, tea on Christmas Day had been at five-thirty and consisted of little bridge rolls with smoked salmon and a little horse-radish, strawberries set in jelly with thick clotted cream, and the Christmas cake which his mother usually made and iced. "It's Marks and Spencer's this year," his mother announced as she put the cake on the trolley.

"I believe they're quite good, mum," David observed eyeing the cake with enthusiasm. He liked the marzipan in particular. "You've not had time this year with moving."

"You know what your father is like, David. He wants everything home-made."

"Well he'll just have to put up with M and S this year, mum or bake a cake himself."

"Now that," said his mother laughing, "would be a miracle."

They waited for the kettle to boil. His mother busied herself putting things from lunch that had cooled into the fridge. David looked out of the window at the basic structure of the new garden that the builder had constructed. There was a lot of work to be done. His father had had a five-foot wooden fence put down each side of the garden to give privacy. Laurels and other shrubs were to be planted in front to break the monotony of it. He thoughts then drifted to Robert. He wondered what he was doing for Christmas. Maybe a grand sex orgy? He thought of Peppino, Eric and Irene, to whom he had sent a card, about Frank, and Jacob in South Africa. He thought of his homosexuality and the priesthood. Could he go ahead and be ordained? His mother brought him back to reality.

"Penny for them, David," she said smiling as she poured water into a silver teapot.

"I was miles away, mum, thinking," he replied.

"Tell me, David," she said becoming serious and looking directly at him. "Is there something worrying you?"

"Why do you say that mum?" David asked.

"Since you came home you're different. You go quiet and into your own thoughts, cutting us out."

David thought for a while. What should he say? Was it so obvious that he was concerned about....

His mother looked at him and quite out of the blue she said, "Is it because you're homosexual?"

It was like thunder in David's ears. His mother knew. How? Here she was asking him outright. Was he that obvious? He looked at his mother and just broke into tears. She came across the kitchen and hugged him. "It's all right, dear. Don't get upset. You are still my David and I shall love you to my dying day. Your sexuality is the least of your worries."

"How did...you...know?" David asked in between sobs.

Oh, I've suspected for a long time. A mother knows her son. It was often things you said in your letters, and now that you seemed so worried and far away, I just put two and two together."

"Oh, mum, what am I going to do?" David asked looking at her beautiful face, tears welling up again.

"Why, nothing dear," his mother replied, ever the sensible person. "There's nothing you can do. Just be the David we all love and be true to yourself." There was a pause while she handed him a tissue from a box to hand. "Let me tell you something. My younger brother, uncle Rex, the one that went to Canada, I'm sure he is homosexual. That's why he went to Canada to get away. He's never married. In those days homosexuality was considered terrible, unlike today."

By now David had pulled himself together. "Poor uncle Rex," he said. "It must have been terrible to be driven out of one's country for something you couldn't help."

"Yes," his mother said quietly. "I didn't understand in those days. Now I do. If it had been today I would have stopped him. Anyhow, can I be of any help?"

David took his mother's hands in his and looked into her eyes. "Not really mum, except be there for me as you always have. I'll work it out in my own way." Then a thought struck him. "Does father know?" he asked in panic.

"No dear, he doesn't. Do you want me to tell him?"

"Not yet mum. I'm not ready for him. You know how....masculine he is. He'll probably be very angry and I can't face that yet," David responded.

"I don't think so, dear" his mother informed reassuringly. "For all his fierceness....and his masculinity as you put it, he loves you. He finds it difficult to show affection but he really loves you. I think he will understand."

"Well......." David reflected a while. "Tell him when I'm back at university. It sounds cowardly and it is, but I just can't face his music yet."

"Of course, dear," his mother smiled, "I'll choose the right moment to tell him when I feel he's responsive."

David kissed him mother. "Thanks mum," he said.

His mother's reassurance, some cold water on his face, soothed and calm David was soon back to normal. As he wheeled the tea trolley into the sitting room his father opened his eyes, yawned and said, "Tea, good. I must have nodded off."

David and his mother looked at each other. His father always nodded off on Christmas day and always seemed surprised that he had done so. "You must have been asleep for an hour," his mother said. She winked at David. "Even Her Majesty at Sandringham could hear your snores."

His father laughed. "Bet she didn't. More likely sleeping like me."

"Well tea is ready," his mother informed him and then we can settle down to a good night of television. I've sorted the programs out."

Surprisingly, the vicar called on Boxing Day morning about midday. He explained that he had been called to a sick bed in the neighborhood and so he decided to pop in and say hello. His father offered him a drink, which he accepted with alacrity. The Reverend Jack Billington was in his forties, distinguished looking and charming.

"My wife and I are not really church goers, David's father honestly explained. "David is. Hopes to be ordained. At King's College, London at present."

"Congratulations, David," he said. "Which year are you in?"

"The second year, vicar," David told him.

I know your Dean slightly," he told David. "Give him my regards when you see him next."

They chatted on about the parish and the various clubs and societies there were for the parishioners. It certainly was a very lively parish and David's parents promised they would go to a service at some time. When the vicar finally left he invited David to visit him at the vicarage. "My wife will love to talk to you being in London. She was an actress on the London stage before she married me and loves to keep up with the latest theatre news." David felt that she would be disappointed with any news he could bring. He could not afford theatre prices, except once in a blue moon, and in any case he was far too busy, but he would meet the vicar's wife nevertheless. What interested him more was the way the parish was organized. It would give him ideas for the future.

Chapter 26

All families have their problems from time to time and the British Royal Family was no exception. The Princess Margaret, (1) sister of Her Majesty the Queen, had fallen in love with a commoner, Group Captain Peter Townsend, an equerry to the then King. The Prime Minister had refused to sanction the marriage unless the Princess gave up her claim to the throne. After much heart-searching, the Princess abandoned her love affair and put her duty to the country first. The incident sparked off media speculation from time to time as to whom the Princess would finally marry.

Not long after David had returned to London after the Christmas break, the Palace announced that the Princess was to marry a Mr. Anthony Armstrong Jones, a professional photographer, and whose father was a barrister. Spring was in the air and a fairytale romance about a Princess who marries her woodcutter was a popular ingredient. The anticipation of a Royal Wedding was just what the country needed and caused great excitement as well as much speculation. Who had proposed to whom and under what circumstances? The media was full of it, but nobody would really know unless a member of the Royals told all, which was highly unlikely, or a palace servant became a media whistle-blower.

Interestingly, there was much discussion in the theological faculty about the sacredness of marriage and the firm stand the Church of Rome took on divorce, and the ambivalence of the Church of England. It was not surprising that Walter and Tom took opposing views. Before they ever started their discussion over coffee, David felt that Walter would take the hard line approach, reflecting his Anglo Catholic sympathies, and Tom would take a view in line with his social philosophy. He was right.

"Marriage is a sacred estate," Walter argued and the Pope is correct in condemning divorce.

"But he's two-faced," Tom told them. "He says there is no divorce, but if you happen to be rich and powerful then he finds some excuse and gives in. Look at the case of the Princess of Monaco."

"There were special circumstances," Walter argued. "The princess was very young, and in any case the marriage was not consummated."

David put his oar in here. "But Walter, if you make a promise before God to be together until 'death us do part' what has non-consummation got to do with it? The promise is broken. The sexual excuse makes it worse."

"Because marriage is for pro-creation and without the production of children the marriage is not really a marriage," Walter explained.

"But that's a load of bullshit," David exploded. "Marriage is the union of two people who are in love and if children are produced then all the better. Surely you don't believe that marriage is just to legalize sex?"

"Exactly, David," Tom agreed. "All the Pope cares about are numbers, more and more little Catholics. Marriage is about the love between two people being blessed by God. There is nothing in the marriage service that says 'thou shalt have children'. Marriage provides a free choice to procreate or not. If we take your reductionist view of marriage, Walter, then you don't get married unless you intend to have kids. I know marriage protects any children in the union but that is not its sole purpose." They were miles apart.

"You've not said much," Walter told David. "How do you see marriage?"

"It's no use asking him," Tom blurted out he's going to be a bachelor all his life.

Walter and David stopped in their tracks. What was Tom saying?

"Oops," said Tom looking rather guilty. "That just came out. I didn't intend it."

"Come on Tom," Walter said. "You can't just let a remark like that slip out and not explain what's behind it."

Tom glanced at David and looked away. "Well, David helped Ziph and me get back together and in the course of our phone conversation he commented that he was not interested in girls, or some such remark. I assumed he didn't like women and wouldn't get married."

"That's all?" Walter asked.

Tom blushed bright red. "No," he said sheepishly. "Sorry, David, but I didn't want to say, but Ziph and I think you're gay." He added very quickly, "But it doesn't matter. We both love you very much."

There was silence for some time. David did not know what to say. Walter was dumbfounded. Tom looked first at David and then at Walter and said, "I want to be completely honest. As a matter of fact I think you're both gay."

It was Walter who recovered first. "So, if it's true, Tom, does it make a difference?"

"Difference? No. Why should it? You're the same as you always were. Don't get me wrong, I'm not anti gay or anything. I have a number of gay friends and you can't go to an English public school without knowing about gays. You David, and Walter are my special friends and I don't really care whether you are or not."

"And I believe you Tom Bowers," David said slapping him on the back.

"Sorry if I put you on the spot," Tom said but I've wanted to ask you for quite a while and today….. You know me, there are times when I lack tact."

"And today is one of those days," Walter laughed. "Yes, Tom, we both are gay, except David has only just admitted it to himself. He worries a lot about it."

David had seen Tom look at Ziph with loving eyes but this time he looked at him. "Oh, David, don't be upset. You're my best friend. Whatever support you need I'll be there for you".

David was moved. "Thanks Tom," he said fighting back his tears.

Having cleared the air with Tom, David found that he was much more relaxed. He phoned Robert on his return and enquired after his health and said he was concerned about him. Robert was brusque, thanked him for his enquiry, hoped he had a pleasant Christmas and rang off. His attitude worried David for some time. Surely he could have apologized for the arrangement he had made with Mitch and said he was sorry. But no, there was not a word about it. Perhaps Mitch was right and all Robert cared about was himself.

Passing the faculty office one morning Miss Prentice beckoned him and he went in to see her. "Are you free at all today, David, as the Dean would like to see you?" David must have looked worried. She immediately went on, "Don't look so concerned. There's nothing wrong…on the contrary."

He agreed to see the Dean at five o'clock after his last lecture.

Now Eric Price-Jones, Dean of King's college and Canon of Southwark Cathedral had a study in proportion to his importance. Huge eight feet double doors led from the main corridor into a vast room lined with books and portraits of past deans. There was a large desk with a swivel chair, four comfortable leather- bound arm chairs and a huge table with chairs for large meetings. Students generally waited in fear for the door to be opened after their tentative knock. David was no exception. The doors opened and the elegant figure, in black suit, appeared. "Ah, David," the gentle voice said, "come in, come in. Punctual to the minute." He waved David to an armchair.

David settled himself down, wondering why on earth he had been summoned to the inner presence. The Dean sat opposite him and put his elbows on the arms of the chair and his fingertips together as if in prayer. "Tell me, David, how are you getting on?"

Fine Dean, thank you. I find Greek a little difficult but that's all."

"How about your lodgings. Are they comfortable?"

"Oh, yes, Dean," David responded. "The Wentworth sisters look after me very well – try to mother me."

"They're good people. Their father was a very famous Anglo Catholic."

"So I've been told. They are very committed Christians but very broad minded – know all the latest pop songs," David replied smiling.

"I take it you're not a pop fan?" the Dean asked.

"Not really, Dean. "I'm rather a square. I prefer classical music – Beethoven or Tchaikovsky.

They chattered generally for a while and the Dean appeared to be genuinely interested in David's life. He was interested to hear about his parent' move back to Sheffield and their new house. David gave him the greeting from the Rev. Jack Billington. "Ah, yes," the Dean replied, "we met at a conference last year. Played professional cricket. He does television work for the BBC, wife was an actress?"

"Yes," David confirmed. "He runs a highly efficient parish. Quite a power house."

"Give him my regards, David when you see him. Ask him to get in touch. If he runs an effective parish he's just the man to talk to our fourth year students at Warminster."

The Dean looked across at David and smiled. "I expect you're wondering why I asked you to come? It's been good to talk but now to business. As you know we have a College Sacristan who looks after the daily services in the chapel. He holds the office for one term, having held the office of Assistant Sacristan for a term. The present Sacristan will finish at Easter and his assistant will take over. How would you like to fill the post of Assistant Sacristan?"

David could not believe what he was hearing. President of the College Union and College Sacristan were the two top jobs at King's and here he was being offered a post. Why him? There were lots of good people in the faculty. What had he done to deserve such an honor?

"Surprised, David?" the Dean asked with a twinkle in his eye.

"Well..., yes, Dean. There are so many others to choose from," he replied modestly.

"And your reply confirms my choice, David. Modesty, honesty and a charitable nature are excellent qualities. So you'll accept?"

"If you think I can do the job, Dean, then I accept. It's a great honour," David replied.

They stood and shook hands. The Dean put his arm round David's shoulder and led him to the door. "I'll get Miss Prentice to type a notice of your appointment and put it on the board tomorrow. Introduce yourself to the new Sacristan and he'll put you in the picture." The big doors opened, the Dean shook hands again and David found himself walking down the main staircase in a daze. College Sacristan of King's College, London. What an honor. He just hoped he could do the job and warrant the trust he had been given.

Even amongst future clergy who are aware that envy is a sin, there were some mutterings of criticism of David's appointment. Of course Tom and Walter were delighted and Ian shook his hand with such enthusiasm that David felt his fingers would be crushed. There were many others who were pleased, including the Chaplain and Father Sumner, however, David noticed that there were others who gave him hostile looks. He was not being paranoid as Tom had noticed too. "And the sods are going to be priests," Tom observed in his forthright way. "You'd expect different from theologs."

"It's human nature, Tom," David pointed out. "None of us is perfect. We all have our little cross to bear." And he winked knowingly.

"I know what yours is," laughed Tom. "What's mine?"

David considered for a while. "Your quick temper and ......over honest disposition,"

"Is it bad, David?" Tom asked with a pained expression on his face.

David put his arm around Tom's shoulder. "If you didn't have a quick temper and an honest outlook you wouldn't be the Tom who's my best friend. Don't worry, it's one of your best traits."

The wedding of the Princess Margaret to Mr. Anthony Armstrong-Jones – made the Earl of Snowdon on his wedding morning by the Queen – took place on a lovely, sunny Saturday morning in June. David decided to watch the procession travel from Buckingham Palace to Westminster Abbey with the crowds on the Mall. After he had seen the carriages taking the Royal family and that of the princess to the Abbey, he rushed back to his lodgings to watch the service in the Abbey on television.

The Princess looked lovely and David was reminded of some years previous when he had met her at a garden party at Lambeth Palace, the home of the Archbishop of Canterbury. He had been selected as a youth representative of the Diocese of Leicester. She was so small and petit as she stood at the side of Dr Fisher, the Archbishop, receiving guests. Now here she was in a fabulous wedding dress being married to the man she loved. Not her first choice. Not everyone gets that opportunity to marry their first love, but here was someone he hoped she could spend the rest of her life with. There was a lump in his throat as the couple exchanged their vows. Such important vows. Marriage was not for him though. Where would life take him he wondered? What was the future to be like for a gay, unmarried priest? He wondered if he could face up to living alone without a partner.

The end of the second year and success in the exams meant that David would be returning to King's and life in the Vincent Square Hostel. He had been persuaded to spend six weeks of his summer holiday in the hop fields of Kent where King's College ran a Mission to Hop-pickers. He would be provided with food and free accommodation in exchange for social work amongst the pickers, who tended to come from the slums in the south east of London. His father was surprisingly quite supportive when David told him.

"It'll be good for you David. Those East Enders are tough and it will be an experience. You never know where you will be sent to for your first parish." He father then looked him right in the eye. "You'll have to be very economical next term, though, as you won't be able to save any money." Typical of his father, thinking about cash. David had been economical and still had some savings left. At a pinch, he could sell his expensive camera with all its extras and raise a little cash if he required it. And so, after only two weeks at home, he set out for the hop fields of Kent.

It had been the tradition of many poor London families from south of the River Thames, in order to get a vacation, to hitch a lift into the fields of Kent and work on the farms. Strawberry picking, hops, peas, and in the autumn, potatoes and turnips were labor intensive and good wages could be earned for the back-breaking work. The families earned money, had a holiday, while the farmers got their crops in. But things were changing. Machinery was driving out the picker. It was cheaper in the long run and farms did not have to provide accommodation and solve the social problems that these deprived people frequently brought with them. There was also the fact that since the Second World War, living standards had improved and old traditions were falling away. However, there were still a few families who were poor enough to require a paid holiday, and some farmers whose crops could not be handled by machines.

Hops are an essential ingredient of beer, although many modern beers contain chemicals rather than the hop. It is a greenish flower of a vine grown on special frames in the fields of Kent. The soil and climate of Kent suits the hop vine. Today, most hops are picked by machine, but quality beers still require the specialist touch of the hand picker. It is to this situation that David traveled, first by train from London, and then by local bus.

The mission was a large wooden hut divided into two sections, one for males and one for females. A lean-to on the side served as a kitchen and fifty yards away a smaller hut with a shower and toilet was used as a bathroom. It was rather like being in the army again. The pickers lived about a quarter of a mile away in converted stables attached to the farm.

There were only ten students at a time, five girls and five boys, and these changed during the course of the six weeks, depending on how much time each student could offer. The Chaplain was to call in from time-to-time and the local vicar supervised the whole project. The original aim of the project when it was set up thirty years before was to convert East Enders to Christianity, but with changing attitudes and a changing society, conversion was not paramount. The idea was to provide support for the pickers and their families. Many families had young children and they got in the way so the students provided a play school for those who wished it. Cups of tea and soft drinks were handed out in the fields free to the pickers out of funds gathered by the student of King's College. The students chatted about Christianity to the pickers, listened to their problems, gave counsel when requested, picked hops alongside them, and provided entertainment in the evening. It was practical Christianity. David found it hard work but very satisfying.

Living in the hut alongside the others was no problem as his army experience prepared him for the lack of privacy. Three of the five males, whom he knew, were theological students like himself from King's and the other two were students from the engineering department of University College. They all blended well together. Likewise, the girls. Two were King's students from the history department and members of the Church of England Council, and the others were girlfriends of the boys and students elsewhere. It was a really happy time. They had a rota of duties and everyone undertook them diligently. David was voted best cook of the group for his stewed steak and onions. The most hated job was toilet cleaning, and although nobody ever refused to undertake it, there were a lot of moans and groans.

Three nights a week some form of entertainment was provided for the pickers. Sometimes it was just a sing-song, another night the very popular 'Bingo' and another a film shown on an ancient 16mm projector. On a Saturday evening the pickers themselves put on an entertainment for the students. Some of them were very talented and the comedy was usually at the expense of the students. Nobody minded. Tradition required that at the close everyone sang 'Maybe it's because I'm a Londoner'. It jogged David's memory of the night in the desert in Aden when the patrol had a singsong round their camp fire.

Every evening, prayers were said in the fields for ten minutes and on

360

Sundays the local vicar celebrated communion in the fields. An altar was set up on a trestle table and everyone sat on the ground. David felt there was something magical about it. The group said prayers for the day before breakfast, everyone taking turns in leading. It was true democracy. Some of the group went into the local village to the pub in the evening but David, not a drinker really, preferred to read, or talk to the pickers who were always willing to chat. They had little one-room houses converted from the old stables and they tended to sit outside in the moonlight and talk to their friends.

In one unit there were two young men in their late twenties. One was obviously a Londoner by his accent and the other was a Scot. At first, he thought they were related to one of the families, but he found that they were independents, come to earn a little money and have a holiday. The weather had been kind. Most days the sun had shone and everyone was looking quite tanned. The two young men worked stripped to the waist and one of them had wonderfully muscular arms and shoulders. Over time, David learned that he had worked in a circus as a trapeze artist and his friend had met him there. His friend explained that work in a circus was the only job he could get when he finished his service in the RAF. David wondered if they were gay.

One evening when he was strolling along the lanes before settling down to read, he met them sprawled out on a bank by the lane. They were just enjoying the evening and each other's company. David stopped and asked if he might join them. They were only too pleased and he sat beside them. The view across the flat fields to the distant village and its church spire was lovely. "Lovely here," the muscle man, whose name he said was Pat, told David. "We often come here for a little quiet. There's no privacy in the camp."

"I know the feeling," David responded stretching out on the grass. "I like my space also."

"You don't go to the pub with the others?" the friend asked.

"I'm not really a drinker and in any case I can't afford to drink, "David told them. "I saved a little cash during National Service but it has lots of calls on it."

It was then that the friend, Grant, revealed that he had served in the RAF. "When I came out I couldn't get a job. The circus came to Dundee. I asked them for a job, any job, and they gave me one assisting in erecting and dismantling the big top. It was bloody hard but I loved the circus. It was there I met Pat." He smiled at his friend.

"One day I saw he was having trouble lifting a huge tent pole so I went over and stopped him killing himself," Pat said, pushing Grant in an affectionate way. "He was such a whimp in those days."

"I wondered who the guy was," Grant went on. He was so strong and had shoulders..." He held out his arms to show David. "....that wide." He exaggerated. "Later I saw him in tights swinging from the roof. Funny really."

"Hey, what was funny about it?" Pat asked.

"You. Tights never really suited you. They....," he stopped and looked at his friend. " ....exposed too much of you."

Pat rolled over and grabbed Grant pushing his face into the grass. "I'll have you know I was very proud of myself in tights. In any case, what do you expect me to wear swinging up there in the big top? My birthday suit?"

Laughing, Grant rolled away from him. "Yes, why not. You would have caused a sensation. Top of the bill."

"You see what I have to put up with?" Pat explained.

"You seem very happy together," David observed.

"We are," Grant agreed smiling at Pat.

"You left the circus then?" David enquired.

"I got worried," Grant told David, "when one night there was an accident – a fall into the safety net. Pat's cousin broke his leg. We talked. I persuaded Pat to give it up. He's far too important to me to break his neck."

They looked at each other with such admiration.

"Now we both work in a car factory in Birmingham," Pat told him. "We live together in our own house, and this is the second year we have taken our holidays picking hops. We like the country life and we get a holiday and some spare cash."

"Besides," Pat chipped in, "the Londoners are wonderful people and we also get to meet people like you."

"On the contrary," David told them. "I get to meet wonderful people like you."

By the end of the six week stint, and three different groups of pickers, the students were glad to pack up and return to their families for a short stay before term commenced. David was tired but well satisfied. He really had met some fantastic people. Saying goodbye to Grant and Pat as well as so many jolly, warm-hearted Londoners was quite an emotional strain. Poor and badly educated they may have been but they had big hearts. David knew now why the morale of London survived during the darkest days of the blitz. It was the resilience and cheerfulness of the Londoner.

At home in Sheffield for the last few days of the holiday, he helped his father with the garden. It was really beginning to look fine. All the family were gardeners, including his brother, and they regarded it as a labor of love. Whilst his mother was house-proud and had a lot to do inside, she was also a good gardener and could be seen in her oldest clothes, on her knees, weeding and planting. They were idyllic days as the weather was reasonably dry. But all too quickly it was time for him to take the train to London. He would be returning as a third year student to the hostel in Vincent Square and as Assistant Sacristan.

The evening before he left his mother took him on one side. "I think your father will understand about your homosexuality," she told David. "With your permission I'll tell him in the next few days."

"He kissed his mother and held her hand. "You've been up to something, mum. Yes, tell him. I think I've sorted things out in my own mind now."

When he got to the hostel, he found that he had been allocated a room overlooking Rochester Row and not Vincent Square itself. But at least it was quite near to Walter. Tom was right at the far end of the hostel near to where the Dean and his family had their private quarters. David set about imprinting his personality on the Spartan room by purchasing a print of a rural scene for the bare wall. 'The Hay Wain' by John Constable was an idyllic representation of country people at work. David knew all too well that farming was hard. However, it did make the room more pleasant. He threw a new cotton bedcover, purchased from Selfridge's, over his iron bedstead. With his books on the windowsill and writing table, a little character was introduced into a drab room. Of course, his room was not so opulent as that of Walter, but it was home.

Immediately life became hectic. He had his schedule of lectures and tutorials as well as the duties of the Assistant Sacristan. There were also duties in the hostel. Every student had to serve at some point at the daily communion as well as read the lessons for morning and evening prayer. They were expected to meditate for a half hour after communion and before breakfast. David found it difficult to concentrate on his meditation as his stomach would always intervene and tell him it was time for breakfast.

One morning, he had read the lessons at morning prayer taken by Father Sumner, the Warden, who sat next to him. When it came to the end of the service everyone got on their knees to meditate. David's stomach rumbled and rumbled. He could not concentrate. He glanced out of the corner of his eye at Father Sumner. He was away in a state of grace. Time dragged and breakfast got more and more attractive. Suddenly the gong went to signal breakfast. The assembled students got to their feet and shuffled out of the chapel. Father Sumner did not move. He had the reputation of being a very holy man and David did not wish to disturb him. However, after a while he knew that if they did not move they would miss breakfast. "Father," he whispered. No movement. "Father," he said louder. No movement. "Father," he said putting his hand on his shoulder.

There was movement. He looked at David with a rather glazed expression.

"Father, the breakfast gong went ten minutes ago," he told him.

"Oh, er..." mumbled the Warden. "I was fast asleep."

A little after three weeks into the term David received a letter with a Sheffied postmark. He knew it was from his father. The handwritten address was so neat and typical of his father. His mother's handwriting was untidy with crossings and many mis-spellings but her letters were lengthy wonderfully informative. It was the letter he dreaded. He trembled a little as he opened it. What would his father say? Would he be hurtful?

"Dear David,

Your mother has just told me about your claim to be a homosexual. I must admit that it came as quite a shock. She assures me that it is true and that you both have talked at length. However, I don't think you are homosexual. If you like I can send you for expert medical advice. It's up to you.

Your mother and I want you to know that whether you are homosexual or not, we love you just the same and our relationship with you has not altered in any way. I know you feel that at times I've been tough with you, and I am aware that showing love is not my best asset, but I do love you and your brother and will always be there for you.

Your ever loving father."

After reading the letter David could not help but shed a tear. The letter was typical of his father, brief and businesslike, but never before had his father said that he loved him. Somehow, his father could not bring himself to show affection. It was something to do with his upbringing and the mores of the Edwardian society into which he was born. For David, it was a wonderful letter, one he would treasure in his heart. His father had accepted his homosexuality and would be supportive in the future. David wrote back by return of post.

"Dear Dad,

Thank you for your lovely letter. It was cowardice not to tell you about my problem. I left it to mum because we had talked at length. So now you know. I have been so unhappy and worried over the past six months since I admitted to myself that I am homosexual. Yes, I am, dad. It is something that I have been aware of since I was about fourteen, but never dared to admit. I have been given expert advice and there is nothing I or you can do about it. I have to accept and learn to live with it.

To know that you and mum accept me as I am, and are supportive of me, is so gratifying and I feel proud that I have such understanding and wonderful parents. The burden on me has been substantially lessened. I am still trying to work out in my conscience whether I can become a priest under these circumstances. Time and God's wisdom will tell.

Your loving son."

With a lessened burden David was able to perform his duties as Assistant Sacristan to perfection and to keep his head above water with the pressures of his academic work. There was little time for recreation. David did keep his running going on Wednesdays and Saturdays as he found it reduced tension, and the joys of London were too expensive and too time consuming. Walter had a new boyfriend, a slim, blond twenty year old who looked all of fourteen. He had met Lawrence at a gay club and they became inseparable. He was a Cockney lad, sweet and unpretentious, and Walter often spent the nights with him at his parents' home. Apparently, his parents were quite happy for their son. David was amazed and thrilled that other parents had the love and wisdom to be supportive.

Quite out of the blue, Tom suggested that they go down to Westwick for a weekend break as his mother had been nattering at him to bring David. There was a shooting party due in and she thought David might like it. "Can't stand these shooting fellows," Tom admitted, " but it's quite fun." They both needed a break so David readily agreed.

Westwick looked lovely with its autumn tints in the trees, and the borders, though not at their best, were ablaze with late roses and Michaelmas daisies. They arrived late on Friday evening and after a cold supper in the big kitchen retired to bed. As usual, Miss Bane brought David his morning cup of tea and drew his curtains. It was misty outside and there was a heavy dew on everything. By the time he got down to breakfast, Mrs. Bowers told him that the shoot had already got under way. "They'll be in for lunch, David," she told him, "eight guns. You and Tom can help to entertain them and then go and watch in the afternoon. You were both so tired when you arrived last night that I let you sleep in." David had finished his breakfast when Tom arrived at nine-thirty or so. David chatted over an extra cup of coffee while Tom ate his usual enormous breakfast.

The morning papers were perused and later David helped Miss Bane and Mrs. Bowers set the huge dining table for eleven. Where the morning went to he did not know. Just before one o'clock he heard voices in the hall and the guests were ushered into the saloon by Miss Bane. They had obviously got out of their waterproofs at Home Farm and walked over to the big house. Miss Bain served drinks and Tom, his mother and David circulated the group offering small talk to the guests.

David had not noticed, but one of the shoot was a Major from the York and Lancs Regiment when he had been doing his National Service, so he was quite startled when he was confronted by the man. The Major looked him up and down with an air of disdain. "And what are you doing here?" he said loud enough for his immediate neighbors to hear.

David was speechless. From the tone of his voice, the man was obviously out to put him down. He did not know how to reply but then a woman's voice chipped in. "David is one of our closest friends...one of the family. He's a frequent house guest." It was Mrs. Bowers at her most haughty.

The Major visibly withered. His tone altered, he said, "Enjoy your stay my boy," and moved on visibly in shock.

"Do you know him?" Mrs. Bowers asked.

"He was an officer when I was doing military service," David told her.

"Rude man," she said. "He'll not come here again."

Tom and David watched the shoot from a bank side overlooking the fields where the guns had been placed. Beaters from the village drove the pheasants over towards the guns and they were shot with a savagery that only the hardened sportsman can muster. David felt sorry for the birds. What a pity the birds could nor retaliate and pelt the guns with lead shot. But that was country life, a tradition centuries old. He could be opposed to it but who was he to stop it? For him it was cruel, just like fox hunting, as the birds and fox did not really have a chance. He thought about human behavior. Humans were capable of wonderful acts of bravery and self-sacrifice, and yet they could also be very cruel. The human race had not really come very far in two thousand years of Christianity. Civilization was really only skin deep.

The weekend in the country proved restful for both Tom and David so that their various pursuits were attached with renewed vigor. The weather in London was getting very cold now and the wind blew bitterly down the Strand. David contemplated buying a warm overcoat. He had a gabardine raincoat but it was not very warm in such cold weather and his usual monkey jacket was not suitable attire for some occasions. He had seen a rather smart black and white Harris tweed coat in an gentleman's outfitters near the Savoy Hotel and wondered if he could afford it. It would have to last him for many years.

He decided to have another look. The price was on a tag at the food of the stand on which the coat was displayed. He knew he could just afford it. Really it was very smart and deliciously warm, but its purchase would take the majority of his precious savings. Never mind. He would sell his camera and equipment. He rarely used it now. As he looked into the shop window, all these thoughts going through his mind, a voice behind him said, "David? David Earl?" He turned round and there on the pavement stood Jacob.

David could not believe what he was seeing and just stared. He had last seen Jacob in Mombassa and assumed they would never meet again. But here he was. "It is David Earl, isn't it?" Jacob asked.

David just inclined his head in agreement. He still could not speak as the surprise was so great.

Jacob thrust out his hand. "I had a feeling it was you, but I wasn't sure." They shook hands and David gave Jacob a bear hug. "I can't believe it's you, Jacob," David said. "What are you doing in London?"

"I'm living here. Been in London six months. What about you? What are you doing here?"

"I'm at university here. King's College. Just along the Strand there." David pointed in the direction of the college."

"Then you are close to where I work. I'm at Bush House in Kingsway, just near you. I'm working for the World Service of the BBC." Jacob told him. "What are you doing here?"

"I was thinking of buying an overcoat. The one in the window." He looked again at Jacob and smiled. "But that can wait. Have you time for lunch?"

And so they walked to St Martin's Lane, near Trafalgar Square, where there are many little restaurants for the hungry office worker and found a convenient corner in which to talk. Jacob explained that he worked on a newspaper in South Africa and was an outspoken opponent of apartheid. He had been hassled on a number of occasions by the security police and had to leave quickly as he was warned about a death threat. Political friends in London had got him the job with the BBC because of his background in journalism and knowledge of several African languages. David told him about his life as a theological student and of his home and family.

While they were drinking their coffee, Jacob put down his cup, looked at David with his big, brown eyes and asked, "Did you ever think of me David after our meeting in Mombassa?"

David smiled and looked into his handsome face. "Yes, I did Jacob, many, many times."

"Did you ever find your true self, David?"

David knew instinctively what he was asking. "Yes, I did, Jacob, but I've been through a lot of pain in finding out."

"And what was your conclusion?" Jacob asked his face showing some anxiety.

"I concluded that I am gay. I must have known for years but I just could not admit it. It has worried me for a long time."

"And what made you admit it?" Jacob asked.

David told him about Robert and the feelings he had for him, the way he was let down and the remorse. Jacob said nothing until David had told all.

"And what do you feel about me?" Jacob asked.

It was such a hard question for David and came right out of the blue. He had strong feelings that had built up since they first met but he was still muddled. He wanted to be honest. He felt Jacob to be a good person and in Mombassa he had respected David's wishes. Such behavior deserved to be reciprocated. "When I met you that night in the bar in Mombassa I was very confused," he told Jacob. "To suddenly find yourself exposed in a gay bar made me afraid as I had spent some years controlling my feelings. That night I had been revolted by the thoughts of making love to a woman and then you came along. I thought you were....so very handsome and I wanted to...hold you...but fear drove me to run, as you are well aware. I have thought of you many times since then and never expected to see you again. You were, are, an ideal, the sort of person I would have liked to meet and with whom I could form a friendship." He had revealed his innermost secrets and he looked into Jacob's face. "There, I've confessed as I've never done before."

Jacob took David's hand under the table and held it. "As I told you in Mombassa, I was very taken with you, David. I knew you were gay, even if you didn't know yourself. Call it intuition if you like. I thought of you a lot and when I came to England I hoped I might meet you somehow. Silly really as England is a big country. I only knew your name. I thought of advertising in the papers but rejected the idea. When I saw you on the Strand I was not sure it was you, but I had to ask. And I was correct. It was you and I'm so happy." He still held David's hand and then gave it a squeeze and looked directly into David's eyes. "Is there any possibility that we could become friends?"

David's thoughts were in turmoil. He had pictured Jacob so many times but never thought they would ever meet again. Now here he was asking for a relationship. He had been hurt once and did not want it to happen again. Robert had given him great pain and made him feel dirty. He had enjoyed the physical experience with Robert and knew it could be equally gratifying with Jacob. But...but would he be hurt again? His experience of Jacob had been a brief one, but his heart of hearts told him that this was a different person. He was an honorable man who had respected David's wishes in Mombassa. He was sure he would continue that respect.....and... he was so very handsome. "Oh yes, Jacob, there is every possibility," David said softly. "It is something I hoped in my imagination might happen. But never thought it would. Oh yes, I would be proud to be your friend."

Chapter 27

The weeks leading up to Christmas were some of the happiest David had ever experienced. As he got to know Jacob he fell more and more under his spell. He was highly intelligent, having been to university in America where he majored in English Literature. His father had sent him there to get him out of the way when there was danger for anyone who spoke out against the regime in South Africa. Jacob had been active in the African National Congress since his early teens and membership grew more and more dangerous. In America he had joined the movement led by Malcolm X (1) and learned how to conduct passive resistance. When he returned to South Africa he had worked for an underground newspaper. Someone had informed on him and he had to leave very quickly over the border into Mozambique and then on to London.

Jacob loved classical music and he and David would spend as much time as they could remaing from their heavy schedules listening to music. David was introduced by Jacob to Carl Orff 's 'Carmina Burana' and to the 'Romeo and Juliet'of Shostekovich. For his part, David took Jacob to a performance of Verdi's 'Requiem Mass' performed in St. Paul's Cathedral under the baton of Leonard Bernstein and got him to listen to church choral music. The wonderful voice of Jessie Norman was also new to Jacob and he marveled at the black singer's power and range. They had such a lot in common.

Jacob Maneto, for that was his full name, was not Jewish as his name might suggest but a Christian. To be accurate, he was a lapsed Christian. His first school was a missionary school where he received his basic education, and then he went on to an all black high school run by Jesuit priests. By the time he was eighteen he had lost his faith, partly because he was bored with all the religion that had been thrust down his throat at school, partly because he was disgusted with double standards of the Christian Churches in South Africa, and partly because of his involvement with the ANC. There were few Churches that actively tried to change the apartheid system. The Anglican Archbishop of Cape Town, Bishop Trevor Huddleston, had been vociferous but was eventually expelled and fled back to the United Kingdom. The rest were pale and insignificant. The Dutch Reform Church actively supported apartheid and bent its interpretation of the scriptures to justify its stand.

One evening as David and Jacob sat listening to choral music, Jacob asked, "Have you reconciled being gay with Christianity, David?"

"What makes you say that, Jacob?" David asked.

"Well," Jacob began rather hesitantly, "I don't have a problem as I'm only nominally a Christian. In fact, I suppose I'm an agnostic. But you are to be a priest and Christianity tends to be hard on gays."

It was something David had been working out in his mind for quite a while, but since Jacob came into his life he had to rethink his position. "I can justify active homosexuality with Christianity," he told Jacob, "provided that it is an act of love and not lust. However, my confessor, Father Sumner, says that if I am to be a priest my gayness should be passive and not active and then it would be acceptable."

"And what do you think?" asked Jacob steering the conversation.

"It's fine for the celibate priest who has no sex drive, but for ordinary guys I don't think it works. I know it doesn't in my case. It can only lead to abuse problems later and embarrassment for the Church."

"So what's your solution?"

"As I see it, there are only two solutions. No gays in the Church is the first. That means that the Church will be the loser as gays have so much to offer. The second is to allow gay priests to live with their lover and exercise their ministry as a couple."

"Wow," Jacob observed, "your second alternative is very radical."

"But what is the other alternative?" David asked.

"I suppose it's to live in a state of negative grace. I won't call it a sin because I don't believe homosexuality is a sin."

"I've discussed that alternative with Father Sumner and he is adamant that to practice physically is sinful. He didn't say gays could not live together but he said anything physical was out," David reported.

"What does he say about us, then. We have a physical relationship. I assume you tell him in the confessional as to lie is not in your nature, David."

David was embarrassed. Yes, he did tell all. That is what confession was all about, being frank with God. He looked at Jacob rather guiltily. "Yes, I do tell. I hope you're not angry. I regard what we do together as beautiful, a means of expressing our love by other than words. For me it's agape, spiritual love, and not eros, lustful love as I had with Robert."

Jacob came across to him, knelt on the floor and took both his hands. He kissed them one after the other. "I wouldn't have wanted it any other way, David. That's one of the reasons I love you so much. Your honesty." David's eyes told all. There was sadness in them and Jacob could see it. "So, David, what does he say."

"He says....." and a tear ran from the corner of his eye. "He says he can't give me absolution because I am not sorry for what I've done. He gives me his blessing and after confession he gives me a big hug." By this time David was quite upset. "Oh, Jacob, what am I going to do?"

Those eight years difference in age and a vast experience of people and situations had given Jacob wisdom beyond his years. He took David into his arms and let him sob and sob. It was a sort of catharsis. The present situation was something he had been expecting, knowing of David's intentions and the Church's intransigence. Yet, it had to be faced by then both. He loved David more than anything else in his life, even father, mother, brothers and South Africa itself. Here was a person with outstanding qualities of beauty, honesty and integrity who had consented to be his friend. What more in life could he wish for?

As Jacob expected, David's emotions would slowly mend and he would let his sharp intellect overcome his emotions. Eventually his tears stopped and he said, "I think Father Sumner has to take the line of the Anglican Church but underneath, in his heart, he knows that it is possible for a gay priest and his partner to serve God. The other problem is that society is not yet ready for gays, particularly priests, to live openly together. The time will come, but not yet."

"You're right," Jacob agreed. He stopped. He knew what he had to ask next but was terrified of doing so. He looked at David with his big, brown eyes. He didn't have to ask the question, David knew.

David looked Jacob in the eye and took his hand. "My love for you is stronger than my faith, Jacob. I shall never desert you. You've got me for ever, if you'll have me?"

It was Jacob's turn to shed a tear. He moved back to his chair desperately trying to fight back his emotions. What he had dreamed of in his pensive moments had come about. He had imagined a handsome white lover who would bring out the beast in him, and David fulfilled every aspect of his imaginings. "What do you mean about your faith?" he asked.

David did not know how to begin. It was difficult to explain. "Since I started my studies," he eventually explained, "there are a number of so-called theological truths that I have difficulty in accepting. When I question the validity of these truths I am told that I must have faith. Faith seems to be the answer presented for all difficult questions. But one can have faith in anything. Faith is not certainty only a belief."

"In life," Jacob pointed out, "there are a lot of uncertainties. We have to have faith in many things. That day will follow night, that love is stronger than hate, that man is innately good."

"True,' David responded, " experience tells us that day follows night, that love is stronger than hate, and that man is essentially good. We are told that God is good and yet all around us is evil. Wars, murders, corrupt politicians who get away with things, sinful priests, and a child dying of cancer. It looks as if the devil is in control. Surely, if God is more powerful than the devil and rules the world, He cannot allow such things? Not that I can accept the devil as an entity. It seems to me that there is evil in all men, only some allow it to distract them. Religion helps to control that evil but religion itself can be evil. Look at the Inquisition, the Borgia Popes, even today the beliefs of Dutch Reform Church in South Africa."

"God gives us free will," Jacob pointed out.

"All right, we have a free will – to be good or evil. But if God is all powerful, why does He allow the innocent to suffer? Vicarious suffering. For me it's a wicked idea that God uses suffering of the innocent as an example to us. I can't accept that we can't comprehend the ways of God. If God wishes we puny humans to understand and do His will then He will make the complex simple – within our understanding. It's a copout on the part of the Church."

Jacob was astounded. "You mean to say that all these things as well as your homosexuality have been milling around in your head for over two years?"

"I suppose so, although some things were beginning to concern me before then." He told Jacob of the child with cancer in the hospital and how his death had made him think.

"You've been under quite a lot of intellectual as well as emotional pressure, David," Jacob pointed out.

"And there's another thing," David went on, "I don't question the figure of Jesus and His teachings in spite of the contradictions in the gospels. More and more I am coming to believe that He was a prophet, like Islam suggests, and not the Son of God."

"Wow, that's radical. What makes you say that?"

"The divinity of Jesus, virgin birth, resurrection and ascension, the so-called 'mysteries' give Christianity an edge over all other religions. God became man and died for man whilst being God. It's a unique concept and very difficult to comprehend. Many other religions have these mysteries but not all together woven into a continuous story in such a unique way. This gives the power, the supreme authority to Christianity. What if...." And the enormity of his suggestion made him hesitate...."What if Jesus was just a man, an exceptional man, who gave us a message of love that can never be improved upon, and it was the early Christians who wove the mystical into the story in order to provide a message stronger than anything before, or after for that

373

matter, in order to get the backing of the Roman Empire?"

"And have you discussed your ideas with anyone?" Jacob asked.

"Tom, Walter and I have had discussions, yes."

"And what were their reactions?"

"As you would expect," David told him, "Walter takes the Anglo Catholic view. Tom, well Tom accepts the teachings of the Church of England without too much difficulty. He does have strong views over divorce and the appointment of bishops but generally they are social reservations rather than theological."

"Have you discussed your views with your tutors or Father Sumner?"

'It's difficult to raise such issues. We seem to be in a brainwashing situation at King's. Asking questions is not encouraged really. When you do, you are told that acceptance is necessary and that faith must be paramount."

"Do any of the other students have reservations like you?"

"Some do," David told him. "For instance, the present college sacristan has certain reservations but admits that he has gone past the point of no return. He feels that if he quits now he will be letting a whole lot of people down. Many students feel that they have obligations to parents or sponsors and to voice their doubts would be to bite the hand that has fed them and to attack the Church itself."

"And God?" was Jacob's comment.

"Yes, we can include God as well," David agreed.

Jacob came and sat on the floor beside David. "The decision is yours, David. I will always be with you. It's up to you. What I do know is that I want to spend the rest of my days with you."

David bent over the side of his chair and kissed Jacob full on the lips. "Whatever I decide, Jacob, it will include you."

Jacob would have been on his own for Christmas and so David rang his mother to ask if he could bring his friend home to stay for a few days. "It will be lovely to meet him dear. You have sounded so happy in your letters since you met him. He's South African?"

"Yes, mum. Any problems?" David asked.

"No dear. Why?" his mother asked.

"Well......." He hesitated.

"Because he's black? Is that why you hesitate?

"Yes, mum. I was not sure how you and dad would take my friendship."

"David Earl," his mother said with mock ferocity, "if after knowing us for over twenty years you haven't learned that a friend of yours is a friend of ours, whatever the color of his skin, then it's about time you did."

"Mum, you're a wonder," was all David could think of. His mother was no pushover and had very well defined standards, but she had a heart as big as the ocean.

They arrived at Broad Elms Lane two days before Christmas in a snowstorm. The train journey from London had been slow due to the bad weather, the carriage was cold and the buffet car over-crowded. David's father met them at the station and fortunately had put snow chains on his car wheels, so getting up from the city to where his parents lived was no problem. The house was lovely and warm from the central heating and so was David's mother's welcome. She soon had them by the fire in the sitting room with steaming cups of tea and newly baked scones to eat. David's father told them that the weather had turned bitterly cold a few days before and the snow had started that morning. It was about a foot deep in places. "Have you seen snow before" he asked Jacob.

Jacob smiled showing his lovely white teeth. "Oh, yes, South Africa can be very cold in places. We have mountain ranges where there is always snow on the peaks. But I first encountered snow when I was at Harvard in America. The snow sometime was four or five feet deep."

"You went to Harvard University?" David's father enquired, very impressed.

David was impressed too. "I never knew that."

Jacob smiled. "Been too busy talking about other things," he laughed and winked. "Yes, I won a scholarship to study English Literature."

"And you turned to journalism?" David's father observed.

"When I graduated I wanted to help the struggle in my country. I was offered a job on an underground paper in Durban, so I took it."

"And he had to escape the assassin's bullet," David half joked.

"Well, I had to leave South Africa or......."

"It's a terrible business," David's father said. "We have stopped buying South African goods as a protest. I know that in some ways it hurts your people indirectly, Jacob, but governments are prone to give in to where it hurts and it is hurting economically."

"Sure," Jacob agreed. "But my people are hurting, economic sanctions or not. It all helps."

"Now stop talking politics and come and eat," David's mother announced. "You two must be starving after that train journey." As always, his mother was practical and knew the way to a man's heart was through his stomach.

His mother had put he and Jacob in the double bed in his room.

"Your father and I have separate rooms now," she told them both. "I've put you together. I hope you don't mind?" David winked at Jacob. "Your father's snoring keeps me awake. You'll hear it, no doubt. He should go and have it seen to but....You know how he is, dear." She wished them goodnight. Jacob and David did not mind. They had never slept together before as David had to be in the hostel each night and so could not stay at Jacob's apartment. That night, their first night, was something David would treasure all his life. To have Jacob's naked body alongside his own with his huge muscular legs around him was perfection. In the night he put his hand on his hairy chest and felt the regular beat of his heart. This was his love, his all, the person he had longed for and the experience was everything he had hoped.

At eight o'clock on Christmas Eve morning his father brought them morning tea. Jacob was embarrassed and pulled the bedclothes over his nakedness. "It's still snowing," father told them. "Breakfast in half an hour."

"Your father brought us tea knowing we were in bed together," Jacob said in disbelief.

"Mm," David responded enjoying his tea. For him, tea in bed was a luxury, but tea in bed with Jacob was paradise. "He likes you. He wouldn't have brought it up unless he approved of us. I'm so happy." He bent across and kissed Jacob who responded likewise.

"In all my years," Jacob said, "I never thought this would happen to me. We think of the British as being reserved, but they're not."

"We are and we aren't," David told him. "When we want to be stuffy, we can be, but if we like someone then we lean over backwards."

"I'm a luck guy," Jacob chuckled, "I've got a wonderful lover and now a new ma and pa."

The acceptance of Jacob as David's lover set the tone of the Christmas period. Having borrowed Wellington boots from David's father, David and Jacob set out to explore the area. Along the main road is the 'Weatsheaf' Pub, a famous landmark and at its side the cricket ground. A little further on, down a road on the left is a huge wooded area that stretches a number of miles. As a youth, David had collected horse chestnuts from the woods for 'conker' fights at school as well a sweet chestnuts for roasting in the winter. Now the trees were bare. Snow covered the ground. With shafts of golden light from the winter sun glinting through the bare branches, it was a magical place. They tramped through the snow enjoying each other's company and the tranquility the wood provided. A rushing stream, edged with ice, barred their path but they waded across with shouts of glee. There was holly with bright red berries. They picked a little to take home. Seen again through Jacob's eyes, David really enjoyed his walk and when they returned home, red-faced from the cold, they were both ready for lunch.

David had not been aware of it, but Jacob was very domesticated. After lunch he helped his mother wash the dishes and tidy around in the kitchen. He suspected that both Jacob and his mother were eager to talk and so he was quite happy when he and his father were shunted into the sitting room. They settled in easy chairs and David was surprised when his father did not switch on the tv but obviously wanted to talk. "Jacob is homosexual like you?" he asked for a dramatic opener.

"Yes, of course, dad. Why do you ask?" David wanted to know.

"He doesn't seem like it. Neither do you for that matter," he added.

"Statistics indicate that one in ten males are homosexual," David told his father. "I don't know what you think homosexuals are like dad but the majority are like Jacob and I. It's just a few who give everyone a bad name."

"Maybe you're right, David," his father commented. "But the very obvious ones do your cause no good."

"Some can't help themselves, dad," David informed his father. "They are what is called 'camp' – rather more female than male. "It's better to feel sorry for them rather than condemn them."

"I've worried a lot about you," his father told him. "Now I've met Jacob I realize there are things about you I have underestimated. Jacob is a fine man and I give you both my blessing."

David was dumbfounded. His father approved and had paid him, although indirectly, another compliment.

"Your mother tells me that you have reservations about ordination. Is that correct or is she reading into your letters something that is not there?"

Yet again, David was amazed by his mother's intuition and his father's obvious concerns. "I have some reservations, dad," David told his father. "I'm trying to work them out."

"Whatever you decide, we'll support you," his father told him. "We've never actively tried to deter you from the priesthood, but we have never been happy about it. It was your decision and yours alone." He looked at David with such understanding. "If you don't become a priest we shall not be unhappy."

David had always known at the back of his mind that his parents had not wanted him to be ordained, but they had never actively tried to turn him away. His final decision would now be easier, whatever that decision was likely to be and knowing that his parents were supportive whatever decision he made was a help.

By five o'clock it was dark but it had stopped snowing. After dinner they watched tv and at ten, after the BBC News, his parents decided to turn in. David suggested he and Jacob go to midnight communion at the Parish Church and Jacob agreed. They would set off early and walk the mile or so. The moon had come up and wrapped against the cold they set off, the crisp snow crunching under their feet.

The church was warm inside and quite full. Most people seemed to have walked and there was a lovely feeling inside. Lights had been dimmed and the huge Christmas tree twinkled at the side of the chancel steps below the screen. The organ played softly as the congregation assembled. David and Jacob slid into a pew half way down the chancel. At the stroke of midnight, the organ suddenly broke into 'Oh come all ye faithful', the choir appeared and processed down the central isle. At the rear of the procession, in festal cope, was the vicar with a life-size baby Jesus in his arms. The choir stopped at the crib on the opposite side of the screen to the Christmas tree and the vicar placed the infant in the crib. The procession moved on, the light came up to heighten the drama, and the service began.

The vicar met David at the door as he and Jacob were leaving. "David!" he exclaimed. Obviously glad to see him, "it's good to see you. A merry Christmas. When did you arrive?"

David told him and then introduced Jacob. The vicar shook hands, wished him a happy Christmas and then asked, "Where are you from?"

Jacob told him South Africa and he was now working for the BBC.

"Oh," responded the vicar. "I do quite a bit of broadcasting for the BBC, but mostly television." He was turning to the next in line when he remembered something and turned to them again. "Thanks David for conveying my message to your Dean. He rang me and asked me to speak about parish organization to your fourth year students at Warminster. He paused and then added, "He has a very high regard for you."

On their way home David and Jacob talked. "Your vicar seems to be well connected," Jacob observed. "Getting into the BBC is no easy matter."

"I believe his wife was an actress," David told him. "Possibly she had connections and he played cricket for Yorkshire for a while."

"That's more like it," was Jacob's comment. "I have to be honest. The only reason I got into the World Service was my ANC connection and the fact that my father is a tribal chief."

"But you have a Harvard degree and speak several African languages," David offered.

"In this life, David, unless you are a genius with a unique talent, connections still count. I bet half your bishops have some form of patronage."

David thought about what he and Walter had discussed. "It's strange you should say that but Walter was saying some time ago that there is hardly a diocesan bishop who has not been to public school. We can safely assume they came from a privileged background and had connections."

"And how do you feel about that?"

"As I told Walter," David began, "I feel that a bishop should be a devout and humble man who gets to high office as a result of election by his peers. What actually happens in the Church of England is that the Prime Minister makes a selection from a list proposed by the senior diocesan clergy. It's laughable really as the Prime Minister can add or subtract from the list at will. He may even be an unbeliever."

Jacob looked amazed. "Why?" he asked.

"Because the Church of England is the established religion of the State and the government has the last word."

"Of course, I forgot about that. And your Queen is Head of the Church?"

"Yes. It seems to me," David explained, "that bishops are appointed for their conservative views. By that I mean conservative with a small 'c'. They tend to be academics or principal's of theological colleges. Few ever come from the parishes and those that do, come from smart, wealthy parishes like ours here in Sheffield. I wouldn't be surprised if our vicar is not appointed as a suffragan bishop quite soon and then ends up as a diocesan bishop with a seat in the House of Lords."

Jacob thought for a while and then stopped, turned to David and said, "Do you know, David, I'm glad I'm not a traditional believer. The Church has so much to answer for. It is so politically motivated rather than being spiritually directed. Look at the Church in South Africa, here in the United Kingdom, and the biggest culprit of all, the Roman Catholic Church. There is so much the Church could do by speaking out but generally it does nothing. When it does speak out, as do many South American bishops, the Church generally fails to support them. Yes, there are a few honest men trying to uphold the true spirit of Christianity but they are a minority. The established Churches crucify Christ every day."

When they reached home a flask of hot coffee and two mugs had been placed on the kitchen table with a plate of mince pies. A note said, 'You will be cold and hungry. Happy Christmas'. They went to bed happy and contented and fell asleep in each other's arms.

David could hear his mother up and about quite early. Jacob was still asleep so he put on his dressing gown and went down stairs. His mother was in the process of getting the turkey into the oven. David kissed her and wished her a happy Christmas. "It needs to cook slowly," his mother told him, "so I got up early.

He made a pot of tea, gave his mother one and took three cups upstairs. His father was awake and sitting up in bed. "I was just going to get us all a cup," his father said.

"Happy Christmas, dad," David said putting the mug of tea on the bedside table. "I beat you to it. Enjoy a cup of tea in bed. Mum has everything under control as usual."

Jacob was still asleep. He looked so wonderful lying there on his back, his muscular chest and arms uncovered. David bent down and kissed him. "Happy Christmas, Jacob, and may we have many, many more."

Jacob opened his eyes. A smile spread over his face like a cloud uncovering the sun and his white, even teeth parted. "Happy Christmas, David."

They had breakfast in the kitchen in their dressing gowns. Presents were opened there and then. Jacob had brought something for everyone and David's parents were quite overcome with his kindness. He gave David a Parker biro and pencil in a rather smart box. David had found a set of two records of Verdi's 'Requiem'. Jacob was delighted. For his mother, David had bought expensive perfume from Harrod's, and for his father, always difficult to buy for, a set of two pairs of gardening secateurs. "You couldn't have given me anything better," his father enthused. "I was saying to mum last week that I need to get another pair as the old ones don't cut properly." His father gave David a cheque. "As you didn't work this summer I thought money would be helpful." David gave him a hug and kissed his mother. They had not forgotten Jacob, much to his embarrassment. A pair of lovely fur-lined leather gloved awaited him.

"We thought you would find it cold here in England," his mother told him. Jacob kissed her and shook hands with his father.

Jacob seemed to like working in the kitchen with David's mum. After he had bathed and shaved he peeled potatoes and prepared the sprouts. David set the special Christmas table, which he decorated with holly round the central red candles. It looked lovely with shining silver and crystal glasses. "I've nothing much left to do now except keep basting the turkey," his mother informed them. "Now off with you and leave me with the last bits and pieces."

"I'll take them to the 'Wheatsheaf' for a drink," his father announced to all. It was not snowing and so heavily wrapped against the cold, they walked down the lane to the main road and on to the local pub.

Lunch was a huge success. David's mother was an excellent cook and the fifteen pound turkey was roasted to perfection. The sage and onion stuffing, bread sauce, sausage meat and cranberry sauce all added to the flavors. The home made Christmas pudding, with a generous amount of whisky added to the custard, specially blended by his father, filled them to capacity. David insisted that he and Jacob did the dishes. His mother gave in on the condition that she finally sorted out her turkey pan and the remaining gravy. "You mum's a wonderful cook, David," Jacob commented as he rolled up his sleeves.

"Last year we had Marks and Spencer's pudding and cake," David told him. "With moving she didn't have time. Poor dear spent her Christmas apologizing to dad and me. This year she has done her usual."

"Where did she learn to cook?" Jacob asked.

"From her mother, I think. I never knew that grandmother as she died a few months after my brother and I were born. According to other family members, she was a wonderful cook, even better than mother."

With his hands in the sink scrubbing plates for all he was worth, Jacob asked, "Can you cook?"

"Yes, I love cooking, although I don't get much chance nowadays. Mum always encouraged my brother and I to mess about in the kitchen. You see, my father is useless and she didn't want her boys to be useless too."

He looked at Jacob, sleeves rolled up to his elbows, dressed in his mother's frilly apron working away on the dishes. He looked so funny. David just stood there and burst out laughing. Tears rolling down his face.

"What's wrong?" Jacob asked, unable to see himself.

"You, you," David giggled. "If only your BBC colleagues could see you now."

David's laugh was infectious. When Jacob tried to look at himself he too began to laugh. He realized how hilarious he looked.

The noise brought his mother into the kitchen. She saw two grown men convulsed in laughter, one in her frilly apron and the other leaning against the kitchen table hardly able to stand for laughing. So this was her son and his new friend. They were going to be fine together.

On Boxing Day his father suggested that they have an early lunch and drive out to Chatsworth Park It was a lovely idea as the roads had been salted and gritted so driving was not too bad. The sun had come out, and although it was bitterly cold, a walk in the fresh air after too much food was a healthy pursuit. The park was only a forty-five minute drive away and David was overjoyed that Jacob could see such a delightful place.

True to form, Chatsworth looked magnificent. The huge mansion with its ornate roof scene, honey-colored stone walls and magnificent proportions sat in the snow like the grand dame that it was. The stark contrast of snow, dark leafless trees behind it, and the sun reflecting on the house making it look as if it was made of gold, was enchanting. Jacob was thrilled. "I've never seen anything like this before," he told them. "It's a palace. It's beautiful."

"They call it the 'Palace of the Peaks," David told him. "The Peak district is this area around Sheffield."

After parking the car and crossing the bridge in front of the house, they made for the wooded slope behind it. There were paths that led to the hunting tower above the house. It was a hard climb but they made it. The round tower is quite large and the views over the estate spectacular. "It's truly spectacular," Jacob enthused as they sat on the inspection seats at the foot of the tower.

"We often come here," David's mother said. "We used to bring the dog until....." She could not go on.

"We had a sheep dog, Laddie," David's father told Jacob. "He was David's dog but because mum was at home with him so much they adored each other. When we moved here he stayed around the house. Usually, after he had been fed, David's mum let him sit on the front porch until we all went to bed. One night when she went outside to get him in he was not there. He just vanished. We looked for him, advertised in the papers, and even paid the Boy Scouts to organize a search party. He was never found."

"The milkman seemed to know something," David's mother added. "He would never say much but I think Laddie was shot by a local farmer who thought he was after his sheep."

"What a sad story," Jacob observed. "And you never thought of having another dog?"

"Oh, no," David's mother quickly responded. "They cause too much heartache when you lose them."

The holiday for Jacob was over and he had to return to London the day after their trip to Chatsworth. It was the whole family that took him to the station and said goodbye. David's mother kissed him and said, "Come back any time, Jacob. You are as welcome as a son." Poor Jacob was visibly moved. He shook hands with David's father and thanked him for a great Christmas. When it came to leaving David tears just poured down his handsome face. "It's not long before I'm back in

London," snuffled David, also moved by events. "Thank you for coming to my home. Have a good trip." He kissed him on both cheeks continental style. At least that was allowed in Britain. As the train moved off, they waved until it slowly passed into the distance. David's father put an arm round his shoulder, something he'd never done before, and his mother took his hand. They walked slowly down the platform and out to the car. Words were unnecessary.

Chapter 28

Sheffield had particularly bad weather in mid January, a raging gale that left a wake of destruction behind it. Chatsworth Park was no exception and whole areas of forest were tumbled like matchsticks. David's mother rang one evening to say that his father had cracked three ribs trying to save a piece of wooden fencing from flying into a neighbor's greenhouse. He was fine but has a lot of pain. They had talked things over and decided to sell the house and move to Torquay where, many years before, they had had their honeymoon, and also where the weather was milder. Another thing that had changed their minds about Sheffield was the imminent death of uncle Bob, his father's brother, who had cancer. Bob had saved all his life for his retirement and within six months he had been diagnosed with terminal cancer. He regretted every day he had failed to enjoy. That was not going to happen to his father and mother.

Life in Vincent Square and at the college went on as usual. David saw Jacob nearly every day as they managed to lunch together, usually in the Chesham, where prices were reasonable. Jacob often came to David's room in the hostel and had been introduced to both Father Sumner and the Dean. Father Sumner still would not give David absolution but talked to him like a caring father afterwards. "I can see why you love him, David," he remarked one day. "He's a lovely person and very handsome. I am happy to personally bless you but in the eyes of God what you do together is a sin."

"Thanks father for being so understanding," David told him. "We can't go without a physical relationship. We've talked about it, but Jacob and I are too male to sublimate our desires."

"So what are you going to do about ordination?" Father Sumner asked. "You can be ordained, hide your relationship, and live in a state without God's grace. Many priests do. Not many are successful. On the other hand, you could give Jacob up." He looked directly at David but went on quickly, "But having seen you two together, I feel that's impossible. You'll have to decide soon."

Walter thought Jacob to be the greatest thing since the world began and always made a fuss of him. "Has he....?" he asked one day.

"Has he what?" David asked knowing exactly what Walter wanted to know but making him suffer a little.

"You know..." he said quite embarrassed but drawing a picture with his hands.

David smiled. "Yes, Walter," he said. "In the front row when they were issued."

"Oooo," said Walter with a big grin all over his face.

Ziph liked Jacob too and was prone to tease him about his sex appeal. "You can't be gay Jacob," she told him. "You're too much of a hunk. All those lovely muscles. It makes a girl come over all funny," and she would pretend to swoon.

Jacob would pick her up in his huge arms, give her a big kiss and then dump her onto a settee. "Elizabeth, you're nothing but a temptress," he would laugh.

"Put me down you big brute," she would yell. "Tom, Tom help."

"It's your own fault, woman," he would say. "Slap her bottom, Jacob, she deserves it."

Jacob never did. He was too kind and they would end up giggling together on the settee.

It was so wonderful to be able to relax with friends and be themselves without having to pretend.

At the end of February his father telephoned one evening to say that the house had been sold. Someone in the area had heard of their proposed move south through neighbors and had offered a ridiculous price. "It's too good to refuse," his father had told him. "We're off to Torquay for a few days to look for somewhere to live." David wished them well and thought no more about it. A week later his mother phoned to say they had bought a new bungalow on the Marine Drive in Torquay with fantastic views over Torbay and would be moving within three weeks. "It's not really what I wanted," she said, "but it will do for the time being. Properties are difficult to find there at the moment. You'll be able to come for Easter."

March saw the arrival of David's twenty-third birthday as well as the end of term, and his tenure as Sacristan. He was determined to have a little celebration and booked a table for six at a small Italian restaurant just off Victoria Street. He and Jacob had eaten there many times. It was family run and the food was excellent and not expensive. So one Saturday evening Tom and Ziph, Walter and Lawrence, Jacob and David sat around a big table in the La Paloma Restaurant tucking into delicious Italian food. David decided that perhaps Italian food was his favorite, although it could be very fattening if you ate nothing but pasta. The Chianti flowed and everyone was in high spirits.

At the end of the meal Tom stood and raised his glass in a toast. "To David," he said, "my best friend and loved by everyone. We have all been touched by your humanity in one way and another. I know that without you David, Ziph and I would not have been together today. You are a giver, David, someone who puts others first and self second.

We love and respect you for it. Now you have been given something - Jacob. We can see he is the greatest joy in your life, and may he be that joy for many years to come. Happy birthday. We love you." They all repeated, "Happy birthday. We love you," and raised their glasses to him.

Then it was Jacob who stood. He looked down at them all, a contented smile on his face. "I want to propose another toast," he said, "if you will permit me?"

"Yes, yes. Go on Jacob," they yelled.

"I came to England nearly a year ago, friendless, but with a vision. The vision of a young man I had met but briefly in Mombassa. He left a marked impression on me. I didn't know if I would ever see him again. Maybe you would call it the will of God, I would call it luck, but I found him again." He looked with such gentle eyes at David. "He is everything I could have wished for, and through him, I met you, his friends who have shown me such kindness. Thank you for all the happy times we have had together, and thank you David for being you." Everyone cheered and clapped and they toasted each other and friendship.

But Jacob had not finished. He produced an envelope from his jacket pocket. He looked at David. "I know you said 'no presents' but I wanted to give you something to remember your birthday, your friends, and your final year at King's. Please accept the contents of this envelope with my love." He passed a long white envelope over to David.

"Open it!" came a chorus of voices.

David did as requested. Inside were two theatre tickets and a note in Jacob's hand. 'You introduced me to opera,' it said, 'and I shall be ever grateful for the experience. Please accept these tickets for a night out to remember. All my love, Jacob' When David looked at the tickets he found they were stalls seats for the opera 'Aida'(1) at Covent Garden Opera House with Montserrat Caballe in the title role. It had been his dream of seeing a live performance of the opera and now it was to be a reality. How did Jacob know? Had he mentioned it at some point? He looked at his lover standing there all smiles. He got up, crossed to the other side of the table where he had been placed next to Tom, took him in his arms and kissed him full on the lips. He didn't care what people thought. "Oh, Jacob," he said very softly, "it's the most wonderful surprise you could ever give me. Thank you."

The party cheered and clapped and sang 'For they are jolly good fellows'. Even the other diners in the restaurant joined in.

Easter came. Jacob could not get the time off to travel to Torquay and in any case he was due to fly to Botswana for a few days to get material for a program. David was not too happy about being parted but there was little he could do. They would have to get used to being apart at times as Jacob's job took him to Africa quite a lot. He took Tom with him instead as he was going through a crisis in his own life. He was not sure whether he wanted to be ordained or not. David felt that some time away from London and some sea air would relieve the tension. He could also talk to his mother whose wise council had helped others with problems. He also had a decision himself to make and bouncing ideas off Tom would help.

Torquay Railway Station is quite small compared with the number of tourists it has to deal with in the summer season. It is planted with flowering shrubs and bedding plants echoing the wonderful gardens of which Torbay boasts. The towns of Torquay, Paignton and Brixham make up the administrative area of Torbay, a superior holiday resort on the edge of a huge bay and backed by the rolling hills of Dartmoor. A 'tor'means a hill and a 'quay' means a harbor. Hence, Torquay is the 'harbour under the hills. It is one of the most beautiful places in Britain with a mild climate all the year round. Wealthy Victorians, like Isambard Kingdom Brunnel,(2) built their mansions on the slopes overlooking the sea, or took lodgings like Elizabeth Barrett Browning.(3) It was into this atmosphere that David's parents had purchased a bungalow.

They were met at the station by David's parents. David introduced Tom who had not met them before. The station lies just behind the famous Grand Hotel, which is featured by Agatha Christie (4) in one of her books. She was born in Torquay and the family still lived in the area. The hotel is situated on the sea front and David's father drove from there, keeping the sea on their right and the gardens and grounds of Tor Abbey, a stately home once owned by the Carey family, on their left. The road goes below high cliffs on the left, now landscaped into a tropical garden, and the Princess Theatre on the sea side. Gardens run all along the promenade right to the Pavilion Theatre (4) at the side of the harbor. Around the old harbor he drove them, climbed the steep Meadfoot Sea Road and then gently ran down to Meadfoot Beach passing the spectacular Hesketh Crescent, a semi-circular block of houses based on the Royal Crescent in Bath.

The beach road, which is directly below the cliff and protected by a huge sea wall, is often closed in the winter as high tides and huge waves wash over it and make access dangerous. In front of them, standing high above their heads, was the huge and incongruous block of the exclusive Kilmorie Flats, a modern architectural monstrosity set in ten acres of grounds. Beneath it is the Marine Drive with views over the bay and an island, magical in a way, called Thatcher Rock. From there David's father turned left up Thatcher Avenue, a very steep road, and at the top turned into the driveway of a modern villa. They were home.

The area overlooking the Marine Drive was just beginning to be developed. The roads and street lights had all been completed and there were newly-built houses scattered on the barren landscape. A number of plots were still for sale. David agreed that the view from his parents' sitting room was spectacular, but he suspected that it could be very windy in the winter as all the properties were exposed. It had French windows that went out onto a balcony, and a further huge picture window so that there was a hundred and eighty degree view. The bungalow sprawled over a half acre site. It had four bedrooms and three bathrooms. The kitchen was not quite as good as the Sheffield house and the dining room, on the rear with no view, except for the unfinished garden, was rather small. The double garage below the bungalow housed the central heating system. The whole bungalow was elevated above the road, which gave it a degree of privacy. "It will do," David's mum told Tom. "There's not much to choose from at present. We sold so quickly. Father and I looked around for a whole week. We could only find this place and a house, which is further along the road. The house only has glimpses of the sea. So we decided on this place. Maybe in a year or two we'll build our own home when we've got to know the area, and then I can have what I want rather than what some builder wants."

The situation of the bungalow was both good and bad. If you enjoyed walking there were many wonderful walks along the cliffs and down onto various little beaches, but on the other hand if you had no car you had to walk a good mile from the bus stop on Meadfoot Beach. Tom and David spent much of their time walking. The weather was cold but sunny. Daffodils and crocus abounded and buds were beginning to break forth on some of the trees. At times the sea was the color of jade and at others a wonderful deep blue. One day was wet and misty. The sea looked cold and gray and mist blotted out everything. The view from the bungalow was not so marvelous then.

Tom had major doubts about ordination, like David, but for different reasons. He had no theological doubts. His problem was that he had cold feet. He was unsure whether his personality was suitable for the priesthood. Yes, he was short-tempered and blunt, but as David pointed out, that was not enough to bar him from ordination. "God accepted all estates of men, except homosexuals," he said. Tom also wondered if he had enough faith to carry him through? He was unsure of himself and frightened at the huge step he was about to take. "I'm committing my whole life and that of Ziph," he told David. "Is it really what I want and what God wants?"

"That is something only you and God will know," David told him. "If you don't proceed, what else could you do, Tom?"

"That's it," he replied rather pained. "What can you do with a degree in theology?" He thought for a while.

"Teach?" David suggested.

"Lord no, not teach. I haven't the patience."

"But a degree is really a yardstick of ability," David pointed out. "It says 'This person is capable up to this standard'. We know that with a science degree it's out of date within five years unless you update all the time. An arts degree is different as knowledge doesn't change at the same rate. You could go into business, become a trainee manager, go into a bank." Tom seemed to relax when he realized that ditching ordination wasn't the end of the world. The seeds of an idea were set. "Why not go on to Warminster and see how you respond there? You could defer a decision and that would give you more time to look at your options," David suggested.

David's own thoughts began to become clearer. He could not and would not give up Jacob. He had found happiness he could never have imagined. A future as a celibate priest would be one of regret. In any case, he was a physical person. Could he be ordained and a practicing homosexual? Yes, he could but....the Church told him that he would not be in a state of grace with God. How could he celebrate communion knowing he was a sinner? He did not think it was a sin to have a homosexual lover but many people did. Did God in His love think so too? What would his colleagues in the Church think of him, his bishop, his parishioners. He had to think of their feelings too. People would be ready for gay priests one day, and gay bishops, but not yet. He also had to think of Jacob and the pressures on him. No, ordination was not possible, given his priorities. He would discuss it with his parents and tell the Dean on his return to college.

Tom and David went to early communion on Easter Sunday morning at St. Matthew's, Wellswood, a church near to where they lived. His father had promised to take them to Buckfast Abbey, a monastery about an hour's drive away and where the Easter service was spectacular. The Abbey and Church, built in honey-colored stone by the monks themselves over many years, was a huge place and a popular tourist attraction. In London Tom and David had visited the Greek and Russian Orthodox cathedrals in order to experience their liturgy. Buckfast would add to that experience.

The service lived up to expectations. Smells, bells, magnificent vestments and the wonderful singing of the large community of monks added to a theatrical as well as a spiritual experience. "Walter would have loved it," Tom observed. "He loves all this ritual. I'm surprised he's not a Roman Catholic."

"And me," David added. "He's very critical of the Church of England. Perhaps Rome is too strict, too inhibiting for him. That's one good thing to say for the Church of England, it encompasses a wide variety of liturgical practice. Perhaps that's its strength."

They met David's father in the car park. He would not come to the service and had spent his time reading the Sunday papers. As they left the monastery he remarked, "Look at the place. All those shops selling souvenirs. It's just a money-making enterprise. Didn't Jesus throw out the money changers from the Temple in disgust?" (5) He said no more and drove home.

Tom stayed a couple more days and then returned to Westwick to spend the rest of the holiday with his mother. He had been well received by David's parents and they invited him to stay any time he liked. "I feel relaxed here," he told David as they waited for his train. "Your parents are so easy to get on with and Torquay is a very beautiful place. Thanks for the holiday and for talking things over. I know where I'm going now." He looked at David with such sorrow. "I'm sorry we won't be going to Warminster together but I understand. Mum wants you to come and stay before the end of term and to bring Jacob."

David was amazed. "Does she know about me then?" he asked.

"Oh, yes, for a long time. You know mum. She doesn't mind a bit. Like your parents. You know, David, we're both very lucky."

David told his parents of his decision one night as they sat in semi-darkness looking out across the bay at the twinkling lights of Brixham. His mother shed a few tears. "It's all right, dear," she told him. "I'm so relieved. I never wanted you to go into that beastly Church. I've watched you change from an open-hearted, fun-loving person into....into an introverted, moody individual. It's not for you, David. Love Jacob and love life as you did before."

His father said nothing. He had little time for the Church, being involved in selling granite, marble and stone to the clergy at times. He regarded them as greedy and corrupt. "What are you going to do then?" he asked.

"Jacob and I have talked," David told him. "He thinks I could get a job with the BBC as a trainee studio manager. We could work together then. Jobs are plentiful in London so don't worry."

It was clear that his parents were happy about his decision and about his relationship with Jacob. As Tom had said, he was a lucky person.

Returning to London, David and Jacob had a tearful reunion. They had missed each other so much. David told Jacob of his decision and they discussed his next step in regard to getting a job. David had met Jacob's boss, Alister Macfarlan, and his wife on a number of occasions and Jacob felt that he would be helpful. "He likes you and so does his wife. They understand our relationship. When are you going to tell the Dean?"

"Next week," David told him. "I want to enjoy our evening at the opera first." And so they did.

The opera 'Aida' was written by Giuseppe Verdi for the opening of the Suez Canal and intended to be a spectacular presentation in line with the greatness of the canal. It tells of the love of a young army captain for an Ethiopian princess and how they offended the Pharoah and were entombed together to die in each other's arms. The whole opera is of huge proportions with the necessity of a large chorus, dancers, and soldiers. On any stage it is spectacular.

Tickets for Covent Garden are difficult to acquire, expensive, particularly the stalls, so David was well aware of the gift that Jacob had given for his birthday. He had heard stories about productions of the opera requiring a cast of hundreds and wondered how the Royal Opera House would cope. Montserrat Caballe was at the height of her career and the tenor Carlo Bergonzi as Radames was a bonus. It was a gala performance and so they both wore a dinner jackets. David thought how handsome Jacob looked. The audience was expectant and excited. The curtain opened on the High Priest, Ramasis, talking with the young captain, Radames, who ultimately will lead the forces of Egypt against the Ethiopians and so the story unfolds. When Radames reveals his love for Aida in the area 'Celeste Aida' the audience was hushed only to cheer and clap at its conclusion. It was a wonderful performance and everything David has expected and more. The Triumphal March in Act 2 was amazing with column after column of soldiers crossing the stage, banners and crowds of citizens as well. Caballe's powerful voice sailed over the huge chorus and her top notes filled the theatre. She was cheered many times that night. The final scene with the lovers entombed and Amneris outside with the chorus of citizens, the trio 'O terra addio' brought tears to David's eyes. Jacob grasped his hand but the tears still flowed. He didn't care. It was so wonderful, so sad, and it touched a nerve that reminded him of his love for Jacob. For him, music was the ultimate expressive medium and the trio said so much. He was drained emotionally when the opera ended but so very happy.

How would he break the news to the Dean that he was not going to offer himself for ordination? It had been a worry at the back of his mind since he had made the decision over the holiday. The Dean had been so good to him over his three years at King's. He would be very disappointed. As luck would have it, an opportunity arose one morning after breakfast at the hostel. The post was placed on a large table in the entrance hall and students helped themselves to their own letters. David was just looking to see if there was anything for him when the Dean emerged from the chapel. "Ah, David, good morning. Did you have a good holiday?" he asked.

"Oh, yes, Dean, thank you. My parents have moved to Torquay so I spent Easter there," he replied.

"Not in Sheffield?" He smiled. "Come into my study, you can tell me all about it." He led David through into his private quarters and to his study.

When they had got settled David told him all about the storm, his father's cracked rib, his uncle's terminal cancer and the quick sale of the house. "It was all a bit rushed, but their new bungalow is quite nice and has super views," he told the Dean with enthusiasm.

"Did you take your friend.....er, Jacob?" he asked.

"No, unfortunately he had to work. Tom Bowers came to stay."

"That was nice of you. I know Tom had some worries. Sea air will blow them away, I think," the Dean added. David was surprised that the Dean knew about Tom's worries but he supposed it was his job to know. He really cared for all his students. "And what about you and your friend?" a voice said. It was the Dean's voice and David had been daydreaming.

"He's fine, Dean," David responded.

"But what about your relationship, David?" the Dean asked.

What should he say? It appeared that the Dean knew about his gayness. "You mean the homosexual relationship that Jacob and I have?" There, it was out in the open.

"Don't look so worried," the Dean told him. "I've thought for a while that you had a problem. You can't be in my position all these years and not spot the signs. When you introduced me to...Jacob.... I knew I was right." He smiled with his gentle eyes at David. "You are too intelligent not to have come to some conclusion about the future."

It was so easy to talk to the Dean. There was a compassion there that encouraged honesty. David furnished his argument. "The Church teaches that active homosexuality is a sin. I'm not so sure that is right, Dean, as I think it can be an expression of deep love. Anyhow, it's a sin according to the Church. It is possible to practice abstinence. For me that is too difficult. I'm left with three alternatives. Become a priest and live out of grace with God. I could never do that as how can I administer the sacraments as a sinner? Be a celibate priest and risk daily temptation. Or.....” He looked at the Dean whose face was expressionless. “Or live with Jacob and not seek ordination. I have chosen the latter.”

There was silence. Both the Dean and David were thinking. At last the Dean spoke. “Your evaluation of the situation is admirable, David, as I would expect from you. However, I’m not in total agreement with your decision. Of course, you are right to believe that unless you are in a state of grace with God priestly functions become a mockery. I’ve seen you and Jacob together and can understand the bond between you, but isn’t the bond between you and God stronger?”

Was the Dean being fair? David felt that his argument was a little below the belt. Should he tell him of his theological reservations? He decided against it. “You know, Dean, the love of God is an intellectual concept,” he told him. “When it comes down to the nitty-gritty of love there is nothing like being in the physical presence of the one you love. Maybe the saints ‘feel’ the physical presence of God, but my faith does not go that far.”

The Dean’s eyes opened wide in amazement. “I’ve never heard it put that way before,” he said. “Maybe you’re right....for you,” he added. “You’re going to finish your degree, though?”

“Oh yes, of course,” David replied enthusiastically.

“And what will you do after you graduate,”

“I think there is an opening for me in the BBC as a studio manager,” David told him.

The Dean stood and David followed. “I’m sorry you will not be going to Warminster as I had high hopes of you. The door will never be closed for you, David, remember that. If you should change your mind then the hand of God is always there.” He put his arms round David’s shoulders and led him to the private entrance into the hostel.

Walter was not surprised when David told him of his decision not to present himself for ordination. “Are you sure you’ve made the right decision?” he asked.

“Yes, Walter, I have,” David told him with confidence. “You know that I have other reservations, theological ones, and I can’t go ahead with so much doubt. I really don’t love God enough to give up Jacob and that is the truth.”

“What did the Dean say?” he asked.

“He was disappointed, of course, but he has left the door open in case at any time I’ll change my mind.”

“And will you?”

"No, Walter. I don't think so. I can reconcile my homosexuality with service to God, but the Church cannot accept it. Until the Church does and stops treating gays like lepers then I turn my back. There are other ways of serving God, and man, without being a priest."

Walter did not take him up on that. He knew David too well to raise an argument he couldn't win. David wondered how Walter could reconcile his homosexuality. He knew he was a practicing gay and was likely to be for the rest of his life. Had Walter accepted living in a state of negative grace, or did he believe that homosexuality was not sinful. He would not ask him, he decided. If Walter wanted to explain he knew he would. They both had a different zeitgeist and thus ended up with differing conclusions with the same problem. David was content.

Tom invited David to stay at Westwick for the two weeks before their final exams. "We can revise together," he suggested. "Two heads are better than one." It was an excellent notion and David's only reservation was not seeing Jacob for a couple of weeks. Tom had another bright idea. "Why doesn't Jacob come and stay for two successive weekends? We've plenty of room and mum won't mind. She'll be delighted to meet him." And so it was arranged. Jacob would travel down on a Friday evening and go back to London on the commuter train on Monday morning.

The weather was bliss and they got into an effective routine. They prepare a schedule of work covering all that was to be examined. The mornings were spent in intense study. One morning David would act as examiner and the following morning, Tom. Where there were problems, a note of the problem would be made and followed up in the evenings when they worked independently. David had read that the span of attention was twenty to thirty minutes, and so he and Tom worked in bursts of intensity and followed by a short period of relaxation. The afternoons were spent in recreation, usually taking long walks and discussing some doctrinal problems that they found difficult. It was an excellent way to study and they hoped it would pay off.

Jacob came for his first weekend. Tom and David met him in Guildford and drove him to Westwick. David had prepared him for the splendors of the house and garden but he was still impressed. "It's lovely, Tom," he said as he stepped out of the car. "David told me all about it but it's much better in reality."

Mrs. Bowers emerged from the direction of the kitchen garden, same hat, different dress, and this time with a trowel in her gloved hands. She was beaming all over her face. "So this is Jacob. I'm so pleased to meet you." Jacob kissed her on both cheeks. "David has talked so much about you. Leave your bag. Miss Bane has tea on the lawn." She took hold of Jacob's arm and led him off. David thought of the way she had welcomed him on his first day.

"Why does my mum always meet visitors dressed like the gardener?" Tom said to himself.

"I heard that Tom Bowers," his mother said turning around as she walked away. "Because she is the gardener and loves being so." She said something to Jacob that made him laugh but David and Tom were too far away by now to hear.

It gave Tom and David so much pleasure showing Jacob around. He was introduced to Billy the bull, who snuffled his hand with pleasure, and thus confirmed him as an honored guest. They had tea with the vicar and his wife, but this time Tom gave them due warning and took a big box of cream cakes as a gift. Mrs. Bowers invited the Mortons to dinner and Jacob got on especially with Frank Morton who knew South Africa very well. They walked the fields, lanes and woods talking and laughing and David had never been so happy in all his life. He was so proud of Jacob. Whilst they had different bedrooms, it presented no problem as David would wait until the household was quiet and then creep into Jacob's bed. Weekends are just weekends and rather short and so Jacob's departure to London came far too quickly.

Then there was a second weekend. It was just as idyllic. The more they were together the more David and Jacob's love for each other grew. Tom had never ever said much about David's gayness, accepting it as an eccentricity of his best friend, but even he had to admit that Jacob was a fine person. "He brings the sun out in you, David" he once said as they relaxed from an intensive revision session. "You two are a pleasure to be with." It was clear that Mrs. Bowers liked Jacob as well. She fussed over him a lot. One morning she commented to David, "He's beautiful, David. We clearly like the same sort of men." They both laughed. Both of them could laugh at his predicament in a state of mutual understanding. In a world where the Church should be encouraging loving relationships and reducing tensions, it was doing the exact opposite. From that moment David knew he had been right about not seeking ordination.

The revision period came to an end and David and Tom returned to London. Vincent Square was quiet over the two weeks of the examinations. Students came together for an examination, launched into an inquest over a quick lunch, and then scurried away into their rooms for more revision. Mealtimes in the hostel dining room were comparatively quiet and the obligatory chapel was regarded by many as a distraction. David and Jacob agreed not to meet for the period of the exams. Jacob phoned him every night. Apart from Greek, David found the exams not too bad but he never really liked formal examinations. He was glad when they were over.

Chapter 29

The period after the examinations was an anti-climax. Most students just lazed about aimlessly filling in time until the results were published. Coffee shops near to the college, full of students, did a roaring trade. The relaxation areas in the Chesham were draped with sprawling bodies. Some students with money left over from their grants went shopping, others just wandered, looking in the windows hoping that one day they would have the finance to buy. The millstone of final examination results was ever present. However, it was not too bad for David as his degree was now not so crucial.

One morning he went for an interview to the BBC. He was placed in a studio by himself and had to read a script. A mystery voice gave him instructions. Later, he was interviewed by a panel of five executives, who asked him all kinds of questions about his personal life and the part the BBC played in it. He had to admit that he rarely listened to the radio, except for the news, as he had been too busy with his studies. In the evening he discussed it all with Jacob who felt that the interview had gone quite well. There was no certainty that he would be offered a job, but there were other things he could do. He had seen a number of trainee management jobs advertised and had put in several applications. With Jacob working, there was no urgency for him to get a job, as finance was not a real problem, however, David wanted to pay his way and not be a burden.

As soon as the results of the exams were published and the official end of term came, David was to move in with Jacob. The availability of a job would determine their future plans. Maybe they would holiday with his parents in Torquay, but no real decision could be made. They could not even decide what to do when Jacob got his annual holiday in September. What they did finalize was that whilst Jacob's apartment was not large, it was comfortable, and they did not consider it wise to move to something bigger.

One evening he and Jacob went to see a showing of 'Ben Hur', the latest epic from Hollywood, starring Charlton Heston in the title role. The trend for pseudo-religious epics, set by the Hollywood producer Cecil B. DeMill, had huge audience appeal and excellent box office receipts. With a cast of thousands, a budget of millions of dollars, and a dynamic publicity campaign, it was a talking point for many and it was only time before David was persuaded to see it. Not that he went to the cinema very much but he had enjoyed 'The Ten Commandments' and 'The Robe' and he and Jacob needed a night out for a change.

True to form, the film was spectacular. The photography was quite wonderful, particularly the crowd and fight scenes, but David felt that Charlton Heston's performance was rather lack luster. He had never been impressed by his acting. It was too wooden, not quite believable. At the end of the film was a chariot race between Ben Hur and his one time friend, now his enemy, where good and evil would be worked out through the medium of the race.

The filming of the chariot race was staggering in its realism and the visual impact rather gory. At one point a figure was dragged underneath a chariot around the Coliseum in Rome while the crowds cheered. The two protagonists lashed each other with whips causing terrible cuts on their bodies and the blood to flow. The director had set out to shock, and it did.

David got bound up in the story. He shed tears when Ben Hur's sister and mother, after years of wrongful imprisonment, returned home only to reveal that they were now lepers. He longed for the evil Roman centurion, a Christian persecutor, to be overcome by Ben Hur, who had been converted to Christianity. The chariot race was the final showdown and David has so much empathy for Ben Hur, that he almost fainted at the sight of all the blood. "I'm going to pass out," he whispered to Jacob who pushed his head between his knees. It was silly really. In the army he had seen so much blood and never flinched, yet the film had made him feel decidedly strange. Why? Was fantasy more powerful than reality? It occurred to him that reality is usually task oriented, and the mind has to concentrate on the task; fantasy has freedom so that the mind can take flights of fancy and has greater emotional impact. He wondered to what extent religious experience, visions, were the result of unfettered fantasy.

They had a meal at a little restaurant just off Leicester Square. David raised his question about fantasy with Jacob. What if religious experience, seeing visions, was merely a flight of fancy, no matter how real the vision might seem, supplanted in the brain by some intense reality? Poor Jacob, he was so frequently amazed by David's agile and enquiring mind. Not that he objected. On the contrary, he loved being challenged and stimulated. Not only was his lover handsome but bright as well. He made him think, and for a man, who also had an excellent brain, it was a bonus.

"If I understand the modern concepts of brain function," Jacob told him, "the ability of the mind to invent new notions is infinite. It is the highest system according to Systems Theory. One idea stimulates another, and that stimulates another and so on. It is the highest system as there are no parameters, except perhaps the intelligence of the individual. Mind can build in all directions. Some ideas are stimulated by reality and others come from what has already been created. Fantasy may stimulate more fantasy. Humans are the only creatures capable of this. That is what makes us unique amongst the animals."

Here David took over. "Suppose an intense human emotion, something like I had in the cinema, unfettered by task reality, initiates a fantasy that is so real as to be believable. When I was in the army I saw some terrible things, but because I had a task to undertake at the time, emotion was reduced or suppressed. In the cinema there was no task, nothing to control my emotions, so I believed what I saw as if I was there. And I nearly passed out because of it."

"I follow you, Jacob responded, but how do you get to your visions?"

"Right," David said. "If a susceptible person, or a deeply religious person, who believes in say the appearance of aliens or the Virgin Mary, is stimulated by the thought of aliens or the Virgin, because the mind is free to fly, and there is no task orientation, aliens or the Virgin will come into view. It will be intense, real. They will be convinced by what they saw. Visions can happen to anyone if they are in a susceptible state. What is different is that the person who sees a vision, and is not limited by reality, actually believes what they see. I believed the vision of blood and gore because I wanted to and there was nothing else to detract me from it. I was so bound up with the story. You see because you want to. You have faith in what you see."

"So you are saying," Jacob added, "that your reality in the cinema was because you were ready to accept it."

"Yes, but now I can see it was a trick of the mind. The person who sees aliens or the Virgin Mary may not accept that the mind has been tricked. What I experienced was real enough at the time, but my rational mind tells me how silly I have been. Those who see things may deny rationality and tell themselves that it all was so clear it must be."

"I agree the mind can play tricks," Jacob told David. "What was your point about faith?"

"I was not necessarily talking about religious faith," David informed him. "Those who want to believe in little green men, or flying saucers, or the appearance of the Virgin will do so even if they are challenged because they have faith in what they have seen. With faith you believe because you want to believe. Faith is the belief in something without rational evidence. It can be very strong. It can also be misguided."

"Can you give an example?"

"Yes," David told him. "Sir Arthur Conan Doyle, the creator of Sherlock Holmes, (1) a convinced spiritualist, claimed that after his death he would return to prove the spiritual world existed. He had faith in his claim. We're still waiting. Thousands of Jehova's Witnesses believed that the end of the world was about to come. They had faith in a particular date. The date passed and they are still waiting."

"And I believe it's time we went home to bed, David Earl, or we'll not be up in the morning. I have faith in your rationality that what I say is true," Jacob remarked as he signaled to the waiter for the bill.

The following afternoon, around three thirty, a student knocked on David's door to say that there was a telephone call for him. The communal phone was in a booth in the main entrance hall and David went down stairs to receive the call. A voice at the end of the line asked tentatively, "David,...... David Earl?"

David did not recognize the voice. "David Earl here. Can I help you?"

"It's Alister Macfarlan," the voice said. David realized who it was, Jacob's producer. "I'm sorry Mr Macfarlan but I didn't recognize your voice." David expected he must be phoning to tell him something about his interview at the BBC.

"David," he said. "I've bad news." David thought he must be referring to the studio manager post. Never mind if he had been rejected, there would be other jobs. "I'm afraid Jacob.... has been knocked down.... by a bus." The words did not really register. What had happened? Knocked down? No, he can't have said that. Then the voice said, "Are you there David?"

"Yes. What did you say?"

"Jacob. He's been knocked down by a bus." There was a long silence while the message sank into David's mind. David was just going to ask which hospital he was in when the voice said, "He's......dead."

David's dull, unbelieving voice said, "Dead.....He can't be....Are you sure it's Jacob."

"There's no doubt, David," said the voice from far away. There was silence again while David took in the enormity of the situation. The voice asked, "Are you all right?"

David let the phone slip so it hung on the end of its cord. A voice at the other end of the line kept saying, "David, David, are you there?" David felt as if it was all part of a bad dream and that he would wake up to find Jacob smiling at him. The phone was talking to itself and then suddenly went dead and purred incessantly.

David opened the door of the booth as if in a trance. He seemed to be walking outside himself. He was floating, weightless, slightly sick. He could see students about but he was not part of their world. There was a rushing sound in his head. He could not hear what they were saying. Jacob...dead. "Oh no, no it can't be. Not his Jacob," he heard himself say. He began to walk unsteadily along the hall. A student, a hazy figure with big, staring eyes, came up to him and spoke. He could not make out what was being said. Someone else came to him. They were in a sort of mist. His eyes were playing tricks. "Are you all right?" asked a hollow voice as if was talking slowly down a megaphone. The rushing sound got worse. Then he felt himself toppling. He could see himself fall. He crumpled in slow motion like the tower of match sticks he and his brother had once built at home. There was no pain when he hit the floor. He remembered saying Jacob's name over and over again. Then there was blackness.

A voice from afar said, "What happened?"

"We don't know," a deep, booming voice said. "He took a phone call and then just collapsed. He keeps saying 'Jacob, Jacob no, no, no...'."

"Help me get him to his room," the first voice commanded. "Send someone for the doctor."

An indistinct face at the end of a long passage looked down at him. David could see the person but he was out of focus. "What... happened?" a voice asked.

"He's... had... some.... kind.... of.... a... shock," another voice said as if a recording was being played very slowly

"Do... you.... know.... what.... it....was?" the first voice asked.

"He... had.... a.... phone... call. He... collapsed. He... kept... saying 'Jacob... no' over.... and.... over.... again," another distorted and yet familiar voice said. "Jacob... is... his.... friend. Someone... has.... gone... to.... try..... to..... phone... him."

"I'll... give.... him... a..... shot.... to... calm..... him.... down," the first voice said. "Someone.... stay..... with.... him..... and.... I'll.... be.... in.... later."

It was evening as the table lamp was lit on his desk. The curtains were closed. Someone was sitting in his armchair. He felt weak and sleepy. What had happened to him? He had passed out. Then he remembered the voice on the phone. 'Jacob ...knocked down.... by a bus.....dead.' Tears began to well in his eyes, to run down his cheeks, to flood like the monsoon rains. He sobbed silently. "Jacob, oh Jacob. My love, my life." His silent sobs shook the whole of his body.

The figure in the chair came over to look at him. He took his hand. The sobs continued and slowly turned into sound. "Oh, no, not Jacob. Please God let it not be Jacob." The sobs were interspersed with words but did not abate.

The figure, a tall lean priest, sat on the side of his bed and took David into his arms. He said nothing, just held the sobbing figure who still kept repeating, "No, not Jacob. Please God, not Jacob."

It was a long time before David's sobs stopped. He was exhausted and dropped into sleep. Father Sumner gently laid him back on his pillow. Tears were in his eyes, as how could he not be moved by such mental anguish? He knelt and started to pray.

There was a knock on the door but the priest continued to pray. Walter came in with a visitor, Alistair Macfarlan. They waited. Father Sumner having finished his prayer got up and Walter introduced him to the visitor. They spoke in whispers. "How is he?" asked Walter.

"Still in mental torment," Father Sumner reported. "The hurt is very deep. He keeps repeating Jacob's name and asking why it happened."

"Poor, poor David," was all Walter could murmur as deep emotion went through him. He left, seeing that Alistair wanted to talk.

"If only I'd come here myself," Alistair told them, "instead of breaking the news over the phone."

"You did what you felt was right at the time," Father Sumner told him.

"I suppose I was upset and didn't think."

Father Sumner waved Alistair to the arm-chair while he sat at the desk. "What actually happened?" he asked.

David stirred and said "Jacob, oh Jacob" in his sleep. The two men looked towards him and Father Sumner smoothed his bedclothes.

Alistair hesitated. He didn't know where to begin. "At about twelve-thirty today," he said hesitantly, "Jacob left Bush House to have lunch. Usually he met David but for some reason today they didn't meet. He was walking up the Tottenham Court Road when without warning a bus mounted the pavement. Apparently, the driver had a heart attack and lost control. It hit Jacob who was looking in a shop window and failed to see the oncoming bus. The police say he died instantly. It's a wonder others weren't killed. Jacob was the unlucky one. The police rang me. How they found me I don't know. As David is Jacob's closest friend I rang him."

Alistair was obviously upset by Jacob's death too, but had had time to regain his composure. "My wife and I knew of their relationship. We liked them both and socialized quite a lot, but we never realized how close they really were."

"David loved Jacob," Father Sumner told him. "None of us knew how much until ...this happened. In fact, David was giving up the priesthood in order to live with Jacob."

"I knew they intended to live together and that David was trying to get a job with the BBC. What will happen now?"

"I'm not sure," Father Sumner replied. "What needs to happen first is to get David well. To make sure there is no deterioration in his mind. Grief can do strange things. I thought I knew David well but he has surprised me. He is such a loving person. The depth of his love for Jacob has put him in acute shock."

Alistair got up to go. He shook hands. "If there is anything I can do just let me know. When David is ready for visitors please phone me. I need to talk to him."

"Thank you, I will," Father Sumner responded. "With God's help, David will recover. Maybe he'll always have the hurt, but he will learn to adjust to it. He is young, life is ahead of him, and he must carry on."

Very slowly and with the loving care of Father Sumner, the Dean, as well as Walter and Tom, David came out of his state of agony. Jacob's death still hurt but he managed to talk tearfully to Alistair Macfarlan who apologized for his insensitivity. David understood what he had been through and the panic that Jacob's death must have caused him. Alistair told him that Jacob's body was to be flown back to South Africa after an inquest, where a tribal funeral would take place, and that his elder brother was on his way to accompany the body. He had asked to meet David and talk with him. David agreed reluctantly and wondered what he had to say.

Alistair went with David to the Hilton where Jacob's brother was staying. They went up to his suite on the fourteenth floor. After introductions, Alistair tactfully left David and Benjamin, for that was his name, to talk. Benjamin must have been about sixty, gray haired and dignified. More stocky than Jacob, he was not as handsome, but he had an imposing presence. He waved David to a chair that had a view across Hyde Park.

Benjamin looked directly ahead of him remembering events far off. There was silence for a while. "I don't know where to begin really," he commenced in beautiful English. "Jacob was one of five brothers and now I am the only one left."

David wanted to say how sorry he was but Benjamin continued.

"He was a bright boy, as I am sure you are aware, and went on to gain a first class degree at Harvard. He could have stayed in America as he had many good job offers, but he chose to return to South Africa. We were all involved in the struggle for freedom and Jacob chose to work for an underground newspaper. Two of his brother had sacrificed their lives because of their involvement in the struggle. Jacob wanted to be part of it. He said it was his duty. Our youngest brother was shot whilst peacefully protesting in Suweto not long after Jacob returned home. It grieved him greatly as he was his favorite. My father pleaded with him to return to America as he had lost three sons. Jacob refused."

"About a year ago we were warned that the South African security forces had put a price on Jacob's head. My father made him leave the country and come to London. Jacob did not refuse this time."

His eyes now focused on David. "What I am about to tell you, David, may embarrass you but I want you to know everything. It may help you in reconciling Jacob's untimely death. Whilst Jacob had never talked about his homosexuality, I knew about it. In Africa homosexuality goes on, like every other country, but in secret. It is not accepted. Just little things gave Jacob away and a brother is sensitive to these things. I make no judgment as I loved him as only a brother can. He went on an assignment to Mombassa and something happened there because he changed. Don't ask me how, but he was a different person when he returned. He still felt strongly about destroying apartheid but there was a new dynamic about him. He talked a lot a bout an Englishman he had met. I realized that this man had sparked something inside him. I'm not certain, but I think he never had a lover. Meeting you altered everything."

He shifted in his chair. "He liked London but missed his family. He wrote frequently. In one letter he said he had bumped into you by chance. He called it a miracle. And so I assume your friendship began. His love for you grew and grew." A tear ran down David's cheek. He could not control himself. "His letters were full of you and he revealed to me the truth about himself. He admitted that he had found 'the love of his life' and wanted to be with you for always." David's tears increased and a sob punctuated the silence. Benjamin looked at him with compassion, but went on. "He said that you were giving up any idea of ordination so you both could live together. You don't know how this sacrifice affected his love for you, David. He had truly found the happiness that had always escaped him. He knew you were true to him. It was, according to his letters, the ultimate fulfillment."

David's tears still rolled down his cheeks. He made no sound other than an occasional sob. Benjamin got up from his seat and went to a briefcase that was on a side table. He opened it and produced a bundle of letters fastened with an elastic band. David wiped away his tears with a handkerchief. Benjamin returned to where David sat. "These are the letters he wrote me. I want you to have them, David." He handed him the bundle and David took them as if in a trance. "You enabled him to find himself. In a short period of time you gave him a depth of love and happiness nobody else could. Thank you, David, for making my brother a truly happy man."

David did not know whether to accept the letters and half offered them back. "But…they are private and written to you."

Benjamin gently pushed David's hand away. "They are for you. His heart was with you and you must have them." Tears rolled down David's face again. Why was Jacob's brother making such a sacrifice?"

"We have both lost him, David. Take the letters as part of him. In time they will give you comfort," he told him. "I will have the comfort of his grave where I might speak with him."

He took David by the hand over to the window. "Look out there," he said. "There is the world. People are going about their business. The countryside here and in South Africa wears its beauty. There is much in life that is good. Don't regret, David. Go out into the world and grasp all it has to offer. That is what Jacob would have wanted. Your pain will eventually dim, but you will never forget his love. It was something special. What you two had together was rare. Such deep love is not easily found. Maybe you'll meet another person and love again. I hope it will be glorious like it was with Jacob. Live and love, David, for Jacob."

Epilogue

With the support of his friends and the wise counsel of Father Sumner and the Dean, David recovered from his hurt and took control of his life again. There were times, particularly when he was on his own, that the hurt came back and silent tears rolled down his cheeks. It was silly really, but he could not help it. He felt as if there was a huge weight pressing on his heart and that it would eventually burst. But it did not. The figure of Jacob was always around in his thoughts, but he got used to it and accepted that perhaps it would be always there. It would become his rock.

When results were published he had done extremely well, except in Greek. He was not surprised as he had disliked Latin at school and Greek was much the same. The Dean and Father Sumner tried to persuade him to go to Warminster Theological College and see how he felt after his fourth year. He refused. He could have lived with some of his theological doubts, but his faith in God had been shattered. His greatest love had been taken away from him. If it was God's punishment for loving Jacob so deeply, then he did not want to know any more. Surely, God could not be so angry as to take Jacob from him. Father Sumner and the Dean called it a mystery and said man was too puny to understand God's ways. David felt that this was another copout as was the explanation for the child's death at Millbank hospital had been. No, he would not be ordained. He would follow the teachings of Jesus Christ as given by a good man, not as the Son of God.

London reminded David too much of Jacob and the life they would have had together and he was determined that if offered a job by the BBC he would not take it. He returned home to Torquay in the County of Devon and into the loving arms of his family. Both his mother and father were shocked when they saw him as he had lost weight and his face was pale and thin. He cried a great deal. His mother encouraged him to get the hurt out of his system. She felt that crying was therapeutic. His father felt crying was sissy, but said nothing

The weather in July and August was wonderful. Devon was at its best and thousands of visitors invaded Torquay which took on the holiday spirit. This was another world of gardens and an abundance of flowers; hills clothed in green splendor; sandy beaches packed with happy holidaymakers; clean, refreshing air that inspired an appetite; and the clothed in greens and blues. David managed to swim and sunbathe and slowly in this idyllic atmosphere, with his mother's good cooking and wise counsel, he regained his old self.

He had changed. No longer did he go to church regularly. He explained to his parents that he was agnostic, and while he believed wholeheartedly in the teachings of Jesus and His moral outlook, he could not call himself a Christian. A true Christian believed that Jesus was the Son of God. He could not accept this doctrine. His mother often asked him how he felt over Jacob's death. The hurt was there, it would always be there but it was getting less of an agony. The memory of Jacob would be in his heart forever. Maybe he would meet someone else, maybe not, but what he had experience over those few short months they were together was a deep love few have had the pleasure of experiencing. He misquoted Samuel Butler saying, 'It is better to have loved and lost, than never to have loved at all'.

Glossary

Chapter 1

1. B.B.C. British Broadcasting Corporation. Government funded radio and television provider. It is independent of the government of the day, funded by the State, and on occasions is in direct conflict.

2. National Service The National Service Act 1948, consolidated previous acts relating to conscription into the armed services. From December 1948 all young men of 18 years and above, who were deemed fit enough by a medical panel, had to served for a period of two years in one of the armed services. Those who refused were imprisoned. Pacifists, known as conscientious objectors were found alternative training, usually down a coal mine. Conscription was abandoned in February 1959 and the last intake was in November 1960.

3. Grammar Schools. In the 1944 Education Act a three tier system of education was envisaged. All children from aged five to eleven would attend a Primary School. At aged eleven children would sit the 'eleven plus' examination, which consisted of three multiple choice elements: reading and writing, mathematics, and a special / logical test. Those with the higher scores would go to a Grammar School where the curriculum was academic and aimed at university or college entrance, while the rest would go to a Secondary Modern School with a more practical curriculum aimed at the world of work. The whole concept was based on the notion that Intelligence Tests could accurately predict ability. The Act was controversial. The problem was that both types of school got the same funding, except that the grammar school had extra for their 16+ pupils. This gave them a financial advantage and so they tended to be better staffed and resourced. The secondary modern schools actually needed the extra funding as their curriculum was supposed to be practical. They never got it and tended to become 'sink' schools.

4. Coronation. The crowning of Queen Elizabeth II took place in Westminster Abbey, London, on June 2nd !953.

5. Nuneaton. It is a small mining town in the county of Leicestershire. The town is surrounded by many slag heaps from the coal mines and was not a pretty place. However, in recent years the local authority has

covered some over and planted trees and shrubs, thus improving the area.

6. Belsen Camp. During the Second World War, the fascist regime in Germany, led by Adolph Hitler, constructed a number of prison camps where they put Jewish prisoners whom they blamed for the economic ills of Germany. These camps had poison-gas chambers, disguised as showers, where millions of Jews were put to death. Belsen, Dachau, and Auchwitz Camps are perhaps the most well known, but there were others.

7.   Richard Dimbleby.   He started out working for his family newspaper and became a war reporter in the Second World War. After the war he worked for the BBC presenting the 'Panorama' program. He became the most famous interviewer on British television. On his death in 1965, the BBC started the annual Richard Dimbleby lecture.

8.   Air-raid Wardens.   Usually men, sometimes women, who for some reason could not go to fight, either because they were too old, or because they were unfit. Their job was to patrol the streets looking to see if any lights were showing from the houses and to help in case there was a bombing raid.

9.   Air-raid shelter.   There were three types of shelter to protect from air raids. The Table Shelter was a table made out of steel with metal netting down the sides. It could not shelter from a direct hit but helped if a house collapsed or there was blast in the area. It was used by people inside their homes where they had no garden in which to build the Anderson Shelter. This shelter, named after its inventor, was made of semi-circular pieces of galvanized steel and could be bolted together to make any size of shelter. It was buried in the garden and often reinforced with concrete. The last form of official shelter were deep cellars, train tunnels, and the London Underground. These were found in cities.

10. Bomb disposal team.   Usually soldiers who were trained to defuse unexploded bombs or land mines.

11.   Evacuees.   Children from London, during the period of the bombing of the city were moved to safer parts of the country and compulsorily lodged with other families.

12. Colditz Prison. The prison was housed in Colditz Castle which was considered to be escape-proof. However, there were a number of escapes. For further information read "The Coditz Story" by Eric Williams, and see the film of the same name.

13. Sunday School. Many protestant churches run a Sunday afternoon Bible class for young people. Before free, compulsory education this was the only chance a poor child had of learning to read and write.

14. Second World War. A European war with the Germany Nazi regime led by Adolf Hitler from 1939-45. In fact the Italian fascists, under Benito Mussolini, joined Hitler. There was also war with Japan during this period.

15. Church of England. It is the established religion of the United Kingdom and its bishops sit in the House of Lords. There has been a Christian community since AD 314 when an English bishop attended the Council of Arles. The severance from Rome came under King Henry VIII. When Rome would not grant him a second divorce, he made himself Supreme Head of the Church and the Book of Common Prayer was introduced in 1549. Much was wrong with the Roman Church and discontent was spread by Cardinal Wolsey. When Henry sacked the monasteries and took their wealth, threw out the clergy who supported Rome, and made himself Head of the Church, there was much support for his actions. Later, his successor, Queen Elizabeth I called herself Supreme Governor of the Church but Rome excommunicated her and the Anglican Church in 1570 To this day the British monarch is Head of the Church of England.

16. Director of Ordinands. A priest whose job it is to look after the welfare and training of men who seek ordination. Today women are included in this group.

17. Matabeliland. An area of Africa where the Matabele people or Zulus lived. It is an area partly in South Africa and partly Southern Rhodesia, now Zimbabwe.

18. Indian Summer. This describes warm weather that comes late in the year in Britain. Perhaps in late September or October.

19. Reading. A university town just west of London where many of its citizens commute to work in London..

20. N.C.O. A non-commissioned officer. One who has not been approved by the Queen. A person who comes from the bottom of the military social scale band is given limited authority. They are lance corporal, corporal, sergeant, staff sergeant, warrant officer in the military.

21. squaddy   It is a slang word for an NCO who is in charge of a group of new recruits in training.

22. Brasso   A proprietary cleaning fluid specially produced for cleaning brass.

23. NAAFI Prior to the formation of the NAAFI there were ad hoc canteen facilities for the services. In March 1920, a committee was set up by the Secretary of State for War to advise upon the type of canteen organization required by the Armed Forces in peacetime. As a result, the Navy, Army, and Airforce Institute was formed on 1st January 1921 to run catering and recreational establishments required by the Armed Forces. It is still in existence today.

24. Savoy Hotel. One of the top hotels in the world. It is situated on the Strand in London. The hotel complex includes the Savoy Theatre which was opened in 1881. Mr Doyle-Cart used the theatre to stage light opera, particularly those of Gilbert and Sullivan, and thus the comic operas are known as 'The Savoy Operas'.

Chapter 2

1.   high camp. A phrase used by theatricals to describe over acting. Homosexuals use the word 'camp' to describe someone who is very effeminate.

2. Sweeny Todd. He was an actual 19th century barber in London who cut the throats of his customers while they sat in the barber's chair. The bodies were then dumped in the River Thames.

3. Commission on Human Rights. This is a part of the United Nations and looks into cases where basic human rights have been violated.

4.   blanco. It can be a liquid or a block that is rubbed with a damp cloth. The idea is that it puts a film of matt, color onto your webbing

belt and gaiters. Most army units use kaki, the Military police and the Royal Navy, white, and the Royal Air Force, blue.

5.   battle dress. This is the usual, every-day uniform of the soldier as opposed to dress uniform used on special occasions. It is the uniform worn in battle. Soldiers have two sets, one for every day and one for best and parades. Both are of the same rough quality, except for officers.

6.   batman. He is the servant of a commissioned officer. Many servicemen regard the job as an easy option.

7.   gaiters. Gaiters are pieces of canvas about six inches wide and fastened by small straps. They are worn round the ankles above the boots. Puttees serve the same purpose. They are long pieces of cloth that are wound round the ankles and usually worn with long socks and shorts.

8.   bull. This is a slang word meaning unnecessary routine tasks. The origin of the phrase is unknown.

9.   Asian 'flu. In 1956 a very virulent form of influenza struck the world. It was thought to have started in China and eventually arrived in Europe. Many thousands of people, mostly the very young and the old, died from its effects.

10. N.A.T.O. The North Atlantic Treaty Organization was set up after the Second World War, with the United States of America playing a major role, together with the major European countries. The intention was that it would defend Europe from the threat of Communist Russia.

11. bumper. It consisted of a long pole with a weight on the end. A cloth was put under the weight and it would be pulled backwards and forwards along a wooden floor to polish it. It served instead of a polishing machine.

12. Albert Schweitzer. A man of brilliance – theologian, medical doctor, musician – who gave up fame to run a mission hospital in Equatorial Africa. He was an authority on Bach and the biographer of Widor. He dedicated his life to fighting disease in Africa.   .

13. Widor Toccata and Fuge. A massive organ work with complex

fingering by Charles Marie Jean Albert Widor, (1844 – 1937), and usually played on large organs as it demands deep base notes in the toccata. To play it well requires great skill on the organ keyboard.

14. Quasimodo. A character in Victor Hugo's book "The Hunchback of Notre Dame". Quasimodo is a deformed cathedral worker who falls in love with a beautiful girl.

15. Jane Russell   A beautiful American film star noted for her red hair, green eyes, and long, shapely legs. She was popular with the American troops during the Second World War and many carried her photograph.

16. Picasso Pablo Picasso (1881 –1973), a famous Spanish modern artist of the Cubist School of painters. His pictures today fetch millions of dollars at auction.

17. Windsor Great Park. The many thousands of acres of woodland and grazing stretched from below Windsor Castle to Ascot. The land belongs to the State but is in the patronage of the Queen. It is open to the public to walk and picnic.

Chapter 3

1. Commonwealth Memorial Gate. The gate, near Hyde Park, paid for by private subscription, remembers those who died in World War II from other nations. It was inaugurated by HM Queen on the afternoon of 6th November 2002, 57 years after the event, rather too long after to really honor these brave people.

2.   United Nations. Established by President Roosevelt after the Second World War as a place where nations could work out their differences through dialogue instead of going to war. Winston Churchill, Prime Minister of the UK during the war years said, "It is better to jaw, jaw than war, war."

3.   public schools. The name is misleading as these schools are privately run and fee -paying. Originally, most of the schools were set up by rich benefactors to provide an education for the poor, but over time they were hijacked and now provide an education for the rich.

4.   riding a horse. The reference is to the First World War where the British cavalry faced German field guns. A horse and rider with a

handgun was no match for modern weaponry. The force and tactics were outdated.

5.   War Office. Now called the Ministry of Defence. It is the government department that co-ordinates all three armed services and where the politicians and the military work together. The building housing the ministry is in Whitehall, London.

6.   Cyprus. The island of Cyprus was acquired from Turkey in 1878 and the majority Greeks believed that Britain would give them union with Greece (Enosis). The Turkish minority did not want this. After years of discussions the Greek Cypriots launched a civil strife against the British in 1931. This was ruthlessly put down. The island's Greek Orthodox Archbishop, Makarios III and a colonel of the Greek army, Col George Grivas, met in 1951 to plot the overthrow of the British. Negotiations took place again but a solution was not found and so hostilities commence on April 1st 1951. After a bloody guerrilla war by the EOKA terrorists, Grivas called a truce in December 1958. Negotiations took place and Cyprus became independent in August 1960. Archbishop Makarios, who had played a double game and fronted negotiations, became the first President.   Unfortunately, in December 1963 fighting broke out between Turks and Greeks and the island had to be partitioned.   It remains so to this day.

7.   Mau Mau. It is not clear what the words mean but it came to represent a guerrilla organization of Kikuyu tribesmen in Kenya of extreme bestiality, led by Jomo Kenyata, who was seeking independence from Britain. They committed terrible crimes against innocent civilians, both black and white, in the name of freedom between 1947 and 1953. In 1953 Kenyata was arrested and imprisoned for seven years for his part in the uprising. After imprisonment, he formed a political party which won the election and he became the first President of the independent Kenya.

8.   President Nasser. Colonel Gamal Abdul Nasser led a coup against King Farouk of Egypt in July 1952 and later became President. He went to war with Britain in 1956 when he nationalized the Suez Canal. War ensued in October with Britain and France and Israel attacked from the east in November and there was a race for the canal. The United Nations and America sided with Nasser and the Allies had to withdraw being only a few miles from the canal. Nasser was hailed as a hero and Egyptian nationalism began to grow and encourage discontent

all over the Middle East.

9. Berlin. In 1948, at the height of the 'Cold War', the Russians would not allow passage by Britain and America to the city of Berlin in Germany, which had been divided into three zones after World War II. The people were starving because of the blockade and a huge airlift was launched to help the beleaguered city.

10. Duke of Edinburgh Award Scheme. The scheme for young people was started n 1956 by the Duke to encourage young people to become more self-reliant. It consists of challenging tasks set to stretch the participant to the limit.

11. Colonel W.R. Lawton (Rtd.). Quoted these words to the author personally when he visited his home on the Island of Ibiza. Col. Lawton was trained at the Royal Military College, Sandhurst.

12. Passing Out Parade. A parade held at the end of basic training where the young recruits can show the results of their training to their families and friends. The salute is usually taken by a senior officer or the Regimental Colonel-in-Chief.

13. Anthony Hancock. A famous television comedian of the fifties and sixties whose weekly series, 'Hancock's Half Hour", was watched by millions. His sketch, 'The Blood Donor', was particularly notable as he passed out before giving blood and yet later bragged that he had given a whole armful.

14. diphtheria. An acute bacterial infection of the throat where the throat may, in extreme cases, become blocked and a tracheotomy – putting an incision in the throat in order to breathe-is required.

15. anurism needle. A blunted needle that goes into a vein to convey blood, through a tube into a bottle to use for blood transfusions.

Chapter 4

1. Portland stone. Honey-colored sandstone coming from quarries in Nottinghamshire and named after the Duke of Portland on whose land the quarries can be found.

2. Dickensian. Named after the 19th century novelist, Charles Dickens, who wrote rather dark, sad, tragic novels with a social message and

means 'old fashioned'.

3.   Victoria. An area of London, south of Hyde Park, named after Queen Victoria and having the huge Victoria Station within its bounds.

4.   QARANC. Queen Alexandra's Royal Army Nursing Corps was formed on 1st February 1949 and officers received commissions in 1950. It replaced the Queen Alexandra's Imperial Military Nursing Service.

5.   State Registered Nurse. Fully qualified nurse licensed by the State as opposed to a State Enrolled Nurse who was only an assistant. Many male RAMC personnel were either SRN or C344, the military equivalent, and yet they did not get a commission like the QARANC's who had the same qualification.

6.   steel erector. The individual who works high up on steel girders erecting the framework for new buildings.

7.   ENT. Ears, nose and throat specialism. Ophthalmic means to do with the eyes.

8.   detached retina. This is where the light-sensitive membrane at the back of the eye become loosened and has to be put back with surgery.

Chapter 5

1.   original sin. A doctrine based on St Paul's teaching in the Epistle to the Romans 5, 12-21, and later refined by St Augustine, so that a newly born child inherits sin from its parents.

2.   Mass. This is the name given to holy communion by high church members and Roman Catholics. [See note 2 for Chapter 21.]

3.   catheterize. A technique where a small sterile rubber tube it inserted into some part of the body.

4.   prostate. The prostate gland it the mechanism that controls the opening and closing of the bladder. In older people it becomes less efficient and sometimes will not open and thus a catheter has to be used to drain off the fluid.

5. Chelsea Hospital. The Royal Hospital, Chelsea, is a home / hospital for retired soldiers who have no dependents to look after them. It is situated in Chelsea, an area of London, and the pensioners are recognizable by the long red jackets they wear. It is also the place where the annual Chelsea Flower Show is held. This international horticultural show is organized by the Royal Horticultural Society.

6. faeces. Waste material discharged from the bowels. Many old people and the chronically sick have no control over their bowels and bladder.

7. correda. The Spanish for a bull fight.

8. Oxford Movement. A religious movement from 1833 – 45, centered at Oxford and led by John Henry Newman, John Keble and Edward Pusey. Its aim was to restore the ideals of the 17th century church. It adopted the concept of transubstantiation in the mass and other doctrinal beliefs that were closely allied to the Roman Catholic Church. The most famous member of the movement, John Henry Newman, transferred to the Roman Catholic Church and subsequently became a Cardinal.

9. Horse Guards Arch. This is a gateway from The Mall, across Horse Guards Parade, where the Queen reviews her Guards Regiments on her Official Birthday, and beyond is Green Park. At the end of the park Buckingham Palace is found.

10. Walsingham. An ancient shrine in Norfolk, revered by both Anglicans and Roman Catholics, destroyed in 1538. It was later revived and became a central place of pilgrimage for the Oxford Movement.

11. Popery. The leader of the Roman Catholic Church is the Pope whose title is derived from the Latin for 'father'. When a Pope is elected the words 'habemus papam' are announced. The word 'popery' became a derogatory word meaning trying to bring back Roman Catholicism or Catholic rituals to England.

12. Maria Callas (1923 – 1977). A famous Greek operatic diva who was noted for her temperamental behavior as well as her voice. She died of a broken heart after Aristotle Onassis, the shipping magnate with whom she was in love, married Jackie Kennedy.

13. Hyde Park. Once a royal park but now given over to the public for their recreation. It covers many hundreds of acres in central London and has a famous boating lake called the 'Serpentine'..

14. G-plan furniture. Furniture with an ultra-modern design popular in the 1950's and '60s.

15. Museums of South Kensington. A fashionable area of London, just south of Hyde Park, having a number of fine museums within easy walking distance of each other: Victoria and Albert Museum, Natural History Museum, Science Museum.

16. Charles Atlas. The first of the international bodybuilders who advertised a course to improve the physique.

Chapter 6

1. Narcissism. Excessive interest in oneself named after a Greek youth, Narkissos, who fell in love with his own reflection.

2. H.Q. Shortened form of the word 'headquarters' meaning the main administrative place.

3. R.A.F. Lynham. The Royal Air Force base at Lynham in Wiltshire, where military personnel were flown out to various parts of the world, instead of using a civilian airport.

Chapter 7

1. Yemen. The northern part of the Yemen in the 1950's and '60s was under communist rule and unofficially at war with Britain over its protection of the south, known as the Aden Protectorate. The Protectorate was given its independence in 1967 and joined with the north to became the Republic of Yemen.

2. bangers. The word used here means 'sausages' as they explode or bang if cooked without their skins being pierced.

3. Chubby Checker. He was a famous American pop singer of Rock-and-Roll music. His hit 'Rock Around the Clock' was perhaps his most famous song.

4. Charterhouse School. A famous public school at Godalming, in Surrey. It was founded by Sir Thomas Sutton.

5. toff. A slang word meaning an upper class person.

6. Die Fledermaus. A comic opera, 'The Bat', by Johann Strauss Jr. in which one of the characters gives a warning not to become entangled with lawyers as they will ruin you financially. First produced in Vienna and New York in 1874.

7. baguette. A long, thin French loaf that is sliced to make a large sandwich.

Chapter 8

1. radiation experiments. It was revealed in recently de-classified documents that British troops were subjected to dangerous radiation levels when an atomic weapon was exploded on Christmas Island as part of the British nuclear program.

2. wadi. Arabic names for a desert valley.

3. tinea. Round white patch on the skin caused by a fungus in the air. Some skins produce oils that the fungus likes and thus the person is more susceptible. Tends to be more virulent in hot and humid climates.

4. Uffizi Gallery. Famous art gallery in the center of Florence, Italy, where Michelangelo's statue of 'David' can be seen as well as other great works of art..

Chapter 9

1. Bessie Bradock M.P. (1899 – 1970). The Labour Member of Parliament for Liverpool Exchange for twenty-four years who seemed to be the only MP at the time who was prepared to take on the plight of the soldiers with the York and Lancaster Regiment. She was noted for her outspokenness and her honesty.

2. Queen of Sheba. The biblical name for the legendry queen of Babylon in Iraq who was said to have visited King Solomon in Palestine..

3.   University College, Leicester. The University of Leicester received its charter in 1957 and its first academic year was 1957-58 onwards.

4.   charades. A game played with two or more people where a team mimes a play, book, film, television program title for the other team(s) to guess. The mime can be the whole word or parts of the title.

5.   Lawrence Olivier (1907-1989). Knighted in 1947 for his services to the theatre he was said to be the nation's greatest actor. He received the highest honor from the Queen, the Order of Merit, in 1981.

6.   Sybil Thorndike (1882-1976). One of the greatest classical actresses of her time and made a Dame of the British Empire for her services to the theatre. She was noted for her Shakespearean roles and for the title role in George Bernard Shaw's play 'Saint Joan'. In later life she appeared in the film 'The Princes and the Showgirl' with Marilyn Monroe and Sir Lawrence Olivier (1957) where she played the dowager Queen mother. She was noted for her wonderful diction.

7.   Marylin Monroe. (1926 – 1962). Famous American film actress. Her blond hair, beautiful face, and perfect figure brought her many fans all over the world. She gained fame also as a singer for her pouting rendition of 'Diamonds are a girl's best friend'. She was the mistress of both President Kennedy and his brother, Robert. She died under mysterious circumstances in 1957

8.   Wizard of Oz . This famous motion picture about a Lion, Tin Man, and a Scarecrow looking for the Wizard in the City of Oz, starred the young Judy Garland, who was to become famous as an actress and singer.

9.   Pride a Prejudice. A classic novel by the nineteenth century writer, Jane Austen and published in 1813.

Chapter 10

1.   Arab Levy Battalion. Arab soldiers and Arab officers under the authority of the British military. Their function was to 'police' the Aden Protectorate against insurgents and terrorists from the Yemen. Many of the troops were actually Yemeni and served for money rather than the ideals of the British.

2.   Naib. A name given to a local ruler in the Yemen who governed under the direction of the British political officer.

3.   jerry cans. Metal cans about the size of a large suitcase with a screw top. Used for carrying spare fuel or water fastened to the rear of a Jeep or Land-Rover. When empty, they could make a loud clanging noise. Useful for storing petrol.

4.   coverings. Muslim males in the Middle East are expected to cover from the navel to the knee and even when bathing will cover up. In Saudi Arabia they wear long white trousers under their robe, and in the Gulf a long cloth wrapped round their waist. In the Yemen, they wear nothing under their 'footah' or long waist-cloth. To show anything below the waist and above the knee is against the dictates of Islam.

5.   Sandhurst. The Royal Military Academy, Sandhurst, at Camberly in Surrey is the top officer training establishment for the British military and turns out potential senior officers.

Chapter 11

1.   Arabian Nights. A famous book of exotic stories in Arabic called 'A Thousand and one Nights' and translated into English in the eighteenth century. Told by Scheherazade to stop her husband from putting her to death, she saves her life. The stories seem to be Persian in origin.

2.   Napoleonic Wars (1799-1815). A period in British history when they fought the French under the leadership of Napoleon Bonaparte.

3.   Norman Evans. A comedian, popular in the forties and fifties for his comedy sketches, namely 'Over the garden wall' and 'The Dentist'. For some years he had a program on BBC television called 'Over the Garden Wall'.

4.   Cecil B. De Mill. A Hollywood film producer famous for his epic, big budget films about biblical subjects.

5.   Widow's mite. A story from the Gospel of St Luke 21 vv1-4 where Jesus tells the story of a poor widow who give her all, a mite, the smallest of coins. It was not the size of the gift to God but the intention behind it.

Chapter 12

1.   Desert Song. A popular musical of the fifties by Sigmund Romberg telling of the love between an Arab and a beautiful European woman at a time when the Arab World was little known and considered exotic.

2.   Edward VII. He was never crowned as King of England as he abdicated for his love of Wallace Simpson, a divorced American. As Head of the Church of England such a marriage would have caused a constitutional crisis as divorce was not allowed then by the Church. He and Mrs Simpson traveled all over the world looking for a role in life. He was not really welcome in Britain because of his abdication and his support of Adolph Hitler. Recent de-classified documents reveal that he made an agreement with Hitler that if the Germans won the war he would become the 'puppet' King of England. The Duke of Windsor, as he was known, died in Paris on 29th May 1972. The Duchess came to London for the funeral but never returned again from her home in Paris where she died. For further details read "The King of Fools" by John Parker (1988) published by Macdonald Futura.

Chapter 13

1.   Frank Sinatra. An American singer of Italian extraction who remained popular for a generation. He died in 1998.   .

2.   Mount Kilimanjaro. The highest peak in Africa -19,340 feet high – to be found in Tanzania. It is an extinct volcano and has three peaks, usually covered by low cloud.

3.   Masai. Nomadic warrior tribe in central Africa-Kenya and Tanzania around Arusha- noted for their height and bravery. Every young man, to prove his manhood, has to kill a lion with just a spear. They are nomadic and follow their cattle and drink both the milk and the blood from a slaughtered animal. Today, there are not enough lions to kill, and they are restricted where they can take their herds.

Chapter 14

1.   National Geographic Magazine. The magazine of the National Geographic Society of America that undertakes research and exploration in various areas of the world in order to enhance knowledge

and improve the environment. The magazine is famous for its photography. Today there is a tv channel giving a similar service to the magazine.

2.   Brylcream boys. An slang expression used to describe members of the RAF. The hair pomade, Brylcream, was used to sleek the hair down so as to look smart. The RAF called the army 'pongos' from the slang word 'pong' meaning a 'smell'.

3.   lady boys. The word is used generally in the Far East where some boys live openly as females and are accepted as females in society. Many have breast implants and undergo an operation to remove their penis. Generally, they are outstandingly beautiful.

Chapter 15

1.   Aldershot. A town in the county of Hampshire. It is surrounded by military camps and thus tends to be regarded as a military town.

2.   Anglicanism. The name given to the practices found in the Church of England, which are generally considered to be Protestant. Full details can be found in the Thirty-nine Articles of the Church of England. Morning and Evening prayer are the main church services on Sunday. Holy Communion, or Mass as the Roman Catholics call it, is usually Celebrated early on Sunday morning. Unlike Roman Catholic priests, the clergy of the Church of England are not obliged to celebrate Mass every day. They are obliged, however, to say morning and evening prayer every day. Clergy are not required to be celibate.

Chapter 16

1.   docks. Aden was annexed by Britain in 1839 as a staging post on the route to India. Later it became of strategic importance in the Middle East. In the port of Aden there are no deep water docks and jetties. Ships are anchored in the deep waters of the bay and small boats ferry goods an passengers to a small jetty. Hence the strategic importance.

2.   ugly duckling. A Hands Christian Anderson (1805-1875) children's story tells of an ugly ducking who was ashamed of his poor appearance and was made fun of by his fellows. Eventually, he was persuaded to look at his image in the clear water, only to find that he had turned into a beautiful swan that was greatly admired.

Chapter 17

1.　'Rebel without a Cause'. Probably the most famous film that the American star James Dean made in his short career that ended in 1955. His early death at the age of 24, when the speeding Porche he was driving crashed out of control, his moody and wild personal character played out in the people he portrayed on the screen, earned him a cult following.

2.　stevedore. A person who loads and unloads ships and known to be tough and use very foul language.

3.　label. The purpose of the label was to identify that the person had been given a shot of morphine, a pain killer. Usually a large M was written on the forehead but in cases where the face is disfigured then a label has to be attached in a convenient place. Too much morphine could kill.

4.　'cracking' tower. A large metal tower used to break the crude oil into different grades.

5.　Lilliput. The capital city of a fictional people, the Lilliputians, who were only a few inches high and feature in Jonathan Swift's (1667-1745) 'Gulliver's Travels'.

6.　Frank Whittle. The inventor of the jet engine. He designed the engine when he an engineering apprentice at R.A.F. Cranwell in 1928 when he was only twenty-one years of age. His idea was rejected by the R.A.F. as impractical. He could not get British Government funding for his idea and so he set up his own company in 1936. The first flight was in 1939 and went perfectly but still the British Government were not interested. At the commencement of the Second World War the Germans were working on a jet engine. Britain then realized the potential of the jet engine, but it was not developed until 1941 when on May 15th the first jet, the Gloucester, flew at Cranwell. The British government took the patent away from Whittle and gave it to the Rover car company. The patent expired and the Americans developed the engine. Whittle died in 1996 a broken and disillusioned man

7.　Father Potter. Canon George Potter, a famous priest during the 1950's who founded a boys' club in his parish in Peckham, a tough area in south London, in order to provide an interest for young men and to keep them off the streets. Over the years he founded many clubs. The Anglican Church suggested he became a bishop but he declined, preferring the simplicity of his parish. He tells the story of his life in his autobiography 'Father Potter of Peckham: A South London Saga', published by Hodder and Stoughton, 1955.

8.   S.P.C.K. Founded in 1698 'to promote and encourage the erection of charity schools in all parts of England and Wales; to disperse, both at home and abroad, Bibles and tracts of religion; and in general to advance the honor of God for the good of mankind...' the Society for the Promotion of Christian Knowledge has a long history of Christian good works. Today it has a large publishing house specializing in the production of reasonably priced Christian literature.

Chapter 18

1.   Comet. The first British sub-sonic jet airliner built by the De Haviland Company and put into service in 1952 by the British Overseas Airways Corporation.

2.   End of National Service. Conscription was abandoned in Britain in February 1959 and the last intake was in November 1960.

Chapter 19

1.   Downing Street. The street where the British Prime Minister and Chancellor of the Exchequer live. It is a street off the Mall, but now it is not possible to walk down Downing Street as, due to terrorist activity, large iron gates have been erected and only authorized personnel are allowed beyond them.

2.   William Morris (1834-96). He was a designer, printer, poet, and prose writer who was part of a movement to revive hand-craftsmanship. He was most famous for his designs and the colors he used.

3.   Rugby School. This famous public school in the town of Rugby gave its names to the game of rugby where it was first played.

4.   INRI. These are the initial letters of the words in Latin written on the Cross – 'Iesus Nazarenus, Rex Iudaeorum – Jesus of Nazareth, King of the Jews. The words were written in Hebrew, Latin and Greek.

They have become a Sacred symbol of Christianity and are found on vestments and altar frontals.

5. reredos. The name of the decorated wall-covering at the back of the altar in a church. It can be made of carved wood, stone or marble or woven hangings, and can be highly decorated or very simple in design.

6. Stations of the Cross. A series of fourteen tableaux depicting the last journey of Jesus from the house of Pilate to His entombment. They are either carved or painted on a the walls of a church and devotions are made in front of them during Lent and Passiontide.

7. reserved sacrament. A consecrated wafer, or host, with a drop of wine on it held in a locked safe, usually on a side altar. Its purpose is to provide a quick means of giving the sacrament when someone is bedridden or about to die. It is carried by the priest, when it is to be administered, in a small vessel called a pix, worn round the neck. It is commonly used in the Roman Catholic Church, and sometimes in the Anglican Church, but permission has to be gained from the bishop.

8. chasuble. A vestment worn to celebrate the Holy Communion and worn by some priests. Derived from the cloak worn in Greco-Roman times, it is basically a circle of cloth of fine quality, like brocade, with a hole in the center for the head. Later it was altered so that the sides were uncovered. At one time it was considered to be a sign of 'popery' and banned. The Oxford Movement worked to overcome this prejudice and nowadays vestments are commonly used in the Anglican Church. However, some very 'low church' clergy still refuse to wear it. The cope, a full cloak, is also used but generally in processions. It is basically a long cloak made of fine material and often embroidered in gold.

9. Stainer. John Stainer (1840 – 1901) began as a choirboy, at aged 16 became an organist and at 19 gained his B.Mus. He took his BA at Oxford in 1863 and gained a D.Mus. in 1865. He became the organist of St Paul's Cathedral in 1872 and spent his life improving the standards of church music. He was knighted in 1888 and became professor of music at Oxford in 1889.

10. Synoptic Problem. The gospels of Matthew, Mark, and Luke are known as the synoptic gospels. Internal evidence shows that they partly drew on each other as well as other source material. It is a matter of

academic discourse as to exactly who wrote what and when. [For a longer explanation see note 1 for Chapter 22.]

Chapter 20

1.   changing of the guard. Each day the guard outside Buckingham Palace can be seen changing. The Scots, Welsh, Irish and Coldstream Guards take it in turns and it has become a tourist spectacle. It used to be held outside the railings of the palace, but because of the problem of the crowds it attracts, the ceremony is now held inside the palace grounds and the visitor has to watch it through the railings.

2.   St. George's Hospital. The building now does not exist and has been replaced by the most expensive hotel in London.

3.   Royal Academy of Dramatic Art. It is the premier stage school in the United Kingdom and many of the best actors and actresses are trained there.

4.   debutants. The name given to girls who are 'coming out' into society. It was a rather snobbish way of finding a husband. The parents of the girl in question would arrange a ball and invite other girls and all the eligible young men of their social class. The crowning moment was the ball given by the King and Queen where the girls were introduced to society. Such an event was abandoned during World War II but some parents still give lavish parties for their daughters even today.

5.   Mount Sinai. A mountain between Egypt and Palestine that is considered especially sacred by Christians and Muslims. It is there that God gave Moses the Ten Commandments.

6.   homosexuality. Whilst the Gospels have nothing to say on homosexuality, the Church takes its stance from the writings of St Paul, St Augustin and St Thomas Aquinas to justify its disapproval of homosexuality. For Paul see: Romans 1 vv 26-27; I Corinthians 6 vv 9-10; I Timothy 1 vv 9-10: Augustin, Comfessions III 8 (15): Aquinas 'Summa Theologia'. It is interesting to note that the greatest of the Kings of Israel, King David, and the chosen of God, had a homosexual relationship with Jonathan, the son of King Saul. On the death of Jonathan, David described his love as greater than that of a woman. 2. Samuel 1.25-26. For a modern academic review of homosexuality see "Homosexuality" by Michael Ruse (1988) published by Basil

Blackwell.
Chapter 21

1.   Quentin Crisp. A famous, flamboyant character in London in the sixties and later in New York where he settled. His outlandish dress and refusal to hide his homosexuality caused him great anguish, both emotional and physical. His story of homosexual persecution was told in a B.B.C. documentary called 'The Naked Civil Servant'.

2.   Eucharist. The word comes from the Greek meaning 'thanksgiving' and is referred to in the Synoptic Gospels: Matthew 26 vv 26-28, Mark 14 vv 22-24, Luke 22 vv 17-20. In Paul's First Epistle to the Corinthians 11 vv23-25. It is also called the 'Mass' in the Roman Catholic Church and the High Anglican Church from the Latin dismissal at the end of the service – 'Ite, missa est' from the Latin verb mittere – to send away. It may also be called 'The Lord's Supper' or 'Communion'.

Chapter 22

1.   Synoptic Gospels. This is the problem of similarities of subject matter and phrasing in the Gospels of Matthew, Mark and Luke, known as the synoptic gospels. Most scholars agree that there has been 'borrowing' between the writers of the gospels but the controversy is who borrowed from whom. There is also internal evidence from the study of the language used that there are more than three writers involved. This is called the Synoptic Problem. The controversy continues.

2.   Essenes. This is a Jewish ascetic sect that flourished at the time of Christ and yet is not mentioned in the Bible or the Talmud but referred to by Philo, Josephus and the elder Pliny. It has been suggested that John the Baptist and Jesus could have been Essenes as their teaching is somewhat similar. Since the finding of the Dead Sea Scrolls in 1947 in caves at Qumran near the Dead Sea, it has led many scholars to believe Jesus was an Essene as much of His teaching runs parallel to Essene writings.

3. What a mess…. The American comic, silent movie stars Laurel and Hardy used the phrase when they got themselves into trouble. It was usually the fat Oliver Hardy who used is to put the blame on the thin Stan Laurel – 'Look what a mess you got us in Stanley'.

Chapter 23

1.   love. The original gospel stories were an oral tradition in the language of Palestine – Aramaic. The 'recorders' of the gospel stories and teachings wrote in Greek, which was the educated language of the day. Greek has three words for 'love'. (1) Eros – meaning physical or sexual love, from which we get the word 'erotic'. (2) Filia – meaning duty or brotherly love from which we get the expression 'filial affection'. (3) Agape – meaning the highest form of love, supreme love, the kind of love that a mother has for her children where the supreme sacrifice might be made to protect them. It is this word that is used in the gospels to describe the love of God.

Chapter 24

1.   Chatsworth House. A stately mansion built by the Dukes of Devonshire near Bakewell in Derbyshire and quite close to Sheffield and Chesterfield . It is known as 'The Palace of the Peaks' as it is so impressive. In 1818 it was rebuilt - as seen in its present form - as tangible evidence of the wealth and power of the Devonshire Family. There are extensive formal gardens with waterfalls, cascades and fountains as well as thousands of acres of parkland. The house and grounds are open to the public.

2.   Peter Pan. The character of 'the boy who never grew up' was created by Sir James Matthew Barrie (1860-1937) in his book 'Peter Pan' published in London in 1904. It is a delightful children's story with an evil one-armed Captain Hook and a ticking crocodile that swallowed an alarm clock. A statue of Peter Pan stands beside the lake in Hyde Park in London commemorating the memory of J.M. Barrie.

3.   Nicene Creed. The First Council of Nicaea was called by the Emperor Constantine in 325 AD to settle a schism within the Christian community. At the meeting the basic articles of faith were determined. The Nicene Creed is the profession of Christian Faith that is made at the Eucharist, Mattins and Evensong by every professing Christian. To not accept any ofits contents is to deny the basic beliefs of Christianity. In its original Greek the word homoousion, meaning 'of one substance' defines the relationship between Father, Son and Holy Spirit.

Chapter 25

1. Queen of England. After the death of William III there was no heir and the government of the time invited a minor German Prince to become king. George I founded the Hanover dynasty. He never learned to speak English. There followed George II, III and IV. Unfortunately, George IV, as well as being mentally deranged most of his life, left only one married, legitimate child, a daughter, Princess Charlotte, who died in childbirth in 1817. The government offered rich incentives to the Royal Dukes to get married and so the Duke of Kent, lured by wealth, made a marriage of convenience to Princess Victoria of Saxe-Coburg. A daughter, Alexandrina Victoria, was born on May 24th 1819 who became the heir to the throne. She was crowned Queen at a great ceremony held in Westminster Abbey on June 28th 1837. She met her German cousin, Albert of Sax-Coburg, when he visited England on a private visit and fell deeply in love. On February 10th 1839 they married. She had thirteen children by him, but not all of them lived. Thus, the British Royal Family has German roots through Queen Victoria and Prince Albert. Victoria's eldest son, Edward VII married a Dane, Alexandra, but their son, George V, married Mary of Tec, another German, and so the German influence within the British Royal Family was maintained. During the 1914-18 War anti-German feeling ran high and a cousin of the King, Prince Louis of Battenburg, the First Sea Lord and of German ancestry, was forced to resign from the navy and lose his title. The King gave him the title of Marquis of Milford Haven when he changed his name to Mountbatten. The Royal Family had to do something to change their name from the Saxe-Coburg-Gotha line. An aid to the King, Lord Stamford, came up with the idea of calling the family 'Windsor' after the castle. And so, on July 17th 1917 the German family became the very English Windsors.

Chapter 26

1.   The Princess Margaret. The younger sister of Queen Elizabeth who fell in   love with a commoner and divorcee, Group Captain Peter Townsend. Due to State pressure, and her feelings of duty to the country, she did not marry him. Later she met Anthony Armstrong Jones, a commoner, and the government of the day gave them permission to marry. The wedding was held at Westminster Abbey on 6th May 1960.

Chapter 27

1.   Malcolm X. He was born Malcolm Little on May 19th 1925 in Omaha, Nebraska, U.S.A. After changing his slave name and replacing it with X, he preached self-reliance, self-respect, and economic empowerment for blacks. He was assassinated on February 21st 1965.

Chapter 28

1.   Aida. An opera by Giuseppi Verdi and first performed in Cairo, Egypt, for the opening of the Suez Canal in 1871. It is a spectacular opera demanding a huge cast and tells of love and tragedy on ancient Egypt.

2.   Brunel. He was the finest engineer of his time. One example of his work is the iron railway bridge over the River Plym at Plymouth, Devon. The bridge is still in use today. He also built the first great iron ship, the SS Great Eastern which was launched in 1906. It was the largest of its kind for 50 years. Like many wealthy Victorians, he built a home, Brunel Manor, near Maidencombe, Torquay, Devon. The house still stands today. The mild climate and beautiful scenery were perfect for retirement.

3.   Elizabeth Barrett Browning (1806-61). An excellent poet in her own right, she eloped with and married another poet, Robert Browning in 1846. Their famous love story as inspired a play, 'The Browning Version' and a musical 'Robert and Elizabeth'. She and her brothers and sisters visited Torquay where one of her brothers was drowned. The house where they stayed can still be seen on the harborside where the Civic Society has placed a plaque.

4.   Pavilion Theatre. The building, based on the design of the Royal Pavilion in Brighton, was designed as a dance hall and home for the Torquay Municipal Orchestra and opened in 1912. Certainly Agatha Christie danced there as a young woman as the family resided in Torquay. Later it became a theatre where Summer Shows were held. The original building still exists and is now a shopping mall.

5.   money changers. In St Mark's Gospel 11 vv15 – 17 Jesus casts out the money changes and those who sold doves for sacrifice and said: 'Is it not written: my house shall be called of all nations the house of

prayer? But ye have made it a den of thieves.'

Chapter 29

1. Conan Doyle. Sir Arthur Conan Doyle (1859-1930) is the creator of the Famous fictional detective, Sherlock Holmes. He was a convince spiritualist and to prove the existence of the spirit world, he said that after his death he would return in order to prove his point.